THE KING'S

ACTORS

By Kaylee Umstead

Golden Age Publishers

Visit the author's website at https://brand.site/golden-age-publishers

The story, all names, characters, and incidents portrayed in this production are fictitious. No identification with actual persons (living or deceased), places, buildings, and products is intended or should be inferred.

This book is typeset in EB Garamond and Cinzel Decorative

Book Cover by Kaylee Umstead

ISBN: 979-8-9987371-0-7

Library of Congress Control Number: 2025908401

First edition 2025

PREFACE

———— • ————

Growing up, my brother and I used to play Legos together. I distinctly remember how wild and fascinating his storylines were. After the Lego Movie 2 came out, our main characters started becoming more and more distinct. Mine was Unikitty, Lucy, and Rex, and his was Techknight. When I was in the sixth grade, we started getting the storylines all muddled and couldn't remember the continuity, so I resolved to write down our characters' adventures from the beginning. Neither of us, however, remembered how it all started, so I invented a beginning. Over the next 6 years, I changed the names, rewrote the story multiple times, and finally created a novel that was my very own.

Once it started becoming an actual book, I had a dream to eventually adapt it into a 2D animated TV series. I drew the characters...and drew them some more....and some more. 6 years and 9 sketchbooks later, they officially have become my most drawn characters.

A big challenge I had when writing was accurately portraying Rex's backstory. I talked to many real life C-PTSD abuse survivors to really get the wide scope of what they went through and what they'd want to see in a novel. This research took about two to three years but was worth every day. I'm proud of how far the book has come from the original source material and am so excited to share it with the world!

Dedicated to a little girl with big dreams whose ideas spurred a life of excitement, imagination, and adventure.

I hope I made your dreams come true.

BOOK I

PROEM

CHAPTER 1

The bodice crashed under the overwhelming weight of ivory silk fabric. Chestnut stepped back. Another thing gone wrong and time was running out. Chestnut picked up the silk mannequin and removed some fabric to lighten the garment. She had worked through the night in tireless sweat to finish her last dress.

Golden ribbons of sunlight painted the hollowed out redwood tree in a vibrant salmon pink. Two books occupied space on her bedside table. A faded hardcover titled *Heights of a Climbing Ivy,* and a sketchbook of designs. If there was an alternative to bland silk tunics, she was determined to find it.

At least she had been. Today marked the end of her time here on Varterra for the next two years.

A shrill scream interrupted the soft birdsong. "Chessie!"

Her chipmunk ears swiveled. *Oh, Mimi. Not so early, please.* Chestnut thought. If she left the room or allowed her sibling in, she would be liable to discuss her upcoming pilgrimage to New Earth, and the very thought of the adventure deepened the pit in her stomach. She had never ventured past the borders of the redwood forest, nevertheless another planet.

Her muscles tightened with a gentle stretch. *A dip in the bathing lagoon might have been a good idea yesterday. If I hadn't been sewing, perhaps I would have had time.* She added a hem to the edge of the layered dress and unpinned it from the frame. The design, Bravery, was the last of her dresses in the Virtue Series. If only she could absorb the feeling through the fabric, then she wouldn't feel so anxious about today.

Chestnut's round face lowered to rest in the folds of her hair. A strand fell over one eye, magnifying the forest's beauty in a screen of dark brown hair.

I should probably look my best for my birthday. She restrained her curly hair in a loose bun and intertwined flowers throughout. Others of her species looked similar, fur covered Chipeermen with long chipmunk tails, round ears, and miniature antlers, yet still human. Her eyes drifted over her beige olive fur. The difference a day could make was fascinating. Her younger siblings pestered her relentlessly the night prior with squeaky chatter of increasing height, deepening voice, maturing thoughts and all such frivolity. If by chance, one night's sleep did add to her height, how useful would an inch or two be to her already stout frame.

A black chalk portrait of her and two of her older sisters, Lola and Sophie, hung on the wall. The past two years had passed by quicker than a blink. Lola's space vessel landed roughly about a week ago and the Mages had been working to repair it in preparation for Chestnut's departure ever since.

Since her landing, Lola had been a stranger in her own land. The beauty of words was lost on her tongue through short responses and her speech had shortened to ugly contractions of "ain't" and "won't". Besides that, she'd taken the oddest fascination with 'shorts' as she called them instead of their long skirts. Chestnut had no doubt her sister would refine over time. They simply had to wash the filth of this alternate world out of her sister.

Chestnut's bare feet nestled in the soft moss lining of their staircase. A leather satchel rested at her hip, empty, but Chestnut slid her comfort book, *Heights of a Climbing Ivy*, securely into the space.

She poked around the corner, wary of any unwanted guests. Her mother sat alone in their parlor, gently weaving silkworm cocoons.

"Good morning," Chestnut said.

At the greeting, her mother's round face turned to her, gray eyes aglow. "Happy birthday, my Gem." Her mother nuzzled her nose against Chestnut's. "How did you sleep?"

2

"Poorly..." Chestnut looked up at her mother with round eyes. "I don't think I am ready to leave."

"You *have* been ready."

Chestnut wasn't convinced. "I will miss you, Mama."

"The pilgrimage only lasts two years, my daughter, then we shall be reunited." A soft finger brushed a strand of hair out of Chestnut's face. "Now, Doe and Mimi made quite the stir looking for you, we should ease their worries, shouldn't we?"

Unfortunately, we should. Chestnut trailed behind her living shield, maybe it would hide her from her siblings.

Her mother failed as a shield at the minute Doe and Mimi spotted her. "Chessie! Chessie! Chessie!" Mimi's hand suffocated her left hand.

"Happy birthday!" Doe said.

"Thank you, girls." Chestnut squeaked as they dragged her through the town with incessant yanks.

"We need to get you to the lake." Mimi said.

"That was our job!"

"It *is* our job because we're so good at it."

Tiffany stood guard outside her new treehouse with a keen eye riveted on the construction crew. The carvers chiseled out a staircase on the outside of the bark, while inside, they carved the top of what would be a couch and counters. Her eldest sister joined the entourage and exchanged quiet words with their mother.

Warm light filtered through the canopy of towering, redwood trees. Sharp edges existed only in Lola and Tiffany's stories. Every round edge of red mushroom, every gentle bend of the willows, every dull blade of grass softened the atmosphere. Dewdrops clung to tips of bending plants, offering their bundles of safeguarded rain to nurture the grass. The thinnest trunk of the redwood trees measured forty feet wide.

Once they broke the treeline, Doe and Mimi led her over undulating hills. "I bet New Earth is covered in diamonds. I wonder if they know what grass is?" Mimi stuffed

3

a handful of grass into Chestnut's satchel. "Take some just in case."

Chipeermen bowed as the Chief's wife and her daughters walked past. Chestnut's hand gravitated towards her hip, comfort flowing from the feel of her book cover.

Chestnut wished her father a good morning. Beside him stood Mimi's twin brother, Ray. Mimi nudged Fawn, her next older sister and brought her out of dreamy stupor.

Ray, in loud whines, complained about the heat. Her mother ushered Doe and Mimi on either side of Ray so they stood in ascending age order.

Doe, Ray, Mimi, Fawn, Chestnut, Sophie, Lola, and Tiffany; the crown jewels of their parent's crowns. The deviation of Chestnut's name was on account of the doctor misdiagnosing her mother with grave news, However, Chestnut had been born by miracle and instead of naming her Fawn, they chose the name of her grandmother, Chestnut.

Mimi flew to Chestnut's feet. "Chessie, tell me the story again, please!"

"Not right now."

"I said please, Chestnut!" Mimi gave an aggressive slap to her shins.

"Mimi. Please does not connote a yes."

Doe broke from the line as well as Ray and joined their sister in begging.

"Oh, do stop. It is unbecoming to beg." Chestnut kneeled.

Thicket, the matchmaker's most favorable match for Chestnut, passed by. "Chestnut, let the children entertain themselves. There are preparations to be made."

One ear pinned back. "Thank you, Thicket." In an act of defiance, she leaned towards her siblings. "Long ago, before Tiffany–"

"Tiffany is *ancient*. I can not wait till I am twenty-three!" Ray interrupted.

Chestnut was pleased by the insulted scowl which creased Thicket's face. *We're not even courting yet, leave me alone.* Chestnut continued "Long ago a strange beast landed on our planet. A metal beast, unlike anything anyone had ever seen. Inside was a furless alien with a long nose and stubby ears. Frozen solid, the alien lay in death. Our brave Mages investigated the craft and concluded it must have been used for travel through the stars. After replicating the small pod with whatever metal they could scrape off the other one, The noble Chief–"

"That's Pa!" Doe squealed.

Chestnut giggled "Yes, yes, hush now. The noble Chief joined his bravest Mage in an expedition to learn the source of the strange alien. They returned with news of a brilliant, inside out planet, and a conclusion that it was indeed a safe and hospitable planet. And now on every eighteenth birthday, the young princess," she tapped Ray's nose, "or young prince must go through this pilgrimage and return successfully in two years time to earn their place in the royal line."

Mimi squeezed Chestnut around the waist. "We will miss you."

Her stomach tied itself in knots. "I will miss you too, Mimi."

The Chief cleared his throat. "Today, we send off my beloved daughter. As is tradition, Chestnut has reached the age of eighteen, therefore my beautiful child, it is now your turn to embark on this rite of passage."

Chestnut smiled, but held her book with a white knuckled grip. A strand of hair fell in front of her face, but her mother was quick to brush it away.

The Mages creaked open the star explorer's door and Chestnut stepped in. Raw metal lined the small 5' x 5' cabin. A control panel of colorful buttons stretched the length of a wall. If Ivy had found the bravery to struggle through opposition, maybe Chestnut could learn to do the same.

The blurry window obscured her family but Chestnut could understand the back and forth motions of their hands. The spacecraft rattled to life and a powerful burst of flames sent it up into the atmosphere. Chestnut's heart shattered as her home shrunk smaller and smaller.

"Four days until I land...in a completely new place." The craving for the comfort of Ivy and Sparrow's adventures outweighed her anxiety.

She read.

———— • ————

Humidity stifled Chestnut's heavy breath. She scrunched her nose and shifted in the leather seat. *I must have fallen asleep.* She slid the novel off her face and peered out a frosted window.

A looming, granite asteroid caught the light of nearby stars and held it close in scattered gems. The barren exterior allowed other spaceships entrance and exit through a metallic man-made hatch.

Words crackled from a perforated radio embedded in the wall. "Unidentified ship, please state your craft tag." A spotless blue and white ship with the words 'New Earth Space Force' painted on its side flew at a steady pace beside hers. Chestnut twitched her ear. The modern spaceship made hers seem like a beaten up trash can. Not even a clean, nice trash can, but one rolled in old bananas with rot eating away at the algae. She leaned over the radio, looking down her nose at it. At its ferocious growl, she panicked and tapped a button which halted the static. "Craft tag?" Her own voice came through on the radio. *Is that what I sound like?* "Identity. Of course... Tangled Ivy?" She slipped her finger off the button. The static resumed.

"Tangled Ivy, you are clear for entry"

Oh, thank goodness.

Blue particles wrapped around her ship as the other pulled forward. The metal teeth closed behind them. The two ships flew through layers of crust and stone.

Another round of metal teeth revealed a blinding majesty.

Soft shades of every color filled the window, greens of meadows, yellows of deserts, purples of mountains, even colors she'd never seen before. The core brought enough light to fill the hollow planet. Three moons, in a pyramid shape, circled on their own axis and eclipsed the sun's rays. Each eclipse sent a section of the planet's interior surface into darkness. *That must be their equivalent of night.*

Trying to discern what upset her insides so much, homesickness or nausea, was a difficult task and one better given up on. She felt less than ready for this new chapter in her life. For the next two years, she'd be reduced to admiring this sun substitute. In the odd case something happened to her...she may never see stars again.

Brown sun-scorched grass sharpened into individual blades as the ship descended into a roofless sphere. Chestnut gripped her book tighter as a uniformed soldier exited the Space Force ship. He cracked open the hatch and offered a gloved hand. She flattened her ears and hugged her book.

The man turned at a woman's shout.

Chestnut remained in her protected environment. *It's not too late to return–*

"Chessie?"

The soldier stepped aside for a young Chipeerman lady. *Sophie!* Chestnut crawled out of the pod, and wrapped her hand and book around her. "Sophie, you have survived!"

"You too. Four days in space, did everyone ration your food well? Are you hungry? Are you cold?"

Chestnut buried her face in her sister's fur, "Not anymore." *Not with this sun's core cooking us alive.*

Sophie cupped the back of her head. "I'm so happy to see you. I've missed you so much. And Papa, and Mama, and Doe, and Tiffany, and Ray, and Fawn."

"They all miss you quite the same."

"Did Lola make it home safe?"

"Oh, yes, about two weeks ago, she was also..." Chestnut pulled away to regard her Sister's revealing clothes "dressed in shorts and a t-shirt."

Sophie did the same. "A traditional silver crown dress? Goodness, compared to this planet's fashion, our rags look so bland." Sophie brushed off her shoulders the way their mother did. "However, this silk would go for a fortune."

"Would it?"

"Yes, this planet is very heavily monetized. Are you hungry?"

Heh...am I hungry... "It has been four days with nothing but alfalfa."

Sophie made a face. "Of course, I forgot how bland food is at home. C'mon, I'll introduce you to Mexican food." She grabbed Chestnut by the hand and pulled her through the airport-like spaceport. Magical moving treads spat out luggage from its mouth. *How interesting!*

"Oh yeah." Sophie said. "That's baggage claim, the gears move the bags around the tread so customers can grab their bags."

Chestnut felt eyes boring into her fur. Multiple pairs of eyes, from everyone in the airport in fact. She tightened her grip on her book, finding comfort in the worn pages. "Sophie, do many people stare?" These inhabitants looked even more alien up close, with no tail. Their ears were stubby little semicircles on the side of their head.

Sophie twitched her ear and wrapped her tail around Chestnut. "You'll get used to it. Although you definitely would fit in with an outfit update."

Chestnut glanced warily outside. The concrete landscape was so unfamiliar from the wooden homes and earthy atmosphere of her home. So few trees rose up here.

The two hurried up flights of stairs to the parking garage. "There are so many, what are they?" Chestnut said.

"Cars." Sophie pulled out a key chain. After a click, a car beeped on the other side of the garage.

Chestnut frowned, wary of the sleeping metal creatures. Some snored before waking up and wheeling away on their treads. When Sophie jumped into one, Chestnut's ears flattened.

"C'mon, Chessie, it won't hurt you."

"We're crawling into its intestines." The thought was enough to make her feel ill.

"They're not alive, They're made of metal and electricity. Much more efficient than walking everywhere."

If Sophie trusts this thing– Chestnut stepped in.

Sophie turned the ignition key and the car roared to life.

Chestnut's eyes rounded. *How can such a large world flash by so quickly.* The buildings grew shorter as they drove away from downtown. Quaint wooden homes and motels lined the street.

Chestnut tried to decipher everything about her strange new environment, but still couldn't comprehend the appeal in such short clothes. Ladies were dressed in skirts, but theirs were much shorter than the ones on Varterra, showing way too much skin in Chestnut's opinion. That was another transgression, they had absolutely no fur to clothe themselves with. She couldn't imagine how cold they all must be.

The city was alive with activity and the mall was no different. People bustled back and forth, up and down the escalators. The unfinished ceiling bore exposed pipes and wires. Chestnut's eyes didn't adjust as quickly to the bright light fixtures as she would have liked.

"Welcome to the mall, your one stop shop for clothes, accessories, and anything else you might need." Sophie pulled Chestnut to the women's fashion aisle, handed her a few items, and sent her into the dressing room. "How do they look?"

Chestnut gently hung her dress on the hook and faced the mirror. "Different."

The clothes were much more flattering than baggy silk dresses. *I don't see the function in a cropped top.*

"Let me see."

Chestnut poked her head behind the curtain and stepped out.

Sophie looked on proudly, "You look 'Christmasy'. What do you think?"

Chestnut's eyes dropped to her burgundy attire. Her crop top gently fell around her shoulder drooping down in long, baggy sleeves. She would have preferred a skirt, but shorts were much more comfortable. White fur lined the rim of her crop top, sleeves, and short cuffs. "It's nice, but where does the fur come from? It feels like ours." Chestnut tipped her head to one side, going back into the dressing room and changing back into her silk dress.

"It, uh, comes from other animals."

"Oh, like wool, they shave them?"

Sophie averted her eyes. "Something like that–"

Chestnut still didn't quite understand, but realized she probably wouldn't get any more out of her. The two returned to Sophie's apartment. It was a small space, without much to boast about. The walls were suffocating, cold and hard, unlike the soft wood of her home. The room had sharp, jagged edges and everything felt synthetic, from the air conditioning to the varnished granite countertop. She felt more trapped than at home.

"Make yourself at home, take off your–" Not shoes. "Stay awhile. I'll make us some coffee."

"Where are we, Sophie?"

"It's someplace called Dellstine Valley. I've lived here for a few months."

Chestnut scrunched her nose. Whatever Sophie was concocting smelled bitter, but sweet. She cuddled with the warm blanket on the couch.

"Oh, how's Tiffany? Didn't she get engaged?"

"Yes, unfortunately. Now she's married and pregnant." Chestnut sighed. "Arthur is sweet...I just know how miserable Tiffany really is. Although, I have to balance my sympathy with judgement. You didn't get to see her much after she came home, but she has returned quite different."

"Different how?"

Chestnut furrowed her brows. "Different like she deserved to be the golden child, like she is ever so special simply because she came here first and survived. She started living in her bedroom, even installing a door. Like we were some incessant vermin who only exist to annoy her."

Sophie didn't answer, but poured some liquid into a cup and handed it to Chestnut. "Well, maybe she'll have calmed down when you return. Motherhood softens people."

"Possibly." Chestnut craned her neck to sip from the cup.

"When is she due?"

"In a few months. You will probably meet when you return."

"I can't believe it's been a year already! Goodness!" Sophie smiled. "Alright, now down to business."

Chestnut took another sip, pleasantly surprised by the flavor.

"The planet is inside out. The three moons eclipse the sun and create night. The countries are divided into districts which are named with which Old Earth time periods they are inspired by. Victorian District, 2000's district, Old World district, just to name a few." Sophie smiled and pointed to a small room. "There's the bathroom, if you want to change. Unless you want to wear a sheet the entire day."

"Oh, no—not at all." Once Chestnut finished the coffee, she changed into her new outfit.

Sophie was grumbling in the kitchen, writing down a list. "Chestnut, could you get some groceries?"

"Alone?" Her stomach sank.

"Yes, I have to go to work. It'll be a good starter task for you. Just go to the store, get these items, and pay with this money."

Chestnut nodded, but rested a hand on her book for support.

Sophie handed her a fat clutch purse. "Mother and Father didn't really help me with money when I arrived, so I worked really hard my first month. Maybe too hard, but I had to eat. Hopefully, this will make it easier. There's $1000 in it, please, don't spend it all at once."

$1000 in one place..."Yes, sounds perfectly safe." Chestnut fiddled with the clutch purse swaying on her feet, not deciding which leg to put weight on.

Sophie waved off her sarcasm."It is. The only threat to wallets are pickpockets and there aren't any of those around here. I mean, what kind of sick person would steal a wallet?"

CHAPTER 2

Leather-back wallets. The salaries of the unemployed. Rex's whistling wove in and through the small rural town. The tone broadened into music notes and soon Rex was singing with the wind chimes, stepping in time with the wind, and creating a melody all in his own head. A cool fall breeze carried his singing up through the fire-colored leaves.

"Good morning," he bid a man on his way to work. "Good morning!" to a group of teenage girls his age.

Dellsstine Valley; Founded in 6982.

His clear, blue eyes roved lazily over the pedestrians dressed in golden hats, beige trench coats, and black turtlenecks. The pale beige of the stone buildings cooled the warm tones of the street and shops. Rex walked underneath a red and white striped awning for an ice cream parlor, then stepped around outdoor café tables. Step by step, he made his way down the sidewalk. A young lady walked past him and his eyes followed her. "Ma'am?"

The lady's red hair fell from her beret in tight curls and draped over her black coat. She had half her hand stuffed in her wallet, pulling out a five dollar bill.

Rex tipped his head "I think that's a counterfeit bill–"

She looked down, "How can you tell?"

"Well, you see, regular five dollar bills don't have color changing ink. If you tilt it like this, ah, you see? From copper to green."

"Oh..."

Rex smiled. "I can take it for you. I'm collecting counterfeit bills as a gift for my girlfriend. She's obsessed with, like, true crime. Says each bill is a story."

She rubbed the bill in her hand. "Oh well...I guess, if it'd make her happy." She handed him the five dollars.

"It would, thank you so much!" Rex waved as she resumed her walking. He pocketed the money.

The heart of downtown was ridiculously busy for a Wednesday afternoon. Park benches were either wet, covered in pigeon messes, or occupied. Rex tossed someone's empty soda can into the recycling, then slung his cloak off his shoulders. The sun was warming up the day, and he didn't want to lie on the bare grass. He spread out the gray fabric and stared up at the trees, content to watch the steady sway of the branches as clouds drifted past against a bright, blue sky. Rex closed his eyes.

Deep breath in.

Deep breath out.

Further down the park trail, a man squeezed his accordion, performing for pennies.

Yeah, getting better, with each passing day. He smiled. Healing took work, but it was worth it. These moments of peace were precious.

Rex was one with the landscape, until his growling stomach alerted him to a pressing matter. He loosened his tie, groaning. *I don't feel like eating–* His stomach growled again. *Ok. Ok, fine.*

The moon had started its eclipse.

Do I want a salad or a hot dog? Both tempting options. The hot dog stand was in the park, but he should probably eat something healthy. On the walk to the grocery store, he shook out his cloak and pinned it around his collar with a lightning bolt pin. The color matched the bleached strand of blonde hair.

A little girl walked with her mother, her small hand tightly gripping a birthday balloon. She gasped and pointed at Rex. "Blueberry!"

Rex gave her a soft smile. "Hi, Anna!" Last week was her birthday party, at which he dazzled her friends with 'magic'. The pay was good. His golden corset was fancy enough to pass off as a costume, but it also made him very recognizable in crowds. The little girl had released the balloon for her much needed pointing. Rex watched it spiral into the air. *Well.*

He felt the five dollars in his pocket. *I guess I won't need the whole amount for a salad...* He gestured to her mother to wait here.

The balloon seller wasn't much farther down the path. Business was booming, it seemed. Rex pulled out the five dollar bill and held it to the man "Could I have another blue one?"

The man counted out the change. "Thanks for stopping by!"

Yeah. He gave him a half smile, then tapped Anna on the shoulder. "Hey, look at what I got!"

Her eyes lit up, she wiped away her tears and hugged him around the waist. "How did you do that?"

Rex looked up at her mother, beaming.

"He's magic! Come on, honey." She took her daughter's hand and led her away. "Thank you."

He waved, then looked at the remaining cash. *One dollar and change.* Salad was unfeasible now, but maybe he could get a bag of chips. He pressed his lips together and shoved the money into his pocket.

He coasted to a halt until the pedestrian crossing light turned green. He was halfway in the road before his attention was drawn to the side he had just come from. *What is that?* Rex's eyes followed an animal, standing upright. The animal in question was a young lady, except her skin was covered in a thin layer of fur. Round chipmunk ears poked from her temples and stubby antlers from her forehead. He doubled back, compelled by his curiosity. *I wonder what science lab she popped out of.* Hands in his pockets, he strolled a good distance behind her.

CHAPTER 3

Chestnut joined the mass of humanity swarming up and down the cement pathway. She lifted her nose at a sweet aroma. *Flowers, and Basil too! Sophie did say there is a market nearby. Logically following, where there are people, there must be food.* She suffocated the swelled coin purse with both hands. Chestnut rounded the corner of the courthouse. Cars waited at a red light.

Chestnut took a deep breath and broke into the crowd of people. "Hello, excuse me, do you know where a market would be?" Eyes turned on her, but no reply came. She withered under their stares. *I don't want to seem a burden to these people by asking directions. If I could only find the way myself–*

A sharp pain shot through her tail and she tried tugging it from someone's shoe. "Excuse me? Please–" She squealed at a hard shove. The impact would have been lessened if the sidewalk was more pedestrian dense. The shove had thrown her off the path. *How rude, does everyone on this planet behave so boorishly? I should probably get back on the path.* Chestnut raised her nose, *Oh, this direction is not the right one. I have to go back across the sidewalk–* Her ear swiveled at the sound of footfall. She looked behind her. Nothing out of the ordinary. *I could have sworn I was being followed. It may be my own paranoia. Oh, Mama, I wish you were here.* She pulled the book out of its holster and hugged it tight. With the leather bound story secure in her arms, she closed her eyes, centerring her focus on the herbs. Blindly, she followed the scent.

The ground gave way under her, and her eyes snapped open. Hot asphalt burned her feet.

Stark white headlights washed the world in white.

She stared, processing the racing car too late.

"Move!"

A body slammed against hers, sweeping her off her feet. The world smeared. *Moss, the car almost hit me–* The car swerved off the road, colliding with a powerline. Smoke emitted from the hood. The scene was hidden by grey fabric sweeping over her face.

She sucked in a hard gasp once she hit the ground. She threw the cloak off her face, looking up at the body weighing her into the ground.

He sat up. "Claws, what are you, crazy?" Heavy breathing exuded from his lips.

Chestnut blinked. "Hi–"

His brows furrowed as he smiled. "Hi."

Hi. She stared up at him. *Humans look even stranger up close. His ears are so round.* Her fingers grazed his cheek. *His skin has the tiniest hairs on it. I wonder if humans ever had fur at some point?* She then noticed the lightness at her hip. *My book. Where is my book!?* "My book!" Chestnut patted the ground around her. "My book, where is it? I need it!"

"Are you okay?"

"My book!"

"Ok. ok." He cautioned her with his hands. After a quick snatch, he handed the book to her. Chestnut embraced the book, tears staining the pages.

Gold-outlined silhouettes passed by the two. The boy sat beside her, head between his knees. "Claws–"

Her book safely acquired, she turned her mind to less pressing matters. The boy's mud crusted hair withheld the deep richness of an oak tree. His blue eyes reflected a fragile sweetness.

"Wish it hadn't rained last night. This mud doesn't wash easily." The boy pulled his hair back only for it to fall over his face again in greased strings. His words flowed out, one after the other, in a relaxed progression of a cut glass accent.

"My coin purse."

"Coin purse?"

Ooooh, Sophie is going to be so upset, she worked really hard for that money and I lost it not more than 15 minutes after our parting. "Can you help me find it?"

The boy gave her a look "There are plenty of pickpockets in this town, someone must've taken it." He added a knowing smile. "I'll keep my eye out for it though"

Chestnut lunged for his ankle "N–no, please don't leave yet–"

"Uh–"

"What's your name?"

He scowled. "Are you planning on turning me in?"

"Turn you in?" Chestnut tipped her head.

"Call me Lucas, Booky" He smiled

That can't be his real name. He doesn't look like a Lucas at all. Where would I turn him in, and why? Is he a criminal? A thief? He did say he'd keep an eye out for it, maybe he knows a person. Or perhaps he's an undercover spy like Sparrow. He certainly looks like Sparrow. Acts like him too, but Sparrow always stayed for Ivy.

The boy snickered.

I wonder what he finds so funny? Is he laughing at me? Oh Moss, what have I done now? I wish he would just tell me my blunder instead of leading me on like such. Is he waiting for me to ask?

He rose with a grunt. "You don't talk much, do you?"

Chestnut regarded the hand he stretched down towards her. *Oh, is that what he was laughing at? I suppose I haven't said much since we met, in fact, what was the last thing I said? Oh, yes, I asked what his name was and he told me it was Lucas. Whatever language it is, it is certainly foreign to my tongue. A strange and peculiar name for a strange and peculiar boy.* Chestnut noted his midnight blue long sleeve shirt. In this heat, she wouldn't dare wear pants or long sleeves, lest she wilt, but the boy didn't seem to care. She took his hand.

Lucas helped her to her feet. "Woah, careful. Unsteady, aren't ya? I never caught your name, Booky."

"Chestnut."

"Charming." His lips pulled into a smirk.

A red blush tinted her fur. *Is he flirting with me? A matchmaker has not even introduced us! Rather soon for a courtship.* She squeezed her book tighter. A cacophony of screams pierced her ears. Chestnut whirled around, only to back into Lucas.

He grabbed her shoulders, eyes round. Lightning pandered across an unstable powerline.

Three thin threads connected the powerline to the pole. Chestnut held her breath.

"We should get out of here." Lucas pulled her away.

It's going to fall– Her eyes lowered to the family crawling out of the car. *They're going to get hurt!* "We have to help!"

"Wait– no we don't!" He chased after her. "Chestnut!"

She reached a hand in to help a woman out of the back seat. Lucas glared at her, "You are insane." He helped her bring the woman out of the car. "Is there anyone else?"

"My sister is in the back," the woman said.

Chestnut looked at the powerline while Lucas crawled into the car. In the third row was a screaming infant with curly, blonde hair.

Another cord snapped.

"Lucas–"

"The seatbelt is jammed!"

"Lucas, It's about to snap!"

She looked in. Lucas yanked at the booster seat, trying to release the buckle. "Almost–"

The second of the two cords snapped. The post jerked lower. "Lucas!"

Click. Lucas yanked the crying child out of the seat and handed her to Chestnut. He clambered over the seats, falling out of the car.

Lucas looked up at her, his blue irises meeting her gray. He lunged upwards in a hard shove. "GO!"

The thread snapped.

Flesh connected with electricity. An array of sparklers lit up Lucas' body.

He dropped, a stricken look across his pale face.

Lucas! Chestnut deposited the little girl with her family and rushed to him. Her breath hitched, his skin was cold, his eyes lifeless. "Lucas!" She reached to remove the powerline from across his body, but feared she might suffer the same fate. *He has to be okay.* She touched his arm, feeling buzzing pinpricks flood through her, her fur stood on end. "Lucas, You have to be okay, you have to be– please–"

"He will be." The deep rasp drew her attention upwards. A man stood over her, his white hair making his pale skin look abnormally saturated in comparison. "Heath. Class 5 Falcon, leader of Limbo's 95th division. Please stand back as I remove the powerline."

What– what does that mean?

Heath kneeled beside Lucas and with bare hands displaced the powerline. "Time to go home, Prince."

Chestnut reached for Lucas as he lifted onto the stretcher by Heath's men, "Wait, wait, wait!"

That could have been me if not for a split second. Mama would never have known, Papa neither. Doe, Ray, Mimi, all of them would have never seen me again. I would never see them again. The workers pulled him away, but Chestnut didn't miss the slight rise and fall of his chest. *He's alive!* She scrambled to her feet and dashed after them. "Wait, Wait good sir! He is alive! You can't take him!"

Heath raised a brow.

"Sir, he is alive. You cannot bury him. He is breathing. Regard him!"

"I'm aware."

"Then...where are you taking him?"

"To the doctor, my dear child."

I want to be there when he wakes up, I know how it feels to be alone, I don't want him to be alone in the hospital. "Take me with him!"

"What?" His sickly thread of words chilled Chestnut.

"I wish to join him."

He regarded her with cold derision before his eyes softened. "Of course, dear. This way." The more they walked, the more confused Chestnut grew. They came upon a storage truck, filled with large dog cages. "Why would you need cages?"

The leader grabbed her elbow with a death grip. "The Prince must have cared deeply for you to sacrifice his life. Are you his lover? His friend?"

Inside the truck, The soldiers fitted Lucas with a muzzle. "What are you doing to him?" Chestnut pulled against Heath's hold. *Why isn't he letting go?* She tucked her tail between her legs. *Oh moss, Oh moss!* Heath jerked her towards the truck. A shrill noise escaped her. "Help! Someone!" A strong hand clamped over her mouth as she was wrestled into a cage.

Lucas, please wake up! This is not what I wanted! Chestnut made a high pitched scream in the back of her throat.

Heath hopped into the back of the truck just as the soldiers lifted the cage. "Was this what you meant, dear?"

Chestnut stared at him. *I trusted him...I thought he was trying to help, I...I trusted him!* "You tricked me–"

"No, you told *me* you wanted me to 'take you with him'. You have no one to blame but yourself."

No one to blame but myself. I only had the best intentions. I promise, I just wanted– She squeezed her book. *Ivy!*

He kneeled next to the cage. "What is your name?"

Chestnut couldn't get far enough away, she wanted to get out of this cage and run, just run as far as she could, back to Sophie, back to Doe and Mimi and Lola. *I'm scared, Mama I'm scared!* She pinned her ears back. "Are you going to leave me here? With a corpse?"

"He'll wake up."

"This. This is cruel and– you're an awful, mean, nasty person!"

"Wow." Heath said. "I'm wounded." His dull gaze drifted off. "Can you cook? Clean? Do maid stuff? I'm sure you'll sell quickly on the trade" He tugged his gloves further down his arm and unclipped a metal canteen from his hip. "Do you want some water?"

"I want to go home."

"But that's no fun."

"Please, let me go," She'd never felt so small.

Heath pulled a vial of purple syrup from his pocket. "I will if you drink this."

"I don't trust you anymore."

"They're vitamin supplements. It'll be cold in the truck for a long time and I need you alive and in good health." He handed her the cup. "You dug the grave, now you can either lie in it, or accept my deal."

I did land myself here. Because I opened my mouth, I might be a slave in a few days. Chestnut looked down at her book. *What would Ivy do? What would she choose?*

"When would you let me go?"

"The moment the Prince wakes up."

"The exact moment?"

"Within a 5 minute window."

Chestnut straightened. "They're not vitamin supplements are they..."

"No."

"What is it?"

"Poison." Heath breathed.

It was a choice between Poison and Slavery.

Chestnut took the vial.

"Good girl." Heath bowed his head. "The drive should be smooth. I wish I had better accommodations for you, but regretfully this is the best I can do."

Chestnut turned away.

Heath jumped out of the truck. The closing door sent the back of the truck into darkness, except for a sliver of light coming from the bottom of the door.

Tears dripped down her face. She hugged her knees, sobbing into her book. Maybe it would wake up Lucas. The sooner he woke up, the sooner she could be free.

CHAPTER 4

R ex gasped. Electricity shot through him. He reached for something to collapse against, hands meeting the powerline. Snatches of the scene moved in and out of his vision.

Heart keep beating, keep breathi–

A boy collapsed on the pavement which looked startlingly like himself. Rex stumbled back, his transparent, icy blue soul lagging in layers of different opacity. He ran one hand along the length of his arm. Cold. The texture of his skin was gone, replaced by a feeling that his arm *should* be there, but all it was was mist. *I can't be dead– I can't be!*

A demon skirted around Rex, draining color from a human with soft whispers. Startled, Rex surged backwards and topped over. *What is happening?* Rex raised his arm to protect his eyes against a shine of armor. An angel vaulted over him, swinging his sword for the demon.

Okay, okay, I'm in the spirit realm. Noted. Why wasn't he being dragged back to the afterlife? His death sealed the final stage of his contract with Limbo.

A glow appeared beneath the fabric of his sleeve. Rex peeled back the cuff and widened his eyes. The symbol on his wrist glowed a sickly red hue. 夭折

It was green before...claws. Red meant expired. *But I'm only 17. I can't die so soon!* His spirit lagged behind in layers of transparency in his quick approach. Rex shoved his weight into his body, but an equally strong force pressed against him. *C'mon!*

"Prince, you should know you have to wait for a Fallen Angel's notarization first." A woman smiled down at him, a broken halo above her head. Six nubs extended from her back where her wings had been sliced off. She stroked her blonde hair over her shoulder. *"Do not be afraid."*

Rex scooted back, hand extended. *"You're here to bring me back?"*

"My name is Destiny." The Fallen Angel smiled, her pink irises softened on Rex.

"That's not an answer."

Destiny looked up. She was thinking for a while, certainly taking her old, sweet time.

Rex lowered his hand *"Fallens are all so flighty–"*

Destiny giggled. *What can I say? After I fell from Heaven, I can't seem to get my head out of the clouds."*

Rex chuckled, his body relaxing. *"So you're not here to take me back?"*

Her eyes were deceiving. The ethereal peace surrounding her was contagious. Despite Rex's best attempts, he couldn't be wary when he was looking at her. Fallen Angels often twisted others' trust, wrapping it in circles until it made the desired shape. "Not exactly." Destiny softened her expression. *"I can't let you back in your body unless you promise to travel to Lavivrus."*

"Lavivrus..."

"The city of convergence."

"I know." Rex frowned. If he went back into his body, a Falcon would be back for him.

Falcons. The generals of hunting divisions. Like the birds of prey, they sunk their talons into expired contracts. Once they were assigned to return a child to Limbo, they never relented. Depending on the child, they were either gentle guides, or sadistic stalkers.

Rex looked down at his body.

A simple lie could get him back into his body. He wouldn't be as alive as he was before, but he'd be able to eat and sleep, and live like a normal human. Once he was back, he couldn't die again. He never would have to see Destiny again. He wouldn't have to stand at the judgment seat and atone for his deceit. If he could just outrun the Falcon, outrun the hunting party, he would be free. He'd just have to keep running for the rest of his life.

A life of running was better than the alternative: Trapped in a Jester's hat, under the thumb of a cruel King. His heart pounded out of his chest, he could feel it pump inside him, but when he touched his chest with his hand– there was no heartbeat.

Rex drew in a long breath *"I, Prince of Limbo, promise to use my body to travel to Lavivrus. I promise to return to Limbo to fulfill my expired contract and use the rest of eternity in loyal, unending service to the King."*

Destiny smiled.

The pressure preventing him from entering his body gave way. Rex gasped as he dropped into the carnal being. This was the right choice.

"Sleep well, Prince."

CHAPTER 5

Flying cars zipped past a penthouse looming above the streets of the city.

Ava yawned and turned onto her other side, in bed. *Mmm, I feel like I should be awake.* Her green eyes shot open. "I should be awake! What time is it?"

She sat up, but quickly distracted, she instead fumbled for the green notebook on her bedside table. "Dreeeam 927, I fell into a well. Ava, One day you're going to publish this into a book!" She tucked the pencil behind her ear for safekeeping. "Good morning, Ziram City!" Her feet hit the floor. Lipstick lined her thin lips, red ruby just like her favorite artist, Dion Zoe. She looked at the reflected magazine version of herself. *Now I look pretty.* "Mr. Alarm clock, what time is it?"

9:36

"Oh, yeah, I'm still late. Hm. I can't believe I overslept *again*. I'm tired of this." Ava shot her mirrored reflection finger guns. "Ha-ha pun intended." She grabbed her backpack.

"Dad?" Her voice echoed in the empty penthouse. "I love you! See you tonight, Dad." She knew he'd already left for work six hours ago, but maybe he'd hear her on the security cameras.

She could imagine him on the other side of his phone watching her on the cameras. Maybe he whispered back, "Love you too, Ava."

What a nice fantasy. More realistically, he was in a courtroom convicting a felon.

Ava used her foot to close the door, her hands occupied with tying her hair in a ponytail. High ponytail made popular by Sarah Hartman.

"Script...check. Character shoes...check. What else?"

Her energy transferred into rapid elevator button clicking. She tapped her foot while cliche elevator music accompanied her ride to the ground floor of her apartment building. Once the doors opened, she rushed out, but skidded to a halt just before the lobby. "Oh wait. Water! I knew I forgot something!"

She rocked back and forth. *Water, job, water, job, water, job.* "Mmmmmmm– It'll be fine."

She burst through the doors, tourists and commuters scattering from her crazed running.

"I should have taken the metro!" A few miles down, she slowed from her run to a brisk walk.

A microphone thrust into her face screeched her to a halt.

Ava blankly turned to the news reporter, the microphone inches from her mouth. The reporter stared at her expectantly. Did he even ask a question? He must have, but she didn't hear it.

"Hi, can you repeat that?" Ava tapped her finger in the air, put it to her lips, and waited for the reporter. He signaled the camera to cut and retake.

Ava made sure to listen this time.

The reporter counted down.

3– 2– 1– "Hello Ziram citizens! I'm Jerry Corduroy here with Ziram Buzz. I'm here this fine morning with everyone's favorite doll! Born to fame, an instant sensation, talented as she is sweet: Ava Charlie Evans. Ava, tell us how you became the most famous child actress this side of the Scarlet Center? And do you have anything you can share about your next project?" he repeated, his question filled with as much energy as the first time.

Ava waited until the camera was on her good side. "Hi Jerry! I enjoy it very much. It is *amazing*!" She flashed jazz hands. "All I can say is I'm very blessed. I'd never be here without my parents' and agent's support and the support of my fans. Remember, your dreams are as wild as you chose them to be!" Ava struck a pose for the photographers.

A crowd gathered, attention drawn to her by the news reporter. Flashes rose around her as more photographers joined. Ava noticed a little girl clinging onto her father nervously, holding a pen and paper. The father gently patted his daughter, and the little girl stepped towards her, "Will you sign dis, please?"

Oh. My. Goodness. She's adorable! Ava cooed. "Aw, of course I will! What's your name?"

"Eliza." She meekly handed Ava a photograph of Ava's last stage production. *Ugh...I hate this picture...I look so...* Subpar was what she was looking for.

"Here ya go!"

Eliza's pink princess watch caught Ava's eye. *Right, Late!* And getting later by the second. Ava hugged the little girl, and sent her on her way back to her father.

"Thank you, all!" She saluted the crowd.

Flying cars drew her eyes to the top of a studio building reflecting the cloudless sky in its mirrors.

Ava stumbled through the studio doors. "I'm here!"

Eyes turned on her. *Yes, look at me. It gives me power!*

Her stomach growled. "Banquet table, banquet table, did they move it? Why did they–oh there it is!" Glazed donuts with sprinkles, jelly rolls, croissants, egg and cheese biscuits, and a whole assortment of things spread over the black tablecloth. She settled on a cinnamon roll.

Chatter resumed around the studio.

Double doors snapped open. The director, dressed like fake royalty, searched the room for her. "My star. Where is my star?" He checked his designer watch. "Late again?"

Ava mumbled a greeting with a mouthful of cinnamon roll.

"There she is! Today we're filming the last scene." The director beckoned his assistant for his coffee.

"Mhm, have you tried these cinnamon rolls?" She took another bite, catching the falling crumbs in a napkin.

The director tapped the coffee machine, but nothing filtered into his cup "...empty again."

The assistant nodded, pulling out her phone to ring a number.

"Ava, your agent gave me a call at 7:30 in the evening," he said through clenched teeth. "He told me he wants you to meet him in meeting room #654 at approximately 12 pm."

"But that's in three minutes!" She tossed the napkin in the trash.

"He said *approximately*, but you should try to arrive on time for once."

"Right, right, yeah, of course." Ava bounced up and down, warming up to take off running again.

"No running in the studio," the assistant said.

Ava cartoonishly stopped mid-bounce. "Well fine then, I'll just walk. Look at me, walking. Walk, walk, waaaa–" Once she was out of view of the assistant, she raced down the hall. *Do I have a new audition? A new stage partner? The last guy was pretty cute. No, focus!*

Ava skidded to a halt in front of meeting room #654 and slung it open. "Hey Noah, when'd they move the breakfast table?"

Noah spun to meet Ava, amusement in his raised brow. "Ava, great to see yHRK!–" He grunted from Ava's tight hug. "I can't breathe–"

Ava pulled away and set her satchel on the centermost table. "What'd you want to see me about? You could have just texted me."

"Yes, I wanted to talk about..." Wild gesturing was apparently an intricate part of his speech. Blah blah blah–legal stuff, blah blah blah–family, her mind was wandering too far, "–and therefore that's why your father decided to send you to your mom."

Huh!?

Regretfully, she should have paid attention "He's sending me away?!"

Noah watched her. "Are you okay?"

Ava spun around in the chair. "Of course I'm fine! But why is he sending me away? Does he not want me around anymore? I don't stay up too late, just one late night...late couple nights. I had a test yesterday, okay? I had to study." She drummed her fingers against the desk. "And I had a few essays to write. And I had to finish reading a book. And I had to memorize the script for that cat commercial and for this scene. But that's it! Nothing a little Monster and cramming can't fix." Her ear itched. She scratched the pencil off her ear. "Huh, forgot about that" she bent the writing utensil.

"I don't think it's your fault, it's mine. I should have known that all this was too much for you to handle, so that's my bad."

A little extra force snapped the pencil in half. "I can handle it. Everything gets done in the end!"

"On time?" Noah raised an eyebrow.

Ava opened her mouth, but every argument was silly. Despite her father's ground rules to be asleep before he returned home, she was always rushing around at 3am to get everything done. The number of extensions on homework, tests, essays, and auditions were hard to keep track of. She sunk into her seat.

"Avalie, you're a *very* capable young lady." His soft hand dropped to her shoulder. "This isn't your fault."

"Isn't it?"

"It's not. I promise... Ava, I've known you since you were a baby. I know when you're putting a chip on your shoulder, but please don't. Your father loves you."

Sure. She pulled a fake smile onto her face. "Hey, chips are like fuel, they fill my veins. They crawl right down into the crevices and say 'Hey fam' to which the rest of the blood's like 'Ayo, join the party'. Now they're all just vibing and having fun, swingin' on the chandeliers. It's a symbiotic relationship."

Noah furrowed his brows. "Right...as I said before, an issue cropped up and some guy wants to sue you for your newest song. For copyright infringement on intellectual property. Your dad thought that, along with everything else, this was too much for a growing, independent woman to deal with. He wants you out of the public eye for the time being and is sending you to spend some time with your mom in Lavivrus."

"Copyright infringement, HAH! All my albums are original. It was probably a tag line he sang for his dog once." Ava tried piecing her pencil back together.

"Ava, it's about time you experienced what a normal teenager lives like. Going to school, skating in abandoned parks, eating spray-can cheese, going to football games–uh– eating nachos."

"Nachos?"

"It's been a while since I was a teenager." Noah smiled. "Come on, Ava, it's an adventure, I thought you'd be happier."

"I'll be happy to see Mom again." She set the pencil aside. "At least that's something, right?"

Noah fervently patted her shoulder. "Now you're getting it!"

Ava squished her cheek against the desk. "Do I have to have a bodyguard?"

"A young, 16-year old traveling by herself? Of course you have to have a body-guard."

She groaned.

"Now get on! You have a finale to shoot."

"Yeah, thanks Noah." She grabbed her satchel and ran down to the main set.

———— • ————

Ava slammed the apartment door behind her. "Worst. Day. Of. My. Life." She rinsed her father's coffee cup in the sink. She scrawled a heartfelt note and signed her name with a heart. *Hope you'll be able to visit for Christmas if the firm gives you time off! Love you, Dad.*

Her fingers lingered on the note.

When he reads it–if he read it, she wondered if he would think it was cute or bothersome? She tried finding a place he couldn't miss it. On the fridge it would get lost in the pile of drawings stuck to the front by weary magnets. On the counter he'd probably throw it away thinking it was trash. She snuck into his room and left it on his pillow.

"Probably should pack– Where is that bubble storage? Aha! Gotcha." Ava pulled out a small key fob and pressed the center. A transparent green bubble materialized out of thin air. She poked the jelly-like suitcase to ensure its firmness. The last thing she needed was for the fob to malfunction, pop the bubble, and spill her articles everywhere.

The following things were deemed necessary for her journey: art supplies, sketchbooks, notebooks, toiletries, and extra clothes. "Better to have it and not need it, than need it and not have it." She muttered, stuffing a princess costume into the large bubble.

She closed the jelly suitcase, clicked the fob, and the bubble was sucked into the trinket. "An adventure..." Another word for distraction. "Yeah, Maybe this can be an adventure." She smiled. *Smile inside and out, put on a show.*

She stepped onto the fire escape, beside a billboard for 'Hand Rejuvenation Cosmetic Procedure'. Ava looked at her hands. Two scars topped her smooth knuckles. One from her failed attempt at carving an owl and another from a bad cooking experience. *Whoever heard of a child celebrity with damaged hands?* None of her coworkers had ugly hands. Maybe that's why they had so many friends.

Noah's familiar gray car flew up to the fire escape and he opened the door. "Hop in."

Ava stepped in, the car dipping under her weight and wobbling. "I love how it does that! Rush of adrenaline."

"Where's your luggage?"

"Got it right here." she dangled the key fob from her lanyard.

"Here's the itinerary." Noah handed her a binder. "You'll take a boat across the Arnan Ocean and should make it to Lavivrus in five days at the latest."

Ava caught a bunch of papers before they spilled out of the binder. She pulled out a boat ticket and a passport. "Cool."

The interior of Noah's Porpoise was lined in expensive, white leather. They passed a billboard for it, the newest model of flying cars. Noah jerked his chin to the backseat. "Miss Ava, meet your bodyguard, Roz"

A mammoth of a woman sat in the back seat, her eyes flicking back and forth suspiciously.

Gee, I bet she can bench press five of me. "Hi!"

Her bodyguard didn't respond, only giving her the old 'once over' with her eyes.

Maybe she didn't hear me? "Hellooo."

"Hi."

Ava looked back out the dashboard. *Oh jeez this is awkward.* "Soooo. What do you like to do for fun?"

Noah cleared his throat. "Roz is a new hire. Been with the company for a year, two if you count training. She takes her job very seriously, so...don't distract her."

"Hehe– great." If her strained laugh wasn't obvious enough, the regretful look she gave Noah was.

"Be nice." He mouthed to her. Noah descended to a dock. Ava reached to open the door, but the car locked. "Avaaa? Do you have everything?"

"Yup!"

"Debit card?"

"Yup!"

"District cheat sheet?"

"Yup!"

"Toothpaste?"

"Uhhhhh–"

Noah drew a fresh tube from the side cavity of the car.

"Thank you, Noah." Ava shoved it in her pocket.

Noah unlocked the door. "Have fun, Ava. Your mom is eager to spend time with you."

"Pfft, better late than never, right?" Ava withered under his critical frown. "Sorry. Just let me know when my next audition is." Once she closed the car door, Noah ascended.

Ava took pictures of the binder's instructions and her phone typed it into a document. "First step, find the boat *Luck* and get tickets punched" She handed the useless binder to Roz.

A placard welcomed them to Ziram City's Community Dock. Houseboats rocked on the murky water.

Ava barely took a step over the vibrant cedar wood before a man catcalled her and approached. *Ew, I'm 16, my guy...*

Roz stepped forward and pinched his neck. "One half inch to the left and I could kill you. I suggest you leave us alone."

Ava giggled. *Yeah, you tell him!*

The man nodded eagerly, then slunk away once he regained his freedom.

Ava approached the window, her chin held high and her bodyguard trailing behind her. "Hi! Tickets for two, under the name Evans."

A heavy set, slothful woman turned to face her. The lady took a heavy breath. "Closest boat to the pier." She embossed the ticket with lazy punctures.

"Thank you. Now let's see, *Luck, Luck, Luck,* there you are!" She approached the white polished yacht. "Rerr, hello there!" She turned to her personal robot. "Roz, have you ever been on a boat before?"

The bodyguard narrowed her eyes.

I guess not. "It's okay! It's my first time on a forty-foot yacht too. I've only ever been on cruises."

"Oh no. However will you cope?"

Ava ignored the sarcasm. "I like your hair."

Roz looked up at her auburn pixie cut. "Thanks."

Success!

The captain welcomed her on board, led her below deck and to her room, but didn't speak much after that.

Ava stopped Roz from entering her room. "Eheh, I...I think I'm safe."

Roz gave her a steely-eyed glare. "You can never be sure–"

"I'm fine. Roz." Ava slipped on the recently mopped wooden blanks and fell on the bed. "Totally fine."

Roz grunted, but closed the door.

Ava opened her bubble storage to grab her sketchbook. She took the pencil from her ear and twirled it to pacify her racing mind. *I wonder if I hired a hitman, my life would rest entirely on who could do their job better.* She illustrated Roz and a bald-headed 1920's hit-man locked in epic combat.

The waves lapped calmly at the side of the boat, but developed into crashing beats of water. Ava peered out of the window. *I didn't know clouds could get that dark.* Roz knocked on the door. "Miss?"

"Come in."

The wooden door creaked open. "There's a storm ahead. Despite my best efforts, the captain is docking in Azodnem until it calms down. May take days. I can call Mrs. Evans if you'd like."

"No, no...I can do it. Thanks Roz." The bodyguard bowed out of the room. Ava dialed her mom.

A faint ringing reached Ava through the noise of the splashing waves. "Hey, Mom." She winced at her high-pitched, cheery greeting. "Yeah, I have bad news, there's a storm, so we're docking in Azo– Amon– Azode– Something, something. I'll be a little late, but once the hurricane passes, we'll get back on the water." Ava rested her chin on the pillow. "Yeah. Yeah, I'll be careful. Mhm, Yup. Thanks. Yeah, love you too, Mom." Ava hung up.

———————•●•———————

Ava sat on her window sill, watching the calmer waves lap against the hull.

The dock floated closer until it was parallel to the window.

Ava joined Roz on the deck "So...we just wait here?"

"Yes, Miss."

An adventure. This is what Noah wanted. Ava tugged Roz's arm. "Let's go explore! We can always come back."

"Let's stay safe on the boat, Miss."

Ava frowned. "If I understand from the last bodyguard, you're not allowed to make me stay here."

Roz matched her scowl. "Yes. Per my contract."

"Then what are we waiting for? Let's go!" She inhaled a long breath of fresh air, along with a juicy fly. "ACK! Ra–Roz" She choked. Ava gasped at the hard slap on the back. "Thanks."

A weather-worn sign pointed to the small tribal village named Azodnem. "That–"

Roz cut her off. "That way."

"Yuppers...I was going to say that," Ava muttered under her breath. A dirt path, overgrown by weeds and grass led into the town. Ava sang openings to her favorite musicals along the way. She even tried to include Roz, occasionally pointing to her to finish the line. The bodyguard didn't.

Ava frowned. "I wonder if I could pay you to be fun."

As they neared the town, the details crispened. The clay buildings only rose two stories high. She didn't think anyplace could be more primitive than the suburbs, but here she was. She expected to be mobbed by fans screaming her name as they did in her city, but the people didn't seem to know her, to Ava's dismay. *Gee Wilbur, what is Roz supposed to do now?*

A real shady looking truck backed into the parking lot of the local event space. The whole shebang, tinted windows, heavy locks, Ava squinted, *Hmmmmm.* People talked in hushed voices, but a thousand whispers equaled one roar.

"Wonder what that's all about?"

Roz blocked her. "Nothing that needs our attention. No need to take risks."

"But what are they doing?"

"Probably another shipment for the slave trade. It's big in this culture's economy."

Ava ducked through the crowd to have a better look. "Why doesn't anyone do anything?"

Roz followed, her eyes dark. "Why would they? Most of these people own slaves themselves. Keep your tongue. It is not our place to cause problems."

The workers threw up the door and dragged a person out of a truck, a boy.

He had a look of deadness about him, his skin pale and his figure thin. Not thin in the way that was attractive, more of a poverty stricken gaunt. Or maybe that was the effect of his corset. *I've never seen a guy wearing a corset.* The workers let the boy's decorative Victorian high-heel boots drag through the powdery dirt.

"Roz, we have to do something. He's my age..." *That could easily be me in that cage.*

Ten or eleven dark-haired men floated around the truck. Wait, now there were just eight– Ava watched two of the workers disappear into thin air, leaving only six. One had a clipboard, and two were handling their new product, she assumed. Two more waited for the next cage and one man with white hair stood by. She figured he was the leader as he was the only one of them that didn't have olive skin and black hair. The leader reminded her of an Albino wolf. The two men fit the boy with a muzzle, leaving red scars where the muzzle had cut into his skin. They laughed.

The leader lingered as two more workers pulled another cage from the truck. From the inside they extracted a girl. From the distance she looked like a poorly designed animatronic, more fantasy than reality, but her ears swiveled on their own and her tail lashed angrier than any technology could imitate.

The men fixed a gag around her neck, and tied her hands behind her back.

A scowl deepened the wrinkles on the leader's face. "Gentlemen, she's my bargaining chip, *please* be careful." He pinched the bridge of his nose. "You can take a demon out of Hell, but you can't take the Hell out of the demon."

The girl screamed but the gag quieted her.

Jeez, she needs someone's help.

Oh wait! I'm someone. Ava furrowed her brows. *But first I have to get rid of the dead weight.*

Ava turned to her bodyguard. "Roz? Do you have a hair tie?"

She supplied one.

Rats. "Roz! *Roz!* He's got a gun!!"

The crowd immediately broke into a number of screams and everyone ducked, including Roz. In the chaos, Ava slipped away. *Hehehehe.*

Ava trailed behind the group.

Plan? No plan in particular, just distract the leader and...uh...run off!

A little lie and a lot of acting, and she'd learn all she needed to know. She hopped in front of the Albino leader with a huge smile. "Hi! I'm a journalist, could I interview you?"

The man sidestepped and turned a fiery red irised glare on her over his shoulder. He looked at one of his workers.

The worker understood and stepped between the two. "Let's keep this out of the press."

Ava's blood boiled. That's not how this works! She ducked around the worker and stopped him again. "Who is this boy? Who are you? Are you involved in the mafia? Gang? Police? What were you saying about demons?"

The man stole her attention with his cold empty stare as he lowered his chin "Move."

Oh– oh jeez, he looks serious. Ava stepped aside and let them pass. They walked out of view.

Ava charged after them.

The leader halted the group and reached for a long dagger on his hip.

Please don't kill me! Ava whirled around and marched away.

A loud voice called out. Ava recognized her bodyguard's rasp. "Miss Ava! Ava!"

Ava stiffened. *Who cares about having a bodyguard? I'll find her after I'm done.* Through market streets and past unfamiliar landmarks, she followed them.

41

CHAPTER 6

Shivers ran up his spine and along his arm. *When did it get so cold?*

Rope bound Rex's hands and feet. With every movement, the rashes worsened. He blinked open his eyes.

Dim light illuminated an empty, concrete room. The room was suffocatingly humid, filled with dust and the smell of livestock.

Where am I? Where's Chestnut? The wallet, the powerline!

Rex wiggled his mouth, trying to dislodge the muzzle.

The door opened. Rex's stomach dropped.

The Falcon.

"Well," the man said. "Finally awake."

Rex held his tongue.

"Heath Elijah Emortus. Class 5 Falcon, at your service, *Prince.*" A staring match ensued.

Rex gulped a hard lump. "As your Prince, I command you to release me."

Heath pursed his lips, a striking pink against a pale frame of his face. "No, thank you." his lashes swooped in a slow blink "A muzzle suits you, Kitten."

The pet name wasn't Heath's invention, yet stung just as much.

"The train leaves in five hours. A one way ticket to Lavivrus."

Rex glared up at him. "You couldn't drag me on that train even if you cut off all four of my limbs." Power surged through him. Familiar pinpricks that reminded him of the powerline. Rex jumped as sparks flew off him. The electricity danced on the concrete, before falling still. He tapped his foot on the ground. Lightning spread from his veins.

Heath remained still. The coldness of his expression was unwavering.

Supernatural dealings and magic weren't foreign to this planet. Demons often interacted with humans with innocent intentions and great displays of power.

Luck tipped on a fragile scale of good and evil, balancing the fortunate with the overdue. Things like this were especially prominent in the afterlives; Heaven, Hell, and Limbo. The living world stifled magic; not completely, but enough that it wasn't a regular occurrence. Rex tapped his foot again to the same conclusion; lightning scattered from his boot.

"Prince, the harder you make this, the more damaged you return to His Highness." Heath furrowed his brows. "I have no intention of forcefully dragging you anywhere. I've been doing this long enough to know that when faced with uncooperative brats," He took Rex's chin in his hand, "one must work smarter, not harder."

Smarter, not harder. Rex's eyes roved over Heath's face.

"Now you may not want my company on the journey, but you have other reasons for travel." Heath knocked a pattern on the wooden door. "I have a bargaining chip you might consider worth the trip."

Heels dragging, fur flying, Chestnut was dragged into the room. She writhed in the arms of Risen Demons before they shoved her to the ground beside Rex.

Her fur brushed against his clothing. Rex stared at her. "Chestnut? Why is she here?"

"She asked to come."

Rex shot her a glare. "You asked?!"

She matched it, her ears pinning, before she looked away ashamed.

Rex leaned forward, but was held back by his own ropes. "Heath, let her go, this has nothing to do with her."

"Actually it has everything to do with her." He leaned against the wall, eyes dull. "Gentlemen, please undo her gag."

They untied the fabric from her mouth. Rex expected her to be screaming the second the gag was off, but she just turned her face down, blinking tears from her eyes. He'd never seen anyone so defeated. "Chestnut–"

She just slumped against him, turning her face into his shoulder.

"I was going to sell her to the highest bidder, but decided to give her a way to redeem her mistake." Heath drew an empty small vial from his black trenchcoat. "Acidic Dragonium. Your little princess drank every last drop.The acid will slowly eat away at her intestines till the very thought of food disgusts her. Psychologically, with each passing day, she'll become more and more...dragon-like." He looked at them out of the corner of his eye. "Until one day– She'll die."

Rex looked at her, wondering how much of the poison had already taken hold. How much would it change her?

"I'm sorry." She breathed.

Rex looked up at Heath, his eyes hardening. "You're going to give us a cure!"

"I'm *going to*? You're really not in a position to demand anything of me. You can't die, meaning I could slowly starve you for months at a time in this dingy cell." He squatted. "Do you get it?"

Rex lowered his eyes.

"Maybe if you asked nicely," Heath whispered.

Rex scowled.

"Maybe if you *beg.*"

Chestnut looked up. "You promised you'd let me go once he woke up."

Heath leaned back, disappointed, but still drunk with power. "Ah, yes. I guess the Prince doesn't care enough about you to help get a cure for an ailment *he* caused. I always knew he was irresponsible."

"Heath," Rex said. "Please tell me what the cure is."

"Now we're making progress" He tipped his head up, eyes gleaming. "The cure is found in Lavivrus and only Lavivrus, Southwater Taephoon. She only needs it blended into a smoothie to flush the poison out of her system."

Rex met Chestnut's eyes. "Could you travel there by yourself?"

45

"Myself?!" Her fur fluffed.

No, she was right. She couldn't even find a grocery store by herself. He'd be risking his freedom to travel so far, but he'd be risking her *life* if he didn't. Even with their combined funds, ticket prices for trains and taxis were too expensive. A dying girl was not exactly the model of fitness and health.

Tears tumbled from Chestnut's eyes.

Rex's breathing quickened. She was so fragile. A feather could have knocked her over and sent her to tears. She chose to take the poison to avoid slavery. Wasn't that just a different version of what he did?

He needed a way to escape. As long as his contract stood, Heath would hunt him till the end of eternity. Without a way to null the terms of his second life, he would need another way to stay out of Limbo. If Heath never caught him in Lavivrus, he couldn't take him through the portal.

Rex blinked. *The portal.*

He twirled his wrist, lightning sparking at his command. *I just need to destroy the portal. Once I destroy it, I'll finally be free.*

He needed to join Chestnut in her journey.

"Let her go, Heath."

After a moment of consideration, Heath moved to Chestnut and gently untied the ropes from her ankles and wrists. With her new freedom, she wrapped her hands around Rex's arm, huddling into him.

Heath then switched to Rex's binds. The ropes came loose.

The two stared as Heath stepped aside. "I truly wish you good travels." His eyes were soft.

Chestnut lunged upwards and raced out of the room. "C'mon!"

Two paces towards the door, Heath caught Rex's wrist and shoved him against the wall "If you don't make it to Lavivrus by yourself, I'll come looking."

He gasped at the switch, the muzzle sliced into his skin. "I'm not going back!" Rex's voice shattered like glass. Rex kicked wildly, his senses yelling different directions at him. *Duck, Kick, Shout, Run, Appease, Go limp, Punch.*

"Oh please–" Heath pressed his head further into the wall. "His Highness grows ever impatient for his little boy. Much to my confusion, he loves you alot. But you know that already, don't you?"

Lightning scattered from Rex's body. "Let me go!"

He finally remembered.

Lips had pressed against his brow *"After you die, Kitten, I give you the gift of lightning for your safe travel home. May it remind you of our spark."* A smirk had curled on His face.

Adrenaline coursed through him, as thick as electricity. He'd finally gotten rid of His voice, and now it resurfaced as silky and treacherous as always. *This...this is his doing.* "Heath!"

"You can *run* and *hide* and *fight*, but I will always find you. The hunt begins if I don't find you in Lavivrus next week." Heath caught hold of his wrist and spun him back around. "Do you understand?" He snarled. "I'm being nice. If you abuse my kindness, there will be fire and torture and Hell to pay."

"I understand– let me go!" Rex ripped his wrist away and chased a fleeting sense of safety down the hallway.

He raced through a winding maze of concrete, Chestnut out of sight already.

The mask of his human form fell away in shattered fragments. The rims of his vision darkened with blurred panic. A scaled tail streamed behind him with 3 golden fins along the top. His heels disappeared and he ran on spike-like feet. He took shallow breaths through two slits in his neck, his nose shape shifting away.

How much farther had Chestnut gone? He should have run into her by now. He shook his head, bat ears pinned backwards. *Just run!* Far away from Heath, far away from the reality of his passing, far from the powerline, far from Limbo, far away from–

Adrenaline shoved flight responses into him, tainting his senses until he was sure he heard footsteps of someone chasing after him.

Rex burst out of the exit door, momentarily blinded by the sun. He raced on.

When his muscles grew weary, he hobbled to a stop in a market. People stared. *Run! Keep going! Get out of here!* He felt dizzy. His heart raced too fast, he couldn't breathe. Whatever air ventilated his lungs turned sour.

"Aw, now what will you do?"

Rex froze. *Sire.* Shivers spread down his spine.

He was hallucinating. He had to be.

Fingers slid onto his waist and up to his neck.

"Can't wait to see you home, pet." His Highness whispered, the soft breath tickling Rex's ear.

The nightmares resurfaced.

Speeding pulse.

Throbbing head.

Rex swiped his tail in a circle, to clear the area around him. The hands didn't disappear– There was nothing touching him, nothing near him. Where was that ringing coming from? *It's not him–just a hallucination–Hallucination, got that! I can't– he can't–*

Someone yanked his tail, and everything snapped.

His feet skimmed the ground in flying steps. The edges of his vision blurred and darkened. Shadows, hallucinations of memories reached out, grabbing him as he passed. *No, No, No, NO! It's all fake! Nothing's real!*

He flew past the place where the truck was, but he didn't stop.

He passed Chestnut, but he didn't stop.

Gasps and screams greeted him as he ran through the streets, but he didn't stop.

He couldn't stop. Sweat trickled down his forehead. He raced between two men in turbans, but they collided with him. Shoved backward, Rex toppled head first into the cold liquid of a concrete fountain.

Water!

He scrambled into the center and gripped the stone religiously. *Don't drown, don't drown, don't drown.* The rain cascaded around him.

Every inch of him trembled. He curled his tail around him in place of a hug.

Strangers gathered around the fountain, offering hands, but shadows covered their faces and their words of comfort spurred terror.

Hands, too many hands! He was safe behind the cascade of water. That's all he cared about.

He put his hand over his heart, but couldn't feel it. He could feel it throbbing within him, but his hand didn't feel anything, even his pulse had stopped.

One by one, the shadows melted away.

He can't get me here... I'm safe. He released a breath. *I'm safe.* Rex clawed at the muzzle. *How'd they even get this bloody thing on?* He ripped it off and let it rest in the fountain.

A shadow blotted out the sun above him and Rex pressed further into the concrete.

"Hey, you okay?" A girl hopped over the edge and dipped her feet into the water, her green highlighted hair pulled loosely into a high ponytail.

Rex looked her up and down.

"It's ok, I'm not going to hurt you, man. I'm Ava." She tipped her head with a warm smile. "Wanna come out of the fountain?"

"No."

"C'mon, I have a towel in my bubble storage. You can get dry."

Rex blinked. *Being dry would be nicer than sitting here drenched.* He shapeshifted away the bat ears and the tail, shifting back into a human. He carefully crept out of the fountain, sitting beside her on the lip.

"There we go." Ava wrapped the towel around him. "Didn't you have a friend?"

"I was right behind her."

Ava surveyed the area. "Stay here, I'll be back."

Rex watched her disappear behind a building. The world moved in a surreal pattern. Reality always looked different after hallucinations. The towel was of rich quality. It basically smelled like money. *Who is this girl?*

Hand in hand, Ava brought Chestnut over to the fountain. Chestnut dove into Rex's side, and squeezed him tight around the waist, her brunette hair falling over her face.

Ava stepped back "It's ok, you're safe now."

"Now?" Rex blinked up at her.

"I saw those guys take you from the truck, then followed you to this weird building. You both ran out looking like you saw a ghost."

"Is that what happened? I must have been asleep—"

Rex felt like he was sitting next to a beehive. Chestnut quivered in his arms. *What should I do?* He looked at Ava.

Ava shrugged.

Chestnut squeezed him tighter "I'm scared, Lucas. I'm scared, I don't want to die."

Rex winced at the fake name. "Rex. That's...my name."

She looked at him as if he were a stranger that had run her through with a dagger. "Rex?"

Rex pulled away. "You're not– hey, look at me." he gently guided Chestnut's chin towards him. "You're not going to die, We're going to get the cure and you're going to be healed, yeah?"

Chestnut gave a small nod, then Rex pulled her back into a hug.

A shout resounded above the streets. "Miss Evans!"

Ava gave a nervous laugh. "I...guess I better get back."

"We better be off anyway. The sooner I get Chestnut to Lavivrus the better." Rex said.

Ava's features brightened "Lavivrus. You're heading to Lavivrus? Me too! We should go together. I'd have to let my mom know, but I'm sure she'll be fine with it."

Rex narrowed his eyes. She was too kind. There had to be an ulterior motive. "It'll be a long trip on foot."

"On foot? Hah, no. You're friends with a superstar, baby, I gotchu."

"That would be helpful." Chestnut said.

"I don't know–"

"Oh, please Rex. Oh please, please, please, *please* let me come!"

Rex looked at Chestnut, then Ava. "It would get us there faster to travel by train–"

"Yeah, as long as you know the way, It'll be a breeze!" Ava tipped her head in his direction. "You do know the way, yeah?"

Destiny's figure appeared in the shadow of a building. She spoke in Rex's mind. "*I can lead you.*"

With Destiny as their guide and Ava as their sponsor, they'd have Chestnut there and healed in no time. "Yes." He pulled his hood over his head. "I know how to get there."

BOOK 2

JOURNEY

CHAPTER 7

Rex followed Ava out of the village. She insisted on going away from the harbor, for whatever reason. Once they headed into the forest, Rex took the lead. Having voices in his head that weren't his was unsettling, but at least it was the voice of a Fallen Angel. If need be, he could order her to stay out of his thoughts. Fallen Angels and Risen Demons were compelled by Limbo's magic to obey every command from the royal family. Rex snorted. Can a collection of two people even be called a family? He and his father were more a couple than a family, not even that. Rex was more of the King's entertainer than His Highness' son.

The tree line broke into a field of saffron carnations. *I wish I had a compass or something. Are we heading west? What if we're completely turned around? We might be better off stopping and waiting for night. Then I could get my bearings on some of the lights.*

After he settled in Dellsstine Valley, he hadn't bothered looking back. He was comfortable in his routine and had been for the past six years. He had grown fond of small meals and sleeping under the stars.

Destiny giggled. *"You're heading west, Prince, trust yourself."*

He did trust himself. That wasn't the problem. The problem was Ava had gotten him completely turned around and now his sense of direction was impaired.

A haunted, thousand-yard stare darkened Chestnut's downturned eyes.

Ava waded through the flowers, phone pressed to her ear. "Hey, Mom. What? I was totally in a good mood before. I'm just in a better mood now. Mhm. Roz?" She looked at Rex "Uh– yeah– Roz is with me. Listen, I just called to let you know there was a slight change of plans."

Rex shot her a look. *Who's Roz?* It seemed strange that Ava was so quick to pick up and leave.

"Yeah, I made some new friends in Azodnem. Yes, Mom, they're my age. Uhh– there's one boy. Yeah. Yeah I know, be careful. Anyway, they were heading to Lavivrus Anyway, so I'm gonna tag along with them." She giggled. "Yeah. Thanks, Mom. ETA? Uh–" She lowered the phone.

Destiny, ETA? Rex thought.

"Two weeks."

He relayed the message, "Two weeks."

Ava pulled the phone back to her ear. "Two weeks. Alright, yeah, bye, Love you!"

"Your mom?" Rex said.

"Yeah." Ava tucked the cellular device into her jean pocket.

She's awfully cagey... She really wasn't though; just oblivious to Rex's attempts at small talk. "What's she like?"

Ave turned "Who?"

"Your mom."

"Oh, yeah. Uh– she's a woman." At the look Rex gave her, she backtracked. "She looks a lot like me, but she's a woman of science. Super high IQ but not the most personable human being. She's the conductor at Ingray Opera House in Lavivrus"

Conductor. Not bad. "Is your father...alive?"

"Oh, yeah, they just don't live together. My parents love each other, but it's just they both have different jobs in different cities. So... y'know long distance."

Rex hummed.

A fresh wave of tears dripped down Chestnut's cheeks and she hugged herself tighter. Her crying had been on and off since they left the town, but every time Ava or Rex offered comfort, she dismissed them.

"Cold?" Rex removed his cloak.

Chestnut looked at Rex, then shook her head.

"Well here, you can hold onto it in case you need it."

Ava nudged him. "So what about you, where are your parents?"

Oh, jeez. Rex stuffed his hands in his pockets. He joined Chestnut in traumatized silence.

A breeze rippled the flowers in waves. *"You should have kept the cloak, it's going to be cold tonight."* Destiny said.

He never understood before why souls fainted at random in colder climates, but apparently there's no such thing as a warm-blooded ghost. Go figure.

"You know what we need to do?" Ava said. "We need to have some fun! Get your mind off things."

At Rex's tap, Chestnut broke out of her mental prison. "Hm? Oh."

"I think we should just keep walking. No use in wasting valuable energy playing." Rex said.

Ava groaned. "You're soooo boring!"

"For the love of strudels!" Rex cursed, "In case you hadn't noticed we've just been *kidnapped.* Now maybe for you that's not a big deal but for the rest of us–" The damage was severe.

"Is that your curse word?"

Of course Ava had only listened to his opening phrase, because the rest of what he said was *totally* unimportant. Rex crossed his arms and looked out over the field.

"Sorry, sorry. Right, kidnapping. I'll try to be more understanding." Ava tried to offer him a warm smile.

Her apology was adequate but hesitantly accepted. Rex sighed. "Yeah, it's one of my curse words. I have a few I picked up from Matthew."

Chestnut tipped her head to one side, her voice dusty, like an abandoned bookcase. "Matthew?"

Rex looked over his shoulder. "He raised me. He was kinda like my adopted father."

Curiosity brought life back into Chestnut's expression.

Rex followed behind the two to keep an eye out for anything moving amidst the flowers.

Trees sparsely dotted the field. Oaks mostly, but there were a few peach trees. "Let's stop for the night. Are you two okay with sleeping on the ground?" He raised his eyes to Chestnut's surprised stare.

"Yes, anything is fine." Her hair fell over one eye.

The tree curled tangled roots beneath its blue fruit.

"Peaches on my planet are pink." Chestnut jumped, but even the low hanging fruits were too high for her.

Rex propped his foot on the trunk and dangled off it, one hand around a branch. "You're a chipmunk, can't you climb?"

"Have you ever seen a deer climb?" She gave him a sharp look.

"Oh, so you're...a chipmunk, deer, and human?"

"Yes." Chestnut nodded. "Besides, I just don't like heights."

Duly noted. Rex swung himself into the tree. Peaches soon fell like blue snow balls to the grass. Like walking a tightrope, Rex balanced himself on an outstretching limb.

The eclipsed sun glowed behind the moon. Lights sprinkled the opposite side of the planet like starlit fireflies.

Ava settled against the trunk. "Chestnut, right?"

Chestnut gave a shy nod, her hand resting on the book bag draped from her left hip. "Why are there stars?"

Rex leaned over the limb like a lazy panther. "What are stars?"

"Flaming balls of *fire*! Those lights aren't really stars" Ava tapped a key fob and a jelly-like sphere materialized out of thin air. "During the night people turn on their lamps and from our perspective they look like floating lights. I'd love to know what real stars look like."

Chestnut settled into the grass and nibbled on a peach. "I count myself fortunate to have seen them. I came from another planet,"

Rex raised his brows. *No wonder she looks like that. She's a bloody extraterrestrial.*

58

"Wait! Really?" Ava gasped "What's it like?"

Thoughtfulness creased Chestnut's face. "Well, on my home planet, we inhabit the outer surface."

"How? Don't you float away? Doesn't space suffocate you?"

Chestnut drew the book from her satchel. "Our mages call it gravity."

"Gravity! That's a fun word! We have Disavity. It repels us from the core, keeping our feet on the ground."

Rex smirked. "Blah, blah, blah, science. Perks of the homeless, no school." Rex shot her finger guns.

Ava blinked. "Hold up, You can't be homeless, you're sooo–"

Chestnut curled smaller, swiping her tail over her book. Her ear swiveled towards him and her eyes promptly followed. "Well groomed."

"Why, thank you." His smile tipped into a cheshire grin. "I stayed near a small town in the early 2000's district. Occasionally, I'd get a hotel room and freshen up."

"Dude, stop." Ava said "You're not allowed to be that hot while being homeless."

Rex choked and clawed for a hold on the tree branch. Wind drove out of him as his back collided with the ground. "I'm sorry?"

"Ava!" Chestnut looked horrified.

"What?" She smiled, "We were all thinking it."

Rex looked at her upside down. "None of us were thinking that."

Ava crossed her arms. "I dunno, man. I think you're cute. What about you, Chestnut?"

Chestnut hugged the book tighter, her cheeks a hot shade of red.

"What the claws, Ava!" Rex cursed.

The jelly bubble clicked open and Ava pulled a pen and paper from it. "Claws. Crossing that off my 'Curse word alternative' Bingo card."

You've got to be kidding me. A snort escaped Rex and developed into a breathless laugh.

Chestnut's gray eyes lingered on him until Ava asked a new question.

"Hey, Chestnut! Do you mind if I call you Chess?"

"I suppose that would be ok. My sister calls me Chessie."

"Oh, How many siblings do you have?" Ava flipped onto her belly, feet kicking behind her.

A chill wafted through and in response, Rex's laughing eased into a tired smile. *That's weird, I'm so tired all the sudden.* His eyelids dropped.

Destiny invaded his thoughts. *"Only the living have warm blood, remember?"*

Rex certainly felt lulled to sleep by the icy current of air. *Hm, you don't-* His thoughts dropped off in a black abyss. "Say– I should make a fire, then, huh?"

Chestnut regarded him with a sidelong glance. "Yes, please." She returned to her conversation. "I dare say I have seven siblings."

"Seven!" Ava squirted peach juice under her teeth, but she used her sleeve *so* cleverly to wipe it off her face.

Chestnut nodded. Her grip relaxed on the book.

"Gosh, I can't imagine. I'm an only child, thankfully. I've heard good and bad things about having siblings, like the constant competition, the annoying older sibling acting all self righteous and in charge. Do you have one of those?"

"Tiffany. She can be quite like that."

Ava looked at Rex. "What about you, any siblings?"

Rex rubbed two sticks uselessly together like he had been doing for the past aggravating *five* minutes! *Why does she keep asking questions about me? It's annoying.* He gave her an unamused tilt of his head. "None I know of. But my parents are divorced. So, y'know, who really knows at this point." He continued rubbing the two sticks together.

"Yeah, I get that. My mom moved away a few years ago...Sometimes I think it's so she doesn't have to deal with me." She paused when Chestnut gave a soft gasp. "Ah! No, don't get me wrong my Mom is amazing. I love being an Evans. It's not what I am, it's *who* I am! Ava Charlie Evans–ACE."

"That's cool, with your initials like that." The two sticks snapped and so did Rex's patience. "Bloody, flippin', piece of rat mcgee!"

Ava checked off more boxes on her bingo card.

"Stop that!" Rex snapped.

She snickered. "Okay, jeez. Want a lighter?"

"And some coffee if you have it, I'm getting sleepy"

"I got blankets, two lighters, and beanbags, but no coffee, sorry." As Ava listed them, she removed the articles from the bubble storage.

Rex organized the wood. "I'll take the lighter then." He balled up lint from his cloak. Another gust of cold wind blasted him in the face and the edges of his senses numbed, including his fingers. With a toddler's grip, he couldn't click the lighter hard enough. "Gah! you–" He broke off in a yawn "You light it! Please." Rex blew on his hands to warm them.

Ava looked over at him "You really are sleepy."

"Light it!" He felt dizzy. *Stay awake, stay awake, stay awake.*

Ava smacked the lighter against her hand. "Oh! I packed the bad one, sorry, it's broken. Lemme grab the other one." She put the lighter back in the bubble storage.

His words trailed off in soft mumbles. He gave over to the savory sleep. He collapsed, eyes slitted open just enough to see Ava light the fire. Too little, too late.

CHAPTER 8

Chestnut squealed. *Rex! Don't leave me alone with my thoughts.* The book suffocated under her grip. *Two weeks then my siblings, my family, will be left to wonder what happened to me. I will not even make it to Sophie in time to say goodbye. My life is over and I can't even give my family the relief of a funeral or even ashes.*

I should have protested or fought back. I am going to die because of my own foolishness. Why, oh why, did I ever try to help him? I should have left my curiosity insatiated. He saved my life twice, only for me to repay the favor and end up dooming myself instead.

Without Rex to fill the void with mindless chatter, she was left with a running palate of self-blaming chaos.

"Want a blanket?" Ava smiled.

Chestnut's gray eyes refocused. "Hm? Oh yes, thank you." Ava draped the blanket over her shoulders. Chestnut's attention trickled into the fire's dance.

Her community had made bonfires like this. Fun filled nights of dancing and merriments. She would twirl Ray and Mimi over and over. Around in circles till her feet grew sore.

The soreness multiplied with this planet's hard floor. Her fur had already thinned with the day's travel.

The floor on her planet was much softer, in fact everything on her planet was softer, especially the people.

The moon donned a placid hue.

She had been content to hearken to the sweetness and saltiness of her companions' voices. Why must it end so soon? Ava's peppy, raspy voice had a zesty twang akin to citrus. Rex's voice was wrought with a sordid beauty, even those wild cackles and snorts.

That boy now lay unmoving on the grass, his facial features lost behind flowers and tall stems of grass. Ava had been out of place to call him 'hot'. It was inappropriate and taboo in Chestnut's modest opinion. Many behaviors Ava exhibited would be considered taboo on her planet. For one, her speech. "Man", "Ayo", "Sup.", "Can't" Silly words that had no meaning, no weight to them. They only completed the fullness of rambling that came from both Rex and Ava's mouths. Chestnut wasn't too fluent in wishy-washy prattle, but she wished she was. Small talk seemed an intricate part of this planet's culture.

Ava unfolded a blanket. "Should we drape this over sleeping beauty?"

Chestnut glanced up at her, eyes void.

"Yeah you're right, it might wake him up. He needs a good night's sleep."

An ethereal blue glow rose from where Rex was sleeping. Blue ashes flickered towards the sky. Chestnut crept forward, intrigue piqued. Her hands peeled back the flowers to reveal a sleeping ghost of transparent blue. A rim of white teeth was visible between his parted lips.

Oh moss.

A stinging rose in her stomach.

Oh moss, oh moss.

A cloud drifted over the moon and Rex's body returned to a living solid body. Chestnut reached her limp fingers to his cheek. Her fur ruffled, and her fingertips lost feeling as cold reached up. She couldn't understand how icicles hadn't formed on his lashes. Frost could have billowed on his skin at that temperature. The rays of moonlight returned and the solidness of his skin melted into mist. Her fingers went through him, the mist curling around her hand. Pinpricks welled in her frozen hand.

As the moon resumed hiding in the darkness of the clouds, Rex's body rematerialized from the center outward, pushing Chestnut's hand to the surface despite her pushback. *What...what is this?* His clothes misted and returned with his body.

Ava yawned. "Whatcha looking at? You look like you've seen a ghost." At the parted flowers, her face paled. "Oh...ghost."

Chestnut stepped backwards. "Oh moss."

"Huh...never seen that before..."

People did not turn into mist back home!

"Chestnut. Did anything happen? Before you were kidnapped?" Ava said.

The words formed on her lips like poison. A different poison than what invaded her intestines. Both made her sick to her stomach. Chestnut breathed and fog betrayed her fright.

"He died."

Ava's eyes widened. "He–?"

Chestnut withdrew her trembling hand. *Escorted by a ghost. This was not anything I could have predicted from the comfort of my room. I hugged him. He kept me safe. Why did I hug him?*

A softness lined his features. A softness that heightened the sturdiness. Perhaps she had been drawn to him because he'd been a solid rock for her. Her eyebrows knit together. *He was there for me when I was scared. He's still here despite not having any reason to be.*

I appreciate that.

Ava covered her mouth with her hand. "How did he–are you sure he was–dead?"

Chestnut's eyes traced from her shoe to her eyes. *Heath had made sure he was dead. But if he was dead, they would have taken him to a mortician instead of locking him up. Perhaps he's not really dead, but...*She brushed a hand through his mistified body. *How curious.*

"He collided with a down powerline. The man who kidnapped us confirmed he was dead. Yes. I do believe he's dead now." Chestnut said.

She returned to her tree corner, book loosely held at her side.

Flowers hid the glory of his bare soul. Without a body to clothe him, the moon stole pieces of him in those glowing ashes. Chestnut ignored reality and dove into the pages of her book. Rex's glowing state was unfixable, therefore unworthy of anxiety. Be solution oriented, not problem-focused, as her mother always said.

Her eyes soaked in the words of her book. *"Blueberry eyes glossed into my soul. "Ivy. I need your focus." Calloused fingers slid underneath my glove, but it wasn't sewn for two hands. Stubble on Sparrow's chin tickled. I never expected a kiss to tickle. "Sparrow, I can't. What if I fall?"*

Sparrow's muscles rippled as he stood, hand outstretched. "I'm not asking you to, Ivy. I am simply asking you to hold my hand and keep your eyes on me." He raised me to my feet.

A canyon of darkness lay between us and our freedom. Sparrow kept his eyes on me and stepped backwards onto the seven inch wide bridge.

"I trust you, Sparrow. Forever and always."

Sparrow's tail curled, "Forever and always."

Chestnut's eyes raised to the sleeping apparition. *Forever and always.*

I suppose Ava's right. With his hair over Rex's eyes, with his lips parted and his shoulders slim. *Perhaps I am not too stubborn to admit he is mildly attractive.*

CHAPTER 9

"Matthew, watch this!" Rex danced through the crowd of Victorian residents. Matthew had saved up so much for the top hat that sagged over Rex's small head telling him he would 'grow into it'.

Matthew's curly black hair towered over the crowd. "Xavier! Wait for me." He laughed, crow's feet scrunching his olive skin.

Rex ducked underneath the gaggle of well dressed ladies blocking the window. He pressed his 11-year-old hands against the glass. "Look, look, look, look, look!"

A large duck dangled from the inside of the butcher's shop. Rex imagined its dimpled skin dressed with brilliant, green feathers. Hands slid underneath his armpits as Matthew hoisted him into his arms. "Silly Goose! I told you to wait for me."

"But it's a duck! Matthew can we get it, please? It's the biggest duck in months!"

"Maybe in another few months. We're saving up, little by little."

"You said that months ago." Rex tightened his hands around the cloth of Matthew's ivory button up shirt.

"And we're closer, okay?" He brushed the hair from the bridge of Rex's freckled nose. "Once we have enough, I promise. We'll find the biggest bird and spend hours turning it on a slow roast. All the spices."

"M'kay." Rex fidgeted with the buckle on Matthew's suspenders.

The orange hair of Matthew's cousin snaked through the crowd. Rex tipped his head watching it flash by. "Where did Uncle William say he was going again?"

Matthew's soft expression darkened. "Nowhere. He went to scout out better locations for busking. Speaking of, how about we head back and you can help me tune my violin!"

Rex peered over Matthew's shoulder as he walked away. *I wonder if Matthew knows he's pickpocketing.* He caught sight of his adopted uncle through the swarm of people. William's pencil mustache pulled into a devilish grin. *I promised not to tell Matthew I was learning how to steal too. I trust William! I'm sure he has a reason for not telling Matthew.* Rex's cheeks scrunched into a smile as he popped the top hat on Matthew's head.

<hr>

Gunshot.

Rex gasped awake, grass flattened beneath his tight lanky fingers.

Chestnut glanced at him with mild curiosity. Her heavy lashes batted with her slow blinks. "We put out the fire." Her eyes dropped down to her open book.

The core provided a comfortable mid-morning warmth. His skin felt less like ice and more like normal living temperature. "Huh?"

"The fire." She angled an ear towards the pile of ash surrounded by stones.

"Oh, yeah. Thanks."

Ava lay sprawled on her back among the flowers.

There was a haunted, empty quality to Chestnut's eyes. He'd never pinned her as guarded before, but that glaze over her expression was a clear enough indicator that his first impression might not have been too accurate. "How– uh– how are you holding up?"

The tip of Chestnut's tail twitched. "It certainly is a lot to process."

"You're taking it well."

"Am I? I have never been kidnapped before"

That was the first full sentence she had said since leaving the village. "Your voice is pretty." Rex smiled.

A wave of blush overtook her. "Thank you."

"If you want to talk about it, I'm always here to lend an ear. I know how hard it is to deal with...stuff...alone." Years of isolation taught him that.

Her hair bobbed with her single nod.

Ava shuffled, waking up. She slit open her eyes and smiled at Rex. "Good morning." She sat up. "Glad you're awake. So you wanna explain this whole dying thing?"

Sweat billowed on Rex's forehead. "The–huh–what?"

"I told her about the powerline." Chestnut said.

"Oh...powerline. Ah. Yeah. Uh–" He covered his wrist. "You see– the powerline, well it, uh– Oh jeez." He scratched the back of his neck.

"Killed you?" Ava finished with raised eyebrows. "Yeah, got that, I just don't understand how."

Rex took up a nervous pacing, tugging on his fingers to relieve stress. "Uh, well. Yes, I did die. The powerline gave me a heart attack."

"How are you here then?" She probed.

"I–" Rex whirled on her. "Since when do you care? Just mind your own business."

Ava raised her hands "Alright. Ok, man. No need to snap."

Like a pouting toddler, Rex crossed his arms and sat down.

"Trust issues?" She leaned towards him.

"No."

"Mhm." Ava raised her brows. "Daddy issues?"

Rex averted his glance.

"S'okay, man." Ava said "We all have stuff we're going through. Talking about it helps."

He turned his nose up at her. Chestnut watched him intently and a look of fear crossed her eyes. *Wait, she's not afraid of opening up, is she? I want her to talk to me, so I can help her.* His arms loosened from their crossroads. *But I can't expect her to open up if I'm allowing myself to stay so closed.* "I–uh– so I should be dead." Rex turned his head to cut Chestnut's deciphering stare out of his peripherals. "I've died before though. When a soul dies a second time, they get to keep their body because spirits can't travel."

"What's beyond it?" Ava scooted forward.

"I was six, so I landed in Limbo." At her blank look he added, "It's the realm between Heaven and Hell. Children under the age of innocence go there."

"You mean all that stuff's real!?"

"Yeah." His eyes were magnetized back to Chestnut. Her stormy eye had dropped to her book. *I have to keep going, don't I...* "Anyway, You can either join Heaven's waitlist, or take a second life in exchange for eternal servitude to– y'know–" Rex was only willing to reveal so much. "If you take your second life, you can choose to resume your life or start it over without your memories."

"And this isn't some–like– crazy dream you had, right?"

Really. Rex sent her a look. "You want proof? I had a heart attack and am still here."

Ava buffered.

Chestnut curled her tail as if invested in a mystery novel. "That's what Heath was talking about. He wants you in Lavivrus so he poisoned me to get you there." She fit her fingers into each other like puzzle pieces. "His motive being he's probably connected to this realm and is responsible for bringing you back to it so you can slave away for eternity."

"Jeez..." Ava said.

The turtle had come out of the shell, just as planned. Rex nodded, trying to encourage this burst of energy from Chestnut. "Yeah."

"Now who's behind all this–?"

Rex jumped to his feet. "Welp! Hahahaha, we had better get going, huh?"

Chestnut's fur poofed to conceal her behind a ball of fur. "Oh–ok."

The bubble storage gurgled as Ava dumped peaches into it. "What? I love peaches." She grinned.

Rex winced. "Don't say that."

"That I love–"

"Don't."

"Love?"

Nails on a chalkboard! Did she understand the weight of that word? It wasn't just 'a word' that you tossed around lightly. Rex pulled his hood over his head. "You shouldn't use such a bad word so flippantly."

"...Yeah, ok man." Ava rolled her eyes.

Rex ushered them on their feet. "At this rate, we'll reach the station by nightfall."

"Cool, then imma charge my phone. It's at 18%"

Ava led the way. Rex stood in front of Chestnut to block her from standing, "Booky". He reached a hand to Chestnut. Hm, how familiar. At least this time they weren't coated in mud. "I want to talk." Chestnut received the invite and like a venus flytrap, his fingers closed around hers.

Rex hoisted her to her feet and led her on by the hand. "Any effects of the poison yet?"

She shook her head, returning to her protective, fortified shell.

"It's only been one day, so I shouldn't expect so." He released her hand.

"What did you want to talk about, exactly?"

"I opened up, your turn. What's going on in that brain of yours."

Chestnut blinked then turned her eyes to Ava in the distance.

Is she really about to give me the silent treatment? Maybe she's just thinking. Claws. Of course she's thinking, that's all she ever does. He found it bizarre. Phrasing things in terms of tales of valiant heroes and awful villains brought a brightness to her usual plaintive expression. Ah, that's how he'd get answers out of her. He just had to speak her language. "What kind of book is that?"

"*Heights of a Climbing Ivy*"

He inspected the cover from a distance. "What's it about?"

Chestnut held her book close to her heart, shielding it from Rex. "About the consequences of not trusting others."

Rex leaned away.

"Yes, like that." She handed him the book. "Perhaps you should read it. You might learn something."

"Uh– no, that's fine." He didn't want some book preaching to him about the magic of friendship. He'd tried singing kumbaya. The ones who don't sing always end up manipulating the ones who do. "Maybe you could summarize it for me."

She looked down at it. "Well, it follows Ivy Thistlethorn, an odd Chipeerman with horns instead of antlers. She meets the wonderful dashing Sparrow. By an accidental explosion of the mage's magic, they end up bound together. Meaning they can't walk more than 6 feet away from each other before the tether restricts them. Any injury that affects one, affects the other. They go on a quest to find artifacts to release their souls from bondage... falling in love." A soft smile stretched across her face.

A darkness entered Rex's eyes. "You psychopath. You enjoy 'love', don't you?"

"I'm sorry?" Chestnut's face screwed up and her tail lashed. "Yes. I think it's sweet and wholesome."

S-sweet? Rex stared at her, head spinning. "Wholesome...Wholesome?! Do you know what 'love' is?"

She pursed her lips, tilting her chin up in defiance "For the sake of having a mature debate, what is love for you, Rex?"

"A chain." Rex thrust his bared teeth into her face. He breathed smoke from his nose. "Like a python, it suffocates its victim and leaves it rotting and craving the same love that left it in that state. It's an addictive, self-destructive drug used to control others."

Chestnut took a deep breath. "Ok."

She has to agree, or disagree. Something! "Is that it? Just okay?"

"Mhm. You're not in the right mindset to listen right now."

I'm sorry?! "How would you know?"

Chestnut watched him.

"Oh, you're *so* stoic." He drew her hand from a long stroke down her arm. "I know what phases the great princess." He pressed a soft kiss against her hand. Just as planned, a flustered bundle of nerves replaced her calm. She pulled her hand away, but Rex cupped her face. "You like it when I treat you like this. Why?"

"I don't– this is– uncouth! And, and, and..." Her eyes widened as he leaned her back into his arm. "Sparrow."

"Oh." He pursed his naturally ruby lips. "I see Booky. You think I'm like your book character."

"Moss! No! Not that I'm interested in loving you, or loving to interest, or– interested in–interesting–I'm not interesting, not really, you probably are. But I–" Her ears pinned.

He had her completely bent over backwards at this point, propped up on his knee. "What if I did this?" He kissed her cheek.

A shrill squeal escaped her. "Rex!"

"Shall I do it again, *Ivy*?"

She writhed like a worm on a hook and ran away in adorable, flustered bounces. Rex wiped off his lips. *That was unpleasant.* It felt like kissing a cat. Thankfully her cheek fur was short. She flashed a wide-eyed glance at him from beside Ava, then her fur fluffed to double size. *At least I got her to show some emotion. Get her mind off things.* He trailed behind the three.

CHAPTER 10

Her fingers ran through her hair. *Oh moss, oh moss, oh moss, oh moss, oh moss, he kissed me!* She raised fingers to the spot where his soft lips had met her fur. Her face warmed again. *Silly! Silly, silly, silly girl! It is not for a lady to engage in such activities with a man so soon after introductions.*

Ava snorted. "Oh, no, what'd he do?"

"Is it normal on this planet to kiss so soon after meeting?!" Chestnut blurted

"You kissed!"

"Help!"

Ava laughed. Somehow, the cacophony of noises from her companions' mouth eased her fluster. Chestnut used her tail to block Rex from her peripheral vision.

"I think he likes you." Ava poked her.

"No, he does not. He just does it to fluster me."

"Hehehee, you like him?"

Chestnut gasped. "Scandalous! No. Moss no, heavens no. He is..." *Smart, considerate, sturdy, comforting...*Chestnut's heart dropped. *But he's also pushy, and self absorbed, and bossy, and, and...dead!*

"Makes sense. You two have been attached at the hip since I met you."

Perhaps I have been too touchy...

Rex came behind them. "The station is just another mile, then off to the Bronze Era district."

Oh, yes. Sophie mentioned these different Eras. It makes it sound like time travel when he says it so casually. I suppose this Old Earth had an immense influence on these people for them to base their entire culture and social standing around it. Chestnut was pulled into the icy blue of his eyes. She could see far into his soul through them, yet so little. She pinned her ears back and hugged her book.

Rex looked over her head at Ava. "We're just stopping by, so no lingering. The minute we get off the train, we're laying over to–" He trailed off as if listening to something else. "The–" His pupils contracted. "No. Not there. Somewhere else." He took a deep breath, shoulders tense. "Victoria." His fingers tightened around his cloak.

"Cool." Ava said.

Why is he so upset about going to the Victorian District? Chestnut pitched forward to see him. "What lies in the Victorian Era?"

"Nothing."

"Maybe the source of his daddy issues." Ava snorted

Rex's furious expression creased lines into his face. "No."

Ava gave him a hard slap on the back. "Aw, it's ok! If you want to talk about it, we're here."

Bringing light to the fact that there is something to talk about only dissuades us from talking about it. "Ava, your offer is appreciated, but I think it's fallen on deaf ears," Chestnut said.

Ava turned to her. "Hold up, was that a contraction? I think that's the first time I've heard you use a contraction!"

"A what?" Chestnut tipped her head.

"You said 'It's', 'it' plus 'has' equals 'it's'."

How curious. "I suppose my dialect is relaxing the slightest bit." Chestnut lowered her eyes.

A track split through the carnations. Wooden beams lay across gravel with large, rusted nails driven through the edges. Chestnut approached with a bobbing head. Rex's hands wrapped around her waist and yanked her back. "Careful!"

"Why?"

"What if a train came by. You want to get run over?" He pulled her further backwards.

"Release me. I understand." His hands unlatched from her waist. She followed him walking along the track, a good ten feet away.

A sharp cramp gripped her side. She wavered from the group pace and keeled over. *I shouldn't slow the group because of my own inability to keep up. I just...* The cramp tightened and pinpricks moved up to her stomach. *Oh moss, I think I might throw up.*

Rex raised a hand to signal Ava to wait.

Chestnut grit her teeth and forced her screaming body to take her forward. "Let us continue."

Rex dropped to walk beside her on the inner side of the railroad track. "Let me know if you need a break."

"I'll rest on the train." Her ear angled towards him. "What does a train look like?"

"Uh– big metal thing. I dunno."

A hard laugh came from Ava. "You don't know what a train looks like?"

"I told you," he pointed at himself, "homeless. Before that, I lived in Victoria. Not many trains there."

Is that why he was so so averse to going to Victoria? Like a leech, Chestnut attached herself to the sliver of insight. "Rex, What were you like when you were a kid?"

"Let's talk about something else."

Another stab erupted in her kidney. Her eyes watered.

Rex gently settled her on the ground. "Don't cry, it's ok. I know it hurts."

"Why did I have to get involved in any of this? I never wanted this when I left my home. I never asked to watch you die or be kidnapped. Or–or." Her eyes dripped in mourning. "Rex, I just want to go home. I just–" She clutched her stomach.

He gripped her hand, which was a fatal mistake. Chestnut squeezed it till his hand was black and blue. Rex gave a halfhearted smile. "Uh– there's gotta be something we can talk about to get your mind off it."

Chestnut tossed her head from side to side. "It hurts–"

"Didn't you– oh. Do you still want to know what I was like as a kid?" Rex plucked a flower and tapped the petals off.

Is he really willing to open up for the sake of my distraction? She wiped her round, curious eyes. "I–I do."

"Alright, alright. Uh– it depends on which childhood. They were radically different."

The strain of her cramp increased with her soft laughs. "Radically. That's a nice word."

"Yeah? I got a lot of other big words. I was temperamental, hot-headed, haphephobic." His mouth twisted in a sad smile. "That's what you call a fear of touch. I've grown out of it for the most part, but occasionally it crops up."

While his eyes were fixated on the carnation, Chestnut reached a hand to his shoulder. A light tap and he jumped, eyes wide. His ears reddened and he turned away. *I didn't mean to embarrass him.* The pain eased and Chestnut released his hand. "Haphephobic. Did your parents do that to you?"

His hand shook over the flower. A terrorized stare entered his face. "He did alot to me." Rex set the flower down. "A–any–anyway. Um...No, once I took my second life my mom had already died."

"Then who did you grow up with?"

"Two–" Rex broke off. "One young man. His name was Matthew. He was like a father, I guess."

"What happened to him?"

Rex looked up, a tearful flush of red entering his cheeks "Now that you're feeling better, let's get back onto the road." He stormed ahead of Ava, nervously pulling on his corset.

Chestnut stood up slowly. *What happened to you?*

CHAPTER 11

Why won't the shaking stop? Rex clenched his hands, but his weak grip only served to increase his frustration. *I'm fine.*

A soft laugh rang in his ears since Chestnut had mentioned His Highness. Of the many laughs He had, this one was the most haunting. A soft amused chuckle. Usually accompanied by petting, Rex felt the glove pull gently on his hair. The hand moved underneath his ear and a wetness pressed against his forehead. *"Kitten, you bring me great delight."* Another kiss pressed upon his brow.

He walked in tortured silence. Tortured by his own hallucination. Rex squeezed his eyes closed, but the darkness only painted the past in neon hues. He flung his eyes open. *Slow your breathing. He's not here. You're fine.*

Think about something else, Rex. Think about any-bloody-thing else. His dream stirred. Matthew never did get him that duck. A familiar anger replaced his fear. The laughter faded away, replaced by a–

Gunshot

Rex jumped.

If Destiny is forcing me to go through Victoria to get to Lavivrus, I'm not going to leave without righting a wrong. He tapped lightning against his leg.

Thanks Sire. This will serve me well.

There were so many outstretched avenues. Knife, noose, breaking his neck, all plausible options. *If I could get my hand on a gun, wouldn't that be poetic justice.* The lightning increased in voltage till it burned his skin. *Ow. Actually, I wonder if I could simulate that powerline. That would do the trick.*

Rex snapped lightning from his hand on the offbeat of his steps. *On Matthew's life, I promised myself I'd do this.*

Ava trotted up to meet him. "So you kissed Chestnut. Rrrrer!"

Rex pulled his cloak further around him.

"So you like her?"

"What?"

Ava waggled her eyebrows.

"Stop that."

"Why'd you kiss her then?"

"She was being all stuck up and stoic, so I just pulled her off her high horse with my good looks and shining armor."

Ava looked back at Chestnut falling behind "Mhm. Mhm. And in Layman's terms?"

"She annoyed me."

Her humor vanished behind Ava's scathing expression. "So you...kissed her."

"She liked it."

"You're leading her on."

"Yeah?"

"What happens if she actually falls for you?"

Falls for him? He'd never had anyone fall for him. Except for– His Highness, but He didn't count. 'Fall in love' is how the expression went, wasn't it? If she was falling in love with him, that meant she would start manipulating him. Maybe she already was and he was too blind to see it. *I didn't see it coming the first time, not even the second time, why would I see it this time?* "I should apologize."

If he let this go on, if Chestnut decided he was her new toy, if she fell in love with him...

Rex's downturned eyes fell on wooden steps. "You did get us tickets, right?"

"Yup, we got first class seats, and a nice, hot meal, baby." Ava smiled, hopping up the stairs like a gazelle. Rex stalked behind her, more cheetah than gazelle.

Chestnut joined the inside. "I've never ridden in a train before. Is there a certain etiquette to follow?"

Rex averted his eyes from her.

"Not really." Ava said. "You sit on seats and the train chugs off."

Chestnut refused to look at Rex too.

Why won't she look at me? I get to not look at her in case she's trying to capture me in a trance with her eyes, but what's her excuse? Rex walked behind them into the station. An outdoor hallway passed between two ticket booths. A collection of women in hijabs, gentlemen dressed in top hats and spats, a summer camp of students wearing sweatpants and t-shirts, and medieval peasants dressed in sackcloth stood with them on the wooden boards. Rex herded the group towards the back corner. Filled chairs lined both booths. Two hands for each person, hands for grabbing, hands for scrolling, everywhere he looked hands were in use.

A hand slid around his elbow, Chestnut clung tight to him. "There's so many people..."

I know. But being clinged to was suffocating, especially by the girl he'd just kissed in an act of self defense. "Ava, could you–"

Ava caught his drift and pulled Chestnut into a hug. "S'okay. Once we board, it'll be less stressful."

"My community only had maybe 100 people. I've never seen so many people in my life."

"Scary, huh?"

Chestnut nodded.

Rex watched them in solemn silence. He rubbed his elbow.

Once the doors opened, the passengers hoisted their suitcases onto the metal stairs.

Ava pulled away. "Do you want me to hold your hand?" At Chestnut's nod, she slid her hand into Chestnut's.

Thank Limbo, Ava was here. He wasn't sure he'd be comfortable holding her hand so casually. In a fake stage performance, he could act anyway he liked; flirty, suave, touchy. However, the stage only extended so far. An audience member would never jump on stage during a show and take up his own routine. Rex considered himself a part of the crowd of onlookers, watching the subtleness of Ava's and Chestnut's act.

He offered a hand to help Chestnut up. Ava joined last, providing proof of their entry.

Ava and Chestnut sat beside each other with Rex opposite Ava. The fourth seat was occupied by a girl wearing headphones. Rex pressed against the window to avoid contact with the stranger.

Chestnut looked up. "When does the train pull out?"

"When everyone's boarded." Ava scrolled tiny candies into explosions on her phone.

Rex leaned over the table. "Chestnut...I wanted to apologize, for earlier."

A heavy suitcase thudded past them, swiveling Chestnut's ears. "Apologize? For the kiss?"

"I just want to make sure we're clear on where we stand."

Ava pretended she wasn't totally eavesdropping.

Chestnut met his blue eyes with hers. "Where do we stand?"

"I know I'm attractive by society's standards." *As Ava so helpfully pointed out.* "But I've had a very bad experience with relationships, especially romantic ones in the past. And...I just want to make sure you're not falling for me or anything."

Chestnut blinked a few times, before she snorted. "You! F-falling...for you? You don't need to worry about *that*, Rex. I would never fall for you any deeper than superficial admiration."

"Uh– Good." Rex turned away. Good. They were on the same page. That's what he wanted. That's what he... wanted. Rex whisked his attention back to her. "Why not?"

She pinned her ears. "I find you reserved, vain, pushy, and impulsive."

Excuse me? Rex leaned forward. "Vain! I'm not vain."

"And I quote 'I know I'm attractive' You also lied about your name at our first introduction." She met his challenge, nose to nose.

"I do that with every stranger. Keeps me out of trouble, Booky."

"Does trouble follow you around, Lucas?" her mouth turned into a passive -aggressive smile.

The table jutted into his stomach as he leaned closer. "You're full of wit, aren't you?"

"I do admit I have an affinity for intelligent sounding words."

"How about disinclined?" Rex smirked.

"Impetuous."

"Platitudinous."

"Extemporaneous!" Chestnut's fur fluffed, brushing Rex's cheek.

Ava snickered. "One more inch, and y'all will be kissing."

They both slumped back into their seats. Rex's arms crossed. *How dare she call me extemporaneous! I always think before acting.*

Chestnut turned her nose away from him.

The train jerked forward, then took off at a steady chug. Chestnut gazed out the window.

Impetuous. Pfft, I bet she doesn't even know what that means. Rex thought.

Cups of water and beverages came by on a cart. Rex took a water.

The countryside rose up and blocked the view behind tall hills. Rex noticed the book jutting out of Chestnut's bag again. *Yeah, I'm bored, why the claws not?* He gestured to it. "Hey, lemme read it."

Chestnut looked up at him. "Let me add rude to the list."

"Please?"

"That's a step in the right direction. Now, rephrase it."

Rex scowled. "I think I'll take you up on your offer, Booky. May I read your book while we wait, please?"

"You may." She gave him the book with a pleasant grin. "Now next time, do that in your thoughts, then maybe I can cross off impulsiveness from the list."

Prissy, stuck up, teacher's pet. Rex opened to the first page. "Do you not have printing presses where you grew up?"

"No. Each has to be handwritten."

"Hm." Rex had a time of it translating the chicken scratch into words, but by page 25, he'd adjusted to it.

The girl beside him lit a cigarette. Rex and Chestnut gagged. Ava gave her a look but was pretty unaffected. Rex held his cloak's fabric over his nose.

A choking sound came from the girl beside him. Her body stiffened like a board, with spasms of movement billowing her chest.

"Ava, what's happening." Chestnut said.

"I–I don't know."

The girl fell limp, on Rex's shoulder. She paled, Rex could feel her spirit leaving her. "She's dying."

One strong push propelled her onto the floor, Rex stooped over her. "Is there a doctor on board!?" Earbuds came out, eyes turned to him. "Doctor!"

Claws, I can't let her die, stay with me, stay with me. No pulse.

A passenger joined him on the ground, a middle aged man. "Looks like a heart attack."

"Doctor?"

"No, nurse."

Rex felt himself falling into panic. *Deep breaths* "How do you deal with heart attacks?"

The man looked above him. "Defibrillator, we need a V-fib!"

"That's the thing with electricity." Rex's eyes widened. "How much voltage comes from a defi–fiber–fiber–the thing!"

Chestnut scooted beside him, sleeves rolled up.

The nurse pumped her chest. "We need at least 300 volts."

"Chestnut lean back." Rex flung his hands on the woman's chest and pumped his guess of what 300 volts were.

The nurse gasped, but chose not to question. "Again, 400."

Rex upped the voltage, sending lightning through his veins into her. *Gently, gently.*

He pulled away and the woman gasped. The nurse leaned over her and whispered soft instructions to her.

Rex snubbed the cigarette on the carpet. Breathing heavily, he turned to Chestnut. "Are you okay?"

The lightning had fluffled her fur to double the size. "Fine. Is she though?"

The nurse looked up. "She'll be fine. She just needs immediate medical attention once we come in."

Soon, the train staff arrived, defibrillator and first aid kit in hand. They leaned the girl back on the two seats, propping her feet up. Rex stood, looking down at her. *That's why you don't smoke, ladies and gentlemen.*

Chestnut stood beside him. "You can take my seat."

"No, you need the rest."

Ava scooted over to exchange seats. Chestnut looked up at him. "We could probably fit the three of us here"

Thighs touching, shoulder to shoulder? No, thank you. "I'd rather stand."

"Okay."

Rex crossed his arms.

Once the train pulled into the station, an ambulance was waiting for the girl. "Stay together. Especially here." *Now we need a place to stay; an inn. Then I can slip away to go hunting.*

He looked down and tried to focus on something other than the nagging memories tugging at the edges of his mind; waiting to be given an inch so they could take a mile.

He wanted to head inward, closer near the heart of the city. However, walking there would be a waste of time. He held out a hand. *C'mon, Taxi.*

He stepped backwards but jumped as he ran into something. He put a hand over his heart, although it wasn't like he could get a heart attack or anything now.

Ava gave a faint smile, "Steady there."

"You startled me, that's all."

Ava stuffed a hand in her pocket and continued scrolling on her phone.

Chestnut rested on a bench. "Moss, I'm glad that lady's okay."

"Yeah, so where'd you get the magic from?" Ava said.

Rex stared at the skyline, his fingers stroking his hand.

"Rex."

He turned to them, "Huh, what?"

Chestnut tipped her head. "Come sit."

I don't even know where to find William. He could be anywhere. He sat down beside her, elbows resting on his knees.

"Rex, are you okay?" Chestnut said.

"Fine."

She searched his face. "Is it something to do with your childhood?"

"No."

"Do you want to talk about it?"

"No."

Chestnut gave him a look, then turned to face the street of horse carriages.

The horse hooves clopped through his mind, steady four beats until a gunshot rang out. The noise haunted his hallucinations like a ghost. Ava hailed a cab. Rex ran his hands through his hair. "Just being here...It's Matthew."

Chestnut watched them as well. "Are you afraid you will not be able to find him?"

Rex's eyes dulled, but he offered no response.

"What is he like?"

Rex's austere expression cracked behind a soft smile. The memories of Matthew were sweet. "Heh– where do I start? Amazing." He could still see his soft expression wrinkling as he smiled down at him. "He did everything right. He was kind to everyone. He was honest, and hardworking and... I was 11, the last time I saw him. He had 3 jobs, just to get a salad on our table. Something healthy and sustaining for a growing young boy." Rex's face dropped. "I never understood back then how much he sacrificed for me. We weren't even related. He just took me off the streets and raised me."

"Was there another person?"

William had made it perfectly clear that he was outcasted from Matthew's family. Every argument that kept Rex awake reminded him over and over that William was only here for free room and board. "There was no one else." Rex shrugged his cloak tighter around him. "He's dead to me. At least he will be." Fire pulsed through his veins. A hot hatred.

Gunshot.

Lightning sparkled off him.

"Whatever happened, as my sister would say, 'It's water under the bridge'." Chestnut did her best impression of what Rex believed was her sister.

She's so optimistic. Her smile was infectious and soon he found himself reflecting it.

Ava yawned. "Oh, yeah, one of your *seven* siblings." She walked backwards along the curb. "Imma get water, be right back."

A boy approached the curb, eyes glued to his phone. He looked about 17, maybe 18, but it was hard to tell underneath the hood of his seafoam green hoodie.

Ava walked behind him as he took a step back. Their feet got entangled with each other. Ava's shoelace caught underneath his sneaker. After a hilarious scene of flailing arms, Ava fell.

Rex bit back a snicker.

"Oh–sorry about zat!" A thick, french accent lingered in his voice. He reeled back and cleared his throat. "Tee. Thuh, thuh, thuh. *That.* Sorry, still working on my 'Th's" He laughed in an American accent. It wasn't a bad impression, but definitely not his natural one. He reached down to help her up.

Rex narrowed his eyes. *He's more worried about his pronunciation than hurting Ava...at least he has his priorities straight.* Mr. French was rather tall, about twice Rex's size; well-built. He had a shy smile that crinkled his amber eyes. His blonde hair mixed with his yellowish skin made him look like banana pudding.

Rex didn't like banana pudding.

The boy's eyes flickered over Ava. He picked her off the ground.

"Ava Charlie Evans, But you can call me ACE. Nice to be knocked over!" She smiled

"H-hey, I said I was sorry."

Chestnut stepped forward. The stranger's eyes glanced over her.

Seeing Chestnut checked out by another guy made Rex's blood boil. "Buddy, eyes up here."

The boy blushed a hot red. "I-I wasn't checking her out! I was just noticing the knotted fur, mud, greasy hair, and the– uh—lack of shoes." He seemed most put off by that last one.

"My name is Chestnut, and this is Rex."

The boy's eyes flickered over Rex, making Rex's skin crawl. He didn't like being scanned. He muttered under his breath "rather...pale. I'm Jason."

Rex rolled his eyes and reached out a hand. *There's gotta be some cab around here!*

A horse-drawn taxi carriage pulled up in front of them. The horse's silky black pelt was lined with gray hairs.

"Jason," Ava smiled, "not a very *French* name."

"I was born in New France. My mother didn't want me standing out too much."

"Huh! Interesting." She said.

Rex ushered Chestnut into the cab. "Ava, we're leaving."

"I know, I know, give me a second."

Jason smiled, "where are you headed?"

Rex stepped in front of Ava, looping an arm in hers. That was none of his business. The closer he came, the more the height difference became more noticeable. It sickened him, like being taller was some kind of power play. "Nowhere. Good day."

Ava resisted his pulling. "Wait, wait." She slipped back to Jason. She gave him a flirty look.

"Hi." He let out a small laugh as his face reddened.

"Gimme your number, nerd!" She smirked.

A quick exchange of numbers later, Rex's patience had long drained. *I wonder if they know having their phones out is illegal.* She could do whatever she wanted. He didn't care. He just wished it would go a little quicker.

"Great!" Ava elbowed Jason. "I think you're *really* cute so I'll see ya later!"

Jason pulled his hood back over his head. "Mhm."

"C'mon." Rex yanked Ava into the cab. He thumbed through the $50 he'd taken from Chestnut on their meeting. "To Victoria, sir."

The driver took the money and handed him back a guinea change. With a grunt, the driver whipped the reins.

Rex settled in, looking at Ava and Chestnut sitting across him. "You know that was illegal, right?"

"Pfft, hurt nothing. Did you see him? He's a model. And there weren't any cops around."

The concrete turned to cobblestone.

The amount of cars were replaced with horse and buggies carrying wealthy Lords and Ladies. *Matthew would never have associated with such prissy, stuck up jerks.*

Now William... Rex could see him guzzling gin while robbing the rich through their own gambling. He'd taught him everything he knew about pickpocketing after all.

Chestnut perked her ears. "Illegal?"

"Each district has strict laws about what's allowed and what's not. If you had a bunch of people with phones in the Victorian Era, it'd take away from the authenticity. Likewise, if you brought a fan into the Bronze Era, you could get fined."

Ava wiggled a nonexistent tie and faked a British accent. "All items have to be kept hidden in a suitcase until in an appropriate Era or in privacy."

"However, some places like restaurants and inns have special permits to have showers or running water for tourists and travelers. However, residents aren't allowed to stay or eat at such places."

Chestnut watched the ping pong of information. "Oh moss."

Rex turned his attention to the window. The ride took the rest of the day. *At least Victoria is in their summer.*

Chimney sweeps, only little boys, stood on almost every home. Some of those children would go down that flue and never see the light of day again. Even a good honest living had its cost.

Rex kept his guard up against pickpockets, or worse, gang members who might recognize him.

Ava and Chestnut gawked and smiled at the trains of dresses and pocket watches.

If they were going to be staying a few days, they better try to fit in. "Follow me, I know a tailor. Pickpockets love nothing more than to steal from tourists. especially if you stick out like a sore thumb. Ava, you still have your bubble storage?"

"Yeah, why?"

"That way we can keep our clothes. How much money do you have?"

Chestnut pulled her coin purse out of her pocket. "$1000"

Rex shushed her. "Keep your voice low! $950, actually."

Chestnut tipped her head "Huh?"

"I took $50 when we first met." Rex searched her face for a change, a twitch, anything, but she remained straight-faced. *Impressive.* "There's a thrift store down the way and a tailor further up." *$1000, what's that, uhh 3 guineas? 64 shillings?* Rex noted his ripped corset and his holey boots. Wearing one pair of clothes for two years seemed to wear them out quickly. He definitely needed new clothes.

"I'm going to go through the thrift store and see what I can find. Why don't you ladies get fit for dresses? It'd make a nice momento."

Ava's face lit up and she darted with Chestnut towards the tailor.

Rex jumped back as a blur of tar dashed in front of him. Oh yeah, he could see angels and demons now– there sure were a lot more demons here than in other areas they have traveled. *Don't judge. Maybe one day they'll rise to a fallen angel status. Risen demon.* Rex avoided another group of demons whispering and headed for the thrift store.

 Rex thumbed through the rack of men's garments. Most of the sizes were too big. He looked across the cobblestone road at a hat store.

He remembered that hat store...

A filter slid over his vision. He saw bullies, standing like vultures over a little kid fighting his hardest, but to no avail. They picked him up by the arms. The lead bully peeled back his fist, then–

Rex turned away.

He heard the punch, he felt the punch. The hallucination faded.

Rex continued his search. There wasn't much for a gentleman. Most of the clothes were practically rags. *I already wore those before. Maybe I'll join the girls.*

Rex pushed his way into the tailor. Ava gawked at a bright red elaborate dress. "Hey Rex, I think I'm going to get this!"

"Don't. That's for a prostitute."

Ava stepped backwards as if the dress was infested with lice or something. Rex waved over a tailor. "What can I help you with, sir?" The tailor's thick British accent flattered him.

Rex matched it subconsciously. "Cravat, breeches, stockings, boots, waistcoat, and a corset, please."

"This way, my Lord." The tailor removed Rex's cloak and unclipped his corset. Rex felt a rush of uncomfort. His spine felt like jello without the whale bone. His dark blue shirt breathed, for the first time in a while.

The tailor fitted him for another corset, this one ivory. Rex took a sharp inhale as the tailor jerked the ribbon tighter. "How does it feel in the tail? The back and the shoulders?" The tailor asked.

"Good, a little tighter though."

The tailor jerked again.

Rex bit his cheek. "Ah, good."

Ava huffed and came beside him, thumbing through the men's small sizes.

"What are you doing?" Rex said.

"I can't move in a dress. Wait 'till you see Chestnut though." She clicked her eyebrows. "Reerr! Anyway, I'm going to check in the thrift store." She ran out of the store.

"Be careful!" Rex called after her. He looked at himself in a mirror. *Not bad.* The tailor brought folded coats, breeches, and stockings and added the amounts to a tab. Rex slid his coat over the corset. It flared at the waist in an oval that stretched to his inner knee. Rex paid for the outfit, then held it in his arms while tapping his foot.

Ava entered the store again wearing sackcloth and second-hand chimney sweep clothes. Her large shirt tucked into her pants with suspenders over her shoulders. "Much better!"

Rex grabbed a newsboy hat and shoved it on her head. "Put your hair in that. Then you'll *really* look like a guy."

Ava stuck her tongue out. "So you gonna hold all that fabric or put it on?"

The dressing room was open now. Rex dressed and pulled back the curtain for Ava to admire the outfit.

Ava's eyes widened "Woah. You look like a prince!"

That hit a nerve, hard and fast. "No, I look like a gentleman." He smirked and cast a sidelong glance at the mirror.

The reflected image reminded him too much of a Prince he hadn't seen in a long while. Xavier looked back at him. *You can't outrun me.* Rex's face paled as he regarded his younger self.

Another hallucination crossed his eyes. His Highness stood over him, holding him close with a charming smirk. *Him.*

The two looked near identical, the only thing separating them was a generation. Rex's face dropped, he could feel the warmth, smell the sulfur. His red eyes glowed in the dark vision. *He* curled his eyebrows, an amused look spreading, and leaned further to whisper into Rex's ear. *"The apple doesn't fall far, does it?"*

Rex, relying too heavily on his instinct, kicked the mirror, sending it toppling on the ground. It shattered into thousands of shards. Rex breathed heavily, his mind fogged by panic.

His hair was teased by his own imagination. A soft tugging. *"Mmm, your hair is soft, Kitten."*

Get away, get away, get away, get away! He ruffled his hair.

"You good?" Rex turned to Ava, who looked a little frightened.

"F-fine. Fine. I'm fine." Coming here was a mistake. *Get in. Get out. Get it done.*

A curtain pulled back, revealing Chestnut. A beautiful long skirt trailed behind her, a bustle adding to the volume. She wore a puffy white shirt that highlighted her hourglass figure. She looked at Rex and blushed.

Wow, she really looks like a lady. Her usually unrestrained mane was now twisted in a bun, decorated with flowers and pearls.

"Is it alright? Oh, I do look ridiculous" She blushed redder and retreated to the dressing room.

Rex stopped her. "You look fine, Booky. Let's go."

She motioned to her bustle. "I do not like this, but the tailor swore by it."

Rex nearly choked from laughter. *I'm sure he did.* "It's just the style." Rex slipped the wallet out of her pocket, without her feeling. He handed the clerk money.

Chestnut gave a bemused sigh. "Rex."

He smirked "Nature of the game, Booky. At least I'm nice enough to give it back."

Ava asked for directions to the nearest inn.

Chestnut drank in every detail of this place.

Rex watched them like a hawk.

Ava pulled her phone out to take a few pictures. She put it in her back pocket and continued talking. The person she was talking to shook his head and walked away.

Ava slumped, dejected. A stocky man with orange hair slid up to her.

He looked too familiar, like someone he'd known. He had to look away, only lending his ear to eavesdrop.

"I can help with directions." The man said.

More talking, but Rex didn't care to pay much attention.

He watched Chestnut gawk at the buildings. *Claws, she really looks lovely in that outfit.* Her eyes were alight with wonder; Rex looked around, The architecture was so normalized from his youth that he'd never taken a moment to look and admire it as a tourist. He had to admit, there was something stunning about the way the sun shone and shined on the gold and brass. Chestnut dashed to him, tail curled. "Isn't it wonderful?"

Fresh roasted walnuts sent a smoky aroma their way. Rex smiled softly at his home. "Wonderful...yeah, I guess it is." Fur covered fingers wrapped around his hand and dragged him to a statue.

"Just look at this masterpiece!" An angel of stone gazed towards the horizon, it's eyes devoid of sadness. Determination rippled in its garments and its furrowed brows.

Rex's eyes lingered on their hands, intertwined by the palms. "Booky?"

Chestnut let out a dreamy sigh, her hair gathering beneath her chin as she raised one shoulder. "Inspiring. Captivating."

She was rather fond of big words, Rex smiled. "Enthralling."

"Yes, exactly. Enthralling is a good word." Her eyes squinted. "What else can you come up with?"

Claws. Rex stared at her. "Uh-" *Think, Rex, think.*

"Never thought I would catch *you* speechless, Rex."

Well if you would stop looking at me with those gray, wide eyes, maybe I could think easier. "Hold on, hold on, give me a minute." He had to come up with a good word, something impressive. "This statue is a simulacrum of an angel's likeness."

"Simulacrum?" She raised one eyebrow.

"It's totally a word." He bumped her with his hip.

She turned on him, fur bristling. "Excuse me, Sir."

"Hm? I didn't do anything."

Her tight lips broke into a smile. "Silly boy."

"Hey, where's Ava?" Rex said. "We should probably check into an inn."

Chestnut swiveled her ears. "Ava's that way"

"Let's go then." *I told her to stay with us!* Rex swam through the crowd. A painter captured the likeness of the statues on a portrait while a band played on a street corner, stirring dancers to accompany them. Rex smiled, Matthew and he had tried that. Every Saturday was spent dancing to the quick fiddling of Matthew's violin, eagerly watching for hands to drop coins into his top hat. Ava danced a swing routine with a chimney sweep dressed similar to her. Her hair swayed into her wide grin, cutting off her riotous laughter in a choking fit. The Sweep laughed at her. "Bloody good fun."

Jeez, that's the third boy. Rex approached them and tapped the chimney sweep's shoulder. "May I?"

"Hey, Rex, there you are," Ava said.

Despite the boy's glare, Rex stole her away. "We better find an inn."

"Oi, I get it, walkin off with some prissy toff." The poor boy took up his sweep and pointed it at Rex.

Rex gave him a sad look. If not for Matthew's death, he probably would have grown up just like this boy, they looked about the same age. *I'm not like the aristocracy, at least not anymore.* He then realized he was dressed head to toe in expensive silk and ornate embroidery. No wonder this boy thought he was rich. Rex offered an arm to

Ava. "Sir, this is my sister, she likes to dress up like commoners as a novelty. I'm not stealing her from you."

The Chimney Sweep's face reddened. "So I'm just a novelty to you. Jolly good." with that he stormed away.

Ava hesitantly slid her arm in Rex's. "I didn't mean to offend him."

"It's hard when the rich expect us to be their slave for a small fee. I feel for him."

Ava held her silence, but didn't stop gawking at the beauty. That's all she'd ever see, her and Chestnut. The poverty, the sewage growing algae on the stone, the garbage piled in alleyways, the drafts of cold nights, were never publicized. They'd never truly get it.

"Quick thinking by the way! Siblings–I think he bought it."

Rex snorted. "You think so? I guess we do look pretty similar."

"We could totally be twins!" Ava skipped with him.

"Maybe if you were an inch taller."

"Wha–take off your shoes and then we'll see who's taller Mr. 2-inch-heel."

"Never." He smirked and turned to Chestnut. "What do you two want to eat for dinner?"

Chestnut averted her eyes. "Oh, I'm not especially hungry."

"No, you, of all of us, need to eat. You're not allowed to starve on my watch." *I'm risking my afterlife for her. She doesn't get to die.* "Not like we can hunt, and food's expensive here. There will probably be options at the inn we find. They usually have bars on the ground floor."

Ava pumped her fists. "Burgers and fries, burgers and fries, burgers and fries!"

Lamplighters revived candles in their glass cages as the moon eclipsed the sun.

I'm running out of time. You and Chestnut find an inn and order us some dinner. I'm going to take a walk."

Ava grunted under the weight of the raptor. "Now?"

"Yeah, I just want to reacquaint myself with the area."

Chestnut took his hand again. "You can reacquaint yourself later. You need to eat too."

Rex cursed under his breath. If he tried to slip away now, it might look suspicious. *It's not like I can just tell them 'Hey, I gotta go kill the guy, be right back'. I'll have to handle this delicately.* He didn't protest being dragged through the cobblestone streets by Chestnut.

※

Rex lounged in the richly decorated chair, fingers drumming anxiously. Ava and Chestnut were trying to figure out how to draw a bath. They couldn't find an inn on this side of the city, so instead, they settled into the nearest pub they could find. They had a small meal, but Rex was too busy warning drunken gentlemen with glares to focus on his food. Chestnut was full by the fourth french fry, but Rex urged her on. Ava's burger made quite the mess though.

"Got it!" Ava exclaimed, followed by the sound of running water. "Now how do I turn it off...? that's the question."

"Oh dear." Chestnut said.

Rex could barely hear his own thoughts over the abused piano and out of tune singing downstairs. There were no walls thick enough to block that amount of noise. A yell echoed through the wooden flooring, followed by shattering glass and gunshots. Rex hopped to his feet by his pounding heart's prompting and quadruple checked that the door was locked. He returned to his chair, breathing heavily. *So that's why Matthew warned against staying in a pub.*

Rex steeled his nerves. Going out at night was dangerous, but if anyone tried anything, he had an electric defense. He needed to find William. He needed to find him tonight.

"I'm gonna go for my walk now."

Chestnut poked out of the bathroom. "Ok, stay safe."

97

"I will. Bye booky" He unlocked the door. "And lock it once I leave." He closed the door behind him and waited till he heard the latch. *Good.*

He pulled his cloak over his head and trotted down the stairs. Burly men blocked the stairwell. "Excuse me." Rex pushed past them.

The night was blustery and took the edges of his cloak up in its breeze. *C'mere William. I just want to right some wrongs.*

Rex stole away into the alleys.

CHAPTER 12

The door latched with a mechanical click. Chestnut's eyes lingered on the door before turning back to the bath.

"I wonder what he's doing?" "Why don't you follow him?" Ava waggled her eyebrows.

Steam rose from the freshly drawn water and fogged the mirror. Chestnut's fur sagged in the humidity. "Oh, no thank you. Last time I followed him we ended up in cages." Her fingers twirled around her curls.

"Alright. I just thought you would want to make sure your *boyfriend's* ok."

He is not my boyfriend. He's far too cavalier and daring...and kind, and gentle, and intelligent... What was she thinking again? Oh yeah. *We're friends and that is all. By any means, even if I were to be somewhat attracted to him for a mere moment, nothing lasts forever. My golden, highlighted version of him is bound to shatter at his first mistake. Then I won't like him anymore.* Chestnut turned her nose in the opposite direction. "You insult me."

"Just saying–"

"He is perfectly capable of handling himself, Ava. After all, he has the–zappy, lightning thing."

"Woah, woah, woah! You don't have, like, a fancy word for that? Tsk tsk tsk. Chestnut, you're slipping."

Moss, what is that word? Electro- Electronic- Lightnic- "Well, apologies, but no one has magic on my planet."

"Same, it's gotta be from this afterlife he told us about." Ava smirked. "Also the word you're looking for is electrokinesis."

"Thank you." Chestnut looked at the door as more screaming came from downstairs. *I'm already fated to die in a week, what more could Heath do to me. And what if he jumps Rex while he's exploring?* "Do you think I should follow him?"

Ava removed her shoes and socks. "Definitely."

A distasteful rot entered the room once her socks exposed her feet. Ava didn't seem bothered. *Perhaps human sense of smell isn't as refined as Chipeermen.* Chestnut gagged. *I'd rather risk getting kidnapped than stay here much longer.* "My return will be timely. Lock the door once I leave, please."

Ava prepared for her bath. "Alright, I'll be here. Don't die."

Chestnut closed the door, resting her head on it for a moment before raising her nose.

Rex had a distinct smell, a sweet blend of apple cinnamon, musty Victorian clothes, earthy tones of grass and rain, and smoky lightning. She followed the trail downstairs before pausing. The smell veered. She turned around until she picked it up again. A tang of blood added to his smell, she spotted a swath of his cloak left on a nail. She took it and inhaled. *Yes, distinguishably Rex.*

Perhaps I ought to smell it again. She did, not because she needed to. The scent pleased her, it reminded her of his smile, his impeccable diction, his witty word-building. She pressed the fabric to her nose again. *He smells vaguely like home.*

She blinked out of her dreamy stupor. *Moss, this swath is distracting. I must focus.* She continued down alleys and backroads. Thankfully, she was alone, however she feared the shadows might take the lack of people as a chance to attack. She hurried faster, her dress lapping in the wind's breath. The scent split down two different roads. He must have gone down one and doubled back to the other.

Chestnut tripped over a bag of trash, and her next step was in a puddle of rainwater. *Ohhhhh, this is utterly revolting. Steel yourself Chestnut. Ivy would never be so scared.*

A mound of trash was piled in the corner. Chestnut gagged.

The scent was strongest down one direction, so she chased it. A corner of Rex's cloak disappeared behind a corner. *Oh, thank goodness!* She followed slowly. A man with red hair wandered underneath a lamp post, his stout frame darkened by the shadows. Rex peered around a garbage can.

Chestnut's eyes widened. Large bat ears swiveled on his head, twitching to pick up the slightest noise. One swiveled to her squishy steps. He jumped, lightning lighting up the corner. Black eyes with wide blue iris turned on her. The lack of pupils in his eyes, paired with the bat ears made her especially sure he wasn't as human as he'd let on.

Rex's eyes hardened. "Chestnut?"

"What are you doing?" She nestled beside him, peering out at the man.

Rex hissed like a slow cooker valve with too much pressure. "Go back."

His snarl caught her attention. "No."

"Chestnut, go back." He growled, his face inches from hers.

"No."

"Claws!" Lightning scattered around him.

The man widened his eyes and raced off. Rex immediately chased after him, tail streaming under his cloak.

Rex! Oh, moss, I guess we're running now. Chestnut sighed and took up as quick of a jog as she could muster.

CHAPTER 13

He'd found him.

As usual William had been wrapping up his Sunday evening smoke on the corner of Curb and Currey. *Old habits die hard tonight, don't they.*

Rex didn't register Chestnut's breathless panting behind him. He had a target. The chill in the air made Rex sluggish, but regardless, he was hard on his heels.

Run little rat, right back home.

Lightning followed in his wake.

A fire lit in his eyes.

Back to our home.

William scrambled around a corner. Rex slid around it, and in one fluid motion, took up running again.

As much as William was trying to outrun Rex, Rex knew he had to shake off Chestnut. She wouldn't understand, even with the longest explanation about all the ways William corrupted him. She still wouldn't understand. William's worst crime? Using a little kid as a willing accomplice. Rex had trusted him with his life, and despite the warning signs, he believed William had only ever had his best interest in mind. Even after the fallout between him and Matthew, if he had just left, Rex could have moved on. But every action had an equal opposite reaction. Each death must be paid for in blood.

William jumped into a crack in the wall.

Rex burst into the crevice, and grabbed his hand.

Furniture sparsely dotted the room. A handmade bar covered one corner with smoking pipes, thread pickers, and dirty clothes hiding the surface. Dim light outlined an old Victorian chaise couch, an olive rug, and handkerchiefs, hundreds of them hanging from the ceilings. The rotting wooden boards had deteriorated more than Rex remembered, but it was home.

His heart raced in his chest.

The man's eyes turned on him, just like they did when he was a kid. "Rex?"

"William–" His voice scored his throat like barbed wire.

"Oh, my boy, I never thought I'd see you again!" He croaked. "No wonder you was chasing me, come to give your uncle a hug after so many years."

William–

Gray streaks lined his orange hair, his whiskers now longer and patchy.

Rex stiffened as William wrapped him in a tight hug. How easy it would be to pretend everything was okay. Matthew was going to walk through that door any minute with his beaming smile that only he could pull off and ask what they were doing. *Everything could have been okay.*

William pulled sharply away as Chestnut entered. "What in the bloody hell is *that*?"

Her ears pinned.

"A shave would do ya well, ma'am" He snickered.

"...thank you."

Rex stepped between the two of them. "William–" he'd practiced for this moment, rehearsed his lines, his blocking, why was this harder than he envisioned it to be? "Chestnut please leave–"

"Rex, I'm not leaving you."

He looked at her, eyes round. "Please– I can't have you here, especially not in your condition"

William's expression dropped. "You ain't gotten her pregnant, have you?" Lightning rocketed off Rex, catching on Wiliiam's hand. He jumped back "Ow, Ay, is that...uh...new?" He coddled his limp hand.

Chestnut hid behind the bar.

"In fact, a lot's new, ain't it? My, you've gotten tall." William looked him over.

"I'm Matthew's height now."

The dagger impaled into William. He flinched. "Xavier, You know that had nothing to do with you–"

"Didn't it? I was a novelty to all your gang friends 'Look at this kid! A prodigy of kleptomania!' Don't tell me you didn't know they would make you choose!"

"Matthew killed Oscar, he earned that bullet."

"But you didn't have to fire it!" Rex screamed.

"It was him or me. Rex, can't we put this behind us? That was six years ago, I've grown, I've changed. Age has made me wiser, almost too wise. I need your help for survival. These thumbs don't work as quick as they used to–"

"You're worried about...getting older?" Rex laughed, a shrill insane trill. "Well, I can fix that." He slammed his foot into William's stomach. "You took *everything* from me."

"Rex!" Chestnut yelled.

The corners of the room blurred in a red centered focus on William.

Hands intertwined in his and pulled him out of the tunnel vision. Chestnut looked up at him. "Rex, let's go. Before someone gets hurt."

"That's the plan."

Chestnut flattened her ears against her head. "This won't help."

"This is the *only* thing that will help" His voice shattered. He tore his hand out of Chestnut's and soon, William's throat was clasped between his hands. Screams filled the darkness of his peripherals. Rex threw him on the ground.

Rex stomped William's hands. "You used those to teach me to steal."

He kicked him straight in the jaw.

"You used that to tell me you loved me!" *Just like His Highness did.*

He drew the thief up by the collar. "You turned me into a monster!"

William begged "Rex please... Matthew had it coming!"

Scales crept up Rex's arms. His tail lashed back and forth.

Rex's boot soaked in sticky liquid.

William coughed. He crawled backwards.

Hallucinations danced around the room. Rex's younger self laughed and played. He heard Matthew's voice, smooth and amused. The puff of cigars, the jingle of coins, the ruffle of blankets. The voices screamed at him, mocking him.

"Are you proud of the monster, William?!" Rex shrieked.

He flung his hands down onto his chest.

Giga-watts pummeled from Rex's veins.

William convulsed. His eyes rolled back.

Smoke filled the room.

Rex didn't care. The voices didn't stop, only darkening. Yelling, screaming, arguing!

Gunshot.

The lightning tapered off.

Rex's breath palpated in mixed laugh and cry. "Matthew promised...he promised."

One memory remained in the room with him, fixed in time by years of mourning. Matthew's hands raised as he looked into the barrel of a gun. "*William, if you do this it'll haunt you to the day of your death. I promise, if you hurt the kid, you'll die by my ghostly hands.*"

I just want Matthew back– Tears streamed down his cheeks.

Rex's shoulders slumped and he breathed in William's familiar scent. Smoky, damp, with a hint of bread.

It faded as the corpse paled.

Blood dripped down his face, down his bloody lip.

Rex fell to his knees, his strength gone.

What have I done?

Why don't I feel better?

That was supposed to fix everything!

Chestnut's shaky gasps remained the only remaining noise. "What have you done–?"

Rex turned dull eyes to her. His heart seized. "Why does it still hurt?"

Chestnut glided forwards. "Come away from there." Her tone soft, she pulled him to the furthest wall. "I told you it wouldn't fix anything."

Rex's eyes quivered over the lifeless form of his adopted Uncle. *I killed him...* His hand went to his lips, covering his mouth. *Claws, I killed him.*

"Rex."

Dead... Even if he had been furious with him, he could have reconciled. Maybe William could have told him why he killed Matthew. Bile rose in his throat. *I killed him.*

"Rex." Chestnut said, firmer.

He looked at her, wide eyes glazed over. "Why don't I feel better?"

Chestnut hardened her eyes. "Xavier."

That name brought back the six year old. The kid who believed the best of everyone, who would cry at a pindrop, who would never hurt anyone.

"In no universe was killing him going to make you feel better."

A pin dropped. Salty tears washed the blood off his face. "What have I done–?"

Chestnut's lips parted in a soft exhale. She leaned forward, hands sliding under his arms. "Something you'll probably regret."

The truth in those words came as a gut punch; he already did. He did, but there was nothing he could do to bring him back. William had always had a knack for keeping demons around, if by Rex's guess, the three of them were fated to be separated for eternity. William in Hell, Matthew in Heaven, and Xavier, as always, stuck between the two in his own kingdom of Limbo.

Xavier trembled, clawing her back as if this hug was his last.

"Shhh, Rex, I'm here," Chestnut cupped the back of his head, her fingers spreading through his hair. "I'm here."

Xavier wiped his lower palm over his eyes.

Chestnut pulled away. "If there's anything I have learned while here on this planet, it's that the world is unfair and cruel. But if met with an equal amount of cruelty, no one wins." Her fingers slid under his ear to cup his face. "No one wins when hate fights itself."

Xavier turned his face into her hand. Soon little drops of water fell on her fur. "No one wins." The number of those droplets increased in frequency. *No one wins.*

"Your name isn't Lucas. It's not Rex either, is it?"

"No...it's not Rex either." Rex was his closest alias, the version of himself so carefully crafted to fool the world. Xavier was his name. Besides the terror, it was all he had left of His Highness. "Xavier is what my father named me...but the less I remember of him the better. Please don't call me that."

Chestnut sighed. "I won't."

"Thank you." Xavier sat exposed, his emotions dressed on his sleeves for her to see. He'd never felt so vulnerable, yet he'd also never felt so safe. "I'm sorry." He wondered if this changed anything. If she would pack up tomorrow and leave. Better to travel alone than with a murderer, right? "I understand if you never want to see me again. I can write down the map to Lavivrus." That is, if Destiny would give it to him.

Chestnut looked him dead in the eye. "Rex. I'm not scared of this side of you. I know there's good in you, and one mistake will not chase me away."

Xavier's eyes dropped. "Matthew said something similar to me."

Chestnut brushed away a rogue tear. "Then he was a wise man."

"He was." William had his moments of clarity too. Rex wiped the remaining tears away. "I want to bury him. I feel I owe that to both of them."

Chestnut tipped her head. "Alright then. I'm right beside you."

Always and forever. That was the motto of her book characters, wasn't it? He wasn't sure why that popped into his mind, but it was a soft place to land. He turned his eyes to William.

I won't let your memory die. I'll always remember you and Matthew.

CHAPTER 14

Rex approached the cemetery. Chestnut grunted and set down William's feet. "I have never had to bury a man before."

"Me neither."

"Really? I thought this was a normal Sunday for you." She gave him a small smile.

Rex frowned. "You know most girls aren't so cheery after watching a murder–"

She shrugged, lifting William up again. "You know little about the thrill I get from adventure."

"Adventure?"

"Oh, yes, how often does one get to bury a dead body?"

When they had reached the gates, the moon slid from behind a cloud and William fell through Rex's blue ghostly hands. "Well that makes things harder..."

Chestnut giggled, her eyes catching the moonlight in silver ringlets.

"Hey–" He laughed along. "We should not be this happy right now."

"Oh, why not? We are quite miserable enough with this whole poison ordeal, and Heath, and you running away from whatever, and now we're dragging a dead body outside of city limits." She pulled back her long curly hair, smudging dirt on her face "I have never felt more alive in my life!"

Rex snorted, and stepped closer. "And now you're here with a vain, pushy, impulsive ghost. How's that adrenaline for ya?"

She stepped clean through him. "Everyone back home will never believe me."

"H-hey! You can't just step through me."

"Shall I do it again, Sparrow?" She tipped her head with a smirk.

The night changed her. It took her shy exterior and melted it into silver strands of moonlight. Without pretense, without hesitation, she spoke and acted. Rex was finally seeing the real Chestnut and she was glowing under the moonlight's encouragement.

He grinned. "That's not fair, I can't kiss you like this."

"And thank goodness for that" her fur fluffed. She stooped to pick up William's shoulders. "Won't we get in trouble for trespassing?"

"Trespassing? Please, so many people die in this city. The cemeteries are free for public use, all you need is a shovel and..." He blinked.

Chestnut burst out in sleep deprived laughter. "We didn't even think of a shovel!"

Rex watched her. Her laugh was a quiet array of bleats, chortling, gasping, and breathless wheezing. Her nose scrunched when she laughed another string...*I guess that's ...kinda cute.* His eyes softened.

"Well what do we do?"

"Steal a shovel?" Chestnut joked.

"Steal–" Was this how she acted in her racing thoughts? He smiled. "Yeah, let's go steal a shovel."

Chestnut dragged the corpse to a plot of land and laid him there. She gagged. "Moss, he reeks of death and cigarettes."

Rex smelled him. "I don't pick up any of that."

"You *are* currently an amalgamation of moonlight, Rex."

He circled around her. "I wonder if I could, like, possess someone?"

Chestnut dusted off her hands and rolled her eyes. "We should be so unfortunate."

Moonlight outlined the stones in lustrous glitter. Each epitaph bore a date and a name. Rex walked beside her. "What's it like, where you grew up?"

Chestnut angled her ear towards him. "Oh, wonderful. Effervescent waterfalls cascading into pools of refreshing, life-giving water. Mushrooms the size of that shed over there. Oh, and the color scheme. Rex, the warmth, the richness of sun streamed forests."

"Sounds like paradise."

"It is, and that's the problem." her fur fluffed. "Everything is so peaceful and wonderful, nothing interesting ever happens, except for in my books. Even then, the stories my community writes are dull at best."

"Yeah, but too much excitement can be permanently damaging..." He covered the symbol on his wrist.

"Yes, perhaps. I invented my own stories while I created gowns–"

"You make clothes?"

Chestnut's eyes gleamed. "Yes, There was no room for variety I'm afraid, as dye is hard to come by for us. But, it truly is amazing the opportunities in off white"

Rex hummed, just enjoying her excitement. Her smile was infectious. "So are there other animal humans on your planet?"

"No, just us."

"You don't have any predators on your planet, do you?"

She tipped her head. "Predators?"

"You know, killers. Animals that eat other animals."

For a moment she looked horrified. "No, everything on my planet thrives off of natural herbs and plants."

"You don't eat meat?"

Chestnut shook her head, her curls bobbing.

Logically, it made sense, deer and chipmunks were herbivores. Apparently there was more herbivore DNA in her than human. He looked forward to the day when he could introduce her to the soft tenderness of a well-cooked duck.

"That sounds lovely." He breathed.

"Yes. Rex? I have come to terms with your reservations. You have a right to your secrets, and I don't want to impose on them, but I do wonder...what did William do?"

"What did William do...?" His hands took up a steady shaking. "Well, for starters, he was Matthew's cousin. Lazy son of a dog who took advantage of his kindness. He didn't work, yet somehow always had so much money. I met him when I was six.

When I was ten, he pulled me aside and taught me a very valuable lesson. He said "You listen here, kid, if you have ever been guessin' about the weight of the jangle in me pocket, I'll tell you exactly how–" He taught me how to steal something innocent at first, just to save up enough for a present for Matthew's birthday." His eyes dulled. "Then I got better. And we trained longer. Matthew never knew about it. If he had, he would have kicked out William and I loved him. I didn't want him to leave. Well, one day, he took me to an upstairs room, introduced me to a bunch of his cartel buddies, they all stole together and shared the goods. Matthew came to find me. They gave William a gun and told him to shoot himself, or Matthew. I escaped just as Matthew dropped dead."

Chestnut's eyes rounded. "I'm so sorry–"

How different things would have been if William had turned over a new leaf and started an honest living. "But it helps keep me alive now, so I guess I owe him."

"Why have you not taken a job yourself?"

"Labor laws." He tried kicking a stone, but his foot went through it. "Here in Victoria, they don't exist, so I was a chimney sweep with Matthew. But I ran far away and in the 2000's district, you have to be older than 18 to get a job...and there was no way I was turning myself in as an orphan. So I survived on my own. Stealing what I needed to survive."

"But aren't you a prince?"

Rex tensed. "Aha–Ahahahaha, well–uh–yeah–technically. Prince of the *afterlife*. Money has no meaning there, I guess I could have taken money with me, but I was quick to escape there too..."

"Why's that?"

And that was enough of a heartfelt chit chat. The walls went back up. "I'd rather not talk about that..."

"Of course. What makes you happy?"

Rex looked at her. "What makes me happy?"

Chestnut nodded.

"Well...I know it sounds silly, but I love animals." A cloud covered the moon, returning Rex to his carnal mask. Rex's eyes roved over his arm and he reached to ensure he was solid. Yup. He was back to himself. Back to a human being.

"Not silly at all," Chestnut poked him. "It really is amazing how that works" Her eyes darted to a shed. "Shovel!"

Leaning against a shed was a shovel, rusted with a long wooden hilt, but it would do. Rex took the handle in hand and they returned to the cemetery. He excavated the damp soil.

Chestnut watched him. "You know, maybe you aren't so impetuous." her eyes softened.

Rex looked up at her. Her penetrating eyes did things to his intestines. They'd be his undoing. "You're not so platitudinous yourself."

She blushed.

While he dug, she watched him, standing so perfectly in the moonlight that her hair glowed in silver strands. Shadows reached into the fresh hole the deeper it grew. When it was six feet approximately, he rolled William in and piled upturned dirt on top. He was thankful the moon had stayed hidden. He'd be bothered watching Chestnut do it herself. "I'm going to stand vigil...for the rest of the night, if you want to go back to the room." He set the shovel aside and plucked a dandelion from among its weed community and set it on the grave.

"I think I'll stay here." She slipped her hand in his.

Her hand was soft. Rex gave her a small smile. "Thank you...for being here with me."

"Shhh, vigils are supposed to be wordless." Her eyes betrayed mischief.

"Yeah." His smile dropped. "Not a word uttered until we get back to the room"

The moon came back out, but they didn't move from their positions. Their hands remained intertwined with air. There was no feeling behind it, but there was understanding.

She stood vigil with him for the next few hours. The dandelion was lost in the bare, raw, upturned earth. He looked around for more. The moonlight poured through his body, making him unable to gather flowers, but Chestnut plucked a small bouquet of wildflowers for Matthew and for William. With Rex's ghostly hand clasped in the stems, he and Chestnut presented the flowers on the mound of overturned earth.

They traveled back into the city as the moon slid gently away from the sun. It'd be dark for another few hours, but at least dawn was coming. Rex gave Chestnut the cloak after the burial to shield her from the cold and from drunken men's eyes. Once hidden by the buildings, Rex solidified, he opened the pub door for Chestnut. The lights of the pub decidedly hadn't gotten the memo that the world was supposed to be dull in a state of morning. Rex squinted his eyes.

The lonely bartender cleaned glasses, keeping a protective eye on his passed out customers.

Rex followed Chestnut up the stairs, even the squeak was much too loud for his taste. Chestnut looked back at him with tired eyes. "Almost there."

He nodded.

Chestnut tapped her knuckles against their door. "Ava? It's us," a loud snore replied. "Oh dear."

Rex raised a fist to pound on the door, but barely touched it. He slid his hand back to him, eyes downcast. *She wouldn't hear it anyway if she slept through last night's riot.*

Chestnut looked at him and hardened her eyes. "Ava!" She slammed her own knuckles against the wooden door. "Ava!"

It opened to a groggy-looking Ava. Her hair was messier than a rat's nest. "Gosh, where have you two been all night?" she yawned.

Chestnut opened her mouth to respond, but broke off in a fit of gagging. She covered her mouth.

Rex guided her to a chair. *I guess that means the vigil is over.* "Careful, where's the pain? Stomach? Sit up, it'll worsen it." Rex set a pillow behind her back.

She looked at Rex, then rushed past him to the restroom, keeling over the toilet. *She doesn't deserve this...*He kneeled and held her hair back.

The fit eased. She leaned back into Rex's arms. "It hurts–Rex, it hurts." She squeezed his hand.

"Yeah, it's gonna hurt."

"I'm so hungry–"

"I know, I know, there are some chips, do you want to nibble on those?"

Chestnut nodded.

"Ok, stay here." Rex eased her on the tile and rooted through Ava's bubble storage. Chestnut wobbled into the room, definitely looking greener. "Here, eat these." He opened the chips for her. "You'll need your strength."

Chestnut accepted the bag and Rex turned to Ava. "We're heading out in a few hours, ok?"

Ava stretched "M'kay, I tried staying up for y'all, but I guess I fell asleep."

Chestnut brushed crumbs off her lips. "We appreciate that, Ava, thank you for trying."

Rex fell into a chair, his eyelids dropped.

Chestnut slid her hand over his. "Well we did it. All night vigil."

"Claws, I'm so tired."

"You should get some rest."

"We don't have time for me to sleep." He sank deeper into the chair. "You need your rest, you go ahead."

Chestnut rubbed his shoulder. "Alright. Ava, I'm going to take a little nap."

Ava yawned, "Ya, we'll be quiet."

The thick duvet cover pulled over her sleeping form and she closed her eyes.

Rex watched her. "Ava, do you have everything ready?"

"Yup, ready when she wakes up."

She seemed to catch onto the solemn atmosphere because she didn't say anything else for the next few minutes. Rex tried prying his eyes open, but the weight of his lashes pulled them closed.

He drifted off, slumping in the velvet chair.

CHAPTER 15

Warm water drenched over his head. Rex gasped awake. The blurry light of a memory drifted over the scene. Xavier sat quietly in a bathtub. Servants scrubbed shampoo into his hair.

He sighed. Despite the endless preening, he still didn't feel clean. Warm water cascaded over his head. The soap washed out and trailed down the prince's face. A servant carefully dried his hair and bat ears. Xavier stepped out of the bathtub and they wrapped a sapphire robe around him.

He nodded, "Dismissed," and the servants hurried each other out. His exhale filled the empty room. *Thank you.* His Highness always rebuked him when he thanked the servants. A forest of greenery lined the unused pool. Xavier normally avoided the body of water. His lions lazily rose their heads.

Xavier smiled and patted the floor beside him. The pride trotted over and resumed their napping around him. Their fur surrounded him in a soft bliss. Xavier snuggled deeper into his robes. *So far no summons, but the day is still young.* Dread kept him alert. His Highness had been in an excitable mood recently. He could usually entertain himself whenever He got like this. Last time, He ate 50 pounds of ice cream, beaming before promptly throwing up.

His father reminded him of his lions. Brutes of size that didn't know their own strength. Xavier didn't mind the scratches or the scars, they were all accidental after all. Children's games suited His Highness in his mania. Life-sized chess, Snakes and Ladders, but His favorite entertainment were Xavier's routines; dazzling acts of knife-juggling, fire- eating, aerial dancing. He liked things involving fast paced pops of color.

His Highness' troughs of depression were the hardest to keep up with. Xavier would do the same ballet routine three times, and still He would stare at him with a blank empty expression. His father barely rose out of bed, except to conduct mandatory meetings with his councils. Xavier performed usually in his father's bedroom for Him to admire from the comfort of His pillow.

He usually cycled through manic excitement and depression bi-weekly. For Xavier this meant two weeks of hard work earned two weeks of relaxation. Between the two moods was a flaming temper than only the fires of Hell could rival.

At the end of the day all the King saw him as was his jester. That's all the kingdom saw him as. *I'm supposed to be their Prince. Do they think I want to be here? I didn't ask to drown. Mom...I miss you–* He had watched the living realm progress in time, something foreign to the afterlife. After the first thousand years, he stopped keeping count. It had been at least 7,000 years in the living world. They were nearing the year 8067, far from the generation of his mother, 1700's. Xavier looked at his bare wrist. *If only I could go back in time and see her again...* His Highness had kept him in Limbo long enough. It was time to sign the contract and take his second life.

In his free time, he'd been studying, researching, ensuring that when he took his second life, he would be best equipped for making it last. *If I can pull this off, I won't have to belong to anyone for at least 100 years. That's about the lifespan of a human, right?*

His heart was set on Victoria. *Waistcoats, servants, it sounds pretty similar to life now. Good, it'll be easy to adjust. I wonder if I'll get a new family!*

He could picture a loving Mother, sitting in the drawing room, reading him a book by a hearth. He wanted to go someplace with as few Limbonians as possible. Even with his regressed age, there was a high probability he'd be recognized. Everyone knew his face. *All the heir has to do is marry whoever the father picks out! That's easy! I don't care about that, I just got out of here.*

Knuckles wrapped on the golden door. "Sire?"

Xavier turned and screamed into one of the lion's mane. When he was composed, he bid the servant, "Come in."

The servant creeped in, her gold garments flowing off her shoulders. "The King wishes you to meet him outside."

"Tell the The King I will be there momentarily."

The servant sheepishly bowed out. The door closed.

Xavier groaned, then changed into his navy uniform. Tassels draped off his shoulder. He breathed a last breath of strength before meeting the servant in the hall. They walked through the decorative halls. Xavier looked outside the large windows at his kingdom's shimmering landscape.

His Highness waited on the stairs, dressed in a winter coat.

Routine: "What will your pleasure be, Sire?" Xavier said.

"Xavier! I want to go for a walk through town. Do join me, please." His Highness gave a goofy smile.

"Of course, Sire." Xavier strained a small, tight-lipped grin.

Xavier took his place beside His Highness. He knew why he was here, to be paraded about like a trophy. Nothing new. Nothing rattled him anymore. He caught curious glances and seering glares from the Fallens, Risens, and souls long since kissed by death's cold lips.

To see the Prince outside of the castle was a rare treat.

Xavier padded on, folding one arm behind his back and keeping the other at his side.

His Highness giggled. "Remember when I told you about the Construction going up in the east. Well I did some more research and it turns out that the word East comes from German meaning 'towards the sun'. I haven't seen the sun in a long time, but I can still remember it. Why, it seems like just yesterday I took my second life. Did I tell you I was a bartender?" He shook Xavier's arm, eyes bright. "That was one of the most fun experiences I've ever had! I would do it here as a hobby if I had time, but alas, my duties keep me busy. I've had the Morphers add a sun stimulant to my room but, what

119

I wouldn't do for some vitamin D!" A crease crossed His Highness' face as he descended into deep concentration. Xavier waited until His eyes lit up. "Oh, Kitten, Isn't vitamin D also in orange juice? Maybe I should start drinking more orange juice. Can one survive on oranges? I'm sure it's some kind of diet. You know, there's a diet for *everything* now. I wonder–"

"Uh–Sire?" Xavier raised a hand in surrender. "Why am I here?"

His Highness blinked. "I...I don't know, I just wanted to talk."

This was new. "Talk, Sire?"

His Highness fixed the golden tassels draped from Xavier's left shoulder. "Yes, everytime we see each other, I tell you what to do and you do it. I haven't seen or talked to you in forever!" He exploded His hands for emphasis.

"Just talk...?" Xavier found solace that his father was ignorant about his comings and goings. No one talked about the Prince as the gallivanting type, but Xavier's books and time were relatively unmonitored unless he was supposed to be in rehearsal or performing. It let him feel like he had protected a piece of himself, kept it close to his chest when everything else had been taken from him.

"Yes. Talk. Oh, oh, oh! Have you ever had sweet cravings? What's your favourite dessert?"

"I like apple strudel, Sire." Xavier smiled.

His Highness spun his fingers and created two strudels from thin air. "One for the charming gentlemen with the gorgeous hair." He took a bite, then handed the other to Xavier. "And the other to my sweet, little boy. You're so funny, I love it." He laughed.

Xavier flinched as his father ruffled his hair. *Thank you–*

"You've come a long way from when you were only a child. Do you remember that far back? You would make up the silliest songs and dances." His Highness smiled. "You were so happy back then." He released a sad, reminiscent sigh. "I still wonder what happened, but I was glad that I didn't have to keep calling in ballerinas, musicians, and mistresses. You proved much more entertaining! Anyway, anyway, all that to say, my advisers said I should let you become more of an available figure, a public figure."

Xavier looked warily at the pedestrians clearing the way for them. Half scowled at him, whilst the other half gawked at His Highness. "Sire, I don't think that's... a good idea."

His Highness pursed his lips, pouting "No? You don't?" His tone sharpened. "And why is that? Do you want to make me look like a fool, do you?"

"No Sire...it's a wonderful idea." Xavier looked down.

His Highness gave a charming smile, looking quite pleased with himself. "Good boy!"

Xavier nibbled at his strudel. *Freedom.* He needed the King's permission first. "Sire, instead of becoming a public figure, it might be a better idea to..." Xavier cleared his throat. "Let me take a second life?"

His Highness choked on his strudel. "You? Pet, look at you. You're an entertainer, *My* entertainer. You wouldn't survive a second life."

Xavier's lips pulled into a thin line. "I disagree."

"You shouldn't. The world is no place for someone as delicate as you, Kitten. Where would you even go?" He tipped his cup with a snide smirk.

Xavier tapped his strudel and in a shy peep told the King "Victoria."

"Victoria!" He nearly fell over, howling in wild laughter. "I love you too much to let you go to such a place."

I need that blessing! "Yes, but Sire–"

"Yeah-buts live in the forest." He used a finger rabbit to make his point.

Xavier swatted his father's fingers away. "Yes, Sire. It'd purely be for exploration, to see what life is like on New Earth. S-So I can better relate to souls, when I take the throne."

His Highness's amusement hardened. "*When* you take the throne? Are you expecting that to be soon? You desire to dethrone me. You wish to do me ill."

Oh boy.

"I see. Well, if it's so important to you perhaps you'd like to rule. I'm sure you are much more knowledgeable than I am. Like having meetings with Fallens, construction, taxers, gatherers, retrievers, welcomers, not to mention the servants?"

He waited for an answer. Xavier stared at him; no, of course, he was right, a second life is stupid. "No, Sire."

"Or I suppose you know how to order servants, charge children, brand, entertain, rule, and gather respect?"

Xavier lowered his eyes. "No, Sire."

"Ah! Of course, but the great Xavier would obviously make a much better King, so go ahead! Go to Victoria! Get your spleen ripped out by wild dogs, get beaten and pulverized in a workhouse, get abused and raped by street rats. That absolutely sounds safe. You have my blessing! Go ahead."

"Wait–on second thought." *Ripped, beaten, pulverized, raped? I-I would be safer here...*

"No, you wanted to go to Victoria. I doubt you'll last more than a week. Then you can come home, and live with me *forever*." His Highness intertwined his hand with Xavier's.

Xavier tensed, his innards twisted in uncomfortable knots, over and over again like that finger bunny was taking his intestines and running circles tangling them.

"Forever doesn't sound so bad, does it?" His Highness smiled, pulling Xavier closer.

Too close. *Am I willing to trade 100 years of freedom for an eternity of slavery?* Xavier stared into his father's face.

I'd trade anything to get away from here. "Not at all. Eternity with the *best* father in any world. I just would need to secure it with a second life."

His Highness jumped to his feet, took Xavier's hand and pulled him back to the castle. "Ohohoh! Then come with me, we'll get you branded right away, Kitten!" Tapestries and walls flew past as his Father took flight, zooming down the halls. "Then once you die, you have to come straight back here!"

Once I die...

The King rang bells on the wall, warning the servants of his arrival.

He opened the door to one of their foundries. Thick gloopy lava poured into large tubs. Precisely in order, blacksmith's dipped pieces of metal in and melted it in a symphony of hammering and hissing. Smoke filled the air and Xavier coughed.

His Highness continued walking, drawing the attention of many servants. Xavier felt hot under his skin. *100 years of no staring...*

Xavier was thrown into a smaller room. A line of children stretched into the next five rooms, maybe nine.

As he entered, a little boy was struck with a searing metal brand. The child screamed as smoke permanently etched a symbol into his skin. Xavier reeled and tripped into His Highness. Strangely, the solidity of his father made him feel secure.

A portal lay open, adjacent to the line and while the symbol cooled, a Fallen instructed the child. He flipped his pages and the portal followed similarly, flipping different scenery across. He recognized Lavivrus, Victoria. The scene halted on an icy blizzard, and the child stepped through, his body solidifying and returning to its human state.

With a cold jab Xavier realized he took priority as the Prince and thus was next.

His Highness pushed him closer to the branding blacksmith and Xavier watched as the rod dipped in lava.

The rod raised, stained crimson, flooded with smoke.

The blacksmith aggressively grabbed his wrist, jerking him closer. With a squeak, Xavier felt the metal impress on the inside of his wrist but it didn't hurt for the first few seconds. It came in a wave of heat. It burned; seething burns that made him instinctively jerk his hand away, but the blacksmith's grip only tightened.

Tears formed and dripped down his cheek, one after the other. He opened his mouth in a noiseless gape. Blood welled on the burn. *100 years of freedom! Remember what you did this for.*

Xavier was pulled to his feet and placed in front of the Fallen. When the Fallen looked up, he stepped back, eyes wide and alarmed. "Sire!" He flashed his look to His Highness. "I-w-w-where would you like to go. Sire?"

"Victoria."

Breathing quick, the Fallen flipped in his book to the Victoria page. "With memories or without?"

Xavier widened his eyes. 100 years of freedom without remembering all this, he–

"He'll remember. Can't have you forgetting me, can we?" His Highness glowered above him.

The Fallen read from the book. "When you step through you'll return to the state in which you died, despite any wounds you may have incurred. Your golden robes will be coveted, so be wary of strangers. When the time comes when you die, a Falcon will meet you to bring you to Lavivrus. From there the portal will return you to Limbo."

That doesn't sound so bad.

His Highness sprinkled magic on his hair. He reached around Xavier's waist and pulled him till the space between their bodies closed. "I give you the gift of lightning, may it remind you of our spark. It'll only take effect after you die, of course. I'll see you soon, son." He stroked a finger down Xavier's cheek then lifted his chin. "I love you."

Love...

His Highness gripped his chin and pressed a warm kiss to Xavier's brow.

That's enough! Xavier shoved himself away, stumbling backwards through the portal. Limbo disappeared behind the glowing red rim of the portal. His Highness's smug grin was the last thing he saw before the portal closed. "Goodbye, pet." The afterlife between worlds was replaced by wet stone walls of a dingy alley.

The light extinguished.

A rat scurried past, and he screamed. He waved his hand to drive a spike through one but nothing happened. He tried again but his royal magic to create whatever he wanted was gone.

Panic welled. His golden garments hung loose from his short frame. He waddled forward, but his long limbs were replaced by stubby awkward ones. It'd been so long since he was six years old, he'd forgotten how to manually function. Xavier screamed, an ear splitting *scree*. He held his hands in front of him. His hands were so small, his grip as weak as a toddler's. He screamed again, looking at himself. *I'm so chubby!* He screamed again. If anything was to happen, he wouldn't be able to fight it off, especially now that he was half his height and half the weight. *I-he's gone. I-I'm alone.*

Xavier felt as if the weight of the world had been lifted off his tiny shoulders.

I'm free.

The Lords that he expected to live with were far from this sorrowful, sad alley. Xavier stepped on cobblestone and slipped.

Having face planted into the cold, hard street, his brow quivered where his father had kissed him goodbye.

Never again. Never again, for the next 100 years.

He heard a clatter behind him and expected to see His Highness emerging from the shadows.

Another squeak set him off. His breathing sped, his heart raced.

Something nibbled his toes. Xavier bolted, He ran faster than the tears could trace his pale cheeks.

The street ended abruptly and Xavier whirled around. His Highness's laugh tickled the wind as it whistled through the alleys. "Leave me alone, sire...please. Please." He sniveled, scurrying deep into the corner and pulling his knees closer to him. He gave a low wail and burst into tears. The tears lasted forever. The change in light scared Xavier. It overwhelmed his senses. He didn't remember that. He pressed his back against a wall and cried for who knows how long.

People passed at least 20 feet away at the entry of the alley but no one seemed bothered by his crying. Good. That meant he was quiet enough. Xavier tucked his face into his knees. He wailed, a low cry. Time passed. Time passed but Xavier was too frozen in fear to know where to go or what to do. He was just a kid.

A voice spoke right beside him and Xavier jumped out of his skin. Xavier's bloodshot eyes shot open to see a young man sitting beside him, smudged and ashy with black curls bobbing on his head. "Hey kid...are you alright?" The man outstretched a hand. Snatches of a hallucination flickered over reality.

Gloved.

Olive.

Gloved. *Sire!* Xavier pulled his oversized golden robe over his head.

"Oi, It's okay. I'm not going to hurt you." The young man eyed him hungrily like a wolf– his arm, his leg, his face. Xavier tucked each limb out of sight. A soft smile spread across the young man's face, warm, despite Xavier's impression of him. "What's your name kid?"

"Xavier..."

"Xavier's quite a strong name." The young man peeled the hood off Xavier's head.

"Strong like a cherry wilted on whiskey." A stout man, more fat than limbs laughed from the mouth of the alley.

Xavier stared buggy-eyed at the two. *What if they force me to–* A whimper escaped him, Xavier rolled up his oversized sleeve, bearing claw marks.

The young man noted the stitches. "My name's Matthew. Charmed." Matthew held out his finger. "That back there is my cousin, William."

William stroked his pencil mustache, a thick cockney accent slurring his speech. "Let's get back, I don't wanna be here all night."

Xavier wrapped his hand around Matthew's finger. He acted so much different from His Highness's taunting snake-like charm. Xavier saw the snake reflected in William's eyes, but Matthew had the demeanor of a puppy willing to trust again. Matthew seemed like a wall, like the ones back home that kept him so carefully guarded from a kingdom that was reviled by his presence. He was protected within Matthew's hold. *Will he take care of me?*

"Yeah, give us a moment..." Matthew gently stood, raising Xavier with him. "Do you need anything, squib?"

Xavier tightened his grip on Matthew's finger. "Are you going to leave me?"

"I–" The finger slipped away.

Xavier reached forwards. "N-no!" He fell into Matthew's arms.

"Careful Squib!"

Xavier's hands tightened around his pant leg. "D-don't leave me alone, please" He hid his face in his knee.

"You know–" A gentle crinkle of bread sounded above him. Matthew kneeled and presented a half loaf of bread to him. "It's a dangerous world for a little kid all alone."

Xavier accepted the bread with small, gentlemanly nibbles. An ash stained hand cupped the side of his face.

"Don't worry, I won't leave you. From this day on, I'll take care of you, I promise." Matthew's face creased into a ruddy smile.

Xavier tipped his head. *This feels different.* Matthew's hand warmed his freckled cheek, so unlike the chilling touch that would send shivers up his spine. This wasn't a chain, it wasn't "love", he didn't feel trapped at all.

William snorted and approached, bringing winter's sting with him. "We can't keep him. You barely make enough to support us."

"You could always get a job." Matthew glared at him.

"I have a job. You won't let me work."

"Stealing is immoral."

"It's me-moral."

Matthew's brown eyes rolled. "Can you walk?"

Can I walk? Xavier double checked to make sure his feet were still attached to his ankles. "I think so." Matthew's hand dropped on his head and ruffled his hair.

"Eh, I'm going to call you Rex. You look like a kingly young lad."

Rex. Latin for King, per the castle's textbooks. He'd spent hours by candlelight flipping page by page of Latin dictionaries. He tipped his head. Matthew's dark eye circles ran around his eye like a mask. Rex pointed at him. "Procyon"

Matthew smiled. "Not you too. The baker calls me Trash Panda. Do I really look like a raccoon?"

Xavier nodded enthusiastically.

"I do not." He turned his nose up.

Xavier tugged his shirt for attention. "Yes you do!"

"Do not."

"You do!" He giggled.

Another ruffle tangled his hair. "Silly goose."

Stars grew in his eyes. *Matthew.* The name of a warrior, a protector, a man who would fight off legions of demons for him and still stand strong, raccoon eyes smudged with exhaustion.

If he were to be a goose, he was going to be one with a full stomach and a roof over his head. *One day I'll pay him back, I'm going to work hard to make this thing humans call life worth it!* Xavier hugged him around the hips. *I'm going to make him proud!*

⁓⚬⁓

The memory faded into a starry night sky. Rex walked through a field of forget-me-nots. The stars of his dream swirled into a mirror image of Matthew. The two walked together.

Rex wiped his eyes. "Matthew...I miss you. I avenged you." He wiped his cuff under his eye. "I fulfilled your promise. That counts for something, right?" A wry smile teased his mouth.

Matthew looked at him, sad eyes swirling with galaxies.

Rex reached to hold his hand like he did when he was a scared little boy, but the stars didn't gather to just be held. No one could hold the stars in their hands. Rex's hand went through him. "I wish you were here...I need you. I wonder what you'd say about Chestnut, about Ava. You always gave the best advice." Chestnut. Would they have gotten along? Rex imagined him bringing Chestnut to meet Matthew, the soft smile, wrinkling his eyes, he'd only be 34 years old now. "You'd like her, Matthew, she's kind and gentle." The words choked Rex and he couldn't continue on. *Why did I have to live? Why did you have to die?*

Rex's lips pressed together. "I miss you."

The stars of Matthew's smile rose to form the crows feet that always wrinkled his eyes when he grinned. *"I promised I'd never leave you."*

"Thank you. Thank you for taking me in. Thank you for making sure I never went hungry. For fighting off bullies. For listening."

Rex reached forward to hug him, but the stars dispersed, floating back to join the ranks in the sky. *Thank you for being in my life.*

CHAPTER 16

Looks like her two love doves were growing closer. Ava was proud of her work. *I still wish I knew where they went. They, like, vanished for the whole night.* Ava had been busy though, calling her mother over and over again in an effort to contact her. She tried reaching her father, but he gave a half-thought-out explanation for why he couldn't talk or relay the message. He was too tired from work.

Chestnut had woken after a few hours and kneeled beside Rex, her hand over his.

"Can we wake him up already?" Ava paced "Gosh, he's been asleep for hours."

"A little longer." Chestnut said.

"I don't even know where we're going next."

"I think Rex mentioned the Medieval district."

Ava scoffed. "I'm looking forward to when we get to Lavivrus, and I can use my phone in public."

Rex shuffled and slit open one eye to look at Chestnut. "Good morning." Rex rubbed his face.

"Is everything okay?" Chestnut said.

"Yeah...yeah, I just had a dream about Matthew."

Jeez, he looks rough– Ava sucked her teeth. "Matthew's the guy who raised you right?"

"Yeah–" He and Chestnut exchanged a knowing glance.

*Well that's not excluding at all...*Ava jumped a few times to shake off the sadness. *Smile inside and out.* She rifled through her bubble storage. "Ay Rex, we're heading to the Medieval era, yeah?"

"Yeah."

She yanked a decorative Medieval dress from her bubble. "Cool. Chestnut, I'd give you a dress but it might be too small for you. What size do you wear?"

"The tag on my clothes says medium."

"Yeah, my stuff is extra small." She pulled out one of Rex's shirts. "Rex, you're a men's small." A chaotic smirk stretched her face. "C'mere!"

Chestnut took the dress from her. "We are not putting Rex in a dress."

Killjoy– "C'mon! We did it all the time backstage."

Rex looked numbly at the floor.

Chestnut dropped her voice to a quiet whisper. "He's mourning. Let him alone, Ava."

Mourning? Seriously, what did she miss? Well now she felt bad for being insensitive. "Right. Sorry." She closed the bathroom door.

Rex took a deep breath then raised his eyes to Chestnut's. "I'll be fine. Ava's right though. We shouldn't bleed time periods into others. We'll probably get new clothes once we get there though, so what we're wearing is formal enough for now." He stood. "Our next stop *is* the Medieval Era. We can stop for a little while before making the final stretch to Lavivrus."

Wow, he's fixed, miraculous luck! Ava trotted to the bathroom and slid on the costume. She winced at her reflection. *Ew, rat.* Maybe she should curl her hair like Chestnut's.

Ava trotted out and struck a pose. "Mhm, yeah, Dang right I look fabulous." It was the irony that made the joke funny.

Chestnut smiled. "Indeed you do, Ava."

She's just being nice.

Rex looked at her. "Ava, can you check out? I'm going to hail a cab to take us to the train station. Chestnut, can you double check the room to make sure we're not leaving anything?"

Ava ran backwards out of the room. "On it!" She pulled out her wallet upon approach to the front desk. "Hello, hello, hello, Good morning" She handed the clerk her card.

After a swipe, she struck up a conversation with the clerk about the weather. *She doesn't recognize me either, Jeez, I even toured here. I get that they don't have any technology, but this is just pure ignorance.* She was going to hire a better advertising company.

Rex and Chestnut waited in the bar for her. "Hey guys," Ava giggled. "Why don't we get a few beers to commemorate the moment?"

Rex furrowed his brows. "You are definitely under age."

"Shut up, shut up, shut up." She wrapped an arm around Rex. "*You* know that. And *I* know that. But that bartender doesn't." She grinned.

"No."

"Dang it."

Ava hailed a cab and paid the last bit of cash she had. The Hackney driver didn't take credit cards. *You gotta be frickin' kidding me. Who doesn't take a debit card!? Backwards, third country peasants.* Ava took the first seat in the back, Rex sat opposite her. She plopped her backpack in the seat beside her so Rex and Chestnut would have to sit together. *Hehehehehehe, Oh yeah, cupid of the year award.* She gave Rex a mischievous look.

Chestnut slowly sat beside him and gazed out the window.

Rex joined her in looking out her window. At one point his eyes lazily lingered on her.

Ava watched intently. *Oh yeah, Rex has it bad.*

Rex averted his eyes to the window when Chestnut turned her head.

Ava snickered. "Soooo, what did you two do last night?"

Chestnut pinned her ears.

Rex looked at the table. "My adopted uncle died. Chestnut and I buried him and stood vigil until the sun came up."

133

"Oh." Ava said. "No wonder y'all were so quiet this morning." The cab dropped them off at the station and like last time, Ava guided the three through the mass of humanity. *It's nice to feel important.* The attention was intoxicating.

The day passed, fading into dark. They had been riding all day and would be riding all night. They passed esteemed gardens, built by generational inheritances. However, once they got out of Era limits, the landscape flattened into trees rimmed in moonlight.

Chestnut fell asleep on the train, curled against the side with her head on the train's wall. Rex slung his cloak off and spread it over her.

Ava played games on her phone, headphones in both ears listening to electro swing. She got a text from Jason. "Hello."

Ava smiled and texted back "Hi!"

It wasn't long before they were engaged in a riveting conversation about True Crime and Detective stories.

"Ava, can you please turn off that buzzing" Rex whispered.

Ava looked up. She dramatically turned her phone on silent. "Jason's so interesting! Did you know, He wants to be a detective? He also loves math and he plays chess. Pretty well actually!" *Green flags, green flags.*

Rex scoffed. "Good for him."

Chestnut's fingertips twitched. She made noises in her sleep. She shivered, tears beading on her lashes. Ava gasped when she turned over and fell on Rex's shoulder, hands wrapped tight around his arm. Rex repositioned the cloak to accommodate.

Ava giggled. "You two are cute together."

Rex looked up at her, brows furrowed.

"Oh, c'mon, she totally likes you!"

"Likes me–" He gave her a look. "I should hope so, if she hated me, why would we be traveling together?"

Men. "No, *Like* like, Y'know, kissy kissy, smooch smooch?"

Rex's expression hardened. "You mean...love."

"Sure I guess. Dude, she buried a body for you. She stayed up all night. No way she'd do that for someone she didn't care about."

"Care..." He considered "So it's not love. More affection? Endearment? Appreciation?"

Whatever you gotta tell yourself, Bud. Ava nodded. "Definitely, do you 'appreciate' her as well?"

Rex brushed a strand of hair away from Chestnut's face. "I don't know. I've never appreciated someone before. Love is bad, but I don't think she loves me."

"Love is bad? C'mon. Love is what everyone is looking for."

"Not me... I was a slave to it two too many times."

Ava leaned closer. "Slave– Dude, what the heck?" She nodded to Chestnut. "What do you think you feel for Matthew?"

"Endearment. Adoration. I cared for him a lot."

"In other words, you loved him."

Lightning jolted off him. "How dare you accuse me of loving anyone! I'd never make him do anything he didn't want to do."

Fingertips together and pressed against her lips, Ava furrowed her brows. *Oh, this guy is a piece of work.* "What happened to you that gave you that impression?"

Rex leaned into Chestnut, resting a hand over hers. "M–my father...would tell me to do something. Or give me lashings for punishment, then say 'It's only because I love you.' William too. It was their excuse for everything."

"Lashings?"

Rex unclipped his sleeve and drew it up his arm, stitched together scars lining his arms. "7,000 years of lashings..."

Oh... She'd figured Rex had some kind of daddy issues, but physical abuse? Not her first guess. "I should be concerned, but by this point this is normal. I'm sorry that happened, but at least you're safe now."

"Get some sleep Ava. We have a long way to walk once the train pulls in."

She yawned "But Jason–"

"Tell him you have to go to bed."

"Yeah, I guess we can talk tomorrow." *And the day after tomorrow, and the day after that.* She giggled. She doubted they could ever run out of things to talk about. Jason was so intellectually acute. "Goodnight Rex."

"Goodnight Ava. Sleep well."

She in fact did not sleep well. Her dress was itchy and her mind raced everywhere from how she was going to explain Roz's disappearance to Noah and Mom to wondering if she'd ever see Jason again.

CHAPTER 17

Rex watched Ava drift off. Destiny appeared and leered over him, eyes rimmed in hurt. *"Why would you ever make up such lies about the King?"*

"They're not lies." Rex said simply.

"His Highness would never treat you like that. He's patient, kind, and just." Destiny was oddly passionate about this.

Sure. Rex forsook the conversation. He had tried to expose His Highness plenty of times before, each attempt more useless than the last. After he'd accomplished nothing but earning the kingdom's scorn, he came to terms with the fact that His Highness would always be everyone's idol.

Rex was the only one awake now. Everytime he closed his eyes, he either saw the barrel of a gun, William's charred body, or His Highness. No way he was going to fall asleep tonight. The orange and red fall leaves were now covered in a light dusting of snow.

A rock flew under the wheel and they were jerked again. Chestnut groggily opened her eyes. She nuzzled deeper into Rex's shoulder. "Are we there yet?"

"Not yet, Chestnut." Her name was sweet on his tongue.

Chestnut looked up at him, loosening her grip and pulling away. "Sorry..."

"I don't mind."

"Even with your haphephobia?"

Rex softened his eyes. "If it were anyone else, yeah I'd hate it. But you're not anyone else." He pointed to the stars. "Here, look at this."

Chestnut scooted closer and leaned over Rex to see through his window. "You can see the lights so much better here than in the city. What's that one called?"

"That's the Azeednom, the smaller variant of Azodnem, that's where we were over there, the early modern era."

"We've traveled so far."

"Yeah– how are you feeling?" He looked down at her.

"I am fine enough. Once we get the fish, I'll be much better then."

"Mhm. And the truth."

Chestnut lightly tapped his cheek. "That is the truth, silly boy."

"No, it's not. Your tail fluffs when you're in pain." He gestured to the mass of fur that had been her sleek chipmunk tail.

"It's not ladylike to admit."

"It's not gentlemanly to murder." He raised his eyebrows.

She rolled her eyes. "My digestion has been most painful. Between the extra gas, gurgling stomach, and stinging kidneys, the moments of rest are becoming fewer and farther between. I can almost feel it eating away at me from the inside out."

"Don't worry, We'll be there in the next few days if everything goes well." He pivoted his shoulders to give her more room to rest comfortably.

"I owe so much to you. I don't know what I would have done without you and Ava."

Her hair fell over his chest and he couldn't resist stroking two fingers along a strand of it. "I'll be happy when you're all healed." Is this the endearment Ava was talking about? No, this feels different. His eyes dilated and his hands sweated.

Chestnut gave a light chuckle and curled her head underneath his chin. "Tell me a story about Matthew."

"About Matthew?"

"Mhm." She mumbled, drifting back into a sleep.

"Oh, there's so many. I used to be a chimney sweep, y'know. I was so small that I could fit in the actual chimneys, well one time I actually got stuck."

"No!"

"Yeah, it was crazy. They actually had to take it apart brick by brick until Matthew could pull me out. William was furious, but not as furious as the landowner was."

Rex continued. One story led to another and then two stories to four. Pretty soon, Rex had Chestnut laughing along. Eventually he told her to fall asleep. She needed her strength, but she insisted the same for Rex. Rex smiled down at her and wrapped his arms around her shoulders. "Alright, Booky."

She hummed a goodnight and Rex closed his eyes with a rare clarity.

For the first time in years, he felt safe.

CHAPTER 18

Chestnut woke up wrapped in Rex's arms. *His skin is colder than I would have expected, but it adds a refreshing coolness to this cabin. I have never been in a more humid place before. I suppose it is the body heat filling the train. I am mostly excited to offboard.*

Their conversation during their search for the shovel replayed in her mind. *I never planned to ever let anyone see myself so thrilled. I completely expected him to ostracize me and never speak to me again, but it seems it has endeared me to him.* She smiled. *There isn't an ounce of selfishness in this. He isn't trying to kiss me, or look at my face, or comfort me, he's just here.* Back home, her culture dissuaded wasting time in meaningless acts of kindness. Her matchmaker would have looked at this and said "How unconventional. How can she do anything when trapped in his arms? How can he go to work without having to untangle from her grip? A woman should not be so needy." But Chestnut enjoyed this much more. *He's so unlike anyone I've ever met. In all his impulsiveness, there's a life behind his eyes, an excitement for something bigger than himself.*

The fall of the eclipse painted the world in violet strings and amber thread. *I would very much love to make a dress such as that, some tulle around the skirt in a colored layering. I wonder if Rex would like it.* Ava had taken off her bracelet during the night and it lay on the table. Chestnut hadn't minded it before, but her eyes caught on it now. Her grey eyes tinted a poisoned purple hue. *Why, it's so beautiful, is it not?* The silver reflected the sunrise. *What beautiful...beautiful shine.* Her hand reached for it. *She wouldn't mind at all if I held onto it. After all, it's so shiny and tempting.*

Rex shifted behind her.

Chestnut jumped and abandoned the bracelet. *Has he seen?* His eyes were still closed. Chestnut hastily nabbed the bracelet and tucked it in her pocket. *Beautiful, beautiful silver. My silver.*

Rex groaned. "Mmm, G'morning."

"Good morning" She gave him a smooth dragon's smile, guiltless.

"How do you feel?"

"It's certainly getting worse, but nothing I can't manage." She hummed.

Rex gave her a look. "You're acting differently."

He knows. "No, you're just groggy." She hissed.

"More dragon-like." He quoted Heath.

Chestnut blinked. *More dragon-like? I'm not– am I? Oh moss!* The reality of what she'd done set in. Chestnut pulled out the bracelet and handed it to Rex. "I took it–"

Rex's eyes hardened. "Just a symptom, okay? It's not your fault."

Isn't it? I'm so ashamed of myself, Mama would be so ashamed. Her daughter, a thief, a willing thief at that. What else am I going to steal? How much longer until the urge strikes me again? "Why did it allure me?" She knew so little of dragons.

"Dragons hoard gold and shiny things. Must be what Heath meant."

First my body, now my mind. I don't believe I'll be able to recover from this even if we did get the cure. She leaned further into Rex. "I'm sorry–"

"We're so close, Chestnut, don't worry." He gave her a small smile.

If only it were so simple.

The train pulled in just as Ava woke up. Immediately, she glued her eyes to her phone.

Rex lifted Chestnut off the train by her waist. "Now let's get something to eat."

Even the mention of food made her horribly nauseous. *I need to eat something.* She knew that, yet her body refused to acknowledge the hunger. A looped recording played over the intercoms, welcoming them to the Medieval era. "Ye faire travelers of thy neighboring countries, Welcome."

The extravagant barrage of erident eloquence reminded her of home. *What a silly way of bidding visitors welcome. I wonder if everyone here speaks like this. Or perhaps it is simply the rulers, King and Queens and all that.*

They walked through the station, stores on both sides. "What do you want to eat?" Rex said.

She made a face. *Nothing. In fact, if there was to be an anti-snack where the consumer gained an appetite, that would be much more appreciated.* "Maybe a small salad, or cheese and crackers." Chestnut's eyes lingered on a keychain of a knight as they passed. *Shiny.*

Her fingers rubbed against each other itching to take it. *That's just the effects of the poison. You must stay yourself, Chestnut.*

Ava was drifting behind, admiring the knick-knacks. Rex pulled Ava to his side. "Stick with the group."

She glowered at him. "I was."

"You and Chestnut can go and get a snack. I'll take like–uh– a bag of chips. I'm going for a restroom break."

"Okay." Ava said.

Chestnut frowned. *What is so important on her phone that she has to stare at it while she walks? She seems addicted to the thing. Why, I doubt she could put it down even if she wanted to.* "Ava–" she said softly.

"Mhm?"

"Food."

"Oh yeah, right, uh c'mon." She looked up and trotted to a convenience store. "Go crazy." Ava leaned against a bookshelf and resumed her texting. She giggled.

Go crazy? "What is the meaning of that expression?"

"Hm?"

"Ava please, would you–" Chestnut tipped down Ava's phone, "Be here right now?"

143

She rolled her eyes. "Ugh– fine, yeah. Ok." she stuffed the phone in her pocket. "Go crazy means splurge. Get whatever you want, okay? And get Rex a bag of chips."

"Won't you get anything?"

She shrugged, "I'll look around."

Okay then. I suppose I'm– her eyes drifted to a display of can openers. *Ava did say to get whatever I desired.* Chestnut spent the next few minutes collecting shiny memorabilia from the display stands. She placed it on the counter for purchase along with a bag of original chips and a fruit salad.

Rex dried his wet hands on his clothes as he returned. His eyes widened at the knick-knacks. He laughed. "Okay, no, no, no, no, no, no, and–"

She looked up at him with round beady eyes. "But I need my can opener."

He regarded her for a second before smiling. "Alright, just the can opener."

"Thank you!"

"Ava! C'mere, we have to pay."

Ava trotted over with a tuna sandwich "Gotchu, Gotchu." She gave Rex the chips.

"Thanks" He popped it open and presented the bag to Chestnut "Why don't you try one?"

Her ears pinned back. "Oh. No thank you." *I intend to just stare at my own food and pretend like I have the intention to eat them.* She caught Rex intently watching. *He's waiting for me to eat this...I suppose a few bites won't hurt.* She managed to eat the entire fruit cup.

Chestnut stepped outside, completely enamored with her can opener. The crisp, mountain air thinned the more she breathed.

Pay-to-look binoculars stood around the wood, offering visitors a better view. Rex leered over the railing. "We're going off road, ladies."

"Because, why not?" Ava hopped over the railing and helped Rex lower Chestnut down.

Oh, moss.

They stepped carefully over the cliffside. On Chestnut's left, cold hard stone, on her right, an endlessly deep precipice. *This is completely safe, except for if I pitch to the right, I would certainly fall so fast I would splatter against the earth–* She hugged her book and looked back at Rex. "What if we fall?"

"If you fall, I'll catch you." His face pulled into the smile only he could pull off. His cheeks crunched his eyes into soft wrinkles that said 'everything was going to be okay'. No matter what happened, everything was going to be okay. A breeze prompted Chestnut to shrug Rex's cloak tighter. Her fur protected her against the frigid blast of wind well, but the pads on the bottom of her feet were vulnerable to the cold. Chestnut hesitated at a gap in the ledge.

"I'm going to lift you over okay?"

"Okay." She squeezed her eyes closed. His hands closed around her waist, pressing uncomfortably under her ribs. Her feet connected with stone again as she landed smoothly. She looked up at him, catching his soft smile. His hands lingered, and she wouldn't have wanted it any other way. *How did we ever end up on this journey? I stepped into traffic and suddenly we were being kidnapped.* She smiled. *I made the right choice. At least if I die by this poison, it'll be in Rex's arms.*

Her knees wobbled and she collapsed on the cliffside with a quiet thud, almost sliding off. Rex knelt down to her, gently placing his hand on her shoulder. "Are you okay?"

Chestnut blinked frost from her lashes. "My legs are still sore from all that running yesterday." She chuckled.

"Can you walk?"

Chestnut braced herself on Rex and attempted to stand but her legs buckled underneath her. Rex spread his arms and stood over her, flattening her against the wall. Rock crumbled beneath him and tumbled miles and miles down. Chestnut screamed, huddling in Rex's body. The wind blew soft, she looked up at him. *Why is he here? After Ava joined our party, he could have decided to leave–*

Rex grunted as jagged stones scored down his back.

Moss! "Rex." She breathed.

"It's okay. You're not able to walk are you?"

She shook her head.

No one opposed when he swept Chestnut up in his arms in a princess carry.

Rex tugged the cloak further around her. "Try to sleep. I won't drop you."

Her eyes welled and she curled her tail around him. *Thank you.*

They navigated the precipices until the sun eclipsed.

Chestnut blinked open her eyes. "Why have we stopped? Are we there?"

"Not yet but almost" Rex searched the horizon for signs of life, a fire or a light. A square stone structure reared itself on the side of a cliff.

Ava grabbed Rex's shoulder, bouncing. Chestnut's hand tightened around his Victorian jacket at the shaking.

"Ava, Quit it." Rex said.

"It's a castle!" Ava jumped around Rex and bounced over boulders and stone.

Castle? Is that what we have been looking for? Chestnut's heart swelled. *A warm bed and hearth sound wonderful.*

A canyon stretched between where they stood and the castle of their choice. A river separated the two.

Rex slid Chestnut to a lower ledge. He followed.

Ava easily scaled down the mountain. "I had to learn rock climbing for my fourth movie, *Hearts of Stone.*"

Chestnut's feet landed on the damp pebble shore, plastering her fur.

The peaks of the river's rapid current frothed and foamed like a rabid animal. A drawbridge stood like a wall on the other side.

Although Rex's demeanor didn't change, his jaw tightened.

Chestnut shook her feet after every step. "How do you open a castle?"

"You knock, duh." Ava said.

"And what, pray tell, do you knock on?"

Ava noted the upright door that blocked the entrance. "Correction: You yell." She raised her voice. "Hey! We need some help! Anyone?"

Shortly after, a man dressed in silver appeared over the castle wall. Chestnut's eyes dilated. *Shiny.*

"Friend or Foe?"

"Thou dearest knight! We hast traveled a long way and seek an audience with thou king." Ava bowed.

"Feudal Lord Larval is not seeking trade at this time."

"We're travelers."

"From where?"

Ava took a deep breath, preparing for the next set of shouted conversation. "Azodnem!"

"And your business in travel?"

"To heal our friend. She's been poisoned, and she needs rest"

Rex wrapped an arm around Chestnut.

The knight paused, looking over the three strangers. "Entry granted." *Oh thank goodness.* Chestnut relaxed. After moments of waiting, the hinges creaked and the drawbridge wound down.

Ava quickly stepped over to the other side.

The rapids didn't slow as they splashed over the wood. The water churned and lapped hungrily beneath them. Rex followed slowly, a shiver in every step.

"Is everything alright?"

"Yeah...everything is fine." Rex raised his eyes to the sky.

"Rex." Chestnut softened her eyes. "I am here for you. What's wrong?"

He gulped, feeling for his next step. "I...I can't swim." He breathed, eyeing the frothy tips of the rapids. Rex's fingers wrapped around hers.

Chestnut stepped closer, connecting with Rex walking shoulder to shoulder, hand in hand. "I won't let you fall in, Sparrow." *Can I truly promise that? Even if I wanted to, my size would surely be overtaken by his if he pitched forward and fell in. I have only swam in shallow water before, I certainly couldn't dive in and save him from such aggressive rapids.*

Rex bowed his head, eyes closed. Then his eyes raised, staying above the waterline. He released a hard breath.

But I would. Despite the most likely scenario being both our deaths, Rex is risking his life to save mine. I would do the same for him.

Once they were all on the other side, two knights led them inside the castle gates.

Fields spread over the precipices peppered white with nothing but chickens. Shepherds watched their goats, who bleated their shrill complaints, while the peasants sprinkled feed to hoards of chickens. An eagle swooped over their heads.

Rex looked at her, his eyes alight. "Isn't he so majestic?"

Those are...sharp talons. Men toted alpacas back and forth on the busy dirt roads. One alpaca's tail flicked into Ava's face. Rex couldn't restrain a laugh.

Chestnut smiled. Sheep scattered from under them and leaped onto roofs with bleats.

Stars danced in Rex's eyes. "Look! Look at them all."

Chestnut giggled. "There certainly are a lot of sheep."

They dragged themselves up a stone spiral staircase, carved from the mountain itself, that reached a dead end at the mansion's marble doors. Halfway up, the group paused to accommodate one of Chestnut's coughing fits.

Fanfare sounded, and more guards closed in around them.

"You'd think they might have realized we aren't a threat by now." Rex whispered to Chestnut.

Yes, It's not too hard to discern our peaceful inquiry. Why, with our lack of weapons and dirty states, any person would be able to see that.

The steps led them to the grand, white, pearl doors of a mansion.

"I'm disappointed," Ava said. "I thought there'd be a King."

"A Lord is just as good." Rex said.

A servant slid open the door. Chestnut's wet fur indented the expensive rug with her footprints. A chandelier hung high over the multiple floors. They were led to what Chestnut believed was the Lord's study. The knight halted in the doorway. "Lord Larval, you have unexpected visitors."

"Our hearth is warm with guests already."

"They seek a place to stay."

Another voice added to the two, a soft husky voice. "We'll come back to this conversation, but for now, you have guests, Lord."

Rex ushered Ava and Chestnut to stay behind him as the door opened again. Ava's smile widened, despite her best efforts to hide it. The husky voice belonged to a detective in a beige trenchcoat and a white button up collared shirt. Behind the Detective was a boy wearing a similar outfit to his companion, taking rigorous notes. A pen tugged at the edge of his mouth thoughtfully.

Ava stood agape " Jason!"

"Ava!" Jason ripped glasses off his face.

"What are you doing here?"

Jason lingered behind while the detective escaped away. "I'm helping my Dad with a case."

"Cooool!"

Panic crossed Jason's face as his father gained more ground. "I-I have to go, I'll find you later."

"Okay!" Ava waved.

Chestnut waved too. *What a wonderful coincidence! It thrills me to see Ava so excited.* She looked at Rex, but judging by his hard expression, he didn't agree with Chestnut's optimism.

"He's trouble, Ava. I can feel it"

"No one cares about you and your gut feelings" She stuck her tongue out at him playfully.

The knight stepped aside and led the three into the large sitting room.

"How may I be of service?" The Lord wiped sweat from his brow.

Rex stepped forward "My Lord, we're travellers bound for Lavivrus. One of our party is ill and we need a place to stay for a day or two."

The lord's white beard stretched to his collar. He looked them over in lazy blinks. "Ill?"

"Poisoned, my Lord."

He hummed thoughtfully. "I can spare a bedroom for two days."

"Thank you, my Lord."

"Join me tonight at dinner. The length of my table is stretched specifically for guests, after all."

"Thank you, my Lord," Rex repeated, bowing out of the room.

Chestnut smiled. *That went well.* Her eyes lined the ornate stone walls. *The sconces have such a warm glow. I wonder how we'll manage the sleeping situation. Surely, there aren't two different beds. Perhaps I can inquire about a second bedroom. That way, Rex can sleep on his own. I know he doesn't like sleeping among company.* "Excuse me–" She tapped the knight. "Perhaps we could have two adjoining rooms?"

"One moment." The Knight bowed back into the room and indistinct conversation between him and the Lord sounded behind the doors. The Knight returned. "Only one."

Chestnut looked at Rex. "Well, then I'll sleep on the floor."

"Huh?"

Ava snorted. "Chestnut, you are *not* sleeping on the floor."

"Well...I don't want Rex to–"

Rex stared at her until it clicked. "Oh, Chestnut, it's okay. You need sleep and besides, we haven't even seen the room yet."

The knight left them with a servant. The little maid led them up three flights of stairs to their bedroom. "May your stay satisfy you." She opened the door.

Chestnut entered last, creeping past the small bed. Curtains hung around its frame, draping down to conserve heat on cold nights. A large tapestry covered the wall, picturing a hunt. Hound dogs chased after deer while riders on horseback raised their guns. Chestnut's heart strained for the deer.

"Two days." Rex reminded. "The rest of today, tomorrow, and then we head out in the morning."

"Got it." Ava jumped on the bed.

Chestnut brushed back the window's curtain. *Oh, my.* Rivers of mist curled through the whitecapped peaks. The sunset painted the landscape in a display of mauves and violets. She sat on the window sill. As much as she felt she was opening up to him, she felt his walls starting to crumble. "Rex?" She twisted to look at him.

"Hm?"

"What is your last name?"

"Clawfada, Xavier DeClawfada."

She tipped her head. *He looks like an Xavier.* "I like that name."

Rex blinked and looked down with a small smile. "Thanks–"

CHAPTER 19

Any other compliment would have meant less. He felt his face warm. She thought he had a nice name. His Highness had told him that his wife chose the name and that it was a subpar name for a prince, but Rex disagreed. Before His Highness had tainted it with nightmares and bad connotations, his name had always been a piece of his mother he held close. A knock echoed through the stone room. Rex exchanged a glance with Ava. *Who could that be?* Rex answered the door.

Chestnut smiled. "Hello–"

"Jason!" Ava yelled.

Rex strained a smile. *Ah, hello Jason...*

His eyes lit up as Ava rushed towards him. She gave him a big hug. "Brooooooo!"

Rex furrowed his brows. *Didn't you meet, like, two days ago?*

Jason gave her an awkward pat, but grinned from ear to ear. "Ava!"

"Jason!"

"I just got away from my father. He's doing some research."

"Oh man! Can I join you for your next interview?" Ava bounced.

"I can ask."

"Yeaaaaah!" Ava did a little dance, which prompted a laugh from Jason.

Rex stepped backwards into the room, deciding he'd rather see what Chestnut was looking at. "Quite the view, huh?" Rex sat on the edge of the window. He breathed on the window, and his warm breath caused it to fog.

Chestnut smiled at him. "Ava taught me a fun trick." She gently poked three circles into the fogged pane, one smaller than the other. She dotted two points inside the tallest circle and drew a sideways 3. "A snowman." She seemed so proud of herself.

"Not yet." Rex drew a hat and two stick arms. "Now he's a dapper snowman." Rex glanced outside at the eclipsing sun. He released a soft breath. The sun had no idea what was happening with its inhabitants, it just shone. On and on it shone steadily, completely oblivious to him. He didn't matter, none of this did. Nothing they could do could stop what happened or what will happen, just like the sun kept shining. Rex noted how the fading light glinted off rooftops, making the mountains sparkle. *Beautiful.*

She chuckled. "You know. you are a lot like Sparrow."

"How so?" Rex shifted from sitting on the window sill to sitting on the bed.

"He's broken too." She gave him a soft smile.

"Hm."

"I thought, instead of calling you Rex, or Xavier...well I thought Sparrow might be suitable. What do you think?"

Much better than Kitten, although that was a pet name too... Xavier shook away the unease. This is different. Yeah, it's different.

"Sure." Xavier gave a weary smile. He was tired of having Rex dictate his trust, dictate his comfort. It exhausted him, but he was tired of fighting. He just wanted to trust her... trust her motives were pure, to trust she had no agenda. "Come on, we have a dinner to get to." Xavier stood up and held out his hand like he did that one sunrise in the Victorian era.

He had to trust her. He would trust her. If he couldn't trust her, who could he trust?

Ava cackled behind them. "I should *not* be laughing this hard at a Dad Joke!"

Jason looked pleased with himself.

They were up all night talking, then texting this morning. I wish I had such an easy time making friends.

"Well," Jason said, "I should start getting ready for bed."

"Womp, must be nice, we have a dinner to go to."

Jason smiled and scratched the back of his neck. "Yeah, you know, if you want, we could...hang out tomorrow?"

Ava bounced. "Oh my gosh, oh my gosh, yes!"

"Okay" He flushed. The gentle giant looked nervous, sweat building on his forehead. "I...uh...gotta go". He paused, then turned back "Rex, could I talk to you?"

Rex was taken aback. What could he do? Say no?

Yeah.

"No." Rex slammed the door, but Jason caught it before it closed.

"W-wait, wait, wait, I really need your help–"

Rex looked back at Chestnut, who gave him an encouraging gesture. "Okay, sure." Rex slid on his coat and stepped into the hall. He looked up at Jason... Rex wasn't sure what was more insulting, that he wanted to talk or that he had the nerve to be taller.

There was an awkward silence, as if Jason didn't know where to start.

"So?" Rex said.

Jason's cheeks reddened. "I want to...we are...uhm...hanging out" He flashed Rex a panicked look, but it zoomed quickly past his eyes. He cleared his throat. "What does she like?"

"You have no idea where to take her and you want my advice?"

Jason blushed.

He looked down. "Well, she likes theatre and affirmation. She's really into sports and high energy activities. Trust me, she will let you know when she's bored." He gave a small laugh.

Jason wrote all that down. "Perfect! Thanks Rex. Oh, and have a good time at dinner."

Rex leaned back with a distrustful look. He wasn't too fond of Ava and Jason hanging out alone, but it'd be irresponsible to leave Chestnut alone. Ava could handle herself. He nodded "You too." *...you too? Ohhh claws– I'm too tired for this.* Rex closed the door and banged his head on the wood.

Rex waited outside the dining room while Chestnut whispered sternly to Ava. "Now, be on your best behavior."

"Alriiiight."

"And say please and thank you."

"Chestnut, you're not my mom."

A servant opened the door and bowed. "Dinner is served." He led the way in for the three of them.

Rex seated himself on Chestnut's left to ensure she wouldn't sit beside the Lord.

At the tap of a glass, the guests rose. A heavyset waitress's smile glinted in the glass. "Now introducing Lord Larval Jane."

Servants led their Lord to Rex's left hand side, across from Chestnut.

The dinner commenced at the Lord's sitting. Servants brought a host of salads from the kitchen, which Rex politely declined. He'd rather have no salad than look like a vagabond picking all the tomatoes out. He never liked tomatoes.

Conversation was slow to start. The girls both looked uncomfortable, so Rex struck up a topic. "Thank you for letting us stay, Lord Larval. You have a beautiful castle."

Chestnut nodded.

"Thank you. It was built by my great-grandfather."

"Generational wealth." Ava commented. She'd worn her monocle down to dinner, despite Chestnut's warning, because she thought it's be funny. "Yes, yes, rich people speak, indeed."

Chestnut shot her a look. "What Ava means to say is that we're greatly appreciative."

The Lord dabbed his mouth with a napkin. "Where's the fourth?"

Rex looked at Chestnut. "Fourth?"

"Oh, I could have sworn there was another in your party. No matter, which one of you has taken ill?"

Chestnut raised her hand.

She looked smaller than usual with her ears pinned back and her hair in front of her face. She looked shy, scared even. Rex tipped his head. *Are you okay?*

Once she shook her head, Rex dismissed himself from the table. "Excuse me, we'll be right back" He led her outside of the room.

Chestnut started a sentence but Rex wrapped her in his arms.

Her words fell away and she asked instead "Wh–what is this for?"

"I just thought you needed this right now"

Moments of shock passed before she returned the hug. "The urges are getting stronger. I feel sicker. I don't know if I'll be able to even finish the salad. I'm starting to worry, Sparrow."

He was too. If he was being honest with himself, staying an extra day may be the difference between life and death for her. The image of that moonlit night resurfaced in his mind, sweat trailing down his brow as he lifted chunks of dirt from the trodden grass. He didn't think he could bury Chestnut. The pain would be too overwhelming for him to do much of anything. "I know." He took a deep breath. "But I also know that you are so brave."

She snorted. "Me? Brave?"

"Yeah" He smiled. "You climbed a mountain today"

"And was terrified every second of it–"

"But you still did it, you also survived a kidnapping with a level enough head to make a major decision." He pulled away and cupped her face. "You are brave, Chestnut, and I know you'll continue to stare this thing down with resilience and patience, because that's who you are."

Her eyes rounded. "I don't know if I can be"

"Then be courageous. In the absence of bravery, be courageous."

She slid between his arms again, squeezing him around the waist. "I will, for you."

He looked down, his stomach clenching. *For me...*

⁂

Rex pulled out the seat for Chestnut, then seated himself. Ava had managed to get the Lord loosened up and howling in laughter.

It never ceased to amaze him how easily she connected with people. Seamlessly she could turn a stranger into her next best friend. It started with a quip, a smile, and then it developed into a meaningful relationship, like she had with him and Chestnut. Rex smiled at the two. *I'm glad Ava decided to join us.*

"Rex, you just missed it. I was telling Larvae about my experience with Basketball."

Rex sat down with a soft chuckle. "Basketball?"

"Oh, yeah. I was this tall, and you know, literally the smallest on my team, so all my teammates looked down on me like this, breathing down my neck. Anytime I did something wrong, it was 'hey'." She breathed heavily in her deep voice. "Pipsqueak" more heavy breathing "C'mere!" Her voice cracked, but the Lord burst out in another wave of boisterous laughter. Chestnut giggled too.

Remarkable. Rex chuckled. 7,000 years of training and refining his craft as an entertainer, and yet Ava was a natural comedian. He was never good at stand-up comedy. Rex sawed a bread roll in half and slathered it with butter. Finally, the servants delivered the main course; Steak, on silver platters, accompanied by red wine.

Rex watched as a servant refilled his glass of wine. Just a half glass, but it set him on edge. He drank the first glass to not seem rude, but he didn't know how comfortable he was testing his limit. The Lord and Chestnut discussed in soft tones their upbringings. Ava pretended like she was listening, but Rex knew what daydreaming looked like.

"You don't like it?" The Lord gestured to his untouched glass.

Not at all. He probably should come up with a better response though. "It's too soft, I usually lean on the harder side." He shrugged.

Ava's eyes brightened. "Cool! I wanna take shots!"

"No!" Rex said. "You're underage."

She sank in her seat.

The legal drinking age in the Medieval era was fifteen, technically, but he didn't want Ava to get carried away.

"A man who can hold his liquor. Haha! I can admire that." He beckoned a servant. "I don't see why we can't have a little fun, Bring out the fine glasses."

Rex raised his hands. "O-oh no, thank you. I have to be in the mood for it."

Ava banged the table. "Shots! Shots! Shots! Shots!"

He shot her a look. *Ava! Shut up!*

The servant returned with a shot glass and a large bottle of what Rex could only imagine was the Lord's hardest liquor. He gulped. *Greeeeat.* Rex looked to Chestnut for support, and she gave an amused giggle. *Yup, you're right...I asked for this.*

The servant poured them both a glass, and the Lord held it out to Rex. "To her healing."

Well he couldn't refuse drinking to Chestnut's healing, could he? Rex reluctantly grabbed the small glass and tapped it to the Lord's. They both downed the shot. Rex gagged, his eyes lighting on fire. *That's...strong.*

The servant poured another glass .

"To my good hospitality."

He couldn't exactly say no to that either, else he'd risk sounding ungrateful. He took the shot.

"To our good health and happiness!" Shot.

"To seeing my mom again!" Ava cheered, looking at Rex expectantly.

These were becoming harder to swallow. He felt sick.

The Lord brightened and slapped the table. "Cheers!"

"Cheeeers–" Rex forced a laugh.

The servant placed the bottle in the middle of the table, leaving it in Rex and the Lord's hands.

A fog settled over Rex's inhibitions.

His Highness's voice rang in his memories. *"Good Kitten!"* He blinked as the same rose poison poured into a glass. His Highness set the bottle down with pristine white gloves, and pushed the glass forward. *"A few more and we'll have a wonderful night."* Rex blinked away the hallucination.

Chestnut reached forward. "Rex?"

"Ya?" He turned his head on the table to look at her. She was so pretty! He furrowed his brows and lifted his hands to mess with her ears. "Doop De Doop. Badaba." He giggled.

The Lord swallowed another glass. "Where did you grow up, son?"

Rex returned the Lord's friendly look. He didn't know when it happened, but he turned around and his barriers, his walls that he protected his secrets with, had crumbled. Rex leaned over the table. "I grew up in Victoria. I lived there for most of my life, with Matthew and William." Rex paused, twirling his finger around the rim of the shot glass. "Until they both died!" He burst out in loopy wheezing.

"On the streets?"

"Yes! I guess you could have called me a ssstreet *rrrat* " Rex emphasized **rat.** He poured another shot. They made him feel lighter, as if he could jump and float to the ceiling. It was freeing. He didn't have to worry about lies and secrets; he could just exist. He smiled and poured another, downing it quickly. *I like existing.* Rex gave a bleary eyed smile. *Am I slurring? I need another shot, that'll fix me up.* Rex took another shot.

The memories washed away. Shot.

The fear washed away. Shot.

Rex reached for the bottle, but Chestnut snatched it, moving it just out of reach. Rex bared his teeth, glaring at her, but she blinked calmly as if to say, *"You'll thank me later."*

Rex reached over the table, whining like a little kid, but still wasn't able to reach. He needed it, he needed it badly to forget, but he couldn't have it.

"Ava, what's wrong with him?" Chestnut said.

"He's drunk. What, you don't have alcohol on your planet?"

Drunk? I-I only had a few shots, five, maybe six, I lost count. Rex noticed the sway and the fogginess, of course. The room spun, proving he was much more tipsy than he thought he was.

Chestnut shook her head with a concerned chortle. "Perhaps we should take him up to the room." She reached for Rex, but he swatted her away.

"No No– Nope! Nah, nah, I don't wanna go to the room." He whined. "I'm perfectly fine, see? I can walk in a straight line."

Ava laughed, starting to record.

Rex, indeed, could not walk in a straight line. Rex's eyelids dropped and darkness consumed him, when he opened his eyes again, he was on the floor with Chestnut stooped over him. *Wonder why she's so concerned?*

"He's awake, Lord, please excuse us, but we're going to take Rex back up to our room."

Rex opened his mouth, but it felt disconnected from his face, he could see his lips moving if he stretched them far enough. *Weeeird.*

Ava trotted beside him and looked down. "Oh, dang, he is *drunk* drunk." She chuckled.

Chestnut slid her arm underneath Rex and helped him up. Suddenly, he was on his feet, being dragged across the velvet castle floor. *What is– why is the leaving the Lord?* He blinked, then slipped on a stair. He made a 'whoop' sound, followed by a giggle.

"Rex, Rex, hey Rex," Ava poked him. "What's your father's name?"

"Felix." He smiled.

Chestnut whipped around to glare at her "Ava!"

"Shh, shh, this is our chance to get out all his secrets"

"No. That's taking advantage of him in this vulnerable state."

Rex pressed a kiss to Chestnut's brow. "Muah. You're so kissable."

Chestnut flushed. She got him safely on the hard floor and slowly helped him hobble along.

Rex hiccupped, tripping over himself. Now on the floor, he wheezed and quoted Russian poetry. He lay sprawled out on the floor.

Chestnut picked him up again, half dragging him. She spoke in soft tones. "Let's get you into bed."

Rex continued quoting, amusing himself until he stuttered into the dark room and Chestnut lay him on the bed. Too cold—the room, it was freezing. Rex shivered, curling into fetal position. A pillow lodged behind his back and in front of him to prevent him from rolling. Rex stuck his tongue out. "Hey, Chestnut?" He gave her a mischievous grin.

"Yes, Sparrow?"

He gestured for her to come closer.

Chestnut leaned in and Rex kissed her cheek. *Hehehe, she fell for it.*

She pulled away, red, but her eyes soft. "You–"

"Heheh, I love you."

Chestnut's eyes rounded.

Ava squealed.

Chestnut pulled the blanket over him. "Goodnight, Xavier."

Xavier purred as her soft lips met his forehead. *Goodnight.*

CHAPTER 20

A va watched Chestnut stoop to kiss Rex's forehead. *I wonder what that feels like...to be loved.* Her eyes dropped to the ground. *I'll learn one day...one day, very soon!* With each passing day, those words were getting harder to tell herself.

She looked outside. *I'm lovable, right?* Maybe she was just incapable of being loved. She'd worked so hard to change everything about her, and she was certain she hadn't missed anything. Her personality was moldable as putty, her hair was the most popular style, and she followed all the latest trends. She didn't understand why people still gave her a once over, then ignored her. She sat down on the bay window, pulling out her phone. Jason hadn't responded–maybe he was busy. She checked her social media, scrolling through her notifications, seeing who liked her post and who didn't. She released a sigh. Her posts exceeded a million followers. So why did she still feel so empty?

Ava looked over at Rex and Chestnut. Chestnut rested on the other side of the bed, reading, with one hand intertwined with Rex's. *Well, Chestnut isn't so special...* Not that she liked Rex, but the attention would be nice. The two of them were so focused on each other, she felt like an afterthought. At least when Jason was around she had someone to talk to. She stared at her phone, waiting for the three dots saying he was replying. She waited five minutes, but to no avail. She sighed. "I'll just sleep in the chair."

Chestnut looked up at her, "Ok, Sweet dreams, Ava"

"Mhm." she hummed.

"Is everything okay?"

"Yeah, everything is fine." *Smile inside and out.* "I got tons of good footage of Rex," She snickered.

"I don't know what that means, but I'm glad it makes you happy" Chestnut smiled, then dropped her eyes back to her book.

That was a narrow save. Ava sighed and looked out at the star-dappled mountain. *I can't wait for tomorrow.*

<hr />

Ava drew in a long snore despite Chestnut's shaking. "Ava, Ava, wake up! Jason is here."

Ava snorted and jumped awake, eyes glazed over. "Huh? Wha–"

"He just knocked on the door. He's waiting for you."

Oh? Oh! Ava jumped to her feet and changed into her dress. Rex was still resting peacefully. "Right okay, Uh– I'll see you later Chestnut!"

"Bye, Ava,. Have fun, and tell Jason I said 'Hi'."

Ava slung her backpack over her shoulder, closing the door with her foot as she tied her hair in a ponytail. She looked at Jason. "Chestnut says 'Hi'."

He laughed. "Good morning to you too"

"Where are we headed?"

"We don't have much time before my Dad's interrogation. I was thinking we could walk around, maybe get some turkey legs, or chestnuts, whatever they have, I'm down to go with the flow."

Ava smiled. "Bro, same."

"How'd the dinner go?"

"Rex took a bunch of shots and passed out." She giggled.

"Jeez! What kind of shots?"

"I dunno. I've never drank liquor before."

"Ah." He averted his eyes.

Ava trotted down the stairs. "C'mon, you're so slow!"

"I'm like twice your size! Give me some slack."

The day was bright with the early morning sun shining above them. Ava squinted her eyes and looked up at it. Her favorite pastime, sun gazing. Jason joined her, holding his hand to his eyes. "You're going to go blind one day."

"Naaah!" Ava said.

"Hey, look, there's the turkey cart."

"Mead too!"

Jason flinched, but followed her. He kept his eyes on the ground.

Ava furrowed her brows. "What's up?"

"I just don't drink." He set a gold token on the counter. "Two turkey legs, please."

"Woah, that's cool, where'd you get that?" Ava inspected the gold. She chomped on it to test the validity of the gold. It didn't dent, *Solid gold!*

"I have a coin collection; at least one form of currency from each district."

Ava pulled on his sleeve, "Bro, that's so cool!"

"Is it?" He smiled. "Yea–uh, thanks." He handed her the turkey leg. "Fresh, caramelized turkey leg."

Ava took a deep breath. "Oh! Delicious, you cook?"

"Yeah, I like to grill."

An alpaca trotted in front of them and Ava hid behind Jason. She'd learned her lesson from the last smack in the face. "So where do you live again?"

"Lavivrus, in the country. We have a big farm with a few cows."

"Ayo, that's where we're headed." Ava tore a strip of her chicken. "My Mom works there so..."

"You're homeschooled?"

"No. She signed me up for Lavivrus Public Academy, wants me to get the whole teenage girl experience."

"Cause you're famous?"

Ava blinked. How long had he known? Why didn't he tell her? He was acting awfully casual for meeting a celebrity. She had assumed he lived under a rock and didn't know who she was, but apparently not. "You know? Why didn't you say anything!?" An autograph or a picture would have at least made her believe she was important.

"Well, I'm not exactly a fan. It would've been a bad look if I ran up to you and asked you to sign my forehead." He snorted.

No, he has a point. "But you have heard of me?"

"Yeah, I mean I think everyone has." Jason checked his watch "It's almost noon. Let's head to the site."

"You're strangely calm about meeting a celebrity." She gave him a look.

"I don't see why I should be. So you can sing. You're still a human being, not a god or anything."

Ava blinked. "But I can sing better than most people."

"And just as well as others."

"Hey!" She smacked his shoulder, laughing "Okay, yeah, I guess most of my fame does come from my parents anyways."

"You do have a great voice though. Do you want to give me an autograph?" He smiled at her.

Do I want to give him an autograph? Pffft, pshh, what kind– what kind of question is that? "Yes."

Jason removed his black ballcap, his blonde hair loosening. He gave her a white sharpie. "Here."

Ava giggled and signed his ballcap. "Yeaaah!"

"Now that I have the official merch, I guess that makes me a fan ."

"Heck yeah!"

They climbed up the mountain, up the dirt roads to a row of smaller homes. Jason peered down a street. "Look for Leif Avenue. It's building A63B.

"A63B?"

"Yeah."

"Found it." Ava pointed to a small shed connected to other small sheds by one long hallway. "Run out of money?"

"No– my father wanted an intimate setting, plus we know the owners."

Ava reached for the door knob, but Jason stopped her. "Er–my father doesn't like civilians in the interrogation room. I didn't tell him I was bringing you."

She shrugged. "I'm interested in criminology. I'll tell him it would be a great honor."

Jason gave her an uncertain look, then creaked the door open. It opened to a large parlor, with a table and some chairs scattered abroad.

Jason's father paced back and forth, his grey hair slicked back and his hands coddling a manilla folder. "Jason. It's 12:03."

Only three minutes late, chill. Ava's eyes swept around the room. Her sneaker crunched thatch, as she inspected the 10x10 foot room. A cockroach creeped in through a hole in the ceiling corner. *Phew, I wish I would have brought a sweater.*

Jason looked uncomfortable. He leaned down to whisper, "Do you feel like there are more people than just us in this room?"

Now that he mentioned it, she could feel it too, like there were a myriad of eyes watching them. *Just nerves. You're imagining it, Ava.* She smiled at Jason's father. "Hello sir, I'm Ava. I'm one of Jason's friends. I'm really interested in criminology and would love it if I could sit in and watch the interrogation."

The man regarded his son, then returned the kind smile "Monsieur Pascal Allons, You can call me Pascal. If you'd like to watch, you may."

Ava beamed. *See, Jason, I told you it'd work out!*

Jason took the manilla folder from his father. "We'll be behind the soundproof glass." He told Ava

She bounced "Lead the way!"

Pascal led the way to the interrogation room. Ava looked carefully at the man in the chair. He looked familiar, white hair, pale skin. She couldn't remember where she had seen him before.

Pascal circled the table.

The criminal didn't acknowledge him beyond an amused glint in his eyes. "Detective, Let me start by say–"

Pascal interrupted him "Wait. Camera, protocol, you understand."

He leaned back in the chair. "Of course. I believe protocol should be followed."

In the corner of the room, his father mounted a camera on the wall.

Jason stood at the glass watching.

"So you're saying they can't hear anything we're saying?" Ava smiled.

"Nope, nothing at all."

She giggled. "You smell!" She yelled at the criminal.

Jason snorted, then broke out in hard chuckles.

Pascal turned to the man. "You do not have to say anything. But, anything you do say will be taken down in writing and may be given as evidence in a court of law."

The man looked up at him, his red irises pinned on Pascal. "Detective, am I a suspect?"

Jason slid his glasses on and pulled out his notebook. "They all ask that."

"We're still piecing everything together. That's why anything you can give me will be of great use. First, let's start with the basics, full name?"

"Heath Elijah Emortus."

Ava's stomach dropped. She'd heard that name before, Chestnut and Rex mentioned Heath. It rushed back to her. "Jason, I know him!"

"What?"

"I know him, he's the one who poisoned Chestnut!"

Jason's expression dropped. He breathed out a quiet "Woah."

Heath's gaze lazily drifted to the mirror, right at her and Jason. "I see your son is friends with the Prince."

"It does seem so, doesn't it?"

"Indeed." It look as if Heath's mind was turning that little bit of information over in his mind like a dagger. "Now tell me Detective, when did the world become so cruel to keep a working man from his trade?"

His father maintained a neutral expression. "Working man, why don't you tell me about that."

"You wouldn't believe me." Heath turned his nose in the other direction.

"I'm open to all stories."

"I'm the humble servant of the King of the second afterlife."

Jason blinked. He wrote 'delusional' in his notes. "Maybe schizophrenic?"

Ava had stopped responding to Jason, fully invested in the interrogation now.

"Are you?"

"Yes sir. Have been for the past 3,000 years."

Jason snorted. "My gosh, this guy needs to be in a straightjacket." Ava shushed him.

"3,000 years of service, congratulations." Pascal said in earnest.

"Thank you. Most recently I was assigned to fetch the soul of the prince."

Jason pressed a button that let him speak through the intercom. "You believe you're the grim reaper?"

Pascal sighed, rubbing the bridge of his nose. "Oh, Jason."

Heath remained unphased. "Your son has a quick tongue."

"And an impulsive wit. Let's get back to your servitude. What does the King want with the prince?"

Jason removed his finger from the radio and furrowed his brows. "This is wasting time. We're here to investigate a murder, none of this information is useful." He pressed the intercom again. "Sir. Could we get back on topic? You know what this is about, yes?"

"Yes, the murdered servant. My squad got carried away, he instigated and they went to redact their dues, just a harmless little blanket party." Heath gave a snide look around the room. "Isn't that right, boys?" He gave a light chuckle.

Ava had a sinking feeling in her gut. "Jason...what if he's not imagining things?" They both felt the eyes, the spirits in the room. Ghosts resided in cool spaces and this room certainly had a chill to it. She was the only one here, besides Heath, who had heard Rex's stories of Fallen angels, and second lives, and Limbo.

Pascal slid a paper across the desk."Mr. Emortus, would you have any objection to putting that in writing?"

"None at all. A pen? Thank you." Heath signed a messy signature at the bottom of the page. "I think it's safe to assume you're on thin ice with the murder squad. Only explanation for why you're here and not a rookie."

Jason's eyes lit with fire. "That's not true at all! He's making things up. The reason you're on this case is because you're training me, not because you're a bad detective."

Ava looked over at him, growing more concerned by the minute. There was no change to Pascals' expression except the slight twitch of his mouth downward.

"Ah! I saw that. Reputation means alot to you, doesn't it?" Heath leaned forward. He cracked the pen and the ink blotted out his signature. "If we can keep this ordeal quiet, I can patch things up. Get you the top detective office. Or, if we're doing things the hard way, I could ruin your reputation with only two truths and a lie."

"Are you attempting to bribe me?" Pascal spat.

"Are you attempting to renegotiate?"

Jason looked at Ava. "That's at least a $100,000 raise! And the respect we would get in the office."

Heath leaned back in his chair. "I'm not asking for a freebie, only a little more time. I want the Prince. Once I get the Prince, even if you do try to take us to jury, you'll never find me and my men again. We'll get out of your already graying hair. You don't need the stress." Heath tutted.

Jason pressed the intercom, but before he could say anything, Pascal nodded politely to Heath. "Excuse me."

"Of course, Detective. Take all the time you need to make the right choice."

Ava jumped when Jason's father opened the door. "Jason. You are here to watch. You begged me to watch so that is what you shall do."

"But, sir, he's handing us the case on a silver platter, primed and juicy like a fat pig with an apple in its mouth. We should take it. Not to mention the promotion."

"And do what, forsake justice?"

"No...But we have plausible deniability."

"Have you ever considered if he's lying? He could be trying to frame–"

"His own men? That's crazy, no one would get their own squad on the chopping block."

"Jason." His father warned.

"Think about it. There are plenty of unsolved cases, and who really cares if this one goes unsolved?"

"The man's family. His wife and his children who just lost their father. We are giving peace of mind to these citizens."

Jason opened his mouth to refute but thought better of it.

Ava looked at Jason and his father. If she ever argued with her parents like that, she wouldn't see her parents for at least a week. They always said they needed time to mentally recover from the strain of arguing with their own daughter.

"I have to run to the lockers to get another copy for him to sign."

"Could I come with you?" Ava said.

"Yes. Jason, you will stand right here until I come back. I don't want you to even *look* at that man. He unsettles me, and I don't trust where your mind is at right now."

Ava looked back at him, *Please don't do anything stupid.*

Jason turned his eyes to the ground. "Yes, sir."

CHAPTER 21

J ason watched his Father leave with a bitter curl of his lip. *I am in my right mind.* Heath's voice echoed from the room, but there was something else- the voice of a girl. Her voice was rich and sweet like honey, soothing to the ear and to the mind. Jason doubled back and pressed his ear to the door.

"May I-"

Jason heard a lighter spark.

"Heath! This is serious. What if he finds out we're working together? The whole plan is ruined." Footsteps paced.

A sharp draw of breath. "Worry on your own time, you're bothering me." Heath sounded unconcerned. Jason smelled smoke through the door.

"He will though, It's only a matter of time. We need a backup in case he kicks me out of his mind. He is no closer to complying than he was in the beginning."

Heath spoke in a low voice "He is."

"He's not."

"It's a process, be patient. One doesn't just jump off a cliff. You have to push them there through little tiny nudges. A nudge here, a nudge there, and soon they're plummeting to their death.

"The King grows impatient."

"Thank you, Destiny, very helpful, telling me what I already know." Despite his scathing words, there was a level of teasing behind it. The chair creaked as Heath leaned back.

"I'm getting tired of playing games with him anyway. I want to make sure the girl lives first, then we can go into phase two."

"Heath! No." The lady let out a shuddering breath

"You're making this so much harder than it needs to be," Heath growled. "Why, on Limbo, the King paired me with a *sensitive* Fallen, I'll never know."

The lady's voice sharpened. "Heath! I'm a choir Fallen, I never asked to be here. I should be singing His Highness's praises, not whatever this is."

"Well then, why aren't you?"

"I don't know. One second I was standing in gold robes, the next I'm going through squad training."

"Destiny, I told you at the beginning of this. If your plan doesn't work, mine will."

"But to go that far—"

"Someone's blood will spill for the Prince's stubbornness. Mark. my. words."

The door creaked underneath Jason's hands. *Crap!*

Both stopped talking.

Jason held his breath, cursing the rundown place. The air warmed up and the ghostly presence disappeared. "Yes?" Heath called.

Jason pushed his way in. "My father will be back soon. He had to grab something."

"You were standing behind the glass, yes?" Heath yawned "I've heard your father's perspective, but how do you feel about my proposal?"

"I think it's something to be considered."

"The two of you are close? You and the prince?"

"We've only really talked twice and he's been mildly pleasant both times."

"You know he's a killer, right?"

Jason's breath hitched.

"Murderer. He's also a pickpocket, so watch your wallet."

Immediately Jason's hand felt his pocket; his wallet was safe. "He seems so mild mannered though."

"Don't be fooled, he's a great little actor." Heath set his feet on the table. "Anyways, enough of the prince. There's a girl in the Prince's party you're awfully fond of, isn't there? Ava Charlie Evans, the actress, yes?"

"W-well, I mean fond– I mean–" Jason stuttered, feeling himself blush.

"Good luck with catching that one, son."

Son? Jason relaxed. The familiarity set him at ease. Curiosity wedged between the wariness. "Why?"

"Between you and me, you've got the same chance as a camel getting through the eye of the needle."

Jason frowned, he was baiting him, waiting for him to clamp his jaw around the worm and hook so he could reel him in. Jason tried to resist but– the bait looked so appetizing. "Why's that?"

"She's an Evans, a pure breed. Her finger is worth more than all your assets combined." He closed his eyes with a satisfied sigh.

"So?"

"So?" He opened one eye "Who are *you*? The son of a nobody."

"My father is not nobody!"

"I never heard of him before this."

"Well–" Heath had run him into a dead end. *He's right.*

"That heart of yours is a pebble chasing after a diamond? You know how many guys she has *just like you* chasing after her? *Nothing* makes you different."

"Shut up." Jason reached for his gun instinctively.

"Slow down there, slick." Heath smiled. "I'm just stating the obvious."

Jason raised his eyes to meet him. Heath flashed a psychotic smile. "As a friend, I say you've got no chance. But as an enabler, I can help. Say the word and I'll have the two of you kissin' at Scarlet Center."

Jason's eyes widened. A candlelit dinner in the fanciest restaurant, with the most expensive meals. Ava's smile, her endearing laughing, her green eyes gazing into his soul. *It's...no, it's too good to be true.* "I can win her heart by myself."

"Sure you can..." Heath turned his eyebrows up looking at him like he was pitiful. *I'm not pitiful.* "There's just one problem, though."

Baiting again. He's trying hard. "What's that?"

"She may not live long enough to return your feelings." Heath took another drag of his cigar, puffing smoke into Jason's face. "Like you heard me say while you were–" Heath flashed a side eye at him "–eavesdropping. Someone's blood will be shed. However, it doesn't *have* to be hers."

Jason waited for the catch and sure enough the next words out of Heath's mouth was "I can guarantee her survival, her safety, if you help me gather intel on the Prince."

"Intel?"

"Yes. My last intelligence suggested a plan B. It always helps to have more ears than less."

"No." His left foot shuffled backwards. "Spying is wrong, This is wrong."

"Oh, of course. The best things usually are wrong. But you need to fight underhanded deeds with underhanded deeds. If you agree, I'll need you to follow a few rules."

"Rules?"

"Just a few: Sorta like a deal, nothing binding."

"Like what?" Jason creeped his hand back onto his gun.

Heath closed his blood-curdling smile and the room chilled again. A spector entered the room, something Jason couldn't see. Worms crawled in his gut. *This is wrong.*

"Rule 1: You'll be my Private Eye. I want a script written documenting every word the Prince speaks from now on. Due every day starting from when you get home."

Heath snubbed his cigar.

"Rule 2: Make sure you keep tabs on the Prince. Maybe invite him to stay in your home. Make sure his window is unlocked."

Claws tapped over Jason's skin. Spirits impeded his personal space.

"And Rule 3: Don't question what I tell you. Don't ask why."

When his phone buzzed, Jason's heart rate spiked. This wasn't right. Whatever mutiny this man was planning against the Prince didn't involve him. It didn't need to, he could step away right now and everything would be alright. He had no business getting entangled within this ruinous deal. But Ava was already deep in consequence without an escape route. *She might die.*

Heath nodded to his pocket. "Go on."

Jason's phone raised to eye level. Heath sent him a text with the rules in writing. His number was saved in his contacts like his phone was hacked.

"In case you forget." He addressed the air, speaking to whatever existed in the room with them. "Thank you, darling, See, you *can* be useful"

Jason caught a glimpse of a silhouette of a woman behind Heath's chair but it disappeared. "I know you have some kind of plan against the prince."

"Oh, Yes. You would too if you knew the circumstances. You seem like an intelligent young man. Precisely why you'll do best. And don't worry about not knowing what to do. I've got that covered. Darling?"

The honey-like voice spoke in his mind, *Jason, I am Destiny. Heath's messenger. Whatever he wishes I can tell you privately. First you must convince your father to accompany the Prince and his entourage home.*

Jason blinked. *O-okay* .

"So, son, what'll it be? Heath watched him carefully.

Ava. He could keep out of it, or he could keep *her* out of it.

Steps pounded outside the door. His Father was returning.

"Now or never, kid."

*I-I don't– this–*His thoughts jumbled in a soup of panic.

"Son, you wanna keep her alive or not?" Heath spat.

Jason saw the knob turn and panic burnt his mind like boiling water. He didn't have time to weigh the cost, even to think. It was non binding, right? He could get out if something goes wrong–

The door creaked open.

He didn't have time!

He thrust his hand out to grab Heath's "Deal!"

CHAPTER 22

Pressure throbbed in Rex's cranium.

"Mmm." He tried to summon enough energy to get up, but his body was content to just lie there in pain. The dark room helped ease his headache but not by much. *Dinner, wine, shots, what happened after that?* His memory fuzzed, like someone had grabbed a chunk of events and ripped it out of his mind. All that remained was a void, where something happened but he couldn't remember what.

When did I go back to my room? He tried to recall the memory, but it was gone. His eyelids dropped again.

Chestnut hummed back "Mmm."

"Mmm?" He blinked his eyes open to look up at her.

"Good morning." She smiled.

He slowly sat up, his legs weighed by the blankets "Claws, I feel awful–"

"You were pretty intoxicated last night I would say. Ava and I brought you up to the room."

He groaned while rubbing soothing circles into his temples. "Thanks– got any water?"

"There should be some on the vanity. The servants left a pitcher for us.'

Rex smelled the water. Mead. It was a wonder that anyone here was sober with all the alcohol available. "It's liquor, don't drink it."

"Why...?"

"They don't have filtered water, so this is safer to drink than what comes out of their wells."

Chestnut paused. "You have to filter your water here?"

"To kill the bacteria" Apparently Chipeermen had a better immunity system than most humans. If they weren't careful, a scientist could find her a curious topic of study. They couldn't afford any more hiccups, not when they were so close to Lavivrus.

Rex peered into the mirror. *Oh jeez, I really do look awful.* His spiked hair stuck up in random places. Veins lined his dark eye circles, and his skin was flushed to the lips. His suit, wrinkled and stained, made him look more like a zombie than a prince. *The walking dead.* Rex chuckled. *Fitting.* He straightened the fabric and leaned against the mirror. "Where's Ava?"

"With Jason."

"I hope they had fun." He picked up Ava's keyfob. "She left her bubble storage."

"We should probably pick out clothes for the next era."

Rex combed over his hair and pursed his lips like a model. "Fashion show?"

Chestnut laughed. "I don't know what that is."

Out of Ava's bubble storage, he pulled a large feathery hat. "How's this?" He modeled it. *Pose, and pose, and pose.*

Chestnut doubled over with hard wheezes. "Rex, please!"

"I've never heard you laugh that hard before" He set the hat aside and drew another item, a feather boa. *Claws, I guess Ava has a thing for feathers.* He slung the boa around Chestnut and pulled her up from the bed. "Would you run away with me, Chestnut?"

She caught his eyes, searching deep in them. "Run away?"

"After we get your cure, after I destroy the portal, let's run away together." He rounded his eyes. Whenever he thought about his future, it became harder and harder to imagine it without Chestnut. He wanted to wake up to her smile. He wanted to hold her as he fell asleep.

Her eyes saddened, "But you have a kingdom. *I* have a kingdom. Don't you want to rule one day?"

Rex's breath hitched. "Chestnut..." How could she tell her? "It used to be my dream, you know, to be King of Limbo." How quickly that had fallen to pieces. First, His Highness crushed his spirit with isolation, then he had given him small meaningless tasks that kept him away from anything a future king would need to know. *I don't think I could be King, even if I wanted to.*

"What changed?"

He sat down on the bed and lowered his eyes. Where to start?

Chestnut sat beside him and rubbed circles into his hand.

"So...my father...The King." He released a heavy breath. "When I was a child, I guess I reminded him too much of my mom. I never knew why, but he practically locked me in my room, giving me pets to entertain me, lions, monkeys, anything we had." He gave a small smile. "I was so desperate for His attention, for anyone's, just to look another human being in the eye. One day I snuck into his private rooms, interrupted a dancer he had hired and showed him my own dance I made."

How much one decision had changed everything.

"I danced my heart out, and at the end, he stood, walked over, rested his hand on my head and called me cute." Tears beaded on his lashes. "He'd finally recognized me, and he didn't throw me out."

Chestnut's eyes softened. "You were seen, that's wonderful."

It had been.

"After that, I took dance lessons, voice lessons, and learned about every form of entertainment under the clouds. I was finally useful to my father, but the space on my schedule dwindled and the workload became stressful. My perfect performances fractured, a stumble here, a fall there..." Rex reached a hand to his cheek. "His Highness thought the best solution...the best punishment..." His other hand tightened around the bedcovers. "Beatings will continue until morale improves, you know? It got worse, much worse, and I got worse because of it. I thought he was the kind benevolent King all the servants told me he was. I looked up to him because I thought how much it would mean if He would teach me how to be kind, how to be a good King."

Chestnut gripped his hand. "Rex–"

"I want to become King, Chestnut... but His Highness would never abdicate the throne to... a Jester. I'm nothing to him but free entertainment."

She pulled him into a gentle hug. "You are so much more than that, Rex."

"I know–" He rested his head against hers. "After William, I tried getting better, healing...but then this whole thing happened with Heath and it all resurfaced."

"Thank you for telling me." She whispered.

"That's why I have to make it to Lavivrus, so I can destroy the portal. Then I never have to go back."

"Won't they rebuild it?"

Rex pulled away and cupped her face. "By that time, we'll be long gone. I don't care how far I have to run... I can't go back."

Chestnut nodded. "I won't let you."

He pressed a kiss to her brow "What did I ever do to deserve you?"

Make a witty joke, keep her out of harm's way maybe, but any decent person would do the same. He only agreed because he had his own business to attend to in the same city. But if he hadn't would he still have joined her? Rex let his lips linger on her forehead. He wanted her to be okay. Her happiness made up for anything His Highness could ever have done to him. By any means necessary, he was going to get her the cure and make sure she returned safely to her family.

CHAPTER 23

J ason escorted Ava back to her room.

"Jeez..." Was all Ava had to say after that disaster of an interrogation.

I can't believe I just did that. He pressed into his palm with his thumb. *I can't believe I just did that!*

"Are you okay? You seem tense." She asked.

Jason looked at her "Hm? Y-yeah. It's a dangerous world, just have to be careful." *I have to keep you safe.*

She looked unconvinced.

Destiny prodded different segments of his mind, searching his memories and gathering information about him. It sent a tingling sensation through his scalp. *Are you going to be much longer?* He thought.

Destiny paused her search to reply *"Not much longer, I just want to investigate your fascination with social drinking. It's an awfully recurrent memory."*

Jason stiffened. *Get out of my mind. Now!*

He was worried she would refuse. Her silence certainly lended itself to that conclusion, but she responded with a simple, *"Okay."*

She didn't understand. What was she? Just a messenger. Who was she to judge? He stuffed his hands in his hoodie pocket. *I did what I had to, okay? High school is fatal if you don't have friends...*

"Fallen angels don't understand such things."

That's right. You don't. Jason scowled. *Now I have a request for you. Why are you hunting the Prince?*

"After the prince's death at six, and after a 7,000 year consideration, the Prince took his second life in exchange for an eternity of servitude to the King. The Prince's contract has expired, and now Heath and I have come to collect."

Jason processed the information, not too worried about zoning out in front of Ava. He'd told her about his social battery. *So you two are just coming to claim what is rightfully yours.*

"Yes."

That seemed reasonable. It was as if he was helping a police officer catch an escaped criminal. He wasn't sure of Heath's alliance with what was lawful and good, but if what they were doing was within the laws, he saw no problem in assisting them. It kept Ava out of harm's way so she could live that normal teenage life her mom wanted. The two stopped outside Ava's room.

"Today was fun. So you're heading back home?"

"Yeah, tomorrow. We're just walking to the train station and then we'll be on our way."

Ava looked both ways, then leaned in. "Could you– Could you pull a few strings to get us on that train? Chestnut's getting worse and I'm really worried about her." She looked at the door.

He blinked. What made her think a nobody would have any more sway than a famous actress. "I could try."

"And then once we get to Lavivrus, if it's not too much to ask, could they stay with you and your Dad?" Her green eyes rounded. "My Mom will cut off my travel expenses once I get home, and I want them to be comfortable."

Two people shouldn't be too much trouble. Isn't that what Heath wanted, Destiny?

"It would make everything much easier, yes."

Jason gave her an encouraging smile "Sure, anything to make sure Chestnut lives."

"Thank you. I'll make sure Rex and Chestnut are up and at 'em bright and early so we don't miss the train. Text me the details and where to meet you!"

"I will!"

Ava slipped into the room. "Good night!"

"Good night, Ava." Once she closed the door, he headed to his own room. *What am I going to tell my father...?*

His suitcase was already packed and ready for the journey. The faded red was more of a pink now, and it was missing a wheel, but the suitcase still held articles just like a brand new one would. Jason looked up at his father who was brushing his teeth. "So...some interrogation we had yesterday, huh?"

"Mhm." He hummed through the suds.

"You know, I really don't think it was Heath who did it." He looked outside at the crisp morning.

After a strong spit, his father dabbled with mouth with a towel. "He admitted to it."

"But he didn't put it in writing, that means we could drop the case?"

His father walked past him, a stern look in his eyes. "What has gotten into you, Jason?"

"Nothing."

His father shot him a look. "You know, they say, 'He that refraineth his tongue is wise'."

"Proverbs 10:19."

"But a lying tongue is much sooner going to get you in trouble."

It's not necessarily lying if you aren't saying anything. "Hey, Dad. Ava asked me last night if we could host Chestnut and Rex once we get to Lavivrus. To help them get on their feet while Chestnut recovers."

"I guess that would be alright."

Oh thank God. Jason opened the window and leaned outside. He took a deep breath as the cool breeze played with his blonde hair. He wasn't as surprised that Rex was a pickpocket as he was about his history with killing. Heath was the paladin who was gracious enough to not lock Rex up for his crimes, instead taking him home. Jason furrowed his brows.

"Ready to go?" Pascal said.

"Yeah." Jason let his eyes linger on the landscape for another two seconds. "I'm ready."

Train wheels thumped against the track. The ride was supposed to be two hours, but two hours didn't last this long. Jason scowled at Rex. *I wonder how he did it. With a gun, with a dagger, concussion with a shovel then stabbed him until he died.* Jason had never felt such injustice for a complete stranger.

"Prince," Pascal stepped towards Rex, "I wanted to ask if you have any plans for lodging."

"Um." Rex swallowed. "I...hadn't thought that fa., I'm sure there is a hotel we can stay in."

"Do you have reservations? Hotels book quickly in this city."

Rex cleared his throat and shook his head. "No."

"Would you like to stay with us?"

Rex exchanged a glance with Chestnut. "Wouldn't that be intruding? I don't want to upset your wife."

Jason went stiff.

"...My late wife wouldn't have minded." Pascal said, his eyes dull.

Mom always loved having guests over. He returned his attention to the landscape. The terrain sloped down in flat groves. Wind danced upon the field of wheat and grass.

"Jason, Jason, Jason, Look!" Ava squealed.

Over the roofs of homes, a skyscraper raised above the horizon. The structures multiplied into a modern city. Flying cars halted in a long traffic line along the border, waiting for clearance to land and assimilate into the duller, less advanced culture.

Chestnut peered around Rex, and tears formed in her starry eyes. "Sparrow...please tell me that's Lavivrus."

"Yeah, that's it." Jason said. *Home.*

Chestnut leaned into Rex. "We finally made it."

Rex pressed his forehead against hers. "I told you we would!"

"You three act as if you have never seen a city before." Pascal looked up from his notebook with a warm smile.

A herd of cows dappled the countryside.

Ava poked Jason with a mischievous grin. "Hey, hey, I think I'm getting deja *moo!*"

"Don't *steer* me wrong." Jason's grin widened as Ava burst out laughing.

Rex, very slowly, turned to the two. "Please. Stop."

"But Rex, The *steaks* are high!"

Jason snorted. "I think Rex wants to *mooove* on to a different subject."

"I *herd* you loud and clear."

"Quite a*mooo*sing"

Rex groaned over Ava and Jason's snickering. *C'mon, don't be a buzzkill, Rex.*

The bullet train deaccelerated into the station. Rex and Chestnut, like glue, offboarded together. Jason watched Rex with an eagle eye. Each gesture could mean death for the four of them. Rex wouldn't hurt Chestnut, maybe not even Ava, but if he suspected that Jason was working against him, he might act emotionally.

Rex said. "Now we need to find that cure."

Pascal raised his brows. "I think she needs a hospital."

"She just needs a fish– uh– Southwater Taephoon? Do you know where we can find it?"

Pascal stroked his stubble. "Southwater Taephoon isn't a readily available fish. Usually miles off shore, they only crop up in the morning. However, Jason and I did catch one once while fishing."

Jason pulled out his phone. "I'll ask Leon if he wants to go out this weekend."

"Leon?" Ava peeked over his shoulder.

"He's my best friend." The only real one he had left.

Ava's phone sounded and she drew it from her pocket. "Oh that's...that's my Mom. She said the chauffeur is on his way. Well...I, heh, guess this is where I say goodbye." She lowered her eyes.

"Now?" Rex exclaimed "You can't, we just got here! Can't you come with us?"

Ava's eyes welled up with tears. She stepped towards him. "I can't, Rex—"

"I'm not good at goodbyes, Ava."

"It's ok. I'll visit all the time. We'll stay best friends. My mom's probably so busy she won't even know."

Jason frowned. *She should choose her best friends better. Keeping the company of murderers is never wise.*

Chestnut wrapped her in a hug. "Thank you for accompanying us. You're something I never expected but couldn't imagine living without."

"Chessie, I'll miss you most. Let me know when you get that cure."

Rex stepped in when Chestnut pulled away. "We'll miss you. I loved having a little sister."

Ava scoffed. "Pfft. You just need to adopt a mom, then you have the whole collection."

He laughed, eyes riveted on her. "Till next time."

Ava's eyes softened. "Till next time."

Pascal gave her air kisses on both sides of her face. "You're welcome to join us tonight for dinner. Jason will send you the address."

"Thanks, but I think my Mom and I are overdue for some girl time."

"Of course, I look forward to meeting her."

Jason gently took her shoulders and pressed kisses onto both her cheeks. "I'll see you at school tomorrow."

Ava giggled. "Ew, Fridays." A myrtle sports car pulled up to the curb. "My ride's here. Bye guys, I'll see you soon."

Rex opened the door for her. "See you soon, Ava."

She gave her signature dimpled goofy grin before Rex closed the door.

Jason's eyes lingered on the car as it drove further away. *See ya.*

"Now we only have two bedrooms and it'd be improper for Miss Oak not to have her own room." Pascal stepped between his son and the prince. "So Jason and Rex, you'll room together."

Jason gave Rex a look, but shrugged. "Okay."

A stricken panic crossed Rex's eyes, but he nodded. "The room will be fine. Thank you sir."

"Now follow me. Our car is just around the corner." Pascal tilted his suitcase and wheeled it away.

Jason saddled beside Rex. "You seem concerned."

Rex looked him up and down. "Why do you care?"

"Why can't I care?" Jason squinted. *Are you trying to hide something?* "My father had a case last week. About a murder." With satisfaction, Jason watched Rex's limbs stiffen.

"Okay."

"Do you enjoy murder?" Jason leered over him.

Rex kept eye contact for a few critical seconds, then looked away. "No."

Jason strode ahead of him. The parking lot beside a concrete financial building was empty except for two cars, a white convertible and a black van.

Pascal clicked his keys and the white convertible beeped.

Rex opened the door for Chestnut.

There wasn't anything to look at that Jason hadn't already seen. The drive took them through the suburbs and into the big city. Trains flew past the highway, as people strolled along the sidewalk. *We should have taken the highway around the city.* It would have added an extra hour, but it would be more efficient than driving through the heart of the city. After they drove over the highway, via the bridge, the landscape flattened into rolling hills. They drove down a long, gravel driveway leading to a quaint, country log cabin. Plains stretched far away in every direction.

By the time they reached the front door, the moon began eclipsing. Jason opened their front door and a golden retriever lurched out of the house. The dog's weight brought him crashing on the wooden boards of their porch. "Chase!" Jason stiff-armed the dog, but his laughter made him powerless to Chase's frantic licks.

"Chase." Pascal said, "Down."

The dog sulked into the house with an apologetic whimper.

Rex rubbed Chase's jaws. "Hey, Buddy."

Books on politics and investigative theory lay carefully stacked on every bookshelf. The kitchen countertop sparkled, but the handles on the oven were worn down

Pascal turned to them. "Tomorrow is Friday. I have work, Jason has school, so you two will be home alone. Showers daily, no eating on the couch, no shoes in the house, and we have a 'no closed doors' policy."

Jason nodded. "Let me give you a tour." The kitchen, on the immediate left, was the first thing he introduced their two house guests to. He presented them with a well stocked pantry of herbs and spices. The rest of the baking and cooking utensils hung along the back wall.

In the living room, the wall-embedded fireplace was surrounded by ornate boulders cemented into it. Jason directed Chestnut to her room right next to the staircase.

A chubby orange cat strolled into the room.

"Yoink." Rex snatched up the cat and sat on the couch. "Aren't you just the cutest thing?"

Paws pushed against Rex's stomach in steady kneads.

"Hey Tigger!" Jason pulled the cat off Rex's lap and coddled him like a baby. "He was my mom's cat." Jason squeezed Tigger tighter, then set him down.

Rex rounded his eyes. "I'm really sorry about your Mom."

That's rich coming from a murderer. Jason hunched his shoulders.

Two twin beds lined Jason's bedroom walls. A mirror on the desk reflected the light from the window.

Rex rested his cloak on the bed closest to the door. Jason watched him inspect the room.

"What are you looking for?" Jason lifted his suitcase onto his bed.

"Bomb, gun, knife, anything you could use against me in the middle of the night."

Jason laughed. "*I'm* not the one who kills people in the dead of night."

Rex handed Jason his gun. "Unload it."

With a sour scowl, Jason undid the gun in a series of clicks and poured out the ammunition. The most curious part of Rex's paranoia was why a ghost would be afraid of dying. "Afraid I'll shoot you?"

Rex averted his eyes. "Not like I could die anyway."

"Right– you're the prince of the afterlife," Jason mocked.

A moment of silence stretched before Rex said, "How do you know that?"

"Ava told me." Jason pulled back the blinds and unlocked the window. Moonlight streamed in, painting Rex in the icy blue. Tiny flakes floated off him like dust.

Jason paled. "Wow. You're really..."

"Dead, yeah, now close the blinds." Once he stepped out of moonlight, his body restructured into a human body. Rex's inspection led him to the closet.

"Rex!" Jason reached over the bed. "Don't open that!"

"Why?"

"Just– Rex!"

Rex flung open the closet and narrowly caught a money bag from falling out. A handful of chunky sacks filled one shelf. "Why do you have money bags–" Rex spilled a few of the coins onto his desk. "They're...pennies?"

Jason coughed into his arm. "It's uh...my penny collection..."

Rex blinked. "People collect pennies?"

Jason yanked the money bag out of his grip "You wouldn't understand." He muttered.

191

"I'd like to try." He looked down at the pennies strewn over the desk.

He'd like to try? I bet he would. I'm sure this is just some kind of ploy to get me to lower my guard. Jason pulled a coin from the sac. "Alright... look, This one is from 1910, from Old Earth. I had to pay a fortune for it. This one is from the Victorian era. See the grit surrounding it? The copper's only been polished once."

The coin in question bore a shotgun on the tails side.

Rex smacked the bottom of Jason's hand and the coin went flying.

"Hey!" Jason's glasses dropped with the motion and he groped on the ground for both his glasses and the penny.

Rex shuffled backwards, "Sorry."

I bet you are. Jason slid his glasses on and shot a glare over his shoulder.

Rex was already distracted, his eyes locked on a framed picture of his parent's wedding. "Who's this?"

Does he never stop? "Put it down! You're getting fingerprints on it." Jason set the picture face down. "She died two years ago..."

"Oh."

"You know what? Just sit in the corner and don't touch anything."

Rex lowered himself onto the bed and undid the laces from his Victorian heels. "I'm not trying to cause any harm."

"Yeah? Well you are. That's what murderers do, they destroy everything they touch." Jason snapped.

Rex's expression hardened. "Are you calling me a murderer?"

"Yeah, I wonder if Chestnut knows."

Stars exploded in Jason's vision as a fist collided with his cheek.

A burning fury had entered Rex's eyes. "Don't you dare say her name in that tone, Filth."

The first punch was thrown and all reason went out through that open window. Jason wiped a stream of blood from his nose, then lunged at Rex, tackling him to the ground.

Lightning surrounded them in a flash. Through Rex's hands, electricity spread into Jason's veins.

Jason fell limp, but swiped his empty gun off the table. He pointed it at Rex, but the trigger only launched air. He cursed and instead knocked Rex's jaw with it.

To let a murderer roam free on the streets was a violation of justice. Jason, since he was a little boy, was determined to be an investigative detective and use his intellect to make the world a safer place. His fists weren't synonymous with intellect, but they worked just as well to pummel his criminal roommate.

Rex grasped Jason's down-stretched hand and flipped him over onto the ground.

The two wrestled on the floor in quiet grunts.

Rex grabbed Jason's wrist and twisted it behind his back. He shoved Jason against the wall. Rex rose on his tiptoes to whisper in his ear. "I could kill you if I wanted, right here, right now." His breath exhaled in short, jerky gasps.

Jason weaseled his foot between his chest and the wall and pushed against Rex with all his strength. "What's stopping you then?" Jason slammed his body on Rex and threw him over his shoulder. He pinned Rex to the floor, his arm and leg held behind him. "Ow, Ow!"

"How did you ever manage to fool Chestnut into loving you?"

Rex struggled. "She doesn't love me."

"That's a relief. I was worried she might be stuck with a lowlife criminal like you for the rest of her life."

Rex yelled, then rasped his tongue over Jason's sneaker.

"Did you just lick my foot? Do you realize how *unsanitary* that is?!" Jason hopped away and chucked the shoe at him. It knocked Rex upside the head and he fell back onto the bed. "What is wrong with you?" Jason spat in a hushed voice.

"I'm a scrappy street fighter, what did you expect?" He ran his tongue over the rim of his mouth and rolled his sleeves up. "And your dad said to take your shoes off at the door." Clawing at Jason's shoulder, Rex brought both of them to the ground.

Crimson blood spattered on the white carpet.

Jason grabbed his waist.

Rex froze.

In his moment of distraction, Jason pinned him by the wrists against the wall. "You can't win a fight with self taught practices." Rex struggled feebly. Jason's figure cast shadows across his face. "You wanna talk about murder? I know over a hundred ways to kill you from quick to slow and painful. If you ever try anything, I will retaliate." Jason kicked his legs out from under him. "Admit it. Admit you're nothing. Admit you cause nothing but pain and suffering to those around you."

Rex scrambled, "No."

"Haven't you had enough?" Jason snarled. "Or are you begging for more?"

Half blinded by blood dripping down his forehead, Rex eyed Jason up and down. "Hm. Kinky."

Jason's amber eyes blazed. "You're disgusting!" He stepped back to gain momentum for a strong kick. "Just a disgusting—" Jason kneed Rex straight in the stomach. "Little."

Bam!

"Rat!"

Bam!

Rex keeled over, raising his knee to protect himself from any more strikes.

Jason threw him on the ground.

Vision blurred.

Glasses shattered.

Body shaking.

Evil never wins. Jason ran his hand through his blonde hair, leaving red streaks.

Rex glared at him behind his ripped bangs.

Destiny slid in front of his raging instincts with soft words. *"One attracts more flies with honey than vinegar."*

Jason curled his lip. *We're not dealing with flies, we're dealing with rats.*

"You need to earn his trust if you're ever going to get any good information from him. You've had your fun, now extend the olive branch."

Doves deserved olive branches. If Jason was sure that Rex wouldn't take the branch between his teeth and tear it to shreds, he would have offered one. Maybe he had crossed the line when he mentioned Chestnut, but Rex started it. Jason furrowed his brows. However, Destiny knew best and if he was going to keep Ava alive, he needed to play by Heath's rules. He wouldn't consider himself the best actor, but for this far off King in an unknown kingdom, he'd wear the mask with pride.

Jason softened his eyes. "I'm sorry. I shouldn't have said any of those things." Jason pressed a cloth against his wounds. "We've got to learn to live together, else we're gonna end up killing each other. I didn't mean what I said... You're not a rat, just a scared little boy. Scared witless, like a cornered animal."

Rex closed one eye as blood dripped off his eyelash.

Jason sighed, then took a set of fresh clothes from his dressers. "It'll take a while to get the bloodstains out." Jason towered over Rex with a sad expression. "Take your shower first, Prince."

Rex rose on shaky feet, accepted the stack of clothes and headed into the other room.

Jason removed the broken glasses from his face. *It's only a matter of time, Prince, before everyone you love finds out who you really are. Sooner or later, they'll all turn against you.*

Only a matter of time.

CHAPTER 24

Ava tapped her card against the chauffeur's register. "Thanks." She turned to a tall apartment building.

I made it guys. I wish I could take Chestnut by the hands and spin her around. Hah! I'm sure Rex would say something like "Not really worth celebrating, you just made it home." All grumpy like, as he does. She could see his doubtful, sardonic frown in her mind's eye. She smiled to herself. After rising 29 floors in the elevator, she looked at her Mom's text, *"Room 2905"*

The golden numbers on the doors clashed with the gaudy yellow paint. *Room 2905.* Ava raised a tentative fist to knock.

Rex would have put a hand on her shoulder and said something like "You got this," with soft eyes and the little half smile he got when he tried encouraging them.

Ava took a deep breath. *I've got this.*

She knocked, then promptly took up nervous pacing. *What am I going to tell her about where I've been, about Roz? I could tell her that it's Roz's fault, I mean she did lose me...technically.*

The door swung open at the whim of a woman bundled in layers of fur coats. Her skin was leathery, but well tanned and dappled with sunspots. She held a mug in her other hand.

Ava lifted her hand in a shy wave. "Hi, Mom."

The women's eyes lit up. "My darling, My baby!" She rushed forward.

Ava threw herself into her mother's open arms. She breathed in the familiar scent of her thousand dollar perfume. "Mom!"

Her mother pulled away and patted Ava down like she was a wanted criminal. "What took you so long? You were supposed to be here three hours ago."

"The train was delayed." Ava was pulled into the double bedroom flat.

"Come in, take your shoes off, make yourself comfortable. Do you want anything dear? A smoothie?"

"A smoothie would be awesome. Thank you, Mom." Ava settled on the white velvet couch. She never thought she'd feel so out of place in a place she once called home. The walls were lined with awards, diplomas, and modern art, but no pictures of her or her mom. *Even Dad isn't mentioned anywhere on the placards—*

Her Mom returned with a smoothie. "Tell me everything. Why did you leave your body guard? Roz got fired. Why didn't you tell us you were running off?" She talked fast. "And with a bunch of traveling hippies! Ava, I taught you better than to wander off with strangers."

"They weren't hippies." Ava lowered her eyes. *Of course. You can't just say you're happy I'm home. Gotta go straight to the lecture, huh?*

"What were they then? Vagabonds?"

Ava smiled fondly. "They were wonderful."

"Wonderful...not a word I expected from my daughter's mouth."

"Why?" Ava leaned back, "Too fancy?"

Her mom raised her eyebrows.

"Right, right, anyway, so there was Rex and Chestnut."

"Ah yes, a boy...how comforting."

"Chestnut is the princess of another planet, she came here on like a right of passage trip? She's a deer, chipmunk, human thingy. Not from a lab! Already asked. She was born that way."

Her mom sipped her coffee. "Hm. Cake, honey?"

"Yes please." Oh, it had been so long since she had anything sweet! Her mom pulled out a cake from the fridge and served her a slice. Ava shoved a big piece into her mouth. The berries from the smoothie perfectly complemented the ice cream. "Now Rex. Phew. Where do I start?"

"Is he named after a dog?" Her mom crossed her legs.

"Uh– no. Rex is Latin, actually, for King."

"Sounds like a hippie name."

Ava leaned forward. "Ha ha...thanks Mom. Again. Not a hippie." Her voice curbed with annoyance. "Rex is just his alias. His real name is Xavier."

Her mom swallowed her coffee down the wrong windpipe and spent the next three minutes hacking. "Xavier. What a lovely name."

"Yeah, he used to be a big tough guy, but now he's really sweet."

"What, by chance, is his last name?"

Ava sat up. What was his last name? Chestnut Oak, Rex Thunder; was Thunder his last name or part of the alias? "Uh, lemme text Jason. He's one of my new classmates. They're staying with him and his father." She scrolled to a new message. *"Hey, what's Rex's last name? Can you ask him?"* Three dots scrolled, but then dropped off. She set the phone down "He's responding."

Her mom nodded. "Right, right."

An awkward silence settled between the two. Ava finished the slice of cake. When her mother reached for it, Ava pulled it away. "It's okay Mom, I'll clean it."

"When did you get so responsible?" Her mother smiled and opened her phone.

"When I started consorting with hippies." She chuckled to herself. "I'll be in my room,"

"Okay, Honey."

Ava dropped off the plate in the kitchen, then opened the door to her old bedroom. Bright pinks blinded her entry. *Ah, yes, the elementary me's obsession with all things pink and princess-y.* She sat on the twin bed. *I wonder what Rex and Chestnut are doing right now?* She rolled on her back and spent the rest of day scrolling through social media, looking at everything and nothing at the same time.

CHAPTER 25

Shiny things. She needed them more than she needed air.

Her search had started after they left the castle. She had been so careful in her technique, removing the lining from the train car pocket, pocketing an old gum wrapper in Jason's car, even now she collected.

She took a trophy off a shelf and placed it on the bed. Her pile grew. *I need more.* The room was large with sparse furniture. A bookcase stood beside a dresser filled with dull books. She swooped past them. *Shiny things. Shiny things. Shiny things. I need shiny things.* A locked chest weighed down a shelf. The corners were protected by metal plates. Chestnut lifted the box off the shelf, stepping over the books that had fallen. With her fingernails she tried prying the metal plates off the box. *This is ridiculous! Who would drill metal plates on a chest? Why not make them detachable so one could easily remove them.* Her nail snapped in half.

Chestnut's squeal was so quiet, yet full of anger. She's always regarded herself as a patient woman, but her temper had shortened. Banging and grunts came from the other side of the house. *The boys must be fighting,* she deduced. But as long as they weren't interested in taking her shiny things, she had no worries to spare for them. Her fur fluffed and she banged the box. "Why won't you detach?"

There must be something to pry the stubborn plate from the screws. Her course veered to the restroom when her gag reflexes caused stomach acid to rise. She rested against the wall. *This is miserable. The poison is festering, and I am more powerless than ever to defend against it.* Her eyes drifted into the bedroom and her hoard of gold and silver. *Oh moss– I gathered all of those things? Can I really say I didn't mean to? I had meant to and I had enjoyed it. Moss, I'm addicted, aren't I?*

Her stormy eyes landed on a metal cow decoration in the restroom. She added it to the stack. *Beautiful, intoxicating, shiny things.*

"Chestnut?" Rex rasped through the door. His voice has lost its beauty behind a dull croak.

"Sparrow, please come in." She slung a blanket over her jewels, then opened the door. Her heart tore itself to pieces.

Rex's eye was stained with darkness, his lip crusted with blood, and his hairline thinner and unevenly torn. A gash from his forehead trickled blood down one side of his face. He was draped in Jason's large clothes, looking like a little boy in the sheets. She stroked his wet hair back from his forehead, eyes round. "Rex–"

He smelled different too. His usual musty scent of grass and mushrooms that always inspired visions of frollicking through rivers of crystal water back home had been washed away and replaced with a pleasanter grapefruit patchouli.

Rex softened his eyes. "It's okay, I just got into a little fight, but I took a shower...that kinda washed off most of the blood."

"Your forehead is still bleeding."

"I wanted to make sure you were settled in." He gave a weak smile.

Chestnut dashed to the restroom and wet a washcloth. "Sit." She sat on the edge of the bed and waited for him to lower onto the floor. "So what happened?" She dabbed the wash cloth to his forehead.

A sharp wince interrupted Rex's chuckles. "Chessie, you don't need to play mother hen."

Mother hen; is that what he sees me as? "I'm not, truly. Can I not care for you?"

He smiled. "You care for me?"

"Of course I do, Rex. I don't bury bodies with just anyone."

"Oh, see? *Now* I feel special." He flashed her a mischievous side eye.

She giggled. "It's surreal we're actually here. To be completely honest, I never thought we would make it."

Rex winced again as she pressed the towel to his face a second time. "I wish they gave out fish here. I assumed the minute we got here you'd be healed, but I guess there's just one more step."

Chestnut looked down. "Rex, what do you intend to do once the poison is cured?" *or once I die?*

"I haven't thought about it much." He said. "I need to destroy the portal back home first. Then, I don't know, go back to Dellstine Valley? Just live the rest of my life in peace."

"But eventually you'll have to go back to your father." *I wish there was some way I could free him from his charge. If only I could trade myself for him, maybe he could be free for eternity and not just an extra 80 years.* She smiled at the thought of Rex's uncontainable joy at his newfound freedom. *I would give him the world if I could. He's already been through so much–*

"That's a problem for future me, yeah? Let tomorrow worry about itself. All I know is that you're going to be healed, I'm going to be free, and Ava is going to be rich and famous."

What a fascinating philosophy. "Yes. That's a pleasant thing to dwell on."

"Speaking of things to dwell on," Rex twisted to look at her, "yesterday I mentioned running away together."

And I had told him that we couldn't. Rex always had a knack for throwing caution to the wind. Charging headfirst into danger without thought for caution or consequences. He was so reckless, but so brave. Chestnut grinned. *Let tomorrow worry about itself.* "Yes, Rex, I'll run away with you."

His expression lit up. "You will?" He jumped up, pulling her with him. "Yes! Yes, you will!"

"Rex!" She laughed. A cramp developed underneath her ribs, but she hid her pain for Rex's sake.

"We can get a dog, maybe some cats, and chickens, and ducks, and we'll have a huge farm with tons of land!" He twirled her.

She pulled away to spare her worsening side. "That sounds thrilling, Sparrow."

"Of course it'll be thrilling–" He cupped her face, "cause I'll be with you."

His sparkling eyes entranced her beyond any of the shiny things she had collected. She leaned into his embrace "I love you, Rex."

The excitement faded as his eyes turned into dull irises. Rex furrowed his brows. "I always thought love was treacherous, but your love is different from anything I've felt before." He leaned forward.

Chestnut's heart bounced through her lungs as he tilted his head. As gentle as falling asleep wrapped in a warm blanket, his lips pressed against hers.

The kiss was short, much shorter than what Chestnut had envisioned her first kiss being, but it meant much more. Unlike the kiss in the field, this was real.

Rex's soft breath buffeted her face. He leaned his forehead against hers. "I love you too, Chestnut."

Colors brightened to vibrant hues. The moon poked from behind the clouds and streamed through the window. The soft touch vanished into a chilling mist, yet Rex didn't move. He simply opened his icy eyes and gazed into her.

A lifetime of looking into those fragile blue eyes awaited her on the other side of this torture. Chestnut could worry about her family. She could worry about what would happen if they didn't get the cure in time, but she didn't. *Let tomorrow worry about itself.*

This moment was perfect enough to keep her mind from wandering.

CHAPTER 26

Jason peered into his coffee as the rooster's call broke through the quiet morning. Jason rubbed his jaw, giving a soft groan. The tip of an incisor had chipped off and left a sharp blade in it's place. His body ached. The day after a scrap was always the worst. Hopefully Rex's pain hurt worse than his own.

I wonder what Heath'll say about our fight. Hopefully Rex didn't notice what I was typing last night.

He had stayed up till 3am on his computer recounting every word, every movement, and every implication that transpired last night. He even included some theories.

The mental image of Rex's icy eyes shining in the darkness clung to his mind. Jason shivered and rubbed his bloodshot eyes. The door opened.

Rex traipsed out and let out a crooked moan, rubbing his forehead. He squinted at the bright light.

And he's still wearing my clothes. Not sure how I feel about that–

Rex averted his eyes from Jason.

Looks like that fight took his ego down a few notches. Jason hummed. "What do you want for breakfast?"

"Nothing. I'm not hungry." Rex's stomach growled as he sank onto the couch. "...maybe a little hungry, but save it for Chestnut. She needs the food."

Jason tied an apron behind his back, "What do you usually like? I could do with some eggs. Want some eggs?"

Rex knit his brows together and muttered an awkward "yeah."

"How do you like them?"

"Over easy."

Jason set the griddle on the counter, slicked the surface with butter, and cracked four eggs over the top, two for both of them. The whites sizzled. "How are you feeling?"

"Sore."

"Same." *Cue faint smile.* "You're a good fighter."

Rex raised an eyebrow. "Why are you being nice to me?"

Because I need to pry your deepest secrets away from you and onto my report. Jason tipped his head. "We're supposed to get along, right? Just trying to be nice."

Rex gave him a look of paranoid caution. He squeezed the pillows tighter.

"So where'd you learn to fight?" Jason said.

"When you grow up on the streets, you pick up a thing or two."

"On the streets?"

"In Victoria. Yeah."

Score! That's going in the report. Jason flipped the eggs. "What was that like?"

Rex lowered the pillow, opening up like a budding flower. "Hard. We usually only had one meal per day, maybe two if we had extra money. Everything was heavily rationed, even with Matthew's three jobs."

"Hm."

"Made me who I am today– I don't wish anything had been different." Rex raised the pillow, reapplying the barrier.

Jason plated the eggs, garnishing it with basil and a hint of garlic salt. He ran a spoonful of orange sauce around the side for aesthetics. "Bon appétit, mon ami."

Rex set the pillow aside and took the plate.

Jason returned to the griddle for his own breakfast. The edges were cooked to a crispy brown. The mustard yellow yolk jiggled under the clover garnish gently set upon it.

A clatter sounded from the living room. Rex slumped on the couch, a rim of white showing between his slightly parted lips. The plate rested on his lap and the fork lay on the floor.

Destiny prowled in the corners of his mind. *"Don't be afraid of the Prince. He's as harmless as a kitten."*

The prince in question rested peacefully against the sofa's armrest. *But kittens still have deadly claws and razor-like teeth.*

Jason settled on the sofa. His father's rules only applied when he was watching.

Rex's shoulder twitched, then again until his entire body jumped awake. He stared, alarmed.

What's he scared of? To say the Prince was odd was an understatement. Each muscle spasmed at the slightest touch, and his eyes were always peeled for a man-eating lion or whatever he thought was after him. Jason had never interacted with someone who didn't assimilate easily into society's standards for living. You wake up, you go to school, you come back and study, you go to bed. At least that was the rubric given to him at birth. "It's okay. You fell asleep. No one bothered you." Jason flashed his eyes to the fork on the floor. "You can just toss it into the sink."

Rex made no movement to pick it up, almost defiantly.

"Fine, I'll do it myself."

"No!" Within a heartbeat, Rex picked up the fork. He riveted furious eyes on Jason and gently set the fork on the empty plate.

He really is just a harmless kitten. He fluffs up and arches back, spitting and hissing, but if challenged, he'll just let whatever happens happen.

Rex wrinkled his nose and crossed his arms telling Jason to go away. *Okay, Kitten...* Jason rolled his eyes and happily left the reluctant house guest alone. "I have to go to school, but if Chestnut wakes up, there are yogurts and muffins in the fridge." He paused, flashing a glance back at Rex, "And...maybe get some sleep?"

He hid his mouth behind the pillow and gave a small nod.

Jason slung his backpack over his shoulder and trotted out the front door. The road from his house to the main road was half a mile, but it was a pleasant, cool, spring morning. The yellow bus pandered down the country road and stopped by his mailbox.

After struggling past rows of students, Jason slung his backpack into the seat beside him. *Reserved for Ava.* The scenery evolved from simple country roads to the bustling city. The bus screeched to a stop in front of a large mass of students. Ava stepped on, dancing and stretching simultaneously. Her glossy hair slicked over her small forehead in a tight ponytail. She pulled a headphone out of her ear and waved at Jason. "Good morning!"

Jason blinked out of his trance. "Good morning." He demoted the backpack to the floor.

"Gosh, you look awful." Ava fell into the seat beside him. "Bad night sleep?"

"Lack of actually. Rex and I are roommates. All night long, a relentless game of chicken, 'Who'd sleep first'?"

"Yeah, that sounds like Rex. Did he end up falling asleep?"

Jason shrugged. "I think he might pass out on the couch."

"That bad, huh?"

"Nothing coffee can't fix."

A mischievous smile spread across Ava's face. "I know how you can make him sleep. How cold can your air conditioner blast?"

"Why?"

"Rex is cold blooded, so when the temperature drops he faints. Out like a light!"

He'd include *that* in his report. "I'll ask my father." At a screech, the bus stalled in front of a large high school.

High school students bustled off the bus, most of them were half-asleep, walking zombies. Some backpacks dropped low, the straps maxed out, the others fit well on the students' backs, straps tight. Jason rested his hands in his hoodie pocket. "So how was time with your Mom last night?"

"Uh– good. We talked for a while, but then things got awkward."

"Ah." Jason spotted red hair in the crowd. *Oh, jeez, I better warn Ava.* "Ava, remember when I told you about my friend, Leon–?" Jason was cut off by a shout.

A boy with long red hair cascading over his shoulders sauntered closer. "Ayo! The detective returns." A smile spread across his face like butter.

"Leon!" Jason slapped his hand against his in a ritual handshake.

Leon wolf-whistled at Ava, "Look what the cat dragged in!"

Back off, pal. "Leon, this is Ava, she's new."

"Matching hoodies. Nice." Ava laughed, "Seafoam green is one of my favourite colors."

Really? He grinned. "C'mon we're gonna be late to class."

Leon pushed Jason aside. "Ava, welcome to Lavivrus Public Academy, more importantly welcome to the clique. I'll get you a hoodie."

Jason slapped him upside the head. "Dude, relax."

The school bell rang. "Fifteen minutes 'till Mrs. 'Watermelon's' class. Don't wanna be late on your first day." Leon blew Ava a kiss.

"Yeah, see ya later, Leon."

Jason felt like banging his head against a wall. *Dude, you have no chill.* Leon always had more energy than Jason could handle, but he was the only student who didn't look at him like he was a monster. Even now as they entered, students parted in the hallway to make a path. Jason's eyes dropped. *I'm never going to live that down–*

"Jeez, you'd think you're some kind of school shooter or something," Ava said.

He hunched over his shoulders. "I just ignore them."

"Right." Ava pulled her backpack tighter over her shoulder. "C'mon, we have class to get to."

The science teacher pointed at a PowerPoint slide. Ava sat on Jason's left, and a sleepy Leon nodded off to his right. The dark room surely made him sleepy, but grades mattered more. Ava doodled Rex and Chestnut. *She should be, I don't know, actually taking productive notes? She and Rex really look like siblings. I've gotta ask her about that later.*

His pencil tapped impatiently on the desk. *Heath wanted to meet after school today. I have my homework finished, and I told my Dad I'll be at the library. All bases are covered.* Jason double checked he had the script he'd written last night. *Perfect.*

Ava looked up at Jason. One look at her vibrant, emerald eyes rejuvenated him. She leaned over and glued a sticky note to his desk. *"Hey Cuty!"*

Jason shook his head. He crossed off the misspelled word and corrected it to *Cutie* in neat, blue handwriting. He slipped it back to her.

Ava giggled. She passed it back to him. *"Aw, thanks!"*

Jason drew an emoticon, –_– ,then leaned over to stick it to her desk. *Oh wait!* He hastily retrieved it and added. *"I'm trying to pay attention."*

She stuck out her tongue. Light blinded the class as the teacher flicked the lights on. "–And that's the effect of the food web!" The teacher concluded, pushing her glasses up. "Class dismissed."

Leon blinked awake. As usual, Jason handed Leon his notes to copy. Once the bell rang, Ava stuffed all her books in her backpack at bullet speed.

Jason carefully packed his bag in descending order of importance. Heath's report, History class, Science, English, and finally Gym.

"Why so glum? School is out." Ava said.

Jason organized his pencils by height. "I like school."

Leon dropped his feet off the desk and snatched one of Jason's pencils. "Teacher's pet." Leon twirled it in his hand.

Jason caught it mid-spin and placed it back into the line. He sunk into his seat, calculating the millimeters of difference. He switched two pencils. "Well, that's why I have all A's."

"That's why you have no friends." Leon swept his long hair out of his face.

"I can't hang out today. I have to go to the library for more volunteer hours." *Heath would kill me if I miss this meeting.*

Leon propped his feet up. "Tomorrow you owe me a pool match."

Jason shook his head and pulled his calendar out of his backpack. "No, no, no."

"C'mon, We haven't done anything for months!" Leon grabbed his calendar, opened it to the date, and scoffed, "So, tomorrow you can't hang out because you have scheduled 'alone time'."

"It's necessary for my mental health!" Jason snatched the book. "We can go fishing after church, okay?"

"That works. I'll just come home with you, then we can head out."

Jason's phone buzzed and he nearly jumped out of his skin. "I have to take this."

Jason pressed the phone against his ear.

Destiny spoke at the end. "Hello Jason. Heath and I are waiting at the coffee shop. Would you like anything when you get here?" Her velvet voice transmitted through the phone without any static.

"No, thank you. I'll get it when I get there. School just got out so I'm heading your way now."

Heath said something faint and Destiny relayed it. "Oh, Heath wants to know if you have the report."

"Mhm! All typed and ready"

"Awesome, goodbye Jason. We will see you soon."

Jason smiled and hung up. *Time to go meet my new friends.*

"Boring, Boring, Boring–" Heath flipped through Jason's pages of dialogue. Heath hummed, "He's willing to fight for that girl? Good to know." Heath highlighted a few lines and wrote it down in his journal. Heath sat in view of all exits, like he wanted to see who was entering and exiting at all times. His eyes flicked up whenever the bell would toll but then returned to the script.

Jason's eyes skimmed the room.

People chatted quietly around them. *I wish Heath hadn't chosen a booth by the front window.* Not that he was ashamed to meet with Heath, but he'd rather not be seen by anyone who might know him. Destiny sat beside Heath dressed in a more casual sundress than her ghosty apparel. She looked more human; the X above her head gone with her nubs. "How was the trip, Jason?"

"It was good. Chestnut and Rex were acting weird."

Heath flipped the page. "Weird how?"

This feels more like an interrogation. "Well, practically attached at the hip."

"Are they dating now?"

Jason blinked. "I guess so. How long have you been following them?" *Stalking them.*

Heath scrawled in his journal "Rule #3: Don't ask questions."

"Yeah but–"

"And don't ask why." Heath raised his eyebrows. "You almost shot him?"

"Uh–" Last night's fight was a blur by now. "Yeah, pretty sure."

"Even with the knowledge that it wouldn't have done much–"

"Yeah."

"Hm." He flashed his eyes at the script Jason had typed out "You're very thorough, kid; makes my job easier."

Jason shuffled. "Thank you." Warmth seeped through his mug and warmed his hands. The barista had even made a frothy soccer ball on the top. It was the little things.

He and Leon often frequented the cafe. They knew the staff by name.

Jason set his coffee down. "Hey, Heath."

"Hm?"

Jason flipped the page back to Rex's reveal about him being dead. "I know I'm not supposed to ask questions, but I'd be able to do my job a lot better if I understood this whole 'ghost afterlife' situation."

Heath set his latte aside. "He died of a heart attack almost a week ago. Why do you think I'm here?" Heath flashed a look at Destiny. "Is there a no smoking sign?"

"Right over there, sir."

Heath frowned.

"So, he really is dead." Jason leaned over the table, his eyes wide.

Heath lifted his latte. "Of course. I thought that was obvious." He put it to his lips and grimaced. "It's cold...lovely. "

"But I can touch him," Jason argued, "he has a physical body."

"Oh yes, second death. You can touch me as well."

"You're..."

"My first death was in 1909, Old Earth. I was three. Hopped on a train, never hopped off. Second time was in a war, I had a wife and kids waiting for me– one bomb took all that away."

"I'm sorry...B-but how are you here then?"

"Clause of the second life. If a child takes a second life, they owe their eternity to service to the King of Limbo. With my background, His Highness decided I would be best leading squads of Fallens in the retrieval of souls. Currently, I am the leader of the 95th division. The leader of retrieval squads are called Falcons." He paused, piercing Jason with his intense stare. "Destiny is one of my team."

Destiny flinched.

"Keep up the good work." Heath stood. "I'll see you here tomorrow with a new report."

Destiny flashed a solemn glance at Jason. "I'm so sorry."

"Don't say that, dear." Heath said. "One more thing, Jason. After Chestnut gets better, I'm sending my boys to stir the pot a little. Hopefully, they won't cause you any trouble. I told them to stay away from you and Ava. But Chestnut might start acting, well...you'll see."

"Wha–what does that–"

"Now I have my own report to give. Wish me luck with the King."

Jason watched him leave, His brain swarming like a hive of bees. "Good luck."

"This–this isn't overwhelming is it?" Destiny said.

"Yes."

"Oh dear. I can't imagine how you must feel right now."

His appetite was waning without anything to lead him on. Starving and curious, any breadcrumb would be appreciated. Jason raised his round eyes to Destiny. "So you're an...angel?"

"Fallen angel."

"So– you were created in Heaven?"

"I was the Prince's guardian angel, before he drowned. I fell for letting him die, so I assume that's why I'm on this assignment. I assume after this assignment, I'll return to being a Choir Fallen."

"Guardian Angels are real? Hold up– Who's my guardian angel?"

Destiny smiled at the seat beside him. "That's not for me to disclose."

Jason scooted over. *That's a whole new level of uncomfortable.* His phone vibrated. *Heath just left, why's he texting me?*

Jason checked the notifications.

Ava had texted him. *"Hope everything's going well at the library. My Mom and I are coming over tomorrow. See ya then!"* Attached was a picture of her and her mom at a nail salon. She looked so happy; her smile brighter than the twinkle in her green eyes.

Jason smiled.

"She's very blessed to have a friend like you." Destiny said. Heath called to her from the doorway. "I have to go, but we'll keep in touch, Jason." She slid out of the booth and followed after the Falcon.

Jason's eyes floated to where Heath had been sitting. He released a rough breath.

Ava's safety was all that mattered.

CHAPTER 27

Ava crunched her cereal.

Her mom had her headset on, scrolling on whatever she saw in virtual reality. "Hm."

Ah, yes. The hum was usually the extent of conversation. Ava rubbed one side of her face. She was so outrageously bored. She couldn't wait to see Chestnut and Rex again. Jason said they were getting the cure for her tomorrow. That meant she was probably pretty weak. Last night her Mom made a point to remind her of her busy schedule this Saturday. "We can't stay long"

"Yes, I know."

"Fifteen minutes at most."

"Fifteen, got it."

"If we stay more than fifteen minutes, I'll be late for lunch with my friend."

Ava had drummed most of last night's conversation out of her mind. She didn't care about the short amount of time. Fifteen minutes was fifteen minutes less trapped in this tower. Ava chugged the last of her milk. "Mom, it's 11:30, I'm ready to go when you are."

"Mhm." Ava tapped her mom's shoulder and she looked at her. "Huh, what did you say dear?"

"We're going to see my friends, remember? You said we'd leave at 11:30."

Her mom turned back around. "Mhm, let me just finish this. Could you get my fur coat for me, dear?"

"Of course, Mom." Ava took the coat off the counter. Articles of clothing fell on the ground, but compared to the mess on the counter, it didn't make it look too different. Ava waited by the front door. Thirty minutes later, her Mom came with jingling keys.

"You have the address?"

"Mhm."

"Did you send it to me?"

"Yes." Ava frowned and stormed down the stairs. *We were supposed to leave thirty minutes ago!* Once in the parking garage, Ava slid into the car and slammed the door.

Silently, they drove into the countryside. "Now tell me your friends' names again."

"Rex, Chestnut, Jason, and Jason's father, Pascal."

"And you said they're French?"

"Yeah, Monsieur Allons is nice. Jason's my classmate. He's the best."

"No dating till you graduate."

Not like you'd notice if I started now. Ava puffed her hair out of her face and leaned against the window sill. The car bounced on the dirt road to a quaint log cabin. *It's really peaceful here.* Ava approached the front entrance and knocked. Her Mom lingered in the car, fixing her makeup.

Jason opened the door, his amber eyes lighting up. "Good morning!"

"Good *afternoon*" she corrected.

"Yeah, shut up. Come in."

Rex sat on the couch, locked in concentrated reading. He looked up "Ava? Claws! You have no idea how happy I am to see you." He hugged her.

Ava laughed, "So you're the one who got in a fight with Jason."

"You missed a lot." Rex opened his book. "Chestnut's resting and Jason–"

Jason wiped off her shoes with a rag. "I was doing homework."

Ava peered into his room. An open laptop filled the room with a white glow. "A script? Did I miss that?"

Jason kicked the door closed. "It's a side project."

Her mom came to the door with a smile. "Hello, I'm Ava's Mom. You can call me Mrs. Evans." She held a hand to Jason.

With great drops of sweat, Jason shook her hand. "L–lovely to meet you Mrs. Evans. My father will be down right away."

Pascal trotted down the stairs. "Ah, you must be Ava's mother. Pascal Allons. Pleasure to meet you, Madame" He gave her mom a nice firm handshake. "Your daughter has impressed me with her quick wit."

"Did she? I'm pleased to hear it." She flipped her sunglasses atop her head. "I'm afraid we can't stay long. I just dropped by to thank you for taking such good care of her."

Ava rocked on her heels. "Chestnut's resting, oh, but this is Rex!"

Summoned into the conversation, Rex poked around Jason.

A wide smile overtook her mother's face. "Felix." She breathed.

Rex didn't seem to have heard. He looked warily at Ava. "Hello Mrs. Evans. Pleasure to meet you."

Her mother swooped forward in a big hug. "The pleasure is all mine! Wh-what was your name again?"

"Rex?" Rex flashed Ava a panicked look.

"Mom, this is Xavier."

Her mom pulled away wearing a lovestruck grin. "Well, aren't you just...the handsomest fellow."

Jason showed Ava the time. "Fifteen minutes. I guess you have to go now."

"No!" Her mother exclaimed. "I mean, I– we can stay a little longer. I'll cancel with my friend." She looked at Rex.

Huh? Ava furrowed her brows. One look at Rex and suddenly her tight schedule isn't so strict?

"Ava, would your friends like to go out to lunch?"

"I'm fine with it." Pascal said.

Her mother stepped closer to Rex. "I'll start up the car. Ava don't dawdle." She rushed out of the house.

Ava stood beside Rex. "Don't look at me! I haven't seen her this excited since she moved."

He shriveled "Eheh– I think I'd rather stay here and finish my book. I want to be here when Chestnut wakes up."

Jason blushed. "Just me? And– and Ava?" A hard lump dropped in his throat. "With your mom?"

Jason stared at Rex.

"No." Rex took a few steps backwards. Jason picked him up like a duffle bag. Rex remained stiff as a board as Jason carried him out.

Ava snickered. "Jason, put him down. He'll come."

Jason looked down at his baggage. "He better."

Rex blinked. "Please put me down."

Aw, I guess Jason's not ready to spend alone time with me and my mom.

Her mom honked. "C'mon kids!" Ava opened the passenger door, but her mother interrupted. "Oh, Ava, great idea. Rex should sit in the front, I'm sure Jason would enjoy your company in the back."

Oh. Okay. Ava's eyes roved over her mother's void gaze. Come to think of it. Had she ever looked her in the eye for more than five minutes?

Ava stepped aside to let Rex sit down. She slammed the door, then sat beside Jason.

The car revved. Ava's mother leaned over. "So Xavier, was it?"

"Yes."

"Xavier's a handsome name. A strong name."

"Thank you."

Ava crossed her arms. *She was never this interested in me.* "You know, Mom, Ava is of Germanic origin. It means desire or wish."

"Is it? Ava said Rex is Latin for king. How did you ever come up with that?"

"It was a nickname."

Her mom burst out laughing.

That wasn't even a joke! Ava grinded her teeth.

"Hey, that's pretty cool." Jason said "So what desire do you have?"

Desire to be important. "I *desire* to get this essay done by Monday." She smiled.

Jason rolled his eyes "I can't believe Miss Watermelon didn't give us a prompt. I mean, Come on! Are we supposed to pick our own topic?"

"Oh yeah, that's absolutely not problematic. I'm sure you'll do cats vs dogs just like the rest of the class."

Jason crossed his arms. "Nope. I'm doing 'The Complexities and Fragilities of Society's Social Standards'."

"Mhm, something easy."

"Like I said, there's a reason why I get all A's."

Ava leaned forward. "N–E–R–D!"

"Shut up!"

"Ah, but you'd hate that." She removed her hair tie, her straight hair tumbling around her. "Admit it, you love the sound of my voice."

"Yeah, cause there's no other reason why I listen to you ramble for hours on the phone."

"Impossible." She collected her hair into a tight ponytail. A strand fell in front of her face. Jason snickered, then tucked it behind her ear. "Thanks," she said.

Jason's face melted into a soft smile similar to her mother's.

Her mom pulled into the restaurant. Ivy tendrils spiraled around beige columns in an Italian garden of flowers.

Her mom exited the car.

Rex tried to drift back to walk with Ava, but her mom kept pace with him. "What would you like for lunch, Xavier?"

"I don't really care, ma'am"

"Do you want a drink? Maybe the pasta. Their Alfredo is my favorite. I used to come here all the time in my twenties with my dates.

"Mom," Ava warned, "I think he's okay."

"Just checking." Her mom ushered them into a booth "So what do you like to do for fun?"

Rex looked too dazed to protest. "I guess I like to sing."

"Oh! That's cool. Have you taken singing lessons?"

"A few."

Poor guy, he looks ready to cry. Praise always improved her confidence; maybe Rex needed a little support. Ava smiled. "Mom, you should hear Rex sing, really, he has the voice of an angel."

Her mom's eyes lit up. "I'd ask you to sing if we weren't in public."

Rex studied the table. "Right."

"Did you ever sing for your father?"

"Often."

Mrs. Evans pressed her lips together awkwardly. "Okay. What else?"

Rex scooted over to accommodate Ava.

Mrs. Evans stared at him and Ava for a long while. "You two even look like each other."

Ava wrapped her arm around Rex. "We get that alot."

Rex whispered in her ear. "Help."

I know, I'm trying, you should be thankful you're getting so much attention from her. Usually, she's glued to her phone. They sat in silence, only communicating through looks and side eyes. *I get Rex is an introvert, but he should at least try to be a conversationalist.*

Rex's eyes were fixed on Chestnut's book. He fidgeted with the pages, his brow creased with distracted worry. *We shouldn't have brought him. He's probably worried sick about Chestnut. We kind of left her all alone.* Monsieur Allons was there to ensure her comfort, but if she woke up without Rex by her side, she may feel abandoned.

Ava stroked her hair, distracting herself with the faded green dye. "I'm actually surprised it lasted this long."

Her mother seemed more than relieved to break the quiet. "Ah, yes! Ava, I already scheduled you for another hair day. Tomorrow we'll go first thing. Xavier, honey, do you need your hair retouched as well?"

"Retouched?"

Ava pointed to his hair. "The little, blonde, lightning bolt. I mean it's not really faded so it should be fine. When did you have it done?"

"Done?" Rex self-consciously covered the lightning bolt with the rest of his dark brown hair. "Never. It's genetic..."

Mrs. Evans smiled like a lovesick teenager. "Yes, Felix had it too."

Rex's breadstick fell out of his hand.

Is he okay? Ava noted the shake in his hand, the wide horror in his eyes. He stared at the table. *Felix is his Dad, isn't he?* Drunk Rex hadn't spilled many secrets, but Ava remembered that little fun fact. "Rex?" She snapped. "Earth to Rex."

Rex's hand spread over his stomach, goosebumps rose on his arms. "Yes, he does."

Ava blinked. *Ah, so they are talking about the same person—*

Her mother's eyes widened "Does. Not did?"

Ava recognized that look of sheer terror on his face. His glazed eyes darted around, listening for hallucinated voices only he could hear. Ava lifted Rex out of the booth. "Excuse us."

Her mom was up in a second. "Xavier!" She grabbed his arm, yanking him around. "Your father is alive?"

Rex's breathing sped. He looked up at her, his nose twitching like a scared bunny. "Let me go–" His voice faltered

She released him. "I'm sorry, I didn't mean– Is your father alive?"

Short hyperventilating gasps came from the scared boy on Ava's arm. Ava fixed her mom with a warning look. "We'll be back." Ava practically dragged Rex along. *Oh, Claws, where's a spot where we can have some privacy?*

"Ava– I can't breathe" Rex wheezed.

"I know, hold on."

At the sight of a family restroom, Rex cast her off and locked himself in.

"Wah– Rex, let me in." *I don't want anyone to see me talking through a bathroom door.* She smiled sheepishly at the waitress.

"No! No, it's safe here. I'm safe. Rex isn't coming out right now."

What do I do? What do I do? Ava groped for a reason, something that would make enough sense to his limited comprehension that he'd let her in.

Ava pressed her temple against the door. "What about Xavier?"

The door unlocked.

Ava closed the door behind her. *Ew...public restrooms.* Rex huddled in a corner, his head tucked against his knees. She's never seen him look so frail.

Ah. Another hallucination. Ava spoke softly "Rex? Breathe in and out slowly. I'm here, Ava. Hear the taps?" She tapped the tile.

Rex's eyes slit open; pupil-less blue irises surrounded by black sclera instead of white. "Taps?"

"Yeah, can you tell me how many taps you hear?" She clicked her long nails three times on the tile.

"Five?"

"Not quite, bud. Try again." She repeated the series of clicks slower.

"One. Two. T-Three taps?"

Ava shuffled closer. "Good job, what about smell? What can you smell?"

The glow of Rex's eyes faded. "Sewage. Dampness." He sniffed. "Strawberry soap."

"Where are we?"

Rex covered his ears. "In His closet. Don't tell him I'm here. He'll kill me, He'll kill me."

"Xavier, why would there be soap in a closet?"

He opened his mouth, but retracted the uncertain answer. "Because...we're not?"

"Can you feel any clothes?"

Rex reached out towards the hallucinated clothes, but felt nothing but air. "N-no. No clothes."

"So where are we?"

"In a restroom?" His buggy eyed stare faded into normal human eyes. "At a restaurant."

Ava smiled. "You want a hug?" At Rex's nod, she wrapped her arms around him. "What did– what did you see?"

Rex's fingers clawed her clothes, pulling her tighter. "Yelling. Lots of loud yelling, He was looking for me. He wanted to discipline me for refusing..." He crossed his legs and pulled his knees tighter.

"No wonder you were so scared. I tell you, If I ever meet this guy, I'll roundhouse kick him in the jaw."

That drew a laugh from Rex, much to Ava's pleasure. *Laughter is the best medicine after all.*

Rex pulled away. "Let's not go talk it out with your mom..."

"Don't worry, we won't. I don't know what's got her all frazzled, she's not usually this demonstrative." She searched his face. "So you good?"

"Better now that...I haven't...His name. Ava, she knows my father."

Ava sighed "I know– I don't know how, but she definitely knows Felix–"

Rex recoiled. "Don't! Don't say His name. It might summon him..."

Ava snorted. "What, like Bloody Mary? Or Beetlejuice?"

"W-well no...but I don't want to chance anything."

Ava stood. "C'mon, we better get back to lunch."

He let out a shrill, hysterical laugh. "But of course, when you get out of the lion's den, the only logical thing to do is throw yourself back in!" His fingers spread in his hair.

My gosh, you need therapy. "I'll stay right beside you."

Ava held a "To-Go" box on her lap. They had dropped Rex and Jason off back at the house after a short, uneventful lunch. With Rex and her mom radio silent, most of the conversation was tossed between Jason and Ava like a good game of badminton. By the time they dropped off the boys, Rex looked like he was near the verge of a mental breakdown.

Fifteen minutes.

Funny how a single look at Rex turned that fifteen minutes into two hours.

Her mom drove through the city.

Oh no. Now that Rex is gone, what was she supposed to obsess over now? Oh, I dunno, maybe her actual daughter? Ava crossed her arms. "So."

"So?"

Despite knowing full well, Ava dared to ask "Who's Felix?"

A far away smile entered her expression. It tainted her movements in the way she sloppily tapped the blinker and let her eyelids fall in front of her eye. She looked tired. Was she disappointed?

Suddenly, Ava was a little girl again sitting shotgun with her eyeline barely above the dashboard, worrying if she had worked hard enough to earn accolades from her parents; her highly esteemed, highly revered parents. The silent car rides always left Ava craving more, wishing she had done better if only to see her mother's beaming expression of pride. Ava felt a stinging in her throat. "Mom, is everything alright?"

"Oh– yes, It was a lovely lunch."

"We probably could have split a dish." She looked down at her "To-Go" box.

"Probably."

Ava smiled. "I'm glad we got Rex home before Chestnut woke up. I know that was important to him."

"Mhm."

"Jason had a great time. And after the whole…yeah. Rex seemed much more at ease." No, he hadn't. If anything he was stressed out of his mind. He second guessed every bite, twirling his pasta, then removing his fork and twirling it smaller.

Her mom didn't answer.

"Mom, there's something you should explain."

"Probably."

Probably? What does that mean? I don't live in probabilities. "Mom…"

Her Mom turned an annoyed eye on her. "Ava, please! Some things have nothing to do with you. I'm sure you had a great time with Jason."

Ava bit her tongue. "Why were you so fascinated by Rex?"

"Ava."

"He had enough on his mind already. You didn't need to give him a panic attack."

"Ava." Her voice was getting dangerously crisp. "I didn't give him a panic attack."

"Yes you did. Mom, this is the least you can do."

"What does that mean?!"

Ava took her good girl silence and refuted herself against it. Maybe Rex's rebellious 'stick it to the man' attitude had rubbed off on her, but she wanted answers. "Well, let's start with putting me in theatre my whole life so you wouldn't have to babysit me."

"We were busy, and I thought you loved theatre."

"I do…but I love you and Dad more…you were never around." Ava sunk into the seat, downcasting her eyes. So often she had come home to an empty house after rehearsal. From second grade, she would pop some leftovers in the microwave and watch it spin around while she counted the minutes until her parents would come home.

An awkward silence settled before her mom said "I'm sorry I wasn't always the most available. It's been hard trying to raise you since your father left."

Ava looked over. "But *you* decided to move away.

Her mothers' temper flared. She aggressively pressed her foot to the pedal, speeding up. "Ava, sometimes I wish you were smarter. Your father is not your father. He's your stepfather!" She snarled.

He–what? Ava remembered sitting at the dining room in their huge penthouse alone...wondering, pondering if her parents had gotten into a car accident and would never return, or if they finally realized what a failure she was and abandoned her. All the memories with her father... *Stepfather* had all been fake. What did that make her? A stepdaughter? Ava's chest heaved with the slow, aching, painful breaths.

"Your real father didn't even stick around for your birth." Her mother finished. "Of course, I'm angry, but I'm also hurt. I'm sorry." She eased off the gas, coasting to a conventional speed. Her mom looked at her. "Long story short, you and Rex share the same father."

Rex is my–

He's–

Pieces of Ava's world crumbled like large stones breaking away from her reality and crashing to nothing more than pebbles. Her last name, her fans, her father, reduced to pebbles. Little teardrops formed in her eyes. "That's why you treated him so special."

"Ava."

"Dad knew too! That's why he's always been so distant... He always looked at me like I was the biggest disappointment on the planet, and that's why, isn't it?" Ava murmured. "You and Dad bounced me back and forth like a ping pong ball because I was a burden. If it were Rex, you'd treat him like royalty just because he's the firstborn to your 'soulmate'! I'm not *good enough* for you." Ava raised her voice.

"That's not true. We love you. Stop acting like a child."

"I'm not an Evans then–" Her entire identity, everything she wanted to live up to, it all was slipping through her fingers like sand. "Does he know? My real father? What happened to him? Why didn't he show up to do anything? Does he not want me either?" Ava continued though the voice cracks.

"People say your father died. If you hadn't dragged Xavier away so soon, maybe I finally would have gotten an answer! He disappeared before I knew about you."

Ava's eyes burned. *It should have been me! I should have been first born–then I could have been important to my family.* "So, am I just a mistake?" Ava tightened her grip on her leg.

"No–" Her mother's eyes softened. "No. I love you so very much."

"I didn't ask if you loved me, I asked if you wanted me."

Mrs. Evans bit her lip.

If Rex's father was the King, that made her a princess. *Rex was wanted by his father. He may have been abusive, but at last he was involved in Rex's upbringing. His Father cared. My Father cared!* "So my life has no meaning– everything I've done and accomplished. It's useless. *I'm* useless." Ava squeaked out. "Mom! Do you realize how sick that is! Is Chestnut my half cousin twice removed?"

"Young lady don't take that tone with me"

"Who cares about my tone?" Ava scrunched her eyes shut. "What is he like?"

"I think you're getting too emotional."

"Am I getting too emotional? You didn't have your entire identity blown up. *Please*, I need to know. Why didn't he come back? Why did he leave? Why didn't he stay for you? What was he like...? Please."

Her mom looked at her, her eyes cradling tears. She turned her eyes to the road and gave a small smile. "He was playful, seductive. The kind of man who knew exactly what you wanted and exactly how to give it to you. Ohh, he was so goofy and silly. He had the most dramatic mood swings. One week he'd be the life of the party, every other word out of his mouth was pure comedy gold. The next month, he'd be dark and brooding. It was the spontaneity that made life interesting. He was a bartender at the club I worked at. He told me stories about his son, Xavier, and his dying relationship with his wife. I really was the best thing for him. He talked of running away together... a-and I believed him. He didn't even tell me where he came from– he just appeared. And as quickly as he came, one day he disappeared off the face of the earth, leaving me alone. I searched for months, getting the police involved, but there was no record of him anywhere."

Ava stiffened. "Didn't it bother you that he was married?"

"He didn't love her anymore." She turned back to Ava. "When I first saw Rex, I thought it was *him*! But– You even look like siblings. And I couldn't resist staring at him. He really does look *just* like his father. The same 'deer in the headlights' charm. The same freckles. The same curl of the hair, the same tiny waist, delicate build. His father has the same lightning bolt in his hair. I never knew his mother. He said she was long dead. Oh, those blue eyes, that dark red tint in his hair."

Ava clenched her fist. She didn't want to hear about how perfect Rex was. *If you think he's so amazing, why don't you adopt him instead? Your standards must be low if you kept me around.*

Her bitter thoughts swirled. *He always did think he was better than me. What does that make me? Rex Thunder-Xavier DeClawfada–Ava DeClawfada*

"I'm a Clawfada?"

"No. You are an Evans– and you always will be! With luck you'll never have to meet your father." Mrs Evans demanded.

I asked for this– why didn't I just leave it alone? "Why didn't you tell me?" She peeped. Ava looked into the rearview mirror at her green eyes.

If her mother loved those 'gorgeous blue eyes' she wouldn't mind if Ava's ugly green ones disappeared. Her eyes darkened. "Mom, when is my appointment again?"

"Your hair appointment? Tomorrow."

I'm not good enough. Ava turned away from her subpar reflection. Deep auburn with a lightning strike. *Maybe with a few adjustments, I can be.*

CHAPTER 28

The front door swung open and Jason and Pascal entered in their Sunday best. A boy walked in behind him, his red hair pulled back in a ponytail.

On the couch, Chestnut had fallen asleep in Rex's arms. At the chatter, Rex blinked awake. *I guess the church service didn't last long.*

Pascal pressed the back of his hand to her forehead. "Still has a fever."

Rex brushed a strand of hair from her face. "I got her to eat a strawberry."

"Baby steps."

He nodded. "Baby steps." Rex kissed her forehead.

Chestnut stirred. "Mm, did I fall asleep?"

"Yes, dear."

"M'kay." She turned over and cuddled back into him, hands wrapped around his arm, and cheek pressed against his collarbone.

"How're you feeling?"

"Tired. " She flicked her ear.

"Do you want some more strawberries?"

"No."

"Would you eat them if I cut them up?"

"I could try."

Rex smiled at her. "I need my arms, dear."

"No. You're my prisoner." Her hands tightened around his arm.

Rex resigned himself to his fate. "And a happy prisoner at that." *Better me than worthless knick-knacks.*

Jason gestured to the redhead. "Rex, this is Leon. Leon, this is Rex and Chestnut."

Leon looked disgusted. "I'll go get the tackle box all sorted."

"Rex," Pascal said, "Jason, Leon, and I are going fishing for the cure. Would you like to come with us?"

Chestnut sighed in his arms. *We came all the way out here to heal her. I guess there's no sense in me staying here.* After all he promised he'd get her the cure. "I'd love to." He gave a nervous smile. "So long as we don't actually go on the water."

Jason rolled his eyes. "Yes, we're going fishing on land. Maybe we can catch a fox or something."

Pascal threw his son a warning glance. "I have an idea." Pascal drew a blindfold from the coffee table. "Rex, you wear this and Jason will guide you. As a trust building exercise."

Why do I have to wear it? Rex picked up the blindfold, rubbing the soft spandex on his fingers. "Trust building exercise. What do you think?"

Chestnut hummed.

"I'll be back, dear. I love you." He slipped her onto the couch and propped a pillow behind her back. Leaning down, he pressed a kiss to her cheek. "Get some rest, okay?"

She had already dozed off.

Rex lifted the blindfold. "Alright, Jason. Lead the way."

⌁•⌁

Rex blindly marched on, Jason guiding him by the wrist. "This isn't fun—"

He felt Jason's grip tighten. "You're going so slow. Just trust me." Jason hissed through gritted teeth.

"I know I'm supposed to 'trust you'. That's the point of a trust exercise."

"Then why aren't you letting me lead?"

Rex twitched his fingertips, "'Cause I don't trust you."

"That defeats the entire purpose of the exercise."

"Well I'd like to know why I'm the one in the blindfold and not you."

A large hand dropped onto his shoulder. "Don't worry, it's all been planned." Pascal spoke beside him. Rex knew his touch was meant to be comforting, but it scrambled his sense of direction.

Salt hit his nose as a breeze picked up. Seagulls cried above them and wood planks groaned beneath their weight. *We are by the water. I should have expected this but*– Rex stepped to the side and the dock dropped beneath him.

"Woah!" Something caught his arm at the last minute. Water sloshed inches from his face as he dangled off the dock with one foot bracing him against it. The blindfold slipped off and Rex stared into the murky abyss of swamp water. Jason pulled him back. "Sorry."

Rex squinted to adjust his eyes to the bright sunlight. Leon stood at the wheel with a fishing pole and a cheesy hat. "All aboard the S.S. Miracle." Leon snapped to get Chase's attention. "Chase, fetch."

At the command, Chase sunk his teeth into Rex's pants and dragged him aboard the boat. "Chase– Chase. Chase!" Rex clawed at the boards.

"Chase, quit it." Pascal said. He helped Rex to his feet. "He gets excited."

Rex huddled on the floor of the boat. At least his eyeline was below the top of the boat. He could pretend that there weren't miles of water surrounding them.

"We're getting that cure, even if we have to stay out all day." Pascal tossed a bag of worms at Jason.

All day? Rex's stomach tied in knots. "Cure yes...Yes! Chestnut needs the–" He peeked above the railing at the watery horizon, "cure." He gulped.

Jason caught the bag. He pulled Rex onto an actual chair and sat beside him. "This is how you bait a hook. If we have four fishing poles, it'll increase our chances."

Rex tried to pay attention, but once the engine roared to life, his focus turned to the life ending ocean. *Don't focus on the water. Focus on fishing. This could be fun, this will be fun, just don't fall in.* Something collided with the ship's hull.

Jason leaned overboard. "Manatees!" He documented it in his journal. The sea cows swam underneath the boat and Jason rushed to the other side.

"Dude, you're rocking the boat." Leon said.

Rex grabbed his shoulders as the little pontoon boat rocked. *Breathe, breathe, calm. Stay calm.*

"Stay seated, especially as we pick up speed and get into deeper water." Pascal instructed.

Jason smiled and continued writing furious notes.

The horrors never ceased. "*Deeper* water?"

The groves passed by as the boat waded through the water. Rex stared over the infinite expanse of hungry lapping waves. Chase's ceaseless barking, the burning sun, the nausea, the dizziness; it all overwhelmed him.

Ice spread under his skin. His vision closed in on itself til he was blinded by darkness.

Rex passed out.

Rex blinked awake in the soft, watery light. His dreamlike memory suspended him in frigid water. The light dimmed as he sunk deeper. Colder by the minute. He paddled upwards in weak, infantile motions. Xavier took a deep breath to relieve his burning lungs, but water flooded into his lungs. *Mom!*

His voice dropped in the water, except for a dull scream. Air.

If he reached far enough, maybe he could reach the surface. His feet touched the bottom and he propelled himself upwards. His head slammed against solid ice, shattering his vision into dark spots.

Air!

Please–

Bubbles escaped his lips.

Xavier resided in void until his spirit split from his body. The cold no longer reached him, and the weight that had kept him tethered to the bottom of the lake had vanished.

To the surface, Air! Xavier propelled himself upwards, floating through the ice.

"Xavier?" His mother called. Her voice quivered as horror melted into her expression "Xavier!" She broke off a branch of a nearby tree and stabbed it clear through the ice. She removed her outer dress, and left in her white frocks and corset dove into the water, one hand clinging to the hole in the ice.

Xavier reached out to her. *Mom, I'm here!* He retreated from the ice as his mother pulled an imposter's body out of the water. *That's me.*

The woman's face contorted and her black hair slicked over her shoulders. Death filled the air. *Mom, it's okay I'm here, I'm right here.* Xavier curled his spirit next to his body. Heat flooded from his mother as she held him close. *Mom. I'm scared. What's happening?*

She wasn't responding,

Mom?

Her tears fell through him. "Please. Please stay with me, child. I need to protect you. Stay alive, please, my son, stay alive!"

Xavier tried to push his way back into his body, to wake himself up and let her know he was okay. He couldn't die now. Grandmother was making his favorite cookies in the cabin. The long awaited fair was coming through town next week. He had been waiting a year for the petting zoo.

However, no matter how hard he pushed against the paling corpse, an equally strong force counteracted. Xavier looked up at his mom. *"Mom! I'm– I'm okay, I'm right here!"*

A red light traced the grass in a square. A staircase opened up, leading down to fiery bowels of Hell. Xavier screamed and hid behind his mother as screams resounded from the staircase. Xavier's face broke out in thousands of tears. *"Mom!"*

A black stained claw reached above the first stair.

"Oh no, you don't." The staircase sealed at the whim of a man in a golden cloak.

Xavier scurried backwards, his heightened sense of terror overwhelming.

The man turned towards Rex, his face obscured in shadow. *"Oh–"* A soft exhale escaped the man. *"You look just like The King."* He removed the cloak from his broad shoulders and wrapped it around Xavier. Six nubs protruded from the man's back, and an X floated above his head.

Xavier burrowed deep into the fabric of the golden cloak. *"What are you?"*

"I'm a Fallen Angel, under division 298 of retrievers. My job is collecting children, like you, and bringing them to my home, Limbo." The man kneeled in front of him. *"My name is Ananiel. At your service, Prince."*

Prince?

"We have to go swiftly. The dead can't stay in the land of the living."

Xavier clung to his mother's sleeve. *"Is Mom coming?"*

Ananiel gave a grieved look. *"No, I'm afraid you won't see much of her for a while."* The Fallen Angel offered his hand. *"You and I have a long journey ahead of us to get to the portal."*

Xavier looked at his mom, then at the Fallen. *"Do I have to leave her?"*

"We'll take care of you from now on."

Xavier tentatively reached forward. He took the Fallen Angel's hand and left behind his body and his mother. He tightened his grip around Ananiel's hand. *"I'm scared."*

"I know, but you'll recover. Then you'll be even stronger." Ananiel smiled and rested a hand on his head. *"Come, little Prince. Time to go home."*

CHAPTER 29

J ason reclined in his seat and finished his crude sketch. The groves passed by as the boat slowly waded through the water.

Rex swooned and fell on Jason's shoulder. "Rex?" Jason stiffened when he didn't respond. "Uh–I think he fainted."

"I fainted once," Leon said. "Not fun. He must really hate water. Hey, he's like a cat!"

"More of a kitten." Jason felt his father's disapproving stare, but ignored it while he baited the hooks.

The mangroves opened into a wide ocean. Pearly white froth surfed on the crests of waves, then dissipated into the depths of the blue. The boat accelerated through the water like a bullet whizzing through air.

Rex shifted and blinked awake. "What happened?"

"You passed out." Jason said.

Wind slicked back Rex's hair as if he was a biker in the 1960's district. He ducked underneath the seat. "Haha– right. Deeper water."

Jason watched him with growing curiosity. "What inspired this deathly fear of water? You took a shower just fine."

Rex averted his eyes.

This was not the time to be cagey. Especially since Heath was getting restless without anything interesting in Jason's reports. "Was it because you fell in when you were a kid?"

"I drowned...when I was six." His voice dulled to a quiet whisper.

Right. And he's here today because of his second life. Jason furrowed his brows. "We interviewed Heath, you know."

Rex's eyes snapped wide "When?"

"At the castle. That's why my father and I were there to begin with. His soldiers had murdered a servant." His Risen Demons, as he now understood. The supernatural had never scared him, but the politics involved certainly worried him. Ava's life hung in the balance between how thorough his reports were and how gracious Heath was feeling. "He explained everything to me, about Fallen Angels, Risen Demons, The King, and why he's after you." Jason's amber eyes stared into the distance.

"He told you about William–"

Jason nodded. "Do the girls know?"

Rex lowered his eyes. "Chestnut watched it happen, but Ava doesn't know."

"Why did you kill him?" The question had burned into the back of his mind for the past few days, keeping him awake at night. Even villains thought they were doing the right thing.

"He killed his cousin," Rex paused, pain deeply rooted in his blue eyes. "my adopted father."

"Why didn't you take him to court? Or do things legally?"

Rex looked at him through the corner of his eye. "They wouldn't listen to a seventeen year old pickpocket, especially because William would have made it look like Matthew had been involved with a cartel."

"Was that his name? Matthew?"

Rex nodded.

From Heath's description he assumed Rex was an mentally unstable serial killer, but he had only been seeking justice. If someone killed Jason's own father, deep down he knew he would do the same. "Heath really doesn't like you–"

Rex nodded, his eyes dulling. "Not many people in the kingdom do."

"And you're just going to let him chase you?" Jason pivoted his torso to face him. There was no justice in that.

"I'm going to destroy the portal to Limbo. Hopefully that gives me a little extra time to be free."

The boat slowed and his father called. "Jason, the anchor is in the back."

"Got it." Jason looked at Rex. The boy was trapped within ultimatums but managed to care for those around him. The compassion he extended to Ava and Chestnut wasn't the compassion of a killer, but of a man. Jason wished he felt like a man. Right now, he felt more like a small little boy, trying to decipher which grown up was telling the truth. Rex was trying to survive, but Heath was pursuing him to complete his task. It wasn't personal, yet Jason felt that someone was wrong. Perhaps the dark secrets of Limbo would forever remain shrouded in mystery. Jason vaulted over the back of the boat and threw the anchor overboard.

"Jason," his father called "Is the anchor set yet?"

"Yeah, just got it!"

"Good."

Jason furrowed his brows as he gazed across the water. *Am I really on the right side?*

CHAPTER 30

Rex noticed Jason drifting away from the group. "Hey."

The boy's amber eyes flickered to him. "Yeah, I'm coming." His voice had drained of self righteousness.

Pascal cast off the fishing line and handed it to Rex. "Here, you just hold it until you get a nibble, then you give a sharp yank and then reel it in using this." He pointed to the spool.

Jason sat next to Leon on the protruding ledge. "How much do you wanna bet he'll drop the rod?" Leon said.

Jason gave a distracted hum "Hm? Oh– $20 he doesn't."

"$20 he does then."

Rex yanked on the line with a grunt. A weight hooked at the end of the line. *It's a fish–* Excitement swelled in his chest. *I actually caught a fish!*

Pascal beamed like a proud father. "Now reel it in."

Rex twirled the spool, dragging the fish through the water. The fish jerked, and Rex folded over the side, eyes level with the fatal waves.

He let go.

The rod disappeared under the murky blue as the fish dragged it to who knows where. Rex turned to them, eyes wide. "I-I'm sorry. I–"

Leon jabbed Jason's arm. "You owe me twenty bucks."

He was going to drown.

The water would envelope him again, except this time he couldn't die and float upwards. Rex moved backwards and sank to the ground, leaning against the cockpit.

"That could've been the fish" Rex said breathlessly "and I lost it! I lost the bloody rod too."

Jason looked at him. "It's okay–no getting it back now."

Rex's breath sped up rapidly, and he closed his eyes. He slid his legs closer and pressed his whole body against it. *Calm down. You're safe on the boat, you're safe.* He drew laboring breaths in through his shaky lungs.

Jason set his rod to the side. "You good?"

Rex squeezed his eyes tighter. "Yeah–fine." His voice squeaked, high pitched and unsteady.

The pride in Pascal's golden eyes faded into disappointment. "It's okay. Here, take my rod. Try again."

Rex looked up. *If I try again, I'll lose that one too. If I knew all I'd do on this trip would be a burden, I wouldn't have come.* But he *was* here. And he wanted to be the one to catch the Southwater Taephoon. Rex stood and wrapped trembling fingers around the metal. "Thank you."

A fish tugged Rex's line.

"There, now reel it in, Rex!"

Okay Matthew. Rex smiled at Pascal. He strained against the fish's strength.

"Is that it?" Leon said.

Rex gave a sharp pull and fins spread, a striped golden and blue fish glided on the breeze.

Jason gasped. "That's it! Rex, reel it in!"

Rex's spirits soared. "I'm trying!" Rex brought it aboard the boat and watched it flop. "That's what'll heal her?"

"Yup."

A smile teased Rex's face and his breathing eased, "She'll be okay." He whispered. "She'll be okay!" Rex whooped. "Monsieur Allons, turn this boat around, we have a smoothie to make!"

Rex tapped the counter watching Pascal cut the fish. *How long does it take to cut a bloody fish!?* "Ready?"

Pascal looked up. "I'm not going to mince it, patience."

Rex bounced, restless.

Pascal slid the fish into the blender and made a face. "Why don't you make sure Chestnut is okay." At the press of a button, the fish grinded into a brown and pink liquid.

Rex gagged. *I'm glad I don't have to drink that–* "Yeah." He headed towards her closed bedroom and knocked. "Chestnut, may I come in?"

No response came.

Chestnut? His heart stopped and he pushed his way in.

She lay motionless on her bed, her body wrapped around a pile of shiny objects.

"Chestnut!" *Please wake up!* Rex barrelled over to her. He rested a hand over the objects.

Chestnut's eyes snapped open, pupil's thin.

In a flash of fur, she arched her back, her spiked unkempt fur appearing more like dragon-like spines. "Don't touch my things!"

Rex jumped back.

Her ribs showed beneath her bony frame and shadows hung from her eyes. She looked weak and tired, but at least she was alive. "Chestnut, it's okay it's just me–" He approached again, but she snarled at him.

"Stay *away*, Rex."

He retreated. "We have the cure. Monsieur Allons is blending it up right now." He said gently.

Chestnut's eyes hardened on him with murderous intent. "I don't want a cure. I want more treasures." She curled tighter around the articles. Her usual soft breath had sharpened into a demonic rasp.

Rex's chest tightened. The toast she ate yesterday morning only lasted for a few seconds before promptly being thrown up. She hadn't eaten in three days. "I know, I know, but this'll make you better, okay?"

They had paid so much for this oppurtunity. Chestnut couldn't afford to refuse.

"I *am* better. I finally understand what's truly important." her eyes rounded on the jewels of metal. "My precious shiny things."

"Chestnut–" He paced a step forward and she hissed. Still he proceeded forward. "This is just the poison. Take my hand, and we can head to the kitchen."

Claws raked over his left eye.

"Thief!" She screeched. "You're just trying to take it from me!"

Rex pressed his hand against the sticky slashes across his face. Chestnut growled when Pascal entered. The man surveyed the scene, then hardened his face. "Rex, hold her down." He whirled around and, within seconds, reentered with a syringe.

Rex blinked. *I'm sorry.* He twisted lightning into a thin thread and aimed it at the compiled junk. The pile lit up in an array of sparklers and Chestnut jumped away, fur fluffing. "Stop!"

He grabbed her around the waist. "This is for your own good, Chestnut."

She thrashed in his arms, screaming. Rex eased her onto the ground and pinned her. Chestnut added a few more scratches to her original slash, but all Rex could think of was how much she was going to regret this once she was healed.

Pascal stuck the syringe into her mouth mid-scream.

Chestnut gagged, but in her gasps for air, she swallowed the liquid.

The two pulled away and left Chestnut to crawl to the corner. "Thieves– thieves." She whimpered.

Rex watched her. This would keep her alive. The wounds were worth seeing her grow stronger.

Pascal rested a hand on his shoulder. "The cure will do the work now...we should give her some time."

Time.

Chestnut remained scarce for the next twenty-four hours. The seconds lasted forever.

Rex had taken the time to plan how he was going to infiltrate the tunnels leading to the portal. They were usually unguarded. He pressed a washcloth to his face, gently dabbing away the crusted blood. Hydrogen peroxide cleaned the wounds but with an awful stinging.

No matter how many things he tried distracting himself with, his thoughts drifted back to Chestnut. Even if she was feeling better, she was more likely to hide in her room out of shame than confront him about what had happened. Rex released a sigh. *Why her, Heath? Out of all the women in the world, why did you choose the one who meant the most to me?*

Jason was in his room, headphones muffling the ruckus that had taken place hours prior. Rex raised a brow at his computer as he entered. *He's been writing for a long time.* Jason stared at the screen, confliction in his expression.

"What's wrong?" Rex said.

Jason looked up and furrowed his brows. "Nothing... Is Chestnut better? It's been a while, hasn't it?"

It had been. "She will be better. We just need to give her time." He removed the towel and Jason's eyes widened.

"Did *she* do *that*?"

Rex nodded. "She didn't mean to. The poison affected her mental state. I don't think she recognized me."

"Have you seen what's happening with Ava?" Jason's eyes dulled.

Rex blinked. "Ava?"

"Rumors are starting to spread that her mom had an affair with another guy. Her fanbase is turning on her because she's not a 'purebred Evans'." Jason mocked "It's stupid. They're all stupid!"

Oh, claws– I hope she's okay. "Have you checked on her?"

"She won't answer my calls, won't even reply to my texts."

That definitely meant something was wrong. "Keep an eye on her, please."

Jason nodded and returned his eyes to his screen.

A soft knock came from the door. "Sparrow...?"

Chestnut stood in the doorway. Her eyes had returned to their dilated roundness, but held a world of pain.

Rex took a step closer, but then stopped. "Chestnut." He wanted to wrap her in a hug and let her know it was okay, but he didn't want to risk getting another slash.

Her eyes welled. "I'm so sorry."

Her tears were permission enough. Rex swooped into a hug, holding her tight. "It's okay. It's okay."

"I didn't mean to–"

"It's okay, Chestnut." He breathed into her hair. "My face will heal, how are you feeling?"

She didn't reply, only squeezing him tighter.

Rex released a soft exhale. "Chestnut, I'm fine, really. I don't blame you. It wasn't your fault."

She gave a small nod. "I'm so sorry."

"Don't be." He smiled. "You're healing now. That's all that matters."

Her stormy eyes rose to meet his. "I'm a little hungry."

Hope swelled in his chest. "Yes. Yes, of course. Let's get you something to eat." He pulled her into the kitchen, relief satisfying the worry that had haunted him for the past two weeks.

They made it. Chestnut was healed.

CHAPTER 31

Jason rode the bus alone. The seat beside him, reserved for Ava, was empty and the girl herself was nowhere in sight. Maybe she skipped? Maybe she was sick? Jason pulled out his phone and scrolled past Destiny's messages.

He'd given up on replying to them. If he ignored them long enough, maybe Heath would forget about the meeting and the report. Jason couldn't, with a clear conscience, give him any more information that he could use against Rex.

Monday hadn't come soon enough. He had been worried sick about Ava. Most celebrities turn to drugs or alcohol when their fame turned against them. Jason knew first hand how easy a trap that was to fall into.

Rex walked into his classroom.

No wait–

Ava walked into the classroom.

Her hair had been cut shorter to her shoulder and dyed to match the darkness of Rex's locks. A lightning bolt framed one side of her face. She wore an ivory Victorian T-shirt with a black vest over.

"A-ava–" The next words fell away at his dropped jaw.

"Hey, good morning." she sat beside him and set a heavy tote bag on the ground.

"Good...good morning, Ava? Did you...get a haircut?"

She pulled out one of the many books from her tote. The spines of each were marked by a library claim. "Yeah, like it?"

"It's–" Did she know it was Rex's hairstyle or was that pure coincidence?

Leon burst out laughing. "You look like an accountant."

Ava stuck her tongue out at Leon, then returned to her book.

"Whatcha reading?"

Ava gave him a feisty look. "Wouldn't you like to know?"

Jason pulled one of the books from her tote. *The Realms of the Afterlife.* He pulled another. *Sorcery for Otherworldly Travel.* How did one weekend change her entire personality? He set the books aside. "Ava? Are...Are you okay?"

She flipped a page. "Mhm."

He nodded for Leon to go sit down. His hand landed on the book, interrupting her reading. "Are you sure?" Mentally stable people didn't dye their hair, change their eye color, and reinvent their wardrobe.

"Fine, Jason." She moved his hand with a hard stare. "Look at this." She gestured to a spell for opening a portal to Limbo.

Why does she want to go to Rex's Kingdom...? "Ava. Magic doesn't exist. None of those 'spells' actually work."

"But it's worth a shot, right? I mean what if one of them actually does."

He noticed the red, espresso-shot rim around her eyes. "How many of these have you tried?"

"Five. Stayed up all night." She wrote down the recipe in a notebook.

Class didn't start for another ten minutes. He had time. "Ava, let's go into the hall."

"I need to finish this."

Jason kneeled by the desk, raising her chin to look at him. "I'm serious. It'll only take like five minutes." He expected another polite refusal, which wouldn't have been bad. Rejection was familiar, although usually it was for an infatuated crush. He'd asked a girl to the prom, but she turned him down flat. Stinging had resulted from his own insecurity over his bravery, but Ava's refusal couldn't sting. It didn't the first time, because he wasn't insecure...just worried; worried for this girl he'd done so much to protect.

Ava softened her eyes. "Ok." She took the book with her and followed Jason out of the classroom.

He led her outside the school to the butterfly garden.

"You tricked me," Ava chuckled, "you said we were going to the hallway."

"I'm sorry. Ava–" he approached her, wanting to take her in his arms and hold her until all this passed, but he only rested a hand on her shoulder. "What's going on?"

"Nothing's going on. What's going on? It's nothing. Going on is nothing, nothing at all. Nothing's going anywhere, or on, or off, or...I should shut up now..."

"No, I love the sound of your voice." Jason pulled one of the drawstrings on his hoodie.

"Pshh, at least one of us does."

"You don't?"

She averted her eyes, hardening her gaze. "Of course I do. I love every part of me."

Jason gazed into her icy blue eyes. He hated those blue eyes. "You're– wearing contacts?"

"Yeah." Her smile wobbled. "Blue suits me, doesn't it?"

"If you loved every part of you, why did you change your eye color?" *I...I liked your green eyes. I loved your hair color.*

Ava looked down, stumbling over her words for a fabricated answer.

Jason pinned her with a hard stare. "You don't have to change yourself to look like Rex."

Hurt multiplied in her expression. "I'm not changing myself to look like Rex. That's stupid. Why would I want to look like *Rex*?"

"Because your mom really liked him."

She whirled on him. "Well, y'know what! Maybe– Maybe Rex stole it from me. How do you know I didn't wear this first? Rex doesn't own brown hair or blue eyes! Lots of people have them."

"Ava, are you okay?"

"Fine!" She snapped. After a second of realization, she turned her eyes to the ground, "–ish."

Jason opened his arms.

As expected, Ava walked into his embrace, banging her forehead against his shoulder.

He didn't stifle the moment with meaningless encouragement. He hugged her tight, wanting to wish this away for her.

Rex might not be a villain, but faced with the decision between him and Ava, he loved her too much to let her get hurt. Ava's own hurt and fears took priority. *I wish you knew how much you mean to me, Ava.* He buried his face in her hair.

"Jason...he's my brother." She breathed.

He's your– Jason's blood ran cold. Heath didn't just pick the next of Rex's party to threaten, he chose his sister. Jason had known there had to have been a reason. In the back of his mind, he knew, but he never thought...

This changed things.

Ava leaned further into his embrace. "Half brother...My father is in Limbo."

The phone in his pocket buzzed at an alarming rate.

Limbo. That's what the books are all for! "You're trying to reach him?"

"I have to know...if I was really just a mistake"

At this he pulled away. "You are not a mistake, Ava. You were carefully crafted. You're one of a kind." *And I love who you are.* "The person you are supposed to be is exactly who you are now."

Ava's posture fell. "I need to meet him. At least..."

The buzzing in his pocket halted and an angry *"Jason! Answer the phone."* rang through his mind.

Ava was more important. Jason ignored Destiny and cupped the side of Ava's face. "I need you to know you are not any less important than Rex, okay?"

She hiccuped and her eyes bled crystal tears. "But I am. He's a good dancer, and singer, and an amazing friend. He's so sweet to Chestnut, he's amazing and I'm...not him."

"And thank goodness, you know why?" He wiped one cheek with his thumb, "Because Rex doesn't watch anime with me. Rex doesn't know how to paint, sculpt, or write. Rex's mind doesn't move in such a chaotic pattern that makes everything beautiful. He doesn't imagine wild ideas no one else could. You literally saved a spider in the cafeteria because he had a wife and kids to get back to."

Ava smiled. "His name was Jimmy."

"Jimmy doesn't wish he'd been saved by Rex. He was saved by you, Ava. You're amazing too." *And Rex has a target on his back. You don't, thanks to me.* If only she knew how high a commodity her life was. Maybe she'd value her individuality a little more.

The school bell rang and Ava looked up. "W-we should be headed back in." She drew a tissue from her pocket.

"Yeah." He finally slid his phone out of his pocket. 56 new messages and four missed calls. He gulped and typed back. *"Sorry…I had to comfort Ava first."*

Destiny replied in mere seconds *"Told Heath. He applauds you for your detective work. We're just a little stunned right now."*

Jason put his phone away once they reached the class. The sinking feeling grew stronger.

CHAPTER 32

A va walked home. She refused to ride in a car with her mom.

As expected, She had finally started to act like a mom. Whether this was because of her guilt or her fascination with Ava's change in appearance was still up for debate. Gossip spread about her heritage, and slowly her fanbase trickled away. Critics that had once praised her for being a prodigy of modern entertainment now slandered her over her mother's affair. Tramp. Mistake. Blemish. All good headlines to draw in audiences. It didn't matter that her life was falling apart, all the media cared about was good ratings. The question on everyone's minds "Where is this man now?"

Safe and tied to a kingdom of the dead.

The alleys of the city were darkened by the shadows of the eclipsing sun. Ava swung the hood of her seafoam green sweater over her head. She had dreaded the upcoming Monday, and to validate her worst fears, fate had decided to make today the worst day of her life.

Students pointed, laughed, and whispered. Her fame was being used against her.

A trash can clattered in one of the alleys.

Is there any point in any of this? None of the books she borrowed from the library had any information. She had reached a dead end and the weight of the animosity was too much for her to bear. *Maybe I should just...end it.* Her dull eyes lowered onto the pavement. *Rex and Chestnut have each other, they have no use for me anymore. Jason would be better off without me ruining his life, and Mom and Dad would be so much less burdened by my existence if I was gone.*

Left would take her home, right would take her to the Houston Highway bridge. She turned right.

The breeze picked up as she walked along the pavement. The ocean lapped far below at the bridge's concrete legs. Ava leaned against the railing and looked down at the white crested tips.

"You can't jump, dear. Who would return those library books?"

Ava spun.

Frosted hair tousled in the gust of wind as Heath leaned against the railing. He inhaled the flames of his cigarette and released a puff of grey smoke.

Ava shuffled backwards. "Who cares?"

"You could end up in Hell for that. Not returning your library books is a serious offense." A glint of amusement rimmed his red eyes.

His joke wasn't funny. "Anywhere is better than here." She draped her forearms over the side.

"How about Limbo?" Heath drawled.

Limbo? Ava twisted to look at him. "You know how to get to Limbo?"

He tapped off the end of his cigarette. "Why of course, Dear. It's my home." His words flowed out in a relaxed progression as if he had all the time in the world. "The King is anxious to meet you, Ava."

Her hands drifted away from the railing. *He is?*

"Oh yes."

This was the man who poisoned Chestnut; the man who let his Risen Demons kill an innocent servant. Rex never talked much about his past, especially not Heath, but she had heard enough to know that getting involved with this man meant doom for either her and Rex.

Yet this was her only lead, and like he said, her father was waiting for her with open arms. "Can you take me to him?"

Heath's eyes lazily drifted to her. "I could."

"What do you want?"

"It's not a matter of what *I* want, but what you're willing to do to be reunited with your loving father."

From Rex's stories, he was anything but loving. "Rex said–"

"The prince is known for his wild stories. Attention seekers often invent stories to smear others' reputations and make themselves look like the victim."

Her eyes widened. "So...all those things he said aren't true?" Now more than ever she wanted to meet this man whose reputation Rex had worked so hard to ruin.

"Not at all. You didn't actually believe him, did you?" Heath slanted his eyes on his cigarette.

Of course I did. He's my brother but– Now she wasn't so certain. "What will it cost to get me to Limbo?"

Heath straightened and unfurled his hand for her. "You have to step away from that edge."

Of course a dead willing body was no use to him. She knew that, yet the softness in his eyes made her think he genuinely cared for her. There was one person worth living for. She took his hand and let him lead her away from the bridge. "Let me walk you home."

Her eyes remained on him. He had the calming effect of a father.

"Tomorrow night, I need you to sleepover at Jason's house." He said gently. "Then at four in the morning I will meet you outside your window. Then I will take you to your father."

She committed the instruction to memory. "Thank you."

He looked down at her, sadness tinting his expression. "You remind me of my daughter."

Her blue eyes rounded. "You have a daughter?"

"Did. She has grown old and died by now, but I did." Once they stepped out of the shadows, the moon's brightness pierced through Heath and he glowed a misty red hue.

"You're just like Rex, aren't you?"

Heath's expression hardened. "I'm nothing like the Prince. Unlike that coward, I follow the rules. I'm loyal to my King and His cause." He gave Ava a side eye. "It's all I'm left with when all is said and done."

Ava looked down. "Rex isn't so bad once you get to know him."

Heath returned his eyes ahead and slowed in front of her building. "Good night, Your Majesty."

The reality of it hit her. She was his superior, the princess of the cause he had so dedicated himself to. She gave him a soft smile. "Good night, and thank you again."

"All in the name of my assignment, Dear. I will see you tomorrow."

"Four a.m."

He bowed his head. "Precisely."

Ava turned into the apartment complex, but looked back at Heath, only to find the ghostly man gone.

CHAPTER 33

"627,001!" Rex exclaimed.

Chestnut added a tally mark to her notebook as she moved the penny into the counted pile. "627,001."

He leaned back in triumph. "And that, ladies and gentlemen, is how to effectively count pennies."

Chestnut laughed. "And it only took us four hours, Thank you, Efficiency!"

Rex smiled down at her. Within the next twenty-four hours, her possessiveness had faded and her intestines had started healing. They were nearing the forty-eight hour mark now and she claimed to feel much better. He just needed to sneak into where the portal resided and destroy it with his electricity, then they could get out of this city and start looking for land to start their farm.

Ava was sleeping over tonight, and after the disaster on Saturday, he was more than excited to spend time with her. He wanted to make sure she was handling the media well too. Everytime Jason turned on the television, there was a new story about how the beloved child actress, Ava Charlie Evans turned out to be the result of an affair between her mother and an unknown man.

Voices sounded from outside and at once he recognized the excited chatter. *Ava!*

Rex scurried to his feet.

"No, I told you, it doesn't matter if they exposition most of the plot, it's supposed to catch up new viewers," Jason said.

Ava groaned. "But who cares about narration? Show me Loid! He's sooo hot!"

"You're weird!" The front door creaked open.

Rex skidded to a halt. Blue eyes met blue eyes. He stepped backwards at a mirror image of himself. The apparition moved forward, giving him a look. "Jeez, Rex. Relax, I just dyed my hair."

It sounded like Ava, it looked like Ava but it couldn't be. Rex steadied himself against the counter. Contacts paled her green eyes into icy blue ones. Her hair was dyed auburn with a blonde lightning bolt framing the left side of her face. He watched her move into the kitchen. Chestnut looked just as startled. "Ava! You look–"

"Yeah, I thought it was time for a change." Ava tugged her vest down.

Rex noticed a striking similarity in their outfits. *What the claws?*

Jason came behind him, reflecting his surprise. "She's staying over tonight."

"You don't say." Chestnut stood and hugged her. "Lovely to see you again, Ava."

"Chessie, you look much better! Much less poisoned."

"I have a slight cold, but nothing time won't heal."

Rex furrowed his brows. *Time doesn't heal all wounds.* He approached Ava warily. *Does she know what she looks like? Why would she intentionally copy me?*

"Boo!" Ava jerked her hands up, and Rex jumped back like a startled cat. "Still jumpy, huh."

That grin, that tone, it was so condescending. "Hehe, yup...Ever since childhood." *You know that.*

Ava spun around, her hair whipping around her. "Chessie, I'll be bunking with you."

"Y-yes." Chestnut flashed Rex a look. "The bedroom is this way."

Rex watched Ava disappear into her room.

Jason sighed after her and leaned on the counter, before gathering himself and trotting after her "Ava, Let me help you get set up."

Ah, yes, lovestruck puppy love. Rex followed. "So, Ava, what inspired this new...look?" Rex said.

Ava shrugged. "Dunno."

"You don't know?"

"Nah."

"I liked your green eyes, they were pretty."

Jason averted his eyes, cueing Rex into his agreement.

Ava's eyes darkened. "Well, I didn't–so, leave me alone."

I wonder what put her in such a bad mood? Rex looked at Chestnut, silently asking her to leave.

"Jason?" Chestnut said. "Why don't you show me the recipe for tonight's barbeque?"

"Yeah, I can do that." Jason blushed and trotted out of the room.

Ava tossed her sleeping bag on the floor, ignoring Rex.

"I saw the news–" He started. "Are you okay?"

"Fine."

Rex dropped his eyes to the floor. "Is this about Saturday?"

"No."

She's so quiet. "You'd talk to me, right? If you were struggling?"

"Why?" She tossed an apathetic glance over her shoulder. "Not like you've been through anything rough."

Was she being serious? "I'd call these rough." He gestured towards his scars.

"Rex, we both know you probably did those to yourself. It's honestly sickening that you've stooped so low as to harm yourself to make the King look bad."

Harm himself? Lightning shattered off his skin. "What are you talking about?"

"You did all of this for attention, but it's okay. We all know just how special you are, Rex. You're the prince who's *perfect.*"

Daggers stabbed into his heart. The wounds were real, the memories were real. She was starting to sound like the servants. Whenever His Highness would leave him with long gashes that spilled gallons of blood, he would beg the servants for help, tell them what happened, but everytime they refuted him. His Highness had worked hard to build his reputation and when he got wind that his son was trying to expose his misdeeds, he isolated him from the kingdom and spread lies that his son was just going through a phase. Meanwhile, Rex sat alone with his lions and his pets, waiting for whenever he would be called out of his room. Eventually he stopped trying. Stopped trying to ask for help, stopped trying to make anyone see him as anything other than the Jester with a vendetta against his father.

Sometimes Rex wondered if His Highness was using a spell to control them, or if he really had that much influence over his subjects.

Rex furrowed his brows. "I don't know who you've been listening to, Ava, but it would be a good idea to make sure you're getting factual information."

She rolled her eyes and turned her back on him.

"Hey." He walked around to her other side and kneeled beside her. "You know I care about you, right?"

She turned her face away from him.

She probably just needs space. Rex's eyes dulled. "I'll be outside helping Jason with the barbecue...if you want to join us."

"Okay."

Rex cast one last look at her, before exiting the room and closing the door behind him.

CHAPTER 34

J ason turned on the bed. He was worried about Ava, and the pit in his stomach
prevented him from falling asleep.

Jason turned on the lamp, looking over at Rex's sleeping form. *He's getting better.*
Every day Rex woke up with a smile and a hop in his step. Jason gave a small smile. He
started being less thorough in his scripts, only adding things that couldn't be used
against him, but Heath must have spotted the gaps in conversation. At their last
meeting he said he would uphold his end of the deal, keeping Ava safe, but Jason no
longer needed to spy on Rex.

Jason pulled out his sketchbooks and flipped to a blank page. He had drawn Ava,
Rex, and Chestnut enough. He needed something new to add to his artbook. Jason
felt Destiny's presence enter the room, the light flickered and the temperature
decreased by at least 10 degrees. He smiled.

"Why don't you try to draw me?" Destiny spoke through his thoughts.

I could try. What else was he going to draw? He envisioned Destiny's soft features,
her blonde hair, her pink eyes, otherworldly sure, but just as captivating. Drawing her
human form seemed too mundane. He needed a challenge. He put pencil to paper to
try and replicate the image in his head of what a fallen angel would look like.

The paper bore renditions of demonic zombies without wings and with broken
halos. Jason grimaced at the horrific beings.

"That looks absolutely nothing like me"

Well, excuse me, It's called an imagination. Jason turned the page in his sketchbook.

"You're excused."

Jason snickered, "Shut up." He tapped his pencil on the paper, Horns maybe? No halo-

"I'm a blonde, for your information."

Blonde– He sketched her human form and added a halo.

"Hm. Add 6 nubs on my back and color in the eyes. Erase the nose, and the ears. There we go! Much more me!"

Jason closed his sketchbook, and leaned back on the bed. His eyes drifted to his alarm clock. *Four a.m. Where did the time go?*

Rex turned over and groaned. "Jason?" He raised his hand to block the light.

"Sorry– is the light bothering you?"

"M'yeah." He mumbled.

"Sorry." Jason leaned over and turned it off.

The house was eerily quiet. So was Destiny. *Why are you here? I haven't heard from you in a while.* There was no response. *Destiny?*

The door slammed open and a breathless Chestnut stood in the doorway, her fur standing on end like she'd seen a ghost. "Ava's gone!"

Rex rubbed his eyes and sat up. "Hm?"

Jason leapt out of bed, turning on the light again. "Gone?! What do you mean gone?"

"She probably just went to the bathroom?"

"No, No! Gone, no trace of her, Rex!" Chestnut paced back and forth. "I woke up and she wasn't beside me. The window was open, I think she sneaked out!"

Jason barrelled out of the room. *Ava, Ava, please be safe, please just be in the closet or something, or upstairs.* The window was open wide enough for a person to crawl out of. A note was left on the window sill. *"Desperation makes for good bait. I told her I would lead her to her father and that's what I intend to do. You know the way, Prince. I'll see you when you get here ~ Your humble servant."*

Heath.

Rex came behind him, clipping his corset over his day clothes. "What's that?"

Jason numbly handed him the note. Heath had promised he wouldn't harm her, he promised! "Rex, it's a trap!"

The creases on Rex's face deepened with his growing confusion. "I don't understand. Who's father? Ava's? Jason, do you know anything about this?"

He looked up, amber eyes vexed. "I– can't– she made me promise not to tell anyone"

"Tell anyone what?"

Jason shook his head.

"Jason, if she dies, that promise won't mean much, will it?"

Dead! No, no, no. Jason pushed his glasses up. "Heath won't hurt her."

"Heath?!" Rex pulled Chestnut closer.

Jason winced. *I'm sorry. I didn't mean for it to go this far. I never intended it to go this far.* He wanted to do the right thing. That's all he wanted, he didn't want all this. Rex didn't deserve all this, He'd floated through his entire life, letting anyone do anything to him. He'd been conditioned to appeasing the biggest dog. He didn't even realize how easily people took advantage of him, how gullible he was. No wonder he took his second life, to get away from everything.

Jason clenched his hoodie's fabric in his hand. "Rex, I love her...I would never wish harm on her."

Rex whirled on him. "What does this have to do with Heath? Why did she dye her hair? Why did she start using fake contacts? Why the heck was her mom obsessed with me?"

"She's your half sister!"

The slow softening of Rex's face was enough to crush Jason. "...What do you mean, Jason?"

"The King and her mother had a..." Jason blushed a hot red, "An affair. And after The King disappeared, her mother found out she was pregnant with Ava. Ava's afraid she's just a mistake...She knows how much her mom and His Highness loves you, so she thought if she looked like you, it would...make them love her too."

Rex's foot shuffled backwards, his face horrified. "And Heath was taking her to meet her father...*My* father" Rex hurled himself out of the window.

"Rex!" Jason flew after him with Chestnut beside. "It's a trap!"

"I don't care, I'm going to protect my sister!"

"But we don't even know where they went."

Rex whirled on him, eyes rimmed with fire. "I know *exactly* where they went."

CHAPTER 35

Rex didn't check to see if Jason and Chestnut were behind him, he had to get to Ava. If she stepped through that portal, he couldn't get to her. The symbol on his wrist given by the King permitted a one way trip to the Living world, which he'd already used. If he returned to Limbo, he wouldn't be able to come back here without another ticket from His Highness. The hallways of the abandoned building brightened closer they drew to the otherworldly expressway. Cold wind funneled through the hallway like a subway, souls of children led by Fallen Angels.

Sister, my half sister. No wonder she was talking like a Limbonian. She's been tricked by Heath. He gripped the crumbled note tighter. *Desperation makes for good bait. He preyed on her weakness!* He whirled around a corner and was blinded by a black hole of a portal. Blue light swirled around the darkness, keeping its shape.

Ava stood in front of the portal, hand outstretched.

"No!" Rex screamed.

She whirled around, eyes wide. "Rex?"

A firm kick shoved Rex to the ground. Heath brandished a sword that stretched down to trap Rex at the tip. "Gotcha."

"Heath, what are you doing?" Ava said. "Rex, How did you find me? Wh–" her eyes flitted to Chestnut and Jason. She inched backwards towards the portal. "You can't stop me."

Jason offered his hand like trying to console a suicidal woman. "Ava, Ava, come away from the portal."

She shook her head. "Jason, this is what I was looking for! I can finally see my father. Ask him about my mom. Ask him if I was really just...a mistake."

Heath grinned, pressing the sword into Rex's throat. "Only one way to find out, my dear."

Ava hardened her eyes. "Only one way." She raced towards the portal, but her body slowed. When she'd reached the portal, she froze and faded from existence. Jason screamed and plunged in after her, slowing then vanishing, just as she had.

Heath slung his sword away "Go get her, Prince. Are you going to let her go all alone in a strange dimension? Will you prevent her from finally meeting her Daddy?"

Rex stepped to his feet and lunged towards the portal, but backed off. *Not even for Ava. Not even for Ava can I sacrifice my freedom.* He backed away from it, but was seized by two Risen demons.

Heath snarled in his face. "You're *so close,* Prince."

Rex's eyelashes, in hard blinks, crusted over his skin.

"Release him!" Chestnut clawed at the Risens, but with one toss she was thrown to the ground.

As he was jerked forward, the dark portal saturated and revealed a tempting red field of downy grass. Rex knew Limbo better than the postcard image pasted in the liquid portal. His ragged breaths shortened. *Sire.*

"Come home, Kitten."

Wheeze in, thudding heart.

"I can't wait to play our games again."

Rex's heels dug into the dirt as the Risens dragged him forward. "No, nono-nonono!" He thrashed. "Stop!"

His heels burned, his wide eyes dried out.

Familiar screams rattled in his mind, the screams of a vulnerable Prince. He scampered on the dirt. *Sire!*

Heath stood beside the portal, eyes solemn.

Footsteps sounded behind him, hands stroked up and down his body. *"Why do you resist, Little Cat?"* His Highness giggled.

Inches away from the liquid, Rex exploded lightning from his being, locking him in place. The two Risens, by their own strength, fell through the portal themselves. Frozen in place, his chest ached from quick whips of inhales.

I'm not going back.

I'm not going back!

"I'm not—"

Hands ripped him from the electric protection. Heath grasped his shoulders. "I will complete my assignment if I have to slice you to bits and wheel you through the portal!"

Black void surrounded them.

Rex blinked at him. "Please don't..."

Heath swung him towards the screen, only for Rex to barricade the way with electricity again. The static crept along the screen, covering it in a cage. "Fine!" Heath took his collar and threw him away from the portal. "Is this what the King chose as his heir? A weak, pathetic liar?" He paced towards Rex. "Your sister was just as weak as you. Do you know where I found her? On the side of a bridge, ready to jump! You weren't enough for her!"

Rex's figure distorted, his grip on his human form completely sliding out of his hands. The blue in his eyes engulfed his pupil and bathed the room in a sickening blue. His sclera darkened to black. *She— no.*

"You aren't enough for Chestnut. You aren't enough for Ava." Heath took his chin in his hands. "You came here to destroy the portal, but ended up destroying everyone you ever cared for."

Rex closed his eyes, hanging limp.

"Even now you refuse to go after her, because in the end you have to admit to yourself, you never truly loved her." Heath stared down at him with red piercing eyes. "In the end, you have no idea what love is."

Heath's words burned in the back of his mind. Scaled wings unfolded from his back. His heels flattened against his foot to create smooth spiked feet, reminiscent of a ballerina's pointe shoes. His clothes melted away into a loose fitted, black top tucked into a red corset. An opaque skirt draped three-fourths around him. Bat ears pinned against his head. Rex split his wings an inch to glare at Heath.

Go back. Anger burrowed deep in Rex's chest. Tunnel vision darkened everything except for those red eyes.

With a yell, Rex flew to Heath, but he sidestepped.

"Come on, Prince!" He snarled.

Rex chased him, lunging only for Heath to step just out of range. His tunnel vision brightened by the portal's light, nearing, closer, and closer.

Heath stood, breathing heavy. "Are you really going to come this far only to leave her alone to die?"

Rex screeched a shrill ear-piercing noise. He flung himself at Heath.

But the man ducked.

Wind rushing past his body, his lunge took him through the portal.

A red grassy meadow softened his fall and greeted him for miles. A castle towered in the middle of hourglass buildings. He spun and lunged at Heath, only to slam his nose on the portal.

Heath approached the portal, chest heaving.

"No!" Rex pounded on the portal, his nails scraped down it. *There's no place I can hide here. No place I can run.* He pressed his back against the barrier.

"I told you I always win." Heath smirked over his shoulder.

No! Lightning lashed from Rex's palm and wrapped around Heath's ankle. "Murderers never win." *William died. I died. There's no exception.* He yanked Heath through the portal.

Heath drew his sword. Rex's hands closed around the blade, pressing the sword towards Heath. Blood trickled from his palms.

Heath's foot planted on his chest and kicked him away.

The injustice burned inside him. Heath whipped him with the broad side of the sword.

Rex grunted, stunned for a second before he grabbed his shoulders and bent him backwards. A loud crack came from Heath's back. The two snakes tangled around each other in a dance.

Heath weaseled out of Rex's grasp, but Rex caught hold of his wrist as he did. Heath raised the sword to Rex's throat. One tap and the hunter would flake away into ash. Rex bared his teeth.

The rush was maddening. Adrenaline coursing through his veins, Rex leaned forward. "I'll kill you for hurting my darling."

A hint of fear flashed across Heath's cold eyes, but only for a moment. "Then kill me. It'll make you a murderer twice over."

Chestnut raced through the portal. "Rex, Stop!"

Rex's eyes swung to her. She was right. He knew she was, but he didn't want to admit it. William's death still prodded the edges of his guilty conscience in the dark hours of the night. One lapse in judgment could mean life or death for Heath. The power cupped between Rex's hands was intoxicating, but he knew what the responsible decision was.

He released Heath and held up his hands in surrender.

Heath slitted his eyes.

Not even a thank you. Wow.

"Heath," Chestnut said, "please, let us go."

Heath's red irises burned into Rex's skin. He remained unmoving, except for a glaze overcoming his eyes as he considered. Rex watched him weigh the odds; consider the options.

Finally, Heath leaned away, sheathing the dagger. "Go." His black coat flowed beside him as he retreated through the portal.

Risens swarmed around him, ensuring their general was unharmed. The portal closed.

Chestnut met his eyes, love beaming in her expression mixed with sadness. "Sparrow…"

Xavier scooped both hands under her and held her in his embrace. Rex wrapped his wings around the two. His tight voice scraped together like metal on metal. "Thank you…I would have regretted that."

Chestnut searched his void eyes. "I couldn't watch you kill another man, even if he was a slimy shape shifting snake."

"I don't know what I'd do without you." A gust blew over the hills, chilling his skin. "I won't let His Highness take you from me." His eyes hardened. Her or Ava.

"Sparrow." She reached to cup his face but he flinched away with a sour expression.

"Don't…don't please." Rex's hiccupped and swallowed. A tear trickled down his face and despite his efforts, Rex's smile twisted into a wobbly cry for help.

She wrapped her arms around him, holding him tight. "It's okay. It's okay, I'm here."

One tear turned to many. "I hated when He did that. I- I hated being His jester." He closed his eyes. Rex's body shook. "…It's my own fault I'm back." His voice quavered. Rex pressed his bat ear against her cheek, and buried his face in the crook of her neck.

"It's not your fault, Sparrow."

Rex coiled his tail around hers, constricting it like a python. He lowered his voice. "He's waiting for me."

She leaned into him, arms wrapped around his waist. "We'll face it together."

Rex turned to Limbo. Wind breathed over the sea of long red grass. A river of fire trickled down rocks. He needed to find Ava and bring her home. Rex looked down at Chestnut's concerned face. "What if He's in a bad mood?" A worse thought entered. "What if He's in a good mood." A hoard of jackrabbits thumped against his chest. Constricted by their thumping, his pulse was sent up to his neck and forehead to throb uncontrollably.

Trembling hands. Why did he always have to have trembling hands in moments like these?

A soft hand landed on his shoulder.

His Highness had once done the same. He would do the same again, and again, and again, over and over in an endless cycle Rex could never escape.

"I can't!" He stepped back.

A wind carried around them and swirled the world into a blur. The floor beneath them quaked. Salt and Sulfur burned the air.

Chestnut pressed into him, her fur standing on end.

Rex's fingers tightened around her. "He's summoning us."

BOOK 3

REUNION

CHAPTER 36

The realm solidified.

Marble tile stretched into the throne room, covered by a single river of a red carpet that climbed up to the crowned throne. The prince's throne stood in the shadow of the King's throne.

The dust settled, but Rex's unease did the opposite. Cross beams ran across the circular rotunda tower moving upwards. Darkness covered the heights.

The throne was empty.

Where was He?

The jackrabbits returned with their incessant heart thumping.

Where was He?!

He took a step backwards towards Chestnut.

Soft chuckles reverberated in his memory, off every towering pillar. The columns bore carved renditions of cats, cherubs, and hourglasses. A voice breathed from high above, smooth and charming. "There's my little kitten."

A sickening shadow of large wings reflected across the tile.

Every muscle screamed at him "*Run!*"

The shadow engulfed the entire red light filtering through the stained glass windows.

Rex stepped faster. *Watch the shadow. Run.*

Like a ping pong ball, Rex bounced off the door and bumped into Chestnut.

She grabbed his hand and spun him. When'd she get so tall?

Not Chestnut.

Fingers slid onto Rex's waist as he was locked into place.

Rex traced the body, from the black polished boots up to the coat tails spreading from a corset, up to the blood red ascot.

Naturally red lips peeled back in a ravenous smile. "Welcome home, son."

A pit dropped in Rex's stomach.

Years of running had led him right back to where he started. He had tried to heal and succeeded for a short seventeen years but no amount of time would be enough to recover from those long nights and splintering wounds. Each scar lingered in his mind, refreshed at the sight of the man who had given them with an iron rod and a psychopathic grin.

Sire.

With a slow inhale, His Highness breathed in the scent of Rex's hair. His exhale carved the grooves of Rex's face with fear. "And now you have nowhere to run." His Highness slid a soft gloved silk finger under Rex's chin. The crimson blood red light highlighted every lock of auburn hair. Light freckles overtook His Highness's flushed grey cheeks and crossed the bridge of his nose. Two slits on his neck opened and closed with each breath. The resounding chuckle grew into a whinnying laugh. "Ohohohoh. Isn't that wonderful? There's nowhere for you to run, Kitten. You're mine." His pursed lips slid past his ear, "Forever."

A puffball stormed around them. Chestnut was half the king's size, but her seething fury wasn't deterred by physical differences. "Let him go!" She slammed her foot against his shins with a fierce kick.

His Highness's eyes lazily drifted to her and He tightened his grip on His son. Like a wave, pearlescent blue mist swirled at the king's command. Heavy iron chains snapped around Chestnut's neck, ankles, and wrists.

His Highness tipped his mouth into a frown with a tut. "Oh goodie. Now that you're restrained, we can be civil." He grabbed Chestnut's chin and ran a hand down her face, tracing down her neck and down her waist. "Welcome to the world of the dead and the morning."

Chestnut's eyes rattled in terrified submission.

Silence rested over the throne room.

Chestnut's inhale scraped over the surface of the tile. "You don't deserve to be a father."

His Highness tipped his head, his lashes lowering in a slow blink. "I'm not a father. I'm a *King*." He swished his hand and a portal appeared, lined in golden thread. His Highness's crisp focus created a vibrant image of a village of giant redwood trees. Chipeermen bearing Chestnut's resemblance walked along a path down the center of the forest.

Chestnut's bravery shattered. "Mama–"

The brokenness in Chestnut's expression gripped Rex. The reality set in. Two weeks ago, Chestnut had left everything she loved, everything she had ever known to come to this new planet. Once she and Rex met, things worsened and now she kneeled at the feet of a King, desperate to go home.

"Tell her to go home, Xavier." His Highness tilted his head.

Chestnut held her hands over her heart, tears beading on her fur.

Rex stared at her.

Cells were made for single occupancy. If he believed there was a spoon he could use to tunnel out, or a plan he could follow to sneak out undetected, he could ask her to wait. But there was no escape. Tethered to a slave for eternity was far from the life he wanted for her. The words slipped out before he could properly convince himself it wasn't selfish to ask her to stay in this prison with him. "Go home, Chestnut."

She broke out of her daze. "No. No, Rex, I'd never *leave* you."

Rex lowered his eyes to the floor, returning to the familiar habit of being the submissive prince. "Sire, may I say goodbye?"

His Highness released him with a noncommittal hum. "Do it quickly."

Rex approached and kneeled to her. "Chestnut, I know you want to go home. Please go home and live happily with your family. You'll be safe there...I want you to be happy."

"I'm happy with *you*."

"But you aren't safe here. Once I find Ava and Jason I'm sending them back."

Her eyes searched his expression. "Two weeks ago, you gave me the choice between safety and love. I would have much sooner wrapped myself in my silk sheets and cowered there, safe. But you showed me what it's like to be brave. You couldn't make me leave if you dragged me by the hair through that portal"

Rex cupped her face and braced himself, "Sire?"

His Highness scowled.

"She'd like to stay."

The scowl deepened. "She would distract you. You have much work to catch up on and cannot afford to play around with servants."

"I would perform better if she stayed."

"Would you?"

Rex returned his eyes to Chestnut. This castle wasn't a farm. He would never be able to build her a log cabin or hold her while the stars danced overheard, but he could love her. He *would* love her. With every word he spoke, with every soft touch, he would never let her feel slighted or ignored.

Heath was wrong. I do know what love is.

"Yes, Sire." Rex said. "I would."

"I'll discuss this with my cabinet, and come up with a more sound answer. Until then, I'll have a Fallen escort you, Miss Oak, to your room."

The chains glowed, dragging Chestnut downward into the tile. "Rex!" She screamed

Rex lunged forward but only caught a strand of her hair. "I'll find you later" Like sand she slipped through his hands.

"No, Rex! Not yet, Not yet!" She screeched, but within moments, she was gone, wherever His Highness had teleported her.

Rex's breath stopped short. The ringing in his ears returned, louder. *Stay safe.*

His Highness bared his teeth, eyes rimmed with fire. "She means nothing to you, Kitten. You are *my* beloved and I can't have you giving away your affection to just anyone." He unclipped his lion fur cloak. "If she does mean anything to you, you know I'll have to dispose of her like the other pets you chose over me. I do need a new fur cloak."

"Sire!" Rex pulled his garments tighter around him, a sick feeling stirring in his stomach.

His Highness regarded him. "Hm. Yes, that might be a problem. You seem to care for her more than me. What about my feelings, my needs?"

"S-sire. I will– I will do everything you want me to, I'll be submissive, I'll– I'll be yours forever, but leave her alone. Don't touch her, please!" He fell on the floor, bowing.

His Highness lifted him back up and slid his hand on Rex's neck, stroking his cheek endearingly. "I'm excited to see what 'perform better' means to you."

Rex froze.

"Need I remind you of your job, Has it been too long?"

Rex stared at the floor.

"Look at me." He squeezed his chin. A fire lit in his eyes. "I expect you to act according to your loyalty to me." He tipped his head "And the Jester said to His Majesty?"

Rex lingered where he was, before leaning forward and pressing a kiss to his cheek. "Anything for the King."

His Highness grinned. "And the son said to his father?"

"I love you."

He patted his head, like a well trained puppy. "Good boy." His Highness lowered a silk gloved hand adorned with rings and gems. Rex pressed his lips to it. "Oh, I missed this." He leaned down. "I'll leave her alone so long as she doesn't tread underfoot. You, however–" He smiled. "Routine beckons. I expect you at my rising ceremonies and my going to sleep ceremonies. At breakfast and dinner you will dine with me, any other sustenance will be provided by the chef. After the courtiers are satisfied and leave, I expect you to remain behind. You and I, Kitten, have some catching up to do."

Xavier nodded. "Y-yes, S-s-s-ire."

In a swirl of His Highness's cloak, he disappeared.

Xavier remained kneeling alone in the great empty throne room. He couldn't count the nights he had been left here to think. The golden seat dressed in satin and velvet with two embellished cats bent over the top, leaning down to reel a mouse in from the floor, was there to remind him he would never be the king. He was the mouse under the claws of an ancient ruler.

Just like he did when he was but a small boy, Rex crumbled, his forehead touching the floor.

Great drops of salt trickled from his eyes down his cheeks. He cried silently, a practice he had perfected in his childhood to avoid garnering concern from the King.

Ava's rash decision had sealed his fate.

Till eternity's end, he was trapped.

CHAPTER 37

Her feet took her faster than she thought she could run. The darkness enveloped her in the portal until she could see a window. The window showed her a sweeping hill of red and orange grass only broken by a river of fire from the under realm, Hell. A soft white glow emanated from the overcast clouds above them. The sky dawned a sunset pink but no sun offered light.

Home. Ava reached forward, even after she heard Jason yelling her name. She couldn't go her entire life without meeting her blood father, the one who had no idea she existed. Her adopted father never paid much attention to her either, but at least he owned a calendar to send her birthday wishes. "I wonder if he'll recognize me." The window was covered by a film of thin liquid. She broke the seal and stepped into the afterlife.

Humidity vanished. The air was crisper than anything she'd breathed before. Her arm hair stood on end from the fall coolness, but the burning river warmed the goosebumps on her arm.

Ava looked up. Hills expanded in every direction for miles and miles until a haze cropped the horizon. Tucked into a shallow ravine, hourglass homes made of delicate pottery covered the red landscape in ivory dots. She looked back at the portal's dark rift as she heard another yell.

Jason pressed through the film and tackled her. "You're okay!"

Her lungs protested his tight hug. "Of course I'm okay."

"Are you hurt? What happened? Why did you follow a stranger? Don't you know gate was opened wide for ceremonial purposes. Ava stepped towards it, but was intercepted by a young man. An X floated above his head and six nubs extended from his back where wings would have been. "Miss, you're not allowed to enter through that door."

Ava's eyes rounded. "Why not?"

"It's reserved for the royal family. Only the Prince and His Highness can walk through." He tipped his head. "You're not unlike a living child, but you're...taller?" He walked around her, then paused, staring at Jason's chest. He looked up at him. "Much taller..."

Jason furrowed his brows. "We're living, and in search of the King."

The Fallen angel looked at them all the more curiously. "The King is in the throne room at present. The Prince has just returned home!"

How did Rex beat us here? Ava followed the Fallen away from the Royal entryway. Seeing her father was more important than breaking rules she already knew she wasn't breaking. "How long will he be?"

"The King often holds long private audiences with the Prince."

"Where will he be when he's done?"

The Fallen ushered them inside the castle through a smaller side door. "Usually in the processing wing." His golden tunic billowed from a spin.

"What's that?"

"It's where First Deceased children meet the King and get blessed for a second life if they desire, or assigned to a house while they wait."

Ava met Jason's wide eyed stare. "Yes, we'll wait there." She leaned over to whisper to Jason. "Then we can find Rex and Chestnut."

"Chestnut?"

"If Rex is here, no way he left her behind."

Jason nodded.

The Fallen Angel smiled at them, his noseless face beaming. "Wonderful. I can lead you there, Miss."

"By the way, what's your name?" Ava said.

The Fallen looked at her softly. "Cael. Pleased to meet you." His eyes swiveled to Jason. "Do you...recognize me?"

"Should I?"

"I was your mother's guardian angel. I fell right before her 47th birthday."

Jason's eyes rounded. "That's–" his voice fell away. "That's when my mom died."

His mom– The woman was so vivid in her memories from family pictures around Jason's house, she could have sworn she'd met her. In the woman's absence, Ava just assumed she was busy. "Why didn't you tell me?"

"We were busy...finding a way to Limbo. You already had enough on your mind."

Was he embarrassed? Did he really think she didn't care or was too busy to share his burdens? That's what friends did! "You should have told me."

Cael wiggled his nubs. "Uh– I'm sorry. Am I intruding?"

"Not at all." Jason said. "What was she like, when she was my age?"

The Fallen definitely looked ready to hide himself in his wings "Well, heh, uh– human?"

Ava guessed Cael was saving Jason from embarrassment. On the subject of parents though– "What is the King like?"

The Fallen's golden eyes turned on her. "His Highness? Oh, he's a wonderful King. Just, kind, loyal, he treats each conflict with a delicacy only The High King in Heaven could rival."

The story sounded so unlike what Rex spouted. Maybe...he was just being dramatic. Yeah. Rex always had a habit of making a mountain out of a molehill. It was much nicer to believe her father was a kind, loving man instead of an iron-fisted tyrant. "How does he treat the Prince?"

"The affairs of the King and the Prince are heavily guarded. On odd occasions, I've heard, the Prince would leave the castle under the King's protection. He's always treated with the utmost respect. Other than that, they're never seen together."

"But such a wise and kind King would never...hurt...his son, right?" Rex's story was still not adding up.

Cael paused. "I doubt His Highness could hurt anyone."

The hallway dead ended into an intersecting hallway at a sharp right turn. Ava's breath caught in her throat.

Fur draped off a man's shoulders, dragging on the ground behind him as he walked down the intersecting hallway.

Cael bowed, so did Jason.

Ava gaped. *Dad.*

The King's white boots slowed their quick steps as he regarded the three. "Rise." He smiled at the Fallen. "Good evening, Cael."

"Good evening, Sire! How are you?"

"Absolutely wonderful, my faithful servant. For the first time in years, the Prince has taught me the meaning of joy again." His eyes shifted to her and Jason. "Oh dear, it seems more living has wandered into Limbo."

Ava stared as her father approached.

The King stooped to be at eye level. His red eyes glowed a soft hue. "Hullo, dear. What's your name?"

There was something warming about his light voice. About the tip of his head. Like wearing a weighted blanket in front of a warm fire with hot chocolate in the middle of the winter. Everything culminated into overwhelmed tears. "Ava."

He chuckled and rested a gloved hand on her head. "Wonderful to meet you Ava. You look like someone I knew once." A wistful gleam hit His eyes.

The weight on her head sent her knees knocking. He was here. Her real father, the one she dreamed of her adopted father being. She always knew in the back of her mind she'd never be important to her parents, but gazing into the eyes of an approving King intoxicated her. To the point when he lifted his hand away, she craved more affection and hugged him around the waist.

"Ava..." Jason said.

The fur of His cloak brushed against her cheek. The King smelled like fall, wearing a cologne that resembled apple cinnamon. The King's chest palpitated under her as he laughed. "Ohohoh! It seems I also remind you of someone. Cael?"

The Fallen Angel gently pulled her from the King and returned her to Jason's side. The King swished his hand and a lollipop appeared out of blue mist. He handed it to her. "Here you go." He then snapped his finger and two servants bustled down the hallway wheeling a basin of water and soap. The transparent souls were children, hardly older than thirteen, but their eyes were marked with age and wisdom. One withdrew the King's gloves and rubbed soap on his hand.

Jason stepped in front of her, acting as a shield.

Ava peered around him. Even the way His fur rippled from his drawn movements was perfect.

He was perfect.

His Highness dipped his hand in the warm water, then allowed the second servant to dry his hand and replace the white glove with a fresh one. He looked at Jason very astutely, deciphering something.

Suddenly the King's face lit up.

He gasped and swooped a wing to propel himself to his other side, eyes aglow like an awestruck child. "Are you– No, you couldn't be the boy Heath so advocated for." He dismissed the servants.

"Jason, sir. Jason Allons. Yes, I worked with Heath."

Ava blinked. *He did?*

He giggled. "Thank you, oh thank you for bringing my son home. He's so much happier now! I knew he would be so lonely and unhappy without me, but he doesn't need to be anymore. You've made a little jester happy, my boy, you should be proud."

Ava tugged on Jason's shirt. "You should be proud!"

Jason, sandwiched between the two, sweated. "Ava... we need to talk."

The King straightened. "Yes, yes, I must be on my way. Cael, do see that they're made comfortable while they stay. Any friend of Heath's is a friend of mine. A noble

284

general."

Ava nodded, catching the words from her father's mouth like nuggets of gold. She eagerly licked her lollipop.

Wings tucked against his back, the King continued down the hallway, the half skirt extending from the side of his hips swaying with every step.

Cael grinned. "Like I said, wonderful."

"Yeah!" Ava took a few steps after him before Jason grabbed her hand.

"Ava? We need to talk."

"Did you see the way he looked at me! Do you think he's proud of me?"

"Cael, could you give us a moment of privacy?" The Fallen vanished and Jason's amber eyes grew more piercing. "Ava, I think your ideals are misplaced."

"Misplaced?" She stood on her tiptoes to peer around the six foot giant.

"Heath isn't...a good man. If the King admired him, what does that say about his character?"

"Maybe he doesn't know."

"Will you just look at me? Ava, remember what Rex said?"

"Rex is dramatic. The King seems sweet."

Jason looked after where he'd left, but turned back to Ava. "Okay..."

"Trust me, in time you'll get to know him, and you'll see just what a great King he is. What a great father he is, Jason! This is everything I ever wanted. I finally have a father now."

He slit his uncertain eyes. "Let's try and find Rex and Chestnut for now."

Ava bounced beside him. The castle seemed brighter and the colors more vibrant. Long tapestries draped from the ceiling, finely woven stories of kings and queens past. Most of them depicted the ruler she'd just met. She admired them.

A sharp scream echoed through the halls and in the next second, Chestnut rose up from a puddle and stumbled to get her bearings. A haunted expression painted her face.

CHAPTER 38

Everything darkened to an empty void.

The warm colors of the throne room were replaced with softer golds. The world solidified in a hallway. Chestnut gulped. "Xavier, Sparrow! No!" She raced down a hall, not a clue where she's going.

"Chestnut!" Ava ran after her and stopped her with a hug, making sure to keep her blue raspberry lollipop away from her fur.

"Ava?" She stared at her, before struggling "No, no, you don't understand, he's alone with him! He–" Chestnut buried her face in her friend's garments. She could still feel the silk glove stroke down her side. "Ava."

"Hey, it's okay, it's okay."

Her wrists and ankles were sore and red, the fur burned away. "His touch..." She blinked and felt it again and again, her fur parting under his finger. She shook her head. "Xavier!"

Jason and Ava exchanged glances.

A Fallen Angel crept to them.

Jason cleared his throat. "Chestnut, this is Cael."

The Fallen's eyes softened. "I'll escort you to your rooms." The soul bowed.

Chestnut looked him over. He had to only be twenty-three years old, wearing a golden suit. She didn't have time to be escorted to a room and locked behind a door. Rex needed her.

Cael bowed, "this way." He looked over his shoulder. "Is it official? Has–has the prince returned?"

How sickening. They are completely unaware of the horrors that the King puts the prince through. Rex's return isn't anything to celebrate, it's something to mourn. If not for Heath, we would have been safe. Her eyes welled. Now they would never have that farm Rex was excited about. With ducks and chickens and–and the other animals he mentioned. Chestnut exhaled. "Yes, he has."

The Fallen's eyes lit up. "I've been waiting so long! I wonder when he'll host auditions next?"

"Auditions?" Ava licked her lollipop.

"The Prince would put on productions for His Highness. Glorious arrays of majesty, so I've heard. Unless the King opens it to the public, no one but Him, the Prince, and the Courtiers ever get to see the performances."

Ava nodded. "I could do that. Has he ever starred himself in a production?"

"Oh no. The Prince performs directly for the King. I saw three seconds through a curtain while the servants were exchanging the King's dinner."

"So that's what the first born grew up with."

"Sounds like torture." Jason said.

Ava looked at her lollipop. "Hey, Cael. The King created things out of thin air. Can everyone here do it?"

Cael shook his head. "The dimension bends to the will of the rulers. Since they created the dimension under Heaven's authority, their line of heirs controls everything that happens here."

Ava swished her hand, "Create an apple." Nothing happened. "How does it work?"

"I'll get back to you on that."

"I bet Rex'll know."

Cael gave her a curious look. "Rex M, Rex A., Rex W., or Rex Q? That's off the top of my head."

Chestnut's heart broke, *I suppose, if this afterlife has been here since the beginning of time, they have multiples of every name.*

"No, no, uh–I meant the Prince."

"Yes, His Highness's Crown Jewel would know, but he's awfully busy."

Chestnut's blood boiled at the sound of his name. "I am almost positive Xavier will–"

Cael's face dropped in horror.

Oh, moss, did I say something wrong?

"You– You can't say his name! Oh, I'm going to get into big trouble." A bell materialized on the wall and rang back and forth. "Oh no, oh no, oh no. I have to go..." Cael raced down the hallway.

Chestnut held her hands over her heart "I didn't mean to get him in trouble."

Jason gave the shrinking servant a glare. "Maybe we should try to be more sensitive to this place's culture, to avoid being locked in the dungeon."

"Indeed–"

Soon an older Fallen hobbled up to them. "Hullo. I'll be leading you to your rooms in Cael's stead."

The Fallen angel led them into the Prince's wing. A long hallway of oak doors stretched before them. A golden, ornate door stood at the end. The Fallen presented their doors.

Ava opened one to a pride of lions sleeping on top of each other. Her eyes widened and she slammed the door.

"The Prince adores his lions." The Fallen said "He's very fond of his pets."

Chestnut smiled. *Yes, Sparrow always was an animal person. I've no doubt I'll get to meet all his pets.*

A door opened for Chestnut to reveal an empty room with oak wood and a large bay window peering over the kingdom. Purple slugs moved about the room, spewing out wood and crafting furniture. They molded the bed into a replica of her shelf back home.

We're not staying here another second more. She had seen the monster that lurked in Rex's nightmares, and now more than ever, she was determined to find something to free him. She peeked out of the bedroom and stole into the hallway as swift as a lark. *There has to be a library somewhere in this stony prison. Hours spent searching won't be enough to make up for how much Rex had done for me. He saved my life, I'm going to save him.* Chestnut turned a corner. *They should label these rooms. How does anyone know where they're going?*

A servant hastened from one room to the next.

"Excuse me," Chestnut hailed, "Can you gesture the way to the li- brary?"

"Three lefts and two rights, should be on the left hand side, three doors down the hall." She then continued about her work.

Chestnut heeded her instructions. She swung open the oak door, her eyes rounding.

Novels stretched in every direction. Servants milled about the library dusting books and cleaning tables. *Never have I seen such an expanse of wonder like this! I wonder if Rex knows the wealth of knowledge right in his own home? Oh–silly girl, of course he does, he lives here.* Her imagination wasn't as sharp as it used to be. It was hard to imagine Rex strolling down these rows, eyes peeled for a title.

She furrowed her brows. *Time to get to work.*

CHAPTER 39

Rex entered his wing, fighting to keep his eyes open. Night and day were divided by Heaven's glow. When the clouds shone bright, it was day. When the clouds shone dim, it was night. Rex guessed it was early morning.

I wonder if the rooms have morphed yet? Rex peeked into the apartments. He found Ava's and cracked it open. Her walls were adorned with golden trophies and awards. Morphers moved like slugs, surrounding the room and molding the features like candles. The room still wiggled and warped, and would continue until she woke up. Picture frames of memories, maybe fake memories, lined the bookshelves. She looked so happy with her parents.

Ava wasn't in her room. Rex sighed. The servants led him here but failed to mention that Ava was probably exploring her new kingdom. Rex would have to find her later, he needed to make sure Chestnut was okay first.

Where's Chestnut's? Rex noticed morphers inching their way to a door. Giant purple slugs about the size of a cat were capable of reading minds and molding the castle like wax. That must be hers. Rex knocked, but there was no answer.

Rex knocked again. *Oh no–* His Highness hadn't taken her, had he? He opened the door. "Chestnut?" The room was spotless, with the crimson curtains peeled back to reveal a village under the canopy of towering redwood trees. A clay cup of tea sat on the window sill and books lined the room. The window played like a movie. Little girls that looked identical to Chestnut played in the fallen leaves. *Is this her home?* The community's population must have been less than 200. Chipeermen bustled to and fro, milking cows, weaving silk, and cleaning farming supplies.

This is what her heart desires. Rex felt a pang of hurt. *She wants to go home.*

However beautiful the landscape was, it lacked the woman he had come looking for. Rex left the room and quickly found a servant. "Excuse me. Have you seen a woman, about five feet, covered in fur, long chipmunk tail with ears and antlers?"

The servant nodded. "Yes, your Majesty. She was asking for the library."

The library. Rex relaxed, *Of course, I should have looked there first.*

The library door was left ajar. "Chestnut?"

Hanging off a ladder fifty feet in the air, Chestnut called his name. "Look what I found!"

"What are you doing here?"

She climbed down the ladder. "I wanted to see if there was any way that you could leave."

"Leave–" His eyes rounded. "Do you think that's possible?"

Chestnut gestured to a pile of books. "I don't know, but it's bound to be in one of these hardcovers!" She placed three more books into the pile and turned back to the ladder.

"Woah, woah!" Rex halted her. "Hold your horses, you look exhausted."

"Pish posh. You *look* more tired than I feel."

"I am... but I have to stay awake for the courtiers." Just as the King's sendoff to sleep was commercialized into a novelty, so was the Prince's. He had forgotten how uncomfortable it was to stand behind a golden gate while Courtiers watched him be undressed and prepared for bed. First thing in the morning, the routine would be redone.

Chestnut rolled her eyes and cracked open a book. "I'm going to find a way for you to be free, Rex, I promise." Her eyes drifted to meet his. "I can't let you live like this."

Rex pressed a kiss to her forehead "Get some rest, deer. The books will be here when you wake up."

"Only if you rest too." She furrowed her brows.

Rex smiled. *She looks so adorable when she's grumpy.* "Okay. I'll call the courtiers, then go back to my room and take a nap."

Chestnut tilted her chin up triumphantly. "And once you wake up, you can come back and help me research."

I assume that means she's not going to rest. "Sounds like a plan, stay safe, Chestnut. I love you."

She looked up from her book. "I love you too, Sparrow. We'll find a way out of this together."

If only we could. He closed the door and headed back to his room. Morphers followed him in, nearly running over his foot. A queen sized bed filled the center of the gold adorned room. The King's apartment was centered in between both wings of the castle and the Prince's adjoined beside it on the west side. Rex dragged through the two antechambers and the large room, finally reaching the bedchambers.

A crowd awaited him, much to Rex's dissatisfaction. This is why he usually slept in the woods, when living. He rolled his eyes and followed his footman through the golden gate, a symbol that the Prince was untouchable and above the average class of peasants. Rex did his best to ignore the courtiers as the servants sat him down at a vanity, combed his hair, washed his face, and rubbed all kinds of beauty serum into his skin. He was dressed in fine silk pajamas and after he walked up steps to his mattress, he sat on the edge and gazed out at the crowd filling the half of the room on the other side of the gate. Rex released a soft sigh, then had the servants close the drapes to enclose the warmth in.

Rex fell, face first, down on the cushion, wings spread over him. Humidity gathered underneath his wings and Rex curled into it. The warmth had never bothered him. Rex drifted into a rough sleep. Finally alone.

Dreams of Matthew and William haunted his mind.

Rex's face felt wet as he woke. He scrunched his eyes and pulled his wing closer around him. He wanted to sleep, but not sleep like that. He wanted the kind of numb dreamless sleep, the quality kind that leaves you refreshed and excited about the day.

He wasn't excited.

All he wanted to do was curl up and fall back asleep. Rex slitted his eyes meeting the velvet canopy that surrounded his bed and dimmed the light. The thick duvet covers had been kicked away and scrunched together, his feet settling in the folds. Rex rolled over on his back and winced as his wings ached. He shapeshifted them away into mist and let it float away. *Better.*

Why don't I just...not invite the courtiers in. He was expertly skilled in readying himself for the day and even if it provoked a stern warning from his father, he would risk it to conserve the small amount of energy he recharged from his sleep.

He heard a soft voice speak from outside the canopy. "Hey Kid, wake up."

A horror mixed with shock riddled through Rex. He ripped open the canopy desperately searching for the voice.

Matthew sat on a velvet cushion, upright with that perfect posture he always had. His face wrinkled in a smile. "It's been a while."

Rex's mind fogged. It fogged beyond belief. He raced towards Matthew, brought him into a tight hug, and squeezed the life out of him. He babbled some unintelligible gobbledegook, spreading his fingers out, and grabbing Matthew tighter. They were the same size now, lithe short twigs, except Matthew was a few inches taller. "Matthew! W-what are you doing here?"

Matthew grunted. "Xavier, I can't breathe!"

Rex released him. He wore the same clothes he was wearing when he died. Rex could even see where he had ripped away the swath. Matthew peeled back his sleeve to reveal the mark of Limbo. Rex blinked. "You- You took a second life?!"

Matthew chuckled.

Something didn't make sense. If Matthew had always had that mark, Rex would have recognized it, he would have seen it. In four years of living with him, did he just never notice? *I'm—I'm so obtuse.* Rex's face contorted and he hugged Matthew again. "I'm just so glad you're here, I need you...I missed you...I– I failed you."

"How did you fail me?" Matthew asked with that million dollar smile.

"I let you die–"

Matthew blinked at him, his eyes blank as if trying to process what he just said. "You did do both of those things. You think I blame you?"

"You do, don't you?"

Matthew's eyes went void. "You've convinced yourself of such, so I suppose so."

"Forgive me." Rex felt tears billow.

Matthew nodded.

A burst of excitement flooded through Rex. Chestnut! He had to introduce the two!! Rex grabbed Matthew's hand and dragged him to the door. "You have to meet my girlfriend."

A panic entered Matthew's eyes, he pulled back, resisting. "Xavier! Xavier, let me go!"

Rex yanked him through the doorway, but felt his strong sturdy hand turn into jello. He looked back, alarmed to see a purple jello in place of Matthew's hand, while he stared at him from the other side of the door. This...this wasn't Matthew. Rex gave another tug and Matthew's head jerked past the doorway turning into a morpher. The morpher was thrown off, decapitating Matthew. Rex screamed as the slimy morpher sniffed around his foot. Matthew, headless now, stepped away from the door, crossing his arms. Rex's nerves shorted out. He slammed the door and slid to the bottom, the tears flowing in closer intervals now. *I'm tired of this! I'm tired of His Highness's mind games! This is too much...It hurts!*

I can't do this anymore!

I'm the Prince. I shouldn't have to deal with this!

The Prince.

His Highness had made sure to remind him over and over again that he was just the jester. Perhaps, that's all he was fated to be. Rex replaced his golden robes with his prince attire, a gold uniform that wrapped around his waist with a white thread. He snapped the cuffs down. *Since His Highness hasn't called me to do anything, I suppose I have a little free time.* Rex returned to the library.

Chestnut greeted him with a wide smile "Hi, Sparrow."

"Alright, let's see what we can find." He rolled up his sleeves

Chestnut pointed to a cream colored page. "I found this."

The chapter detailed the succession of the heir to King or Queen. In order for the current ruler to be dethroned, their contracted symbol needed to be pressed simultaneously by two heirs of the current ruler. Two heirs could cremate a ruler, 1,000 souls could cremate an heir, and 10,000 clouds could cremate a ruler. *Two heirs. Me and Ava.*

Chestnut matched his beaming smile. "You could be King, Rex."

His Highness was a noble ruler, and he could be too. *I've watched His Highness, studied his methods. I could make this Kingdom greater than it ever has been before.*

More importantly, he'd be free.

"I'll go find Ava. Because of this–" Rex released a light breath. "I could finally be free, Chestnut, you did it!" He twirled her.

This future may not be the farm the originally dreamed of, but it was better. With Chestnut as his Queen, the possibilities were endless.

Chestnut leaned against him. "No, *we* did it."

Freedom was closer than it ever had been before. He just needed to find Ava.

CHAPTER 40

Ava looked around for the King, asking servants about his whereabouts. Her mind took her to places she wasn't used to being. Bitter places. From her understanding, the heir had to put on a few plays, sing and dance for the king, and govern over a small plot of land. She could do that, after all, it wasn't rocket science. She already had an impressive resume with musical theatre. Surely her father would be impressed.

She and Jason had taken to exploring the castle grounds. It was a maze of endless history that was in desperate need of labelling. They both had spent a good hour staring at a painting, trying to discern what was happening. A war of some sorts? By the end, they shrugged and moved on.

Ava had been paying attention to the castle buzz about the rebellious prince skipping the Waking Up Ceremony. The courtiers weren't so thrilled about being brushed off. Ava heard many of them talking about complaining to the King about it. Desperate for another warm smile and gentle touch, she and Jason followed them. Jason had stopped to gaze at another painting, lost in its sickly beauty. Ava told him they'd meet later on and he answered "Don't talk to strangers."

Ava smiled "I will!"

She followed the courtiers, but took a sharp right turn to avoid looking like she was stalking them.

Down the hall, a shorter mirror image of the King paced down the other direction, power in his narrow shoulders. *Rex.*

He spun, his eyes finding Ava. "You're okay!"

A few seconds was too much to hope for before Rex had dashed to her and wrapped arms around her. "R-rex, yeah I'm fine."

He pulled away. "Good." The fire in his eyes intimidated Ava. "What were you *thinking* going with Heath? Do you realize how much danger you were in? And why didn't you tell me?"

"Tell you–?" Ava pursed her lips.

"You're my sister."

Ava stared at him until she was sure her eyes had dried out and fossilized. "Yeah–"

"Is that why you changed everything about yourself? Ava, you are beautiful. You *were* beautiful."

"I wasn't–"

"Ava" Rex softened his eyes. "Your beauty was unmatchable, because there's only one Ava."

She looked down. "It's too late to fix it anyways."

Rex tipped his head and swished his hand. His magic extended her hair, returning the dye to her signature green. He gave her a soft smile "Just as exotic as I remember it."

Ava looked at her hair, amazed. "How did you–"

"Imagine what you want to create, see it in your mind's eyes, every corner, every crevice. Snaps are more immediate. I usually just wave my hands. It creates it slower so I can control the rush of magic better." He clicked his hands around one another and a peach slowly materialized out of thin air. He caught it. "See? Versus, y'know." He snapped his fingers and the chandelier poofed into a fan.

Incredible. The realm was quite literally at her beck and call. She just needed her tiara and the only way to get it was to be crowned by the King himself. Ava nodded. "Now I'm off to tell the King I'm his daught–" At Rex's snap, a piece of tape shut her mouth.

Rex's blue eyes widened in horror. "Ava! You can't say that here."

She peeled back the tape. "You did–"

"I whispered." He grinned. "I've been looking for you since morning to talk to you about that very thing. There's a way we can get rid of him if we work together."

Ava's expression darkened. *Get rid of him?* She had just met him and Rex was planning a mutiny.

"Two heirs can cremate a King, we need to both press the symbol on his left wrist. I have a plan. Next summons, you come in and pretend to be all 'Rah, Rah, I'm ready to overthrow the empire'. Then we'll fight each other to distract him. Then we'll turn on him and–"

"I don't want to get rid of him."

Rex's eyes dulled. He blinked. "What?"

Fitting that Rex should try and hog all His attention. Ava gave a sardonic smile. "Heh, you want to get rid of him because you're scared that now that I'm here, there's not enough love for both of us. Yeah?" She patted his head. "Don't worry, Rex. You'll still get a lot of attention. You'll just have to split it with me."

Rex grabbed her arm. "Ava, trust me. I want you to meet your father as much as you, but His Highness doesn't give 'attention' he gives infatuation. And if he's infatuated with you–" A bell interrupted him. He squeezed his eyes closed. "You have no idea what he asks me to do for him...Ava, I'm trying to protect you from that."

No, I see exactly what this is. You're trying to keep him all to yourself. Ava looked at the bell as it angered. "What's–"

"His Highness is waiting...Ava, I need you to trust that what I'm doing is the right thing."

"In what universe is this a good thing? Rex, he's doing so much for the kingdom. He's kind and understanding–"

"He's not, Ava, he's not! That's just what everyone believes."

Ava clenched her fist. Theatre was cutthroat. If you don't stomp on the competition's necks, you won't get anywhere. In real life, there was never enough 'love' to go around. She'd just said that to hopefully ease Rex's worry. If Rex was so worried about Felix, shouldn't he be happy to have her step in to relieve him from the attention he so desperately wants to be free from? Rex didn't understand. He didn't understand what it was like to be shunned, to have to fight for every accolade. Nothing she ever did was good enough for her fans, for her family, for her producers. They always asked more of her. It sounded like His Highness only asked what was expected. And maybe Rex was being too self centered. He had a tendency to make things *all* about him. He may not have even considered that their father had feelings.

After all, why was she here if not to get closure on her Father. How was she supposed to do that if he didn't even know they were related?

Rex was being irrational. "If everyone else in the kingdom loves him except you, that means there's something wrong with *you.* "

"Ava, you're not listening. He doesn't love anyone but himself. We're just playthings to him."

"Maybe I want to be a plaything. If that's what it'll take for him to love me"

Rex ran in front of her and spread out his left wing to block her. "He loves what I can do for him. Let's keep it that way. If he found out you're his daughter, he'd do the same things to you as he's done to me. He'll find a 'use' for you."

Ava summoned a knife and swiped at Rex's wing. She was so mad, she would have cut open his wing to get to her father.

"You'll just get hurt, then I'll have to clean up the mess."

"Oh, so you think I just cause messes. That's how it is, isn't it?"

"Ava, You don't have to be the best!" Rex dodged.

Ava's eyes gradually faded into red. She pushed past Rex. "I do! Who am I if I'm not the best! I've tried so hard! Always done everything right, I've never made a mistake! And for what? Everyone hates me. My fans have turned on me, my own parents hate me! I need to know who I am! I need to know if my existence really is just a mistake! I *need* to know!" She raised her voice.

Rex grabbed her shoulders and curled his wings around him. "No, you *need* to keep quiet. It's for your own good. Trust me," Rex pleaded. He shapeshifted into a human, his blue eyes wide with desperation.

"Trust you? I've been trusting you! I trusted you were human! I trusted you weren't my brother! I trusted you were on my side! I trusted that you cared! Since when have I *ever* been able to trust you?" Ava shoved Rex away with all her strength. "I would make a much better heir than you. I deserve to be the heir! I make things better, you destroy them. You're a villain." Her bloodshot eyes glossed over as tears began to form. She furrowed her brows in raw anger. "No, you're just a weak kitten!" Ava screamed.

The world froze.

Rex's breath was fast and shallow, and so was Ava's.

Rex stared at her, his eyes hurt and emotional. Blank stare. Empty stare.

Ava spun and pounded through the halls, running in any direction away from Rex. Long windows stretched from the ceiling to the floor. She ignored Rex's warning flaring in her mind. *This is what I came here for! I need to know! I need Him to know!*

"Ava, wait!"

The louder she argued, the louder the warning got. Over and over. *I'm sure he only thinks that way because he's just the jester.* Servants flooded down the hall like rats flushed out of a sewer. "The King is coming!" they murmured in hushed whispers.

He's coming!

The King's white polished boots stepped down the hallway. Servants carried his long purple train.

Ava walked toward the fur-lined fabric and reached out with shaky fingers.

Rex spun a corner. "Ava!" He tackled her through the double French doors.

"Rex, stop trying to change my mind!"

"Ava!"

I don't have to listen to you! "I don't care, he deserves to know!"

The King's shadow darkened the french doors. "Kitten, is that you?" His soft voice carried through the wood.

Ava's fist vibrated, shaking violently. She whirred to her feet, a deep seated anger engraved in her scowl.

"Ava!"

She threw open the door.

His Highness blinked. "Oh, it's you again."

"Sire." Her breath left her. "I need to talk to you. It's about something really important."

His Highness' red irises roved over her face. "Alright. You have my attention. I'm listening." He folded his hands together, eyes soft.

"I'm the daughter of one of your...flings."

His Highness tipped his head. "Which one?"

"Charlotte Evans. She lived on New Earth. Pole dancer in Jimmy's club off second and third. She went by Charlie."

His Highness stepped into the room, his shadow casting over Ava. "Yes... I see the resemblance. In my second life, I worked as a bartender at the same club." He forced her to walk backwards. His eyes slid to Rex, shriveled in the corner. His heels clicked on the tile as he neared.

Ava's stomach dropped. If He knew that she was his daughter, why wasn't he treating her as more important? Why wasn't she loved?

Rex met face to face with the laces of His Highness's white boots. "She was much more fun than your mother." His Highness said as if it was Rex's fault.

Rex turned his face away.

His Highness returned his attention to Ava. "In any case, why are you telling *me*? What do you want?" His Highness said.

"I...I want to be loved."

Rex's breath echoed on the floor and returned to him.

"Loved?" His Highness gave a hard laugh. Rex looked up to see the King chasing her around the table, his wings outstretched and hair on fire. "Dear, mere pleasantries are my specialties, but I have no patience for a traitorous mole infiltrating my kingdom. You were never supposed to exist. There's nothing I can do about that *now*."

Tears formed in Ava's eyes. Her hands shook as she scrunched her clothes. "What?"

"Must I spell it out? Are both my offspring complete idiots?" The King bared his teeth, "You. Are. Worthless. And I really don't have time for this, so if you'll excuse me. Xavier, come here. I need to have a word with you as well."

Ava tripped on a chair. "P-please Dad."

"Don't call me that!" Craters deepened with each of His Highness's steps. "Let's make one thing clear- I can *sound* however I like" He said in Jason's voice. His steps came slowly. "I can *say* whatever I like. I can *do* whatever I like!" The King hissed. He disappeared into a cloud of red smoke. He twirled around her and reformed with his finger under her chin and his hand a few inches away from her arm. He was a teenager, he looked almost exactly like Rex. His light brown hair bobbed in front of her. Him, Ava, and His Highness looked like triplets. "I can *look* however I like" He cooed.

Ava blushed as leaned her backwards over the table.

"I am the King. You are not!" His Highness reverted to his normal age. "You have no voice. You have no say. You have no choice." His slow sliding fingernail drew blood from a thin line on her neck. "You have no purpose."

Ava dropped to her knees, hand gently going to her neck.

The world shook like an earthquake as red engulfed everything in its shade. *Maybe Rex wasn't lying–*

CHAPTER 41

The emptiness in Ava's eyes evoked anger from the depths of Rex's spirit. "Don't talk to her like that!"

Time stretched as His Highness slowly turned his head to look at his son. His wispy words came out in a snake-like hiss. "Excuse me?"

Rex's strength evaporated into the sulfur-constricted air. "Nothing Sire."

The calm patience in His Highness's eyes was replaced by a flaming tempered red. "What did you say, Kitten?" He paced forward, Rex shuffled backwards in response. "Say it again."

Rex's back pressed against the wall. "I said...don't talk to her like that." A backhand knocked his jaw loose.

His Highness bared his teeth, "You don't *get* to speak to me like that!"

Ava raised her dull eyes to them. Rex couldn't stand by while his younger sister was degraded to nothing. He turned a defiant scowl into his father's face, "And you don't have any right to speak to her like that."

Another slap sent him to the ground. His Highness created a cat of nine tails in his fist.

The teeth scored against his back. Fresh liquid bubbled to the skin's surface. These lashes were for Ava. Another score ripped the flesh of his legs. Rex's mind fogged. His strength ebbed away with every rip.

Ava winced at every crack. "Stop!" She threw herself between the two.

Ava? Rex propped his back against the wall and looked up at her, outlined in red light. "What are you doing?"

Her green eyes softened on him. "Protecting the people who really love me." She stared down the King, sweat trailing down her forehead. "I'm not afraid of you, Felix."

His Highness's face reddened. "Get out!" He screeched a bloodcurdling noise. He shoved her aside and created an iron maiden around her.

The sides snapped together.

No. Rex swished his hand and a metal rod materialized to pry it open. *Stay alive, stay alive, please-* The spikes gleamed in the candlelight.

His Highness turned a fiery glare on him. "Remove the bar."

Rex's eyes remained on Ava. His Highness' magic forced the side closer together. The strain of keeping the rod unbent was more than he could bear in his state. His unsteady hand shivered. Ava fit her hands between the spikes, avoiding them the best she could, but they pressed in on her.

"Remove the bar. *Now!*" The King snarled, his teeth savage.

Rex's eyes shook, flickering over His Highness's furious face. *I can't do this.* The flames in His Highness' eyes would only be quenched with blood, or passion. *No. I need to do this. For my freedom.* He lodged a foot underneath him and despite the stinging protest in his legs, he lunged for Ava. Upon contact with her skin, Rex teleported her out of the room into the hallway.

The spikes slammed closed.

His Highness turned towards Rex, purple veins in his neck strained and tunnel vision locked. "Wrong answer!"

CHAPTER 42

Ava toppled over headfirst into the quiet hallway. "Rex!" She screamed. This hallway was unfamiliar. She darted down the hallway in the first direction she spotted. Rex had taken lashes for her. He'd defied the King of this sickly kingdom for her.

I can't believe I fell for it; that kind smile, the softness in her father's eyes. It seemed too good to be true. Her quick pace was interrupted as she collided with a body.

Jason grabbed her shoulders. "Ava! There you are. I've been looking everywhere for you! Are you okay?"

She stared into his amber eyes. The hopelessness of their situation finally collapsed on her. She swept into a hug and squeezed him tight. "He knows, Jason. He knows."

Jason wrapped his arms around her. "You told him. Ava–"

The disappointment in his voice shattered her and her eyes welled up. "I really am just a mistake Jason. He doesn't want anything to do with me...I'm just a worthless nobody." And a fool. For trusting someone like that, especially so soon after Heath. She'd been tricked twice, and despite Jason's warnings, despite Rex's, she persisted, blinded by a desperation to be loved.

"You're not a worthless nobody, Ava." Jason breathed into her hair. "You've changed so many lives with your work."

"My fans all turned on me, Jason. Everyone has. Everyone I ever loved has turned on me...for once I just want to feel loved. Is that so much to be asked for? To be acknowledged for how hard I try to be perfect?"

He pulled away and gazed softly into her eyes. "You are loved." His face pulled into a smile. "By Rex, by Chestnut, by me. You don't have to be perfect for us. We've seen just how broken and imperfect you really are and we still love you."

Ugly tears traced lines down her face. "How can you? I'm a mistake."

"A beautiful–" Jason wiped the tears from her cheeks, "wonderful, kind, smart, loyal mistake."

Her eyes stared into Jason's.

Chestnut had also supported her unwaveringly throughout the journey. Her smile had been real, her laughter genuine. *I should have done more to contribute to her healing.* And yet, Chestnut appreciated her presence. Chestnut loved her.

Even now Jason's soft hands held hers and comforted her. He had always made time for her, listening to her ramble on the phone about silly nonsense. He had welcomed her into his inner social circle, and even when she changed everything about herself, he didn't leave. He didn't call her insane and ostracize her, he gently pulled her to the side and asked if she was okay. She'd really taken him for granted. Jason loved her.

And Rex. From their meeting, he had always tended to her and Chest- nut's needs. Their midnight conversations about family and their fears had meant more than any gift her father could give her, more than any half hearted compliment her mother could grace her with. They may have loved her deep down, but she'd never felt important around them.

She always wondered what family sacrifice looked like. Her older brother had thrown himself into the clutches of a lion for her sake.

For their sake.

"We have to find Rex." She breathed.

Rex had come to her asking for help, and she cast him aside for her own selfish reasons. He was hurting. He was trapped. Even now she was certain that His Highness was tearing him apart for his defiance.

Two heirs can cremate a King.

Ava's breath hitched.

"Two heirs can cremate a King!" She slid the contacts out of her eyes, returning her irises to their brilliant, vibrant green. "Jason, Rex needs my help! I need to find him"

"Are you sure it's safe?"

Since when had she been bothered by what was safe? "Rex sacrificed himself for me. It's about time I did the same for him."

The plan? Fight each other until the King lowered his guard, then strike when he was pacified watching the two heirs.

Jason paced forward. "I'm coming to help."

"No, go find Chestnut and meet me in the west wing. That's where they are." Now how to *get* to the west wing– hehe–"This is something I have to do alone, for Rex."

Jason nodded. "I'll be there."

With her heart full, Ava turned on her heels and raced down the hallway. The world's praise meant nothing if the people she loved most didn't love her back. Rex had proved his love for her, now it was her turn.

CHAPTER 43

"Sire–Sire!"

"You disobeyed me–directly!" Lightning sparkled around the King. He lumbered forward. "You need a lesson! Since you've returned, it's like you have a mind of your own!" His lips vibrated in a growl.

Rex dodged a vase, and swiped a shield into existence. "Sire."

"Don't take that tone with me." The cat of nine tails slashed against the shield and His Highness yelled in frustration. He slammed his fist against the holographic shield. "Take this down, now!"

"No!" Oh claws, that felt good! "No! You'll hurt me."

His defiance did nothing except add oil to the blazing fire. "You don't get to say no!" The King swiped his hand and dissolved the shield, grabbing Rex by the arm. He gave Rex a swift backhand.

"You..."

Slap.

"...are my jester."

Slap.

"My pet!"

Slap.

"You don't get to say no!"

Rex's cheeks burned. He hung limp in his father's grip. "Sire, you're angry."

"You wish I was angry, Kitten. I'm *furious*!" Spit flew into Rex's face followed by a sharp scratch. The old voice came back *Appeasement.*

Not this time. Rex weaseled away from him, and created another sphere around him as a shield.

Felix regarded Rex. His hair exploded into a crackling fire. He yelled and punched his arms wildly in a tantrum. He tried forming words, but each syllable only served to tighten the bloodthirsty tunnel vision. This was usually the part where His Highness would relieve the rebellious servant of their contract, reducing them to ash. Rex protected his wrist. This was new though. Apart from spitting curses and pacing, the King wasn't acting. Rex finally realized what he should have millenia ago.

The King had no *real* power.

Empty threats and physical abuse were the only ways he maintained control. He reigned through fear.

And Rex wasn't afraid anymore.

"I am your King, my word is law! I say jump and you say how high! You do what I tell you without question!" He yelled, his eyes intense. Rex could see his mind working, spinning.

It's...nothing but words. Rex stood straighter. Ava had done it, why couldn't he? "No."

His Highness dissipated Rex's force field, but Rex created another. Seven spheres later, His Highness screamed and slammed the shield. "Fine– If you want to be in a hamster ball, I'll put you in one!" He shoved the shield, sending the hamster ball rolling.

Rex's body slammed against the side.

His Highness's anger subsided as the chess board finally tipped back into his favor. He halted the spinning by placing a hand on it and gave an amused snicker. "Run." With a strong kick, the ball went flying, Rex tumbling with it. He bashed against the wall and was thrust across the sphere. Rex fell on his back, letting the sphere spin him around and around and around. The force pressed him against the side, squishing him like a 2 ton elephant. His lungs screamed, and Rex did too. He knocked into a wall, smashing against the opposite side. "Sire!" Rex yelled, begging, groveling. Anything to release the pain.

Felix stopped the ball. "It's the girl, isn't it?" He hissed.

"What girl?" Rex's defenses rose.

"The one with the fur-" His Highness breathed, his tone high pitched and sickly. "She poisoned you." His eyes lit up as if everything finally made sense.

"N-no, she- she didn't do anything." Bile rose in Rex's throat "We made a deal!"

The power transferred. His Highness smiled, "Deals are only illusions of choice. That's how I'll get through to you." His teeth glimmered in the dim candlelight.

Rex slammed himself harder against the curved side of the ball. "If you touch her, I'll–" Tears billowed in his eyes.

"Kitten, oh Kitten. Now, why is she so important?" His Highness mocked, stepping around him.

Rex lashed out at him with his free hand. He rocked the ball hoping to run over His Highness. "Don't touch her!"

The King stopped. "Why?"

"I love her." The words slipped out of his mouth before he could do anything about it. "I love her. Please don't take her from me." His voice faltered, the pressure in his head building as emotions manifested in tears.

Jealousy crept into His Highness's face. "You...love her? You love me!" Sulfur strengthened as a frown deepened the creases in his face "You can only love me. I love you too much to let you go. I'll get rid of her. And once I do- never speak of this again- never talk about her again. I know you don't understand right now, Pet, but one day you'll see. It's only because I love you." He stroked his gloved hand down the reflection of Rex's cheek.

Rex's stomach dropped. He needed Chestnut. He needed her *alive*. The image of his father dressed in his robe and slippers stepping on her fur pelt just because he wanted Rex's love for himself. Rex's blood boiled. He threw himself at his Father like a wild dog. "You don't love anyone but yourself!" He screamed.

The King stepped away, a mix of disgust and power mixing in his eyes. "Is that what you think?"

"I think too much about you! Every day is a living nightmare because of you!"

"I didn't know you had dreams, much less nightmares. If that's what it takes to get the respect I deserve, I'll be your worst nightmare."

The doors thrust open.

"Rex!" Ava snarled.

His father's eyes shook as if not sure what to make of this. The room chilled, and His Highness dispelled the sphere. Rex fell.

The plan.

Ava's green eyes softened, but for a second.

Alright we're doing this! Rex stood shaking out his tense muscles. "Leave, Ava! You heard what the King said. You have no purpose."

"Then I'll carve myself one from your paling corpse."

"There can only be room for one of us in His Highness' heart."

His Highness' expression softened into a proud father. "Well, look who changed their tune so quickly."

Ava's expression hardened. "I will be adored!"

Two actors.

One stage.

One goal in mind.

Rex stepped in front of the King, blood streaming off his sliced skin. *Showtime.*

Ava charged.

Rex caught each one of her messy throws, waiting for an opening. His fist collided with her stomach, and she keeled. He grabbed her shoulders and brought his knee up as fast as he could.

She screamed in agony, stumbling backwards. Recovering, her foot swung around and kicked over the top of Rex. He ducked. *Straighten your leg, we're fighting not dancing. We have to at least look realistic!* Rex grabbed her leg and caught her off balance. She fell to the floor.

Rex stumbled backwards. He dashed behind the safety of his towering father.

His Highness raised an eyebrow and swirled red magic into a blinding mist.

This is my chance. "Ava!"

Rex reached forward, yanking His Highness's wrist down. He pressed a thumb on it. *Ava, where are you! Where are you?!*

She had been following the plan, right? His stomach dropped. *What if she wasn't acting? What if she really wants to kill me to take the throne?* She always craved love and power. What if His Highness' admonishment had tipped her over the edge?

He raised his eyes.

Orange fire lapped His Highness' hair. "What is this?"

This is freedom. It was supposed to be.

The trembling intensified. "Sire–"

"Remove your thumb, or I'll chop both your hands off!" His voice split into seventeen harmonies, all growling.

Rex's eyes darted around, searching the mist for his sister. *We're supposed to do this together!*

Xavier tensed every muscle forcing him to hold his ground in an act of revenge, but Rex fought with equal strength. *A world without my father.* He had a taste of it when he took his second life, but he never was truly free from him. Xavier still heard his voice, felt his hands, and saw his face. Even though he wasn't there, He still was. Wouldn't that be how it would be again? Is there any sense in taking away that presence only to have his memory replace it?

And he was barely a prince. He couldn't be a King. He didn't know the first thing about being a King. His father always made sure he was as clueless as a rock. This must have been why.

Felix shuffled on the floor. "Kitten– think *very* carefully about this. Everything you've done and accomplished has been because of *me*. *You'll* forever drown in your

315

own failure. I'll make your life a nightmare simply by disappearing! If only you knew how much I protect you. Remember that Fallen, Fulfur, was it?" His Father's venom tainted his decisions. "If you disintegrate me, make no doubt, I look forward to watching your world collapse and burn around you! The Kingdom will betray you, and the girl will forsake you. It'll all die with me! All because *you* knew best."

The mark of Limbo shone on his wrist. His Highness smiled at his son's stress. "You know I'm right. You *need* me, All you know is serving me. Surely you must know you're unfit to rule, Hah! A Jester for a King? Whoever would have thought of such an absurd idea?"

Rex's breathing sped up. "Absurd?" *Who am I? I-I'm a performer, I'm a dancer, I can't lead a kingdom...*

Xavier eased on the pressure making Rex's finger drift further away.

But Chestnut believes in me.

She believed he could be a great successor. After everything they had gone through, to throw that away now... If Rex stepped away, His Highness would lock him up, kill Chestnut and Ava, increase security. The plan hinged on the element of surprise which was quickly fading. This was their only chance.

Ava...please.

A body slammed against Rex's "Now!" Ava's thin fingers lay over his.

Two thumbs pressed on His Highness's symbol.

Two actors.

A light trickled out of His Highness's wrist like water. It ran down his arm, consuming him as a whole. A crown floated above his head, particles of the actions he's caused. An unholy screech echoed through the ballroom.

Xavier hardened his face. He'd dreamed of this moment when he'd be free. He didn't need to remind himself of why this was justified. The pain His Highness caused, the hurt, the nights of yanking and demanding. Even now, Rex's blood stained the marble tile.

Felix flaked away, bit by bit, into ash. Worthless, meaningless ash. "You need me!"

Xavier looked down at him. "No."

Flames erupted from His Highness's hair, he outstretched his wings before the edges dropped off.

Felix swished his hand, and a bracelet appeared around Xavier's wrist. Permanent and etched into the gold was a Latin phrase.

"Memento quod ego feci tibi"

Xavier looked back at his father.

A smug smile found its way onto Felix's face. *"Remember what I've done for you. You'll always be my sweet, little Kitten."*

Xavier watched as The King faded into the wind.

He was gone. Everything he'd gone through-was over. His father's words had some truth to it. Memories of his wing, his chess matches with his father, the banquets and parties.

"What now...?" The Prince whispered.

Ava stood above the pile of ash, her face solemn and remorseless. "He's gone...We're free."

Xavier looked at the pile of ash. Light particles rose from it and reconstructed itself into a new crown. Ava and Xavier's eyes traced it as it floated above the ash. Ava swiped a hand through it, but it burst into nothing upon contact. "What?"

Xavier slowly stepped forward. He reached forward and cupped the crown in his hand.

He lifted it above his head. The light broke like an egg and spilled itself over Xavier's hair, anointing him.

He felt his father's power envelope him.

A mad rush dizzied him.

"I'm free..." The ash of his father scattered at his feet. The silence suffocated the two of them.

Chestnut and Jason burst into the room. "Ava!" Jason screamed. They slowed their run as they neared the siblings.

Chestnut's scared stare released into a smile. She looked down at the ash. "Sparrow–"

"We did it." The Prince murmured. "He's gone."

Ava slapped his back, whooping. "Rex! We're free!"

He laughed, for the first time, a light, joyful, unburdened laugh.

"Now we can heal..." Chestnut leaned forward and kissed his hair. Her lips lingered, and Xavier leaned into her hug.

And so the jester became the King. Xavier pulled out of the hug. "Chestnut– " Doors opened before him miles of opportunities. "Chestnut, we're free!" He felt like a little boy again.

Matthew would be proud.

At Xavier's summon, a bell rang.

A little servant girl came in. "Yes, Sire?"

"Alert the Kingdom! Limbo has a new King." Xavier led Chestnut closer to him, and she wrapped her arms around his waist.

Ava tackled Rex. "Rex, you're free!"

His eyes met her green irises. "*We're* free."

Jason grinned behind her.

"Sparrow." Chestnut said.

"Yes, deer?"

She looked up at him with stormy eyes, "You're going to make a wonderful King!"

Rex smiled. "With you by my side, nothing could be more wonderful"

Gossip spread through the halls as coronation plans were being made, all for the new King

King Xavier DeClawfada.

ACKNOWLEDGEMENTS

This journey has been incredible, for my debut novel. To Christ, for saving my soul, and God Almighty, the Lord of my life, for giving me the inspiration and the desire to write this. It's truly been one of the best experiences of my life.

To my parents, Michael Umstead and Elizabeth Umstead. Thank you for teaching me patience, discipline, kindness, and confidence; skills that have helped me become the woman I am today. You raised me to believe that you can do anything so long as you dedicate yourself to it. You always pushed me to be better than I already was and you taught me what real love is! Thank you for believing in me and giving me all the unconditional love in the universe.

To my older brother, William Michael Roberts Umstead, who was my real life Rex growing up. Thank you for setting me on this journey 6 years ago when we were just wide-eyed kids. You whisked me on adventures and storylines and made them come to life around me. Growing up with you was the best gift I could ever want. Thank you for being the Dipper to my Mabel, the Steven to my Amethyst, the Rex to my Ava. "I'm gonna be right by your side no matter what!"

To all the real life C-PTSD survivors who inspired Rex's story and conflict. You all are braver than everything and stronger than the world around you! Thank you for sharing your stories with me, and teaching me compassion and empathy! I pray the best for you all!

To my fourth grade teacher, Mr. Forrester at Grace Christian School, for encouraging my writing career. During class, you'd let me write my first short story about cats and illustrate it. As a little fourth grader, it meant the world to me. Thank you for planting that seed.

To the story itself; Thank you for helping me find myself as I grew up through Middle School and High School. Be it Rex's loyalty, Ava's optimism, Chestnut's persistence, or Jason's intuition, I wouldn't be the person I am now. Thank you for being my friends, even when I didn't have many.

Finally, to all my friends, teachers, beta readers and mentors. Every conversation, every experience helped shape me and this book. Special shoutouts to Randi Olsen, Vince Vanni, Samantha Sanborn, Jewel Ivie, Ava McKissick, and Andrew Davis. Thank you for listening to my long ramblings and always supporting me. I look forward to the future and all the things that the Lord has in store!

The Author, Kaylee A. Umstead

ABOUT THE AUTHOR

Kaylee's writing career took off at the age of 12, when she decided to record the stories she and her older brother had created while they played. 6 years later, now a High School Graduate, Kaylee Umstead is ready to share her debut novel with the world. Having traveled the world as a little girl, she learned how to stretch her dreams beyond the horizon and pursue her passions with the fervor of a pitbull. She's a two time winner of the VFW's Voice of Democracy in her community, and a Blue Ribbon winner in Equestrian competitions. Kaylee prides herself on achieving excellence in everything she does. All the glory and honor to her personal Lord and Savior. Joshua 1:9

Follow her on Social Media!
   Blog: https://the-homestead-blog.blogspot.com/
   Website: https://brand.site/golden-age-publishers
   Facebook: https://www.facebook.com/profile.php?id=1000689 95113313
   Instagram: @kayleealexandraumstead
   Youtube: @Toastymouse0329
   Discord: toastymouse777

Printed in Dunstable, United Kingdom